GW01463997

MANUAL

OF

Classical Erotology

(De figuris Veneris)

BY

Friedrich Karl Forberg

LATIN TEXT AND LITERAL ENGLISH VERSION.

TWO VOLUMES IN ONE

University Press of the Pacific
Honolulu, Hawaii

Manual of Classical Erotology
(De Figuris Veneris)

by
Friedrich Karl Forberg

ISBN: 1-4102-0620-3

Copyright © 2003 by University Press of the Pacific

Reprinted from the 1884 edition

University Press of the Pacific
Honolulu, Hawaii
http://www.universitypressofthepacific.com

All rights reserved, including the right to reproduce this book, or portions thereof, in any form.

In order to make original editions of historical works available to scholars at an economical price, this facsimile of the original edition of 1884 is reproduced from the best available copy and has been digitally enhanced to improve legibility, but the text remains unaltered to retain historical authenticity.

Foreword

It is perhaps well to state at once that the « Manual of Classical Erotology » is intended only for Students of the Classics, Lawyers, Psychologists and Medical Men. Those persons, we think, who may peruse it as a means of awakening voluptuous sensations will be severely disappointed. Never did a work more serious issue from the press. Here we have no curious erotic story born of a diseased mind, but a cold, relentless analysis of those human passions which it is ever the object of Science to wrestle with and overthrow.

As a basis also for the correct interpretation of the drama of the ancient world, Forberg's

studies are most valuable. Apart from that extraordinary book, Rosenbaum's *History of the Esoteric Habits, Beliefs and Customs of Antiquity*, we know of no other compilation which casts so intense a search-light upon those Crimes, Follies and Perversions of the « Sixth Sense » which transformed the olden glory of Greece and Rome into a by-word and a reproach amongst the nations.

The present English translation now offered to Scholars is entirely new and strictly exact. No liberties have been taken with the text. It was felt that any attempt to add more colour, or to increase the effect, — involving a departure from the lines of stern simplicity laid down by Forberg, — would have detracted from the scientific value and character of the work.

The late Isidore Liseux issued in 1882 a French version with the Latin text *imprimé à cent exemplaires* « for himself and friends ». This work is now very seldom to be met with because the whole edition was privately subscribed by Scholars and Bibliophiles before its appearance.

The thieving copyists went of course immediately to work and some wretched penny-a-liner, utterly ignorant of both Latin and Greek, produced an English transcript full of faults, based only on the French text.

There is no need to add that such a book as this is of no value to the Student as a work of reference, for the faulty and forceless renderings often to be met with in Liseux' version are reproduced with charming exactness, while the absence of the original text makes it all the more perilous to accept the work as a guide. Having said this much concerning the only two translations known to us, we proceed to give some account of good master Forberg and what is known of the inception and building up of his chef-d'œuvre.

The eminent Author of this book never became famous. His name is mentioned occasionally in connexion with the « Hermaphroditus » of Antonio Beccadelli, known by the surname of Panormitanus, which he edited. Brunet, Charles Nodier, and the *Bibliographie des Ouvrages rela-*

tifs aux Femmes, à l'Amour et au Mariage, speak of him in this connexion; while a list of his works appears moreover in the *Index Locupletissimus Librorum* or *Bücher-Lexicon* (Bibliographical Lexicon) of Christian Gottlob Kayser, Leipzig, 1834. But with the exception of the *Allgemeine Deutsche Biographie*, the publication of which was commenced in 1878 by the Historical Commission of the Munich Academy, and which has devoted a short notice to him, all Dictionaries and Collections whether of Ancient or of Modern Biography are mute with respect to him. The *Conversations-Lexicon* and the vast Encyclopaedia of Ersch and Gruber do not contain a single line about him, while Michaud, Didot, Bachelet and Dezobry, Bouillet, Vapereau, utterly ignore his existence. For all that he well deserves a word or two.

Friedrich Karl Forberg was born in the year 1770 at Meuselwitz, in the Duchy of Saxe-Altenburg, and died in 1848 at Hildburghausen. He was a philosopher and a collaborator with Fichte, hwile he devoted a part of his attention to

religious exegesis : but above all he was a philo-
logian, and a humanist, — at once learned and inquisitive. He followed first the career of a Uni-
versity-teacher ; *Privat-docent* in 1792, Assistant
Professor in the Faculty of Philosophy at Jena
(1793), he was installed in 1796 as Co-Rector
at Saalfeld. His inaugural thesis : « Dissertatio
inauguralis de aesthetica transcendentali », is
dated 1792 (Jena, 8vo.); this was followed by
a « Treatise on the Original Conditions and
Formal Limitations of Free Will » in German
and an « Extract from my Occasional Writings »
also in German (1795). From 1796 to 1800 he
wrote extensively in defence of the teachings ot
Fichte in Journals, Reviews, particularly in the
Philosophical Magazine of Schmid, and in sundry publications emanating from Fichte himself.
He published moreover : « Animadversiones in
loca selecta Novi Testamenti » (Saalfeld, 1798,
4to.), « an Apology for his pretended Atheism »,
in German (Gotha, 1799, 8vo.). « Obligations
of Learned Men », in German (Gotha, 1801,
8vo.), etc.

The second part of his life seems to have
been devoted entirely to Literature. In 1807 he
was appointed as Conservator of the Aulic Library at Coburg, and having had enough of
philosophy, he turned his whole attention to the
study of Latin and Greek antiquity. Previously
to this his tastes had already been revealed by
the publication of several pretty editions of the
minor Latin erotic poets ; these form a collection
of six or eight volumes in 16mo., with red mar-
gin-lines, and are now very difficult to procure.
The discovery he made in the Coburg library of a
manuscript of the « Hermaphroditus » of Panormitanus, offering important new readings
and variants from the received text, suggested
the idea to him of producing a definitive edition
of the work, with copious commentaries.

The said « Hermaphroditus » so called, « because », says La Monnoye, « all the filth in connection with both sexes forms the theme of the
volume », is a collection of Latin Epigrams filled
out with a patchwork of quotations from
Virgil, Ovid and Martial, in which memory has

a much larger share than imagination, and
which has never appeared to us to possess any
great literary value. But the mishaps the book
has had to encounter, its having been publicly
burnt in manuscript in the market places of Bo-
logna, Ferrara and Milan, the anathemas hurled
against it by some savants, and the favour with
which it was received by others, who were glad
to awaken by its perusal old reminiscences, have
given it a kind of reputation. The Abbé Mercier
de Saint-Léger was the first to publish it in
Paris, together with the works of four other
poets of the same sort : Ramusius de Rimini,
Pacificus Maximus, Jovianus Pontanus, and
Joannes Secundus (a). But Forberg, whilst fully
appreciating the work and particularly the courage of the learned Frenchman, found much to
find fault with; the Epigrams of Panormitanus

(a) *Quinque illustrium Poetarum, Antonii Panormitae; Ramusii Ariminensis; Pacifici Maximi Asculani;
Io. Joviani Pontani; Io. Secundi Hagiensis, Lusus in
Venerem, partim ex codicibus manuscriptis, nunc primum editi Parisiis, prostat ad Pristrinum, in Vico
suavi*, (at Paris, at Molini's, Rue Mignon), 1791, 8vo.

were not numbered, which made citations from
them troublesome, a great number of readings
were faulty, and, thanks to his manuscript, he
could correct them; lastly, Mercier de Saint-
Léger had omitted to give any running commentary on his author, to explain his text by
means of notes and the comparison of parallel
passages, whereas according to Forberg a book
of this character required notes by tens and
hundreds, each verse, each hemistich, each
word, offering matter for philosophical reflections and highly interesting comparisons. He
therefore took the book in hand and began to
collect with inquisitive care everything the Ancients had written upon the delicate subjects
treated in the « Hermaphroditus ».

But having come to the end of his task, he
found that his commentary would drown the
book, that hardly would he be able to get in a verse
of it every two or three pages, all the remainder
of the book being taken up by his notes, and that
the result would be chaos. Dividing his work
into two parts, he left the smaller one in the

shape of annotations, reduced to the merest in-
dispensable explanations, to the « Hermaphroditus », while of the second and more copious
harvest of his erudite researches he composed a
special treatise, which he had printed as a sup-
plement under the title, « Apophoreta », or
« Second Course »; this treatise being in his
eyes only a kind of dessert, following upon the
substantial repast furnished by the Latin Poet of
the XVIth. century. The whole forms a volume
much sought after by amateurs : « Antonii
Panormitae *Hermaphroditus*; primus in Germania edidit et Aphoreta adjecit Frider. Carol.
Forbergius. Coburgi, sumtibus Meuseliorum,
1824, 8vo. » (*b*).

Forberg, good, simple man, was mistaken,
owing to his too great modesty ; the true feast,

(*b*) To certain copies are added some thirty engravings,
representing the principal erotic postures ; these engravings are taken from the *Monuments de la Vie Privée des
douze Césars*, and from the *Monuments du Culte Secret
des Dames Romaines*, two works, now becoming every day
rarer.

at once substantial, nourishing and savoury, is his own work, the work which he elaborated from his own resources, from his inexhaustible memory and from his astonishing knowledge of the Greek and Latin authors down to their minutest details. On reprinting this excellent work, which undoubtedly deserved to be translated, we have given it a new title, one that is much more suitable than the old, « The Manual of Classical Erotology ». In virtue of the charm, the abundance, the variety of the citations, it is a priceless erotic Anthology ; in virtue of the methodical classification of the contents Forberg has adopted, it is a didactic work, — a veritable Manual. He began with collecting from the Greek and Latin writers the largest number possible of scattered notices, which might serve for points of comparison with the Epigrams of Beccadelli ; having possessed himself of a large accumulation of these, it occurred to him to set them out in order, arranging them in conformity with the similarity of their contents, deciding finally upon a division into eight chapters, corresponding with the same number of special

manifestations of the amorous fancy and its de-
pravities :

    I. — Of Copulation.
   II. — Of Pederastia.
  III. — Of Irrumation.
  IV. — Of Masturbation.
   V. — Of Cunnilingues.
  VI. — Of Tribads.
 VII. — Of Intercourse with Animals.
VIII. — Of Spintrian Postures.

He found that he had to make subdivisions in
each class according to the nature of the subject,
to note particularities, individualities; and the
contrast between this scientific apparatus, and
the facetious matters subjected to the rigorous
laws of deduction and demonstration is not the
least amusing feature of the book. Probably no
one but a German savant could have conceived
the idea of thus classifying by categories, groups,
genera, variations, species and sub-species all
known forms of natural and unnatural lusts, according to the most trustworthy authors. But

Forberg pursued another aim besides. In the
course of his researches he had noticed how re-
ticent the annotators and expounders generally
are in clearing up matters which would seem to
require it the most, some in consequence of a
false reserve, others for fear of appearing too
knowing, and others again from ignorance; also
how many mistakes and gross blunders they have
fallen into, by reason of their not understanding
the language of erotics and failing to grasp its
infinite shades of meaning.

It is precisely on those obscure and difficult
passages of the Ancient poets, on those expressions purposely chosen for their ambiguity,
which have been the torment of the critics and
the puzzle of the most erudite commentators,
that our learned Humanist has concentrated his
most convincing observations.

The number of authors, Greek, Latin, French,
German, English, Dutch, whom he has laid under
contribution in order to formulate his exact and
judicious classifications, mounts up to a formid-
able total. There are to be found in the *Manual*

*of Erotolog*y something like five hundred passages, culled from more than one hundred and fifty works, all classified, explained, commented upon, and in most cases, enveloped in darkness as they had been, made plain as light iself by the mere fact of juxtaposition. With Forberg for a guide no one need henceforth fear to go astray, — to believe, for instance, like M. Leconte de Lisle, that the woman of whom Horace says that she changes neither dress nor place, « *peccatve superne* » « has not erred beyond measure »; what a mistake! — or with M. Nisard to translate Suetonius expression « *illudere caput alicuius* » « to attempt some ones life » (*c*)!

Forberg, a philosopher, has treated these delicate subjects like a philosopher, namely, in a purely speculative manner, as a man quite above and beyond terrestrial matters, and particularly so with respect to the lubricities which he has made it his task to examine so closely. He declares he knows nothing of them personally,

---

(*c*) See below pp. 41 and 195 respectively.

has never thought of making experimental inves-
tigations on them, but derives all his knowledge,
from books. His candour is beyond suspicion.
He has not escaped censure; but having a reply
ready for every objection and authorities to quote
on every point, he found an answer to his de-
tractors ready made in the phrase of Justus Lipsius, who had been reproached with taking pleasure in the abominations of Petronius : « The
wines you set upon the table excite the drunkard
and leave the sober man perfectly calm; in the
same way, these kinds of reading *may* very like_
ly inflame an imagination already depraved,
but they make no impression upon a mind that
is chaste and disciplined ».

MANUAL

OF CLASSICAL ERO TOLOGY

FIRST VOLUME

DE

Figuris Veneris

———◦✠◦———

VARIAS Veneris figuras recensere consilium
est, non omnes omnino illas quidem : qui
enim fieri posset, ut mille modi Vene-
ris (1), mille figuræ, per quas ingeniosa libidinis

---

(1) *Ovidius*, de Arte amatoria, *I, 435, 36* :

> Non mihi sacrilegas meretricum ut prosequar artes,
> Cum totidem linguis sint sat s ora decem.

Aloisia Sigæa : « *Quot inflexiones, quot corporis conver-*
siones, tot sunt Veneris figuræ. Nec numerus iniri, nec doceri
aptior voluptati potest. Quisque a libidine sua, a loco, a
tempore, quam indui figuram velit, capit consilium. Sed non
omnibus idem amor. » (*Colloq. VI.*)

THE

Metamorphoses of Venus

—◈◆◈—

W E propose to pass in review the different metamorphoses of Venus, — though truly not all of them. For how is it possible to specify the thousand modes (1),

<hr>

(1) Ovid, *Art of Love*, I, 435, 36 : « To fully expose the ungodly wiles of harlots, ten mouths, and as many tongues to boot, would not suffice. »

Aloysia Sigea : « The body in sacrificing to Venus can take as many postures as there are ways in which it can bend and curve. It is equally impossible to enumerate all these, as it is to say which is best fitted to give pleasure. Each acts in this respect according to his own caprice, according to place, time, and so on, choosing the one he prefers. Love is not identical for each and all. » (Dialogue VI.)

satietas audeat Venerem jungere, numero compre
henderentur? sed eas ita per certa genera digestas,
ut suo quæque loco facile aptari posse videatur.
Noli vero, Lector curiose, aliena forte spe animum
pascere. Neque enim nos ii sumus, qui gloriolam
petamus experta aut nove tentata prodendo in palæs-
tra, qua tirocinium nequaquam posuerimus; neque
est instituti nostri, oculis auribusve accepta tradere;
neque etiam, ut maxime vellemus, ita tibi satis-
facere ullo modo possemus, qui toti pendeamus a
libris, toti simus in libris, vix versemur inter
homines. Lusimus hæc otia primum animi causa,
aliud ex alio nectentes, philosophia, in qua olim
quasi tabernaculum vitæ collocare putabamus,
nunc jacente; an floret, cujus quæque prope
dies nova videt dogmata cito peritura pullulare
ut quot philosophi, tot fere hodie philosophiæ,
sectæ nullæ pro cohorte singulares exstare videan-

the thousand forms of Love, on which the inventive satiety of pleasure ventures? But at any rate such as fall into distinct and definite kinds admit of being easily and methodically classified. Do not, inquisitive reader, hope for more than this. We are not of those who seek after a petty personal glory by unveiling the results of their own experience or by describing novel *tours de force* in the wrestling-school; we are not so much as raw recruits at this game. Nor yet is it our intention to reveal things we have seen or heard in this connexion. If we *would*, we could not, — to your satisfaction, for books are our only authorities. We are solely and entirely bookmen, and scarce frequent our fellow creatures at all.

These trifles engaged our attention first as a mere pastime. We were led to them accidentally, as we roamed from subject to subject; for Philosophy, the garden we had hoped to set up our tent in for life, lies desolate. How *can* Philosophy flourish in times like ours, when almost every new day sees new systems sprout forth, to die down again to morrow; when there are as many philosophers as philosophies, when schools have ceased to exist, when instead of

tur ? Deinde vero etiam propterea, ut eorum ratio-nibus aliquantulum consuleremus, qui in liberiore scriptorum veterum simplicitate salibusque nudis haud raro hærentes deseri se quercrentur pudica in-terpretum aut brevitate aut taciturnitate, licet qui pueris scripserint, eos jure suo abstinuisse ab obscenis voluptatibus diligentius et explanatius enarrandis infitias iverit nemo.

Si quidquam peccaverimus, ignoscas quæsumus cum supellectili nostræ curtæ, tum insolentiorum libidinum imperitiæ, quæ solet regnare in oppidis parvis, tum vero etiam mentularum Melocaben-sium, si placet, probitati.

Non nostrum est exemplum. Præivit Astyanassa, quæ Suida teste (2) primo scripsit περὶ σχημάτων

---

(2) *Suidas in* ᾿Αστυάνασσα : « ᾿Αστυάνασσα ῾Ελένης τῆς Μενελάου θεράπαινα, ἥτις πρώτη τὰς ἐν τῇ συνουσίᾳ κατα-κλίσεις εὗρεν, καὶ ἔγραψε περὶ σχημάτων συνουσιαστικῶν, ἣν ὕστερον παρεζήλωσαν Φιλαινὶς καὶ ᾿Ελεφαντίνη, αἱ τὰ τοιαῦτα ἐξορχησάμεναι ἀσελγήματα. »

groups only individuals are to be met with? Our second motive was to provide some satisfaction, however little, to the claims of those readers who very often find themselves disconcerted by the unconventional raciness of Ancient authors and their out-spoken witticisms, and justly complain of the prudish brevity or entire silence of the Commentators who leave their difficulties unexplained. Of course these latter wrote for the young; and no one can blame them under the circumstances for not having dwelt carefully and curiously on shameful secrets.

It we have fallen into any mistakes, lay the fault, we beg, first on our insufficient intellectual furniture, secondly on our ignorance as to the more uncommon forms of lust, an ignorance prevalent in small towns, and lastly, if you please, put it down to the honest simplicity of our Coburg citizens' *members*.

We only follow others' example. We have predecessors in Astyanassa, who according to Suidas (2) first wrote « of Erotic Postures »;

---

(2) Suidas under *Astyanassa* : « Astyanassa, maid of Helen the wife of Menelaus, who was the first to invent the different positions in the act of love. She wrote « Of Erotic Postures » ; and was followed and imitated by Phi-

8 THE MANUAL

συνουσιαστικῶ) : *præivit Philænis Samia* (3), *vel potius, ne de aliena fama detrahere videamur, qui librum* περὶ ποικίλων σχημάτων ἀφροδισίων *matronæ honestæ nomine inscripsit, Polycrates, sophistes Atheniensis : præivit Elephantis* (4) *sive Elephan-*

---

(3) Priapeia, *LXIII.*

> *Ad hanc puella, pœne nomen adjeci,*
> *Solet venire cum suo futuore,*
> *Quæ ut tot figuras, quot Philænis enarrat.*
> *Non invenit, pruriginosa discedit.*

Vindicem famæ nacta est Æschrionem, quo auctore exstat epitaphium Philænidis ab Athenæo libro VIII, cap. 13, servatum, in quo extremo :

> Οὐκ ἦν ἐς ἄνδρας μάχλος, οὐδε δημώδης ·
> Πολυκράτης δὲ, τὴν γονὴν Ἀθηναῖος,
> Λόγων τι παιπάλημα, καὶ κακὴ γλῶσσα,
> Ἔγραψεν ὅσσ᾽ ἔγραψ᾽ · ἐγὼ γὰρ οὐκ οἶδα.

Præ manibus fuerunt Philænidis libelli Timarcho Luciani, in Apophrade, *p. 158, tomi VII, Operum a Jo. Petro Schmidio editorum :* « Ποῦ γὰρ ταῦτα (ὀνόματα καὶ ῥήματα) τῶν βιβλίων εὑρίσκεις ; ἐκ τῶν Φιλαινίδος δέλτων, ἃς διὰ χειρὸς ἔχεις ; »

(4) *Suetonius in* Tiberio, *cap. 43.* « *Cubicula plurifariam disposita tabellis ac sigillis lascivissimarum picturarum et figurarum adornavit librisque Elephantidis in-*

and in Philaenis of Samos (3), or rather, to deprive no one of his due, Polycrates, an Athenian sophist, who brought out under the name of an honourable matron a book « On the various Postures of Love ». Then there was Elephantis (4) or Elephantiné, a Greek girl, whose li-

---

laenis and Elephantiné, who carried further the series ot suchlike obscenities ».

(3) *Priapeia*, LXIII : « To her a certain girl (I very nearly gave her name) is wont to come with her paramour; and if she fails to discover as many postures as Philaenis describes, she goes away agaiu still itching with desire ».

Philaenis has found a champion of her good name in Aeschrion, who wrote an epitaph for her that is still extant in Athenaeus, bk. VIII, ch. 13 : The last lines read : « I was not lustful for men nor a gad-about; but Polycrates, by race an Athenian, a mill clapper of talk, a foul-tongued sophist, wrote — what he wrote; I know nought ot it all ».

Her works were familiar to Timarchus in Lucian (*Apophras*, p. 158, — vol. VII, of Works of Lucian, edit. J. P. Schmid : « Tell me where you find these words and expressions, — in what books ? is it in the volumes of Philaenis, that are always in your hands? »

(4) Suetonius, *Tiberius*, ch. 43 : « He decorated his various and variously arranged sleeping-chambers with pictures and bas-reliefs of the most licentious character, and furnished them with the works of Philaenis, that

tine, puella Græca, cujus lascivis libellis Tiberius

*struxit, ne cui in opera edenda exemplar imperatæ schemæ
deesset.* »

Priapeia, *III*.

> *Obscenis rigido Deo tabellas*
> *Ducens ex Elephantidos libellis*
> *Dat donum Lalage, rogatque tentet,*
> *Si pictas opus edat ad figuras.*

*Fuerunt igitur, qui figuras ab Elephantide enarratas
pictis tabulis, ipsa forsan præeunte, exprimerent. Hujusmodi tabulas dicat Priapo, rogatque velit ipsam permolere, et
tentare, num docilis sit discipula pictis istis coeundi modis
omnibus fideliter imitandis. Tales tabellas lascivarum figurarum, sive ex Elephantidos, sive Philænidis libris, sive
aliunde ductas, quis enim dubitet, in tam blandi argumenti
illecebris artificium ingenia desudasse certatim atque elabo-
rasse?* respexit Ovidius de Arte amatoria, *II, 680.*

> *... Venerum jungunt per mille figuras,*
> *Inveniat plures nulla tabella modos...*

*et auctor veteris epigrammatis a Josepho Scaligero ad Pria-
peium III, in lucem protracti :*

> *Inque modos omnes dulces imitata tabellas*
> *Transeat, et lecto pendeat illa meo.*

*Nihil frequentius fuisse Romanis, quam tecta parietes-
que obscenis picturis adornare, intelligere est ex Propertio
II, VI, 27, seqq.*

> *Quæ manus obcenas depinxit prima tabellas,*
> *Et posuit casta turpia visa domo,*
> *Illa puellarum ingenuos corrupit ocellos,*
> *Nequitiæque suæ noluit esse rudes.*
> *Non istis olim variabant tecta figuris,*
> *Quum paries nullo crimine pictus erat.*

centious writings Tiberius is said to have fur-

---

no one in performing should want a model of the posture required. »

Priapeia, III : « Taking pictures from the licentious treatises of Elephantis, Lalagé presents them an offering to the stiff-standing god, and begs you prove if she performs agreeably to the pictured postures. »

It would seem then that artists depicted the postures described by Elephantis, she herself possibly setting the example. Paintings of the sort Lalagé dedicates to Priapus, and asks her lover to have her and see if she is a docile pupil in faithfully imitating all the modes of connection depicted in them. No doubt such representations of licentious postures, taken from the works of Elephantis or Philaenis or elsewhere stimulated the ingenuity of Artists to work out in emulation these enticing *motifs* to the highest degree of finish. *Ovid* alludes to such works of art in his *Art of Love*, II, 680 : « They unite in Love in a thousand postures ; no picture could suggest any fresh ones... » : as also the author of an ancient Epigram quoted by *Joseph Scaliger* in his Commentary on the *Priapeia*, III : « And when she has thrown herself into every posture in imitation of the seductive pictures, she may go : but let the picture be left hanging over my bed. » Nothing was commoner with the Romans than to decorate the walls and partitions of rooms with licentious paintings, as may be gathered from Propertius, II, vi, 27 sqq. : « The hand that first painted filthy pictures, and exposed foul sights in an honest home, corrupted the pure eyes of young maids, and chose to make them accomplices of his own lubricity. In old days our walls were not daubed with fancies of this vile sort, when never a partition was adorned with a vicious subject ».

Cæsar cubicula, instruxisse fertur : præivit Paxa-
mus (5), *qui* Δωδεκάτεχνον *composuit de figuris*
obscenis : præivit Sotades Maronita (6), *Cinædo-*

---

(5) *Suidas.* « Πάξαμος Δωδεκάτεχνον · ἔστι δὲ περὶ τῶν
αἰσχρῶ) σχημάτων.» *At sine causa huc referri puto Cyre-*
nen quandam δωδεκαμήχανον *dictam. Videtur enim me-*
retricula illa duodecim Veneris figuras non tam scripto
quam facto expressisse. Suidas in Δωδεκαμήχανον « : Κυ-
ρήνη τις ἐπίσημος γέγονεν ἑταίρα δωδεκαμήχανος ἐπικκλου-
μένη, διὰ τὸ τοιαῦτα σχήματα ἐν τῇ συνουσίᾳ ποιεῖν. »
Aristophanes in Ranis *1361-63*:

Τολμᾷς τἀμὰ μέλη ψέγειν
Ἀνὰ τὸ δωδεκαμάχανον
Κυρήνης μελοποιῶν ;

Nominatur etiam Thesmophoriis, *104, sed nominatur*
tantum. Ceterum nos semper laudamus Aristophanem Bur-
mannianum. Dubito, num scriptoribus de figuris Veneris
adnumerandus sit Musæus, cujus pathicissimos libellos, Syba-
riticis certantes et sale pruriente tinctos, Instantium Rufum
legere jubet Martialis XII, 97, ea tamen lege, ut puella ejus
præsto sit, ne thalassionem indicat manibus libidinosis, fiat-
que sine fœmina maritus.

(6) *Athenæus, XIV, 13* : « Ὁ δὲ Ἰωνικὸς λόγος τὰ Σωτάδου
καὶ τὰ πρὸ τούτου Ἰωνικὰ καλούμενα ποιήματα, Ἀλεξάνδρου
τε τοῦ Αἰτωλοῦ, καὶ Πύρητος τοῦ Μιλησίου, καὶ Ἀλέξου,
καὶ ἄλλων τοιούτων ποιητῶν προφέρεται. Καλεῖται δὲ
οὗτος καὶ κιναιδολόγος. Ἤκμασε δὲ ἐν τῷ εἴδει τούτῳ
Σωτάδης ὁ Μαρωνίτης, ὥς φησι Καρύστιος ὁ Περγαμηνὸς ἐν
τῷ περὶ αὐτοῦ Σωτάδου συγγράμματι, καὶ ὁ τοῦ Σωτάδου

nished his sleeping-room with ; also Paxamus (5) who composed the *Dodecatechnon* on lascivious postures; and Sotades (6) of Maroneia, sur-

---

(5) *Suidas* : « Paxamus wrote the *Dodecatechnon*; the subject is the obscene postures. » But I think he has no good reason to connect with this the epithet *Dodecame-chanos* given to a certain Cyrené. The said wanton damsel seems to have practised rather than described the twelve postures of Venus. *Suidas* under *Dodecamechanon* : « There was a famous *hetaera*, Cyrené by name, further known as *Dodecamechanos*, because she practised twelve different postures in making love ».

Aristophanes says in the *Frogs*, 1361-63 : « Do you dare to criticize my songs, you that modulate your cadences on the twelve-fold postures of Cyrené ? ». Her name occurs also in the *Thesmophoriazusae* (104), but merely her name. (Our invariable rule is to quote from Burmann's edition of Aristophanes.) I am doubtful as to whether Musaeus should be counted among writers on the Erotic postures. Martial (XII, 97) recommends Instantius Rufus to read his (Musaeus') books, as being of the most advanced lasciviousness, vying with those of the Sybarites in obscenity and full of the most suggestive and spicy wit; warning him at the same time to have his girl ready to hand, if he did not want his hands to perform the wedding-march and consummate the marriage without a woman at all.

(6) *Athenaeus*, XIV, 13 : « Also the Ionic dialect has to show the poems of Sotades and the « Ionic » poems preceding his, those of Alexander the Aetolian, and Pyres of Miletus, and Alexis, and others of the same class. The last mentioned is known as the Cinaedologue. But in

*logus dictus, a quo Sotadeorum nomen mansit omni
generi librorum, nimiæ impudicitiæ nota insi-
gnium : præivit Sabellus, in quem Martialis, XII,
43 :*

> *Facundos mihi de libidinosis
> Legisti nimium, Sabelle, versus,
> Quales nec Didymi (7) sciunt puellæ,
> Nec molles Elephantidos libelli.
> Sunt illic Veneris novæ figuræ,
> Quales perditus audeat fututor.
> Præstent et taceant quid exoleti :*

υἱὸς Ἀπολλώνιος. Ἔγραψε δὲ καὶ οὗτος περὶ τῶν τοῦ πατρὸς
ποιημάτων σύγγραμμα. » *Vitæ exitum miserabilem habuit :
nam cum procacioribus dicteriis Ptolemæum Philadelphum,
regem Ægypti, lacessere ausus esset, quam pro irritabili natura regiarum aurium, vase plumbeo inclusus mari mersus est.*

(7) *Quænam fuerint Didymi puellæ, nescitur. Dum aliquis
certiora protulerit, conjicere interea licebit, fuisse in quatuor
millibus librorum, quos Didymum grammaticum conscrip-
sisse Seneca epistola 88 tradit, et unum aliquem de pathicarum
puellarum figuris, dignum, qui juxta Elephantidos libellos
nominaretur. Certe qui tantum subtilitati tribuit, ut quæ-
reret, libidinosior Anacreon. an ebriosior vixerit, Sappho
publica fuerit, nec ne, poterat etiam in Veneris modos inqui-
rere.*

named the Cinaedologue, from whose name a whole class of literature, remarkable for its excessive lubricity, is known as the Sotadic; and Sabellus, of whom Martial speaks : « Copious verses, only too copious, on scandalous subjects you have read me, O Sabellus, such as neither the maids of Didymus (7) know, nor yet the wanton treatises of Elephantis. Therein are new postures of Love that the desperate fornicator tries, and what debauchees use, but never tell of, — how grouped in a series five copulate at

---

this *genre* the most eminent writer is Sotades, of Maroneia, as is stated by Carystius of Pergamus in his work on Sotades, and by Apollonius, Sotades' son, who also wrote a work on his father's poems. « His end was a miserable one. Having assailed Ptolemy Philadelphus, king of Egypt, with witticisms too independent for the sensitive ears of princes, the king caused him to be enclosed in a leaden casket, and thrown into the sea. »

(7) Who were these « maids of Didymus ». Nobody knows. Failing any more plausible supposition, it may very well be conjectured that among the four thousand works written according to Seneca (Letter LXXXVIII.) by the Grammarian Didymus, there was one on the postures of lascivious girls, worthy to be named side by side with the treatises of Elephantis. Undoubtedly a man who devoted himself to such subtile questions as whether Anacreon was more libertine than drunkard, whether Sappho was a public woman or not, was quite likely to discuss the Erotic postures.

Quo symplegmate quinque copulentur,
Qua plures teneantur a catena,
Exstinctam liceat quid ad lucernam ;
Tanti non erat esse te disertum.

Præivit vir divini ingenii Petrus Aretinus, quem tabellas (8) *sedecim obscenissimas a Julio Romano pictas, a Marco tum Antonio in ære incisas, carminibus intemperantissimis, ut nihil supra, illustrasse iniqua fama canit : præivit Laurentius Venerius* (9), *nobilis Venetus, auctor li-*

---

(8) *Vide sis* Lexicon Bælianum, *sub* Pierre Arétin, *et Murrii* Journal zur Kunstgeschichte, *tomo XIV, pag. 1-72.*

(9) *Petrus Bælius in* Lexico, *sub* Pierre Arétin : « *Il y a un dialogue de Magdalena et de Giulia, qui a pour titre* la Puttana errante, *où il est traité au long de i diversi congiungimenti jusqu'au nombre de trente-cinq. L'Arétin, quoique l'ouvrage ait toujours été imprimé sous son nom,*

once, how a greater number still can make a chain. It was hardly worth the pains to be erudite ».

Moreover amongst our predecessors was the famous Pietro Aretino (8), a man of an almost divine genius, whom ill-natured report represents as having illustrated sixteen plates painted by Julio Romano and engraved on copper by Marc-Antonio with verses indecent beyond all expression; Lorenzo Veniero again (9), a Ve-

---

(8) See *Bayle's* Dictionary, article : *Pierre Arétin*; also Murr's *Journal zur Kunstgeschichte* (Year-Book of the History of Art), vol. XIV, pp. 1-72.

(9) *Pierre Bayle*, in his Dictionary, under *Pierre Arétin* : « There is a *Dialogue betwen Maddalena and Giulia*, entitled *La Puttana Errante* (The wandering whore), in which are exhaustively treated *i diversi congiungimenti* (the different modes of intercourse), to the number of thirty-five. Aretino, though the book has always been printed under his name, disowns it, declaring it to be the work of one of his pupils named Veniero. » *Brunet*, Manuel du Libraire (Book dealer's Handbook). « The *Puttana errante*, a little book, very rare, quite worthy of Aretino in view of the obscenities it countains, but which has been erroneously attributed to him. Lorenzo Veniero, a Venetian nobleman, is the real author. He published it to avenge himself on a Venetian courtesan named Angela, whom he designates under the insulting name of Zaffetta, that is to say, in the Venetian dialect, daughter of a police-spy ».

[*Bayle, Forberg* and many other writers have confused

belli Italico sermone conscripti, cum indice La
Puttana errante, *quo coeundi non minus triginta
quinque modos enumerare sibi sumsit. Præivit denique Nicolaus Chorerius, juriconsultus Franco-
gallus, qui Aloisiæ Sigææ, virginis Hispanæ,
nomen præfixit* Satiræ Sotadicæ de arcanis Amoris
et Veneris, *quanquam et fertur libellus sub nomine
Joannis Meursii cum epigraphe :* Elegantiæ Latini
sermonis; *in quo libello nescias, utrum Latine
loquendi accuratam et sine molestia diligentem ele-
gantiam, an festivitatem et facetiarum leporem, an
eruditionis Romanæ scintillas identidem micantes,
an multam et copiosam orationem, exquisitis et verborum et sententiarum luminibus, antiquitatem*

---

*le désavoue, et dit qu'il est d'un de ses élèves, nommé le
Veniero. »* Brunet *in* Manuel du libraire : « Puttana
errante, *petit ouvrage très rare, bien digne de l'Arétin par
les obscénités dont il est rempli, mais qui lui a été fausse-
ment attribué. Lorenzo Veniero, noble Vénitien, en est le
véritable auteur. Il le publia pour se venger d'une courtisane
de Venise, appelée Angela, qu'il désigne sous le nom injurieux
de Zaffetta, c'est à-dire, en langage vénitien, fille d'un
sbire. »*

netian nobleman, author of a little work in Italian, bearing the title *La Puttana Errante* (The Wandering Whore), in which he has undertaken to specify no less than thirty-five modes of loving. Lastly there was Nicolas Chorier, a French lawyer, who under the name of Aloysia Sigaea, a young Spanish lady, has given us the *Satirae Sotadicae de arcanis Amoris et Veneris* (Sotadic Satires on the Secret Rites of Love and Venus); though the book also appears under the name of Joannes Meursius with the title *Elegantiae Latini Sermonis* (Graces of Latin Prose). In this book you do not know which to admire most, the style at once elegant, correct and careful, yet free from pedantry, the wit equally gay and graceful, the brilliant sparks of Latin erudit-

---

the *Puttana errante*, a poem by Lorenzo Veniero and a burlesque parody of the Romances of chivalry, with the *Dialogue between Maddalena and Giulia*, a prose work to which the Elzevirs gave the title properly belonging to the poem. Neither one nor the other is the work of Pietro Aretino. See note at end of vol. VI. of the *Dialogues du divin Pietro Aretino* (Dialogues of the divine Pietro Aretino), Paris, Liseux, 1879, 3 vols. 18°, and London, 1880, 3 vols. 18°. [Note of French Translation of Forberg, *Manuel d'Erotologie classique*, Paris, Liseux, 1882.]

*redolentibus, velut gemmis distinctam, an præcla-
ram artem prodigialiter variandi rem unam magis
admireris. Alios mittamus.*

*Non defuerunt prædecessoribus nostris (antiquio-
rum quidem, quos laudavimus, omnium opera
tempus nobis invidisse dolemus) censores tetrici, nec
tamen lectores studiosi. Neque forsan deerunt utrique
et nostræ paginæ. Hominem illa sapit, ac famæ
securi hominibus scripsimus, naturam subducto
supercilio furca expellere non consuetis, sed qui semel
vivere auderent, quicquid et in tenebris non essent,
nec in publico videri vellent, atque etiam, uti in
omnibus rebus, ita in Venereis, auream potissimum
tenendam putarent mediocritatem. Valeant ceteri
habeantque sibi sapentiæ nomen!*

ion that glitter everywhere, the rich and copious eloquence graced as with jewels by polished and luminous words and phrases of a pleasant antique flavour, or lastly the pre-eminent skill displayed in varying with such manifold versatility one simple theme. The others we need not mention further.

Our predecessors, whether the more modern, or those of Antiquity whom we have cited, and all whose works alas! envious time has robbed us of, did not lack severe critics, nor yet studious readers. And our own treatise will no doubt in its turn meet with both these classes. It is a man's book; we have written it, fearless of censure, for men, — not for such as are wont with frowning brow « to pitchfork nature out of doors », but rather for such as have once for all dared to live their lives, who neither wish to lurk in darkness nor yet to defy the open day with effrontery, in one word for those who think that in Love as in all else the golden mean is the course to choose. Let others go their way, and arrogate to themselves the title of sages!

FDI potest opus Venereum aut per mentulam aut sine mentula. Si per mentulam, frictio mentulæ, in qua omnis voluptas versatur, effici potest aut cunno, aut culo, aut ore, aut manu aliisve cavis corporis; si sine mentula, cunnus fodi potest aut lingua, aut clitoride, aut alia quacuuqne re, virili veretro simili.

THE work of Venus may be accomplished with or without the help of the *mentula* (virile member). If with the mentula, the friction of this organ, in which friction the whole pleasure consists, can be effected either in the *vulva* (female organ), in the *anus* (arse-hole), in the mouth, by the hand or in any cavity of the body. If without the mentula, the vulva may be worked either with the tongue, with the clitoris, or with any object resembling the virile organ.

———

CAPUT I

DE FUTUTIONE

C primum quidem videamus de opere, quod fit per mentulam cunno commissam. Id quidem proprie dicitur futuere. Varius autem modus futuendi. Potest enim fututio fieri aut proni cum supina, aut supini cum prona, aut supini cum aversa, aut sedentis cum adversa, aut sedentis cum aversa, aut stantis vel ingeniculantis cum adversa, aut stantis vel ingeniculantis cum aversa. Jam singula dispiciamus.

Coitus proni cum supina est modus communis

CHAPTER I

OF COPULATION

ND first of all let us consider what is accomplished be means of the mentula introduced into the vulva. This is, properly speaking, to effect copulation ; but there are various ways of doing it.. As a matter of fact copulation can be effected :— the man face downwards with the woman on her back, the man on his back with the woman face down, the man on his back with the woman turning her back to him ; the man sitting with the woman turning her face towards him, sitting with the woman turning her back to him ; the man standing or kneeling with the woman turning her face towards him, standing or kneeling with the woman turning her back to him. Let us examine each of these methods separately.

Coition with the man face down on the woman

atque etiam ad naturam maxime accommodatus.
Aloisia Sigæa (Colloq. VI) :

« *Ego vero communem Veneris usum et figuram*
unice laudo, ut in supinam vir procumbat, pectus pec-
tore, ventrem ventre comprimat, pubes pubi colludat,
diffindens rigido conto teneram rimam. Nam quid
dulcius cogitando fingi potest, quam resupinam ama ti
corporis blando pondere ad irrequietæ sed suavis impa-
tientiæ molles incitari furias ? Quid gratius, quam
amantis vultu pasci, osculis, suspiriis et patrantium
oculorum incendiis ? quid præstabilius, quam amores
suos fovere complexibus, sensibus quidem, quos non
ætas, non vitium ullum obtudit ? Quid utriusque libi-
dini, utriusque voluptati lætius concutientis et succutien-
tis lascivis motitationibus ? Quid opportunius præ vo-
luptate emorientibus, quam flammescentium suavio-
rum vivida vi reviviscere ? Qui aversa ludit in Venere,
uni tantum alterive sensui gratificatur, omnibus qui
in adversa. »

who lies on her back is the ordinary method, and the most natural.

Aloysia Sigaea says :

« For my own part I like the usual custom and the ordinary method best : the man should lie upon the woman, who is on her back, breast to breast, stomach to stomach, pubis to pubis, piercing her tender cleft with his rigid spear. Indeed what can be imagined sweeter than for the woman to lie extended on her back, bearing the welcome weight of her lovers' body, and exciting him to the tender transports of a restless but delicious voluptuousness ? What more pleasant than to feast on her lovers' face, his kisses, his sighs, and the fire of his wanton eyes ? What better than to press the loved one in her arms and so awake new fires of desire, to participate in amorous sensations unblunted by any taint of age or infirmity ? What more favorable to the delight and enjoyment of both than such lascivious movements given and received? What more opportune at the instant of dying a voluptious death than to recover again under the revivifying vigour of burning kisses ? He who plies Venus on the reverse side, satisfies but one of his senses , he who does the same face to face satisfies them all ». (Dialogue VI.)

*Formosas fœminas potissimum hac figura uti ju-
bet Magister Amorum* (De Arte amatoria, *III*,
771-73) :

> *Nota sibi sint quæque : modos a corpore certos
> Sumite. Non omnes una figura decet ;
> Quæ facie præsignis eris, resupina jaceto.*

*Induitur vero hæc ipsa figura non una ratione.
Nam potest aut eques intra femina recipere supinam,
aut supina equitem, et posterior quidem ratio rursus
fingi potest aut ita, ut supina jaceat pedibus divari-
tas, ciaut sublatis.*

*In illum quidem modum, quo supina jacet pedi-
bus divaricatis, Venerem figurare Octaviam jussit
Caviceus* (*Aloisia Sigæa, Colloq. V*) :

> « *Nolo te motitare clunes, et mutuis motibus meis
> respondere. Immo nolo te crura tollere, nec ambo simul
> nec alterum alterumve, cum super te conscendero. Sed
> hæc sunt quæ volo. Primum divariceris et aperias quam*

Ovid, the Master of Loves' Mysteries, invites pretty women to take this posture by preference :

« See you reckon up each of your charms, and take your posture according to your beauty. One and the same mode does not become every woman. You are especially attractive of face ; then lie on your back. » (*Art of Love* III, 771-773.)

This posture is by no means limited to one mode. The woman lying on her back, the rider may clasp her between his legs, or she may receive him between hers. Yet another position may be adopted, according as the woman lie back with legs stretched wide apart or with the knees raised.

It is this position, — lying on her back with legs wide apart, that Caviceo asks Olympia to assume for making Love :

« I do not wish you », he says, « to work your buttocks, or to respond with corresponding movements to my efforts. Neither do I wish you to lift your legs up, whether both at once, or one after the other, when I have mounted you. What I do wish you to do is this : First stretch your thighs as far apart, open them as

aptissime poteris femina. Vulvam ostentes mentulæ fi-
gendam, et eo corporis situ non mutato ad finem usque
libidinem perduci meam patiaris... Numeres omnes
concussiones meas. Vide ne pecces in numero. »

Imaginem desideras? evolvas fabulæ Romanensis
inscriptæ : Félicia, ou Mes fredaines, *caput* xxv
partis II, et fruaris tabulæ adjectæ argumento.

In hunc autem modum, quo supina jacet pedibus
sublatis, Tulliam disposuit Callias (Aloisia Sigæa,
Colloq. IV) :

« *Cum me effudero in amatum istud pectus, brachiis*
amplectere me. Nulla res complexum tuum solvat.
Quin etiam tolle quam altissime poteris crura, ita ut
lepidissimi pedes admotis calcibus politissimas nates
exosculentur. »

Si quis supinam pedibus sublatis jacentem vult
inire, potest is alia quoque ratione ac Tulliana et
forsan multo suaviori collocare amicam ita, ut pedes
supinæ in lumbos equitis decussatim tollantur : cujus
figuræ imaginem jucundissimam, qua possit cuique

wide as a woman well can. Offer your vulva to the member which is going to pierce it, and without altering this position, let *me* complete the work... Count my thrusts one by one, and see you make no mistake in the total » (Aloysia Sigaea, Dialogue V).

Would you see a representation of this? Take the tale *Félicia ou mes fredaines*, part II, chap. xxv, and look at the plate facing the text.

The other position, in which the woman is lying with her knees raised, is the one which Callias makes Tullia take:

« After I am lying upon your dear body », he says, « press me fast in your arms, and hold me thus embraced. Draw your legs back as far as you can, so that your pretty feet touch your buttocks, smooth as marble » (Aloysia Sigaea, Dialogue VI).

If you would enter the woman lying on her back with her legs in the air, it may be done in yet another way than Tullia's mode, and one perhaps still more delicious, by placing your mistress so that she rests her legs crossed over the loins of her rider. A representation of this very pleasant posture, which would rouse the

vel Hippolyto inguen concitari, adspicias Feliciæ
laudatæ partis IV capitii xxv *adjectam. Neque in-
venusta est ejusdem figuræ imago, quæ paulo ante
caput* xxi *comitatur. Hoc schemate videtur usa esse
Doris in epigrammate Sosipatri, p.* 584 *tomi I* Ana-
lectorum *Brunkii :*

Δωρίδα τὴν ῥοδόπυγον ὑπὲρ λεχέων διατείνας
Ἄνθεσιν ἐν χλοεροῖς ἀθάνατος γέγονα ·
Ἡ γὰρ ὑπερφυέεσσι μέσον διάβᾶσα με ποσσὶν,
Ἤνυεν ἀκλινέως τὸν Κύπριδος δόλιχον.

Non equitasse Doridem, patet ex διατείνας *: strata
jacebat pedibusque sublatis constringebat equitem.*

*Possunt vero etiam pedes supinæ tolli ab aliis. Sic
Aloisius Venerem Tulliæ juvit subactore Fabricio
(Aloisia Sigæa, Colloq. IV)* :

« *Ecce advolant,* » *inquit,* « *Aloisius Fabriciusque.* »
— « *Tolle* » *crura,* » *ait Fabricius, machæram in-
tentans. Tollo. Tunc effundit se in pectus meum, et*

numbed tool of a Hippolytus, is to be found in part IV. of the *Félicia* mentioned above. There is another similar plate in chap. XXI, not without charm. Doris, in the epigram of Sosipater, vol. I. of the *Analecta* of Brunck (p. 584), seems also to have made a trial of this figure :

« When I stretched Doris with the rosy buttocks on the bed, I felt immortal in my youthful vigour ; for she clipped me round the middle with her strong legs, and unswervingly rode out the long-course of Love. »

Doris did not bestride him ; the expression, « When I stretched » shows this ; she was lying on her back, and with her feet lifted up clasped her rider.

But again the feet of the woman lying on her back may also be held up by others. In this way Aloysio enjoyed Tullia with the help of Fabrizio, in the VI. Dialogue of Aloysia Sigaea, where Tullia expresses herself as follows:

« Aloysio and Fabrizio come running towards me. « Lift up your legs », says Aloysio to me, threatening me with his cutlass. I lifted them up. Then down he lies on my bosom, and plunges his cutlass in my ever open wound. Fabrizio raised my two legs in the air, and slipping a hand

immergti in ulcus insanabile machæram. Utramque mihi Aloisius tibiam sustollit, et sub poplitibus altera et altera missa manu agitat ipse lumbos mihi nullo meo labore. Procax ridiculæ motitationis genus! Incendi me dixi, sed dicto citius restagnans Veneris spuma restinxit incendium (10). »

Pedibus, nescio sua an aliena ope, sublatis se dedit Leda medicis indulgente marito admissis (Martialis, XI, 72) :

> *Hystericam vetulo se dixerat esse marito,*
> *Et queritur futui Leda necesse sibi,*
> *Sed flens atque gemens tanti negat esse salutem,*
> *Seque refert potius proposuisse mori.*
> *Vir rogat ut vivat, virides nec deserat annos,*
> *Et fieri quod jam non facit ipse sinit.*

---

(10) *Nec Aristophanis ætate artes ejusmodi incognitas fuisse, discimus ex versiculis 889, 90, in* Pace :

> Ὥστ' εὐθέως ἄραντας ὑμᾶς τὼ σκέλη
> Ταύτης μετέωρα καταγαγεῖν ἀνάρρυσιν.

Adde v. 1254 in Avibus :

> Τῆς διακόνου
> Πρώτης ἀνατείνας τὼ σκέλη διαμηριῶ.

under each of my hams, moves my loins for me
without any trouble on my part. What a singular and pleasant mode of making you move! I
declared I was on fire, but before I could end my
sentence, the overflowing foam of Venus quen-
ched the fire (10) ».

So too was it with feet in air, whether of her
own accord or seconded by another, that Leda
gave herself, with her husband's consent, to the
doctors who had been called in, as Martial describes the scene :

« To her old spouse Leda had declared herself
to be hysterical, and complains she must needs
be f...cked; yet with tears and groans avers she
will not buy health at such a price, and swears
she had rather die. The husband beseeches her to
live, not to die in her youth and beauty; and
permits others to do what he cannot effect himself. Straightway the doctors arrive, the ma-

----

(10) This method was not unknown at the time of Aristophanes, as we see from the following passage of the
Peace :
« So that you may straightway, lifting up the girl's
legs, accomplish high in air the mysteries » (v. 889,
890).
And in the *Birds* he says :
« For this girl, your first messenger, why! I will lift
up her legs and will in between her thighs » (v. 1254,
55).

Protinus accedunt medici, medicæque recedunt,
Tollunturque pedes : o medicina gravis !

Licet prono et rem habere cum semisupina, aut oblique, sive in lecto, sive in sella, effusa, aut in latus jacente.

Et in lecto quidem effundijubet Ovidiusobliquam, cui femur sit juvenile, careant quoque pectora menda (De Arte amat., *III*, 781, 782) :

Cui femur est juvenile, carent quoque pectora menda,
Semper in obliquo fusa sit illa toro (11).

Coitum autem proni cum oblique in sella effusa belle et festive more suo depinxit Aloisia Sigæa (*Colloq. V*) :

« *Lætus festinusque accurrit Caviceus, mihi* » (Octaviæ verba sunt) ; « *indusium tollit manumque procacem parti meæ admovet. Dehinc sedere jubet. Ut sedebam, utroque ponit sub pede sellam, ita ut cruribus altius sublatis horti porta ad speratos impetus obversa*

---

(11) *Alia figura prodit ex lectione quorundam librorum :*
     Stet vir, in obliquo fusa sit ipsa toro.

trons retire ; and up go the wife's legs in air : oh ! medicine grave and stern ! » (XI, 72.)

Face downwards to her the man may do the woman's business, while she is half reclining, either obliquely in bed, or on a chair, or lying sideways.

The latter position is recommended by Ovid to the woman with rounded thighs and faultless figure :

« She that has young rounded thigh and flawless bosom, should ever lie reclined sideways on the couch » (11) (*Art of Love*, III, v. 781, 782).

Copulation face to face with the woman sitting obliquely is described by Aloysia Sigaea with her usual elegance and vivacity :

« Caviceo came on, blithe and joyous » (it is Olympia speaking). He despoils me of my chemise, and his libertine hand touches my parts. He tells me to sit down again as I was seated before, and places a chair under either foot in such a way that my legs were lifted high in air, and the gate of my garden was wide open to the as-

---

(11) Readers will find another figure given in some of the books : « The man should be standing, while the woman reclines sideways on the bed. »

*pateret tota. Dexteram tamen subtus nates insinuavit,
paulo magis admovit me ad se... Læva sustinebat hastæ
pondus. Tunc procubuit in me..., applicuit arietem
foribus meis, in rimam priorem, cujus labra diducebat
digitis, inseruit mutonis caput. Hic vero hæsit, nec ultra
quidquam conatus est. « Octavia mea dulcissima, »
« inquit, « complectere me, dextrum femur tuum suble-
« va et in lumbos meos mitte ». — « Non intelligo
quid velis, » inquam. Sub hæc femur ipse meum sub-
dita manu superinjicit in lumbos suos, situ quo vo-
luerat. Demum adigit in Venereum scopum mentulam
et principio quidem impellit levi concussione, mox for-
tiori, ac postremum eo nisu, ut summum mihi non du-
bitarem imminere periculum. Rigida ea erat ac si cor-
nea... Tanta vi ruebat, ut lacerari me exclamarem.
Paululum requievit ab opere. — « Sile, amabo, cor-
culum, » inquit, « ita hæc res agitur : obdura immo-
ta. » Iterum subter clunes manum misit, promovitque
ad se, quæ videbar in fugam converti. Nec mora, cre-*

saults I was expecting. He then slides his right hand under my buttocks and draws me a little closer to him. With his left he supported the weight of his spear. Then he laid himself down on me... put his battering-ram to my gate, inserted the head of his member into the outermost fissure, opening the lips of it with his fingers. But there he stopped, and for a while made no further attack. « Octavia sweetest », he says, « clasp me tightly, raise your right thigh and rest it on my side. » — « I do not know what you want », I said. Hearing this he lifted my thigh with his own hand, and guided it round his loin, as he wished ; finally he forced his arrow into the target of Venus. In the beginning he pushes in with gentle blows, then quicker, and at last with such force I could not doubt that I was in great danger. His member was hard as horn, and he forced it in so cruelly, that I cried out, « You will tear me to pieces ! » He stopped a moment from his work. « I implore you to be quiet, my dear », he said, « it can only be done this way ; endure it without flinching ». Again his hand slid under my buttocks, drawing me nearer, for I had made a feint to draw back, and without more delay plied me with such fast and furious blows that I was near fainting away. With a violent effort he forced his spear right in, and the point

*bris concussionibus ita me fatigavit, ut fere animo
deficerem. Rapido post impetu hastam impulit, sum-
musque mucro hæsit in summo ulcere. Clamorem
tollo... In sudorem defluxit Venereum Caviceus. Sensi
me imbre fervido irrigari... Cum jam deficeret Caviceus, incessit me quasi micturientis pruriens libido :
tum et ipsa ultro clunes tollo, et illico sensi magna
cum voluptate excerni ex me nescio quid, quod mira-
biliter me ea in parte demulcebat. Conniventes mihi
oculi, crebri anhelitus, vultus mihi ignescere, totum
corpus dilabi. « Ah ! ah ! ah ! deficio, Cavici, » excla-
mo ; « siste fugientem animam ! »*

*Coitum denique cum semisupina jacente in latus,
et dextrum quidem latus, Naso judicat simplicissi-
mum esse et minimi laboris* (De Arte, *III*, 787, 88) :

> *Mille modi Veneris : simplex minimique laboris,
> Cum jacet in dextrum semisupina latus.*

*Præcipue hanc figuram inire jubet longiores fœmi-
nas, ibidem versiculis* 779, 80 :

> *Strata premat genibus, paulum cervice reflexa,
> Fœmina, per longum conspicienda latus.*

fixed itself in the depths of the wound. I cry out... Caviceo spurted out his venerean exudation, and I felt irrigated by a burning rain... Just as Caviceo slackened, I experienced a sort of voluptuous itch as though I were making water; involuntarily I draw my buttocks back a little, and in an instant I felt with supreme pleasure something flowing from me which tickled me deliciously. My eyes failed me, my breath came thick, my face was on fire, and I felt my whole body melting. « Ah! ah! ah! my Caviceo, I shall faint away », I cried; « hold my soul — it is escaping from my body » (Dialogue V).

Finally the conjunction with the woman lying on her side, particularly on her right side, is deemed by Ovid the most simple, calling for the least effort:

« A thousand modes of Love are there; the simplest and least laborious of all is when the woman lies reclined on her right side » (*Art of Love*, III, 787, 88).

Above all this position is the most convenient for tall women :

« Let her press the bed with her knees, with the neck slightly bowed, she whose chief beauty

Hoc modo Phyllis videtur esse fututa (Mart. X, 81) :

> *Cum duo venissent ad Phyllida mane fututum,*
> *Et nudam cuperet sumere uterque prior,*
> *Promisit pariter se Phyllis utrique daturam,*
> *Et dedit. Ille pedem sustulit, hic tunicam.*

Pedem igitur semisupinæ in latus jacentis sustulit fututor, tunicam pædico.

Pergamus ad eam figuram, qua supinus rem habet cum prona. Parte equitis versa vice hic sustinet fœmina, equi vir. Hanc figuram dicunt Hectoreum equum, ex illo Martialis, XI, 105 :

> *Masturbabantur Phrygii post ostia servi,*
> *Hectoreo quoties sederat uxor equo.*

Negat autem Ovidius (De Arte amat., III, 777, 78) *diserte, placuisse eam figuram Andromachæ,*

is her long shapely flank » (*Art of Love*, III, v. 779, 80).

It seems that the Phyllis of Martial allowed herself to be done in that way :

« Two arrived in the morning, who wanted to lie with Phyllis, and each was fain to be first to hold her naked body in his arms; Phyllis promised to satisfy them both together, and she did it; one lifted her leg, the other her tunic » (X, 81).

She was lying on her side; the f... lifted her leg; the pederast her tunic.

We now come to the manner, in which the man lying on his back has connection with the woman face downwards. The parts are interchanged; the woman plays the rider and the man the horse. This figure was called the horse of Hector.

Martial says :

« Behind the doors the Phrygian slaves would be masturbating, every time Andromaché mounted her Hector horse fashion » (XI, 105).

Ovid, however, with much sagacity denies that this posture could have pleased Andromaché; her figure was too tall, for this to have been

*neque potuisse aut debuisse illi ut lŏngissimæ placere;
vehi enim decere parvas :*

> *Parva vehatur equo; quod erat longissima, nunquam
> Thebais Hectoreo nupta resedit equo.*

Non nostrum est componere litem.

*Certe hanc figuram induit Sempronia cum Chry-
sogono* (*Aloisia, Colloq. VII*) :

> « *Impatiens moræ Chrysogonus :* « *Exuisti vestes* »,
> *inquit;* « *nunc figuram illam, Sempronia mea, qua
> nosti tantopere delectari me, indue.* » « *Exsilit in su-
> pinum, et sedens obversa spiculum candens divaricatis
> femoribus vibrat ipsa in se sua manu.* »

Idem schema servus ille Horatii Satir. II, VII,
50, *imperavit meretriculæ, quæ :*

> *...sub clara nuda lucerna,*
> *Clunibus... agitavit equum lasciva supinum.*

*Matronæ tamen quæ in illa ipsa Satira, versi-
culo* 64, « *non peccat superne* », *id schematis*

agreeable or even possible for her. It is for little women, that it is pleasant to be thus placed :

« A little woman may very well get astride on her horse; but tall and majestic as she was, the Theban bride never mounted the Hectorean horse » (*Art of Love* III, v. 777, 778).

It is no business of ours to decide the question.

At any rate Sempronia takes this posture with Crisogono.

« He could wait no longer : « Are you undress-« ed », said Crisogono. « Now, my Sempronia, take the position, which gives me so much pleasure, you know which. » He stretches himself down on his back, she gets upon him astride, with her face towards him. and with her own hand guides his burning arrow between her thighs » (Aloysia Sigea, Dial. VII).

This is the same attitude, which in Horace is imposed by the slave upon the little harlot, who :

«..... naked in the light of the lantern, plied with wanton wiles and moving buttocks the horse beneath her » (Sat. II. vii, v. 50).

As to the matron spoken of v. 64 of the same satire as « never having sinned *above* », no doubt

nequaquam arrisit : nam diversa diversas juvant.

Neque valde placuisse videtur illi, qnam Xanthias jusserat κελητίσαι *in* Vespis *Aristophanis, v.* 499, *quærit enim indignabunda, ludens tamen ambiguitate nominis, tyrannidemne Hippiæ moliatur :*

> Ὀξυθυμηθεῖσά μοι
> Ἥρετ' εἰ τὴν Ἱππίου καθίσταμαι τυραννίδα.

Huc etiam spectat illud in Lysistrata, *v.* 678, *quo obscenitatum auceps fœminarum genus dicit aptissimum esse ad equitandum curruque vehendum :*

> Ἱππικώτατον γάρ ἐστι χρῆμα κἄποχον γυνή.

Haud multo secius tangit illas, quæ versu 60 *ejusdem fabulæ :*

> Ἐπὶ τῶν κελήτων διαβεβήκασι,

nam κέλητες *et navigia sunt, et equi. Eadem figura delectabatur Plango Asclepiadis in* Analectis *Brunkii, I,* 217 :

> Νικήσασα κέλητι Φιλαινίδα τὴν πολύχαρμον,
> Ἑσπερίων πώλων ἄρτι φρυασσομένων.

this posture did not suit her. Women have not all the same taste.

Evidently, it was as little to the taste of the girl whom Xanthias in Aristophanes' *Wasps* (v. 499) asked to ride him; for she asks him indignantly, and playing on the double meaning of the word (Hippias and ἵππος, a horse), if he was for re-establishing Hippias' tyranny : « Irritated she asked me if I wanted to revive the tyranny of Hippias. »

Again in his *Lysistrata* (v. 678) this master of wanton wit points to the same thing, declaring the female sex to be very good at riding and fond of driving : « Woman loves to get on horseback and to stick there. »

Aristophanes mocks similarly those, of whom he says, in verse 60 of the same play, that « They are aboard their barks ». « They are mounted on their chargers ». For κέλης signifies both a ship and a horse. Plango in Asclepiades , Brunck's *Analecta*, vol. I, p. 217, affects the same figure :

« When she in horsemanship vanquished the ardent Philaenis, whilst her Hesperian coursers foamed under her reins. »

*Plures hæc equitando Veneris palæstra exhibere
figuras docta, quam ipsa Philænis, multiformis
illa gaudiorum artifex gratias agit Veneri in illo
epigrammate, quod Hesperios quosdam juvenes, supinos ipsam subeuntes, nuper ita emeruerit, ut fati-
gatis mentulis lascivientibus neutiquam pruriginosi
discederent. Supinos exercere moris etiam erat Lysi-
dicæ, non ita facile in Veneris stadio lassandæ, quæ
proximo Asclepiadis epigrammate :*

Πολὺν ὕπτιον ἵππον ἐγύμνασεν, ὃν ποτε δ' αὐτῆς
Μηρὸς ἐφοινίχθη κοῦφα τινασσομένης.

*Quod flagellum, frena, calcar istæ Veneri dedicant,
ad significandam faciunt eam figuram, quæ sibi
coeuntibus potissimum in usu fuerit, ut veherentur,
non veherent. Nihil profecto amplius.*

*Nec alia ratione pendulæ Veneris fructu Fotis
satiavit Lucium suum (Apuleius, Metamorphoseon
libro II, p. 122) :*

« *Hæc simul dicens, inscenso grabatulo super me
cossim residens, ac creba subsiliens, lubricisque gestibus
mobilem spinam quatiens, pendulæ Veneris fructu me*

Yet more expert in this kind of amorous riding than Philaenis herself, this ardent votary of pleasure thanks Venus in this epigram, that she has been able so to exhaust certain Hesperian gallants, whom she had mounted, that they had left her with wanton members all drooping, and feeling no desire left in them. To bestride men was also the favourite pastime of Lysidicé, who was never tired in the service of Venus, of whom the following epigram of Asclepiades treats :

« Many a horse has she ridden beneath her, yet never galled her thigh with all her nimble movements. »

Courtesans consecrated to Venus a whip, a bit, a spur, in order to signify, that with their clients they liked best to pose themselves in that way, and that they preferred riding themselves to being ridden, — nothing more.

It is the same when in Apuleius, Fotis satiated her Lucius with the pleasures of the undulating Venus ;

« Saying this she leaped upon the couch and, seated upon me backwards, plying her hips, vibrating her lithe spine lasciviously, she satiated me with the delights of the undulating Venus,

satiavit, usque dum lassis animis et marcidis artubus defatigati simul ambo corruimus. inter mutuos amplexus animas anhelantes. »

Proximam figuram, supini cum aversa, finxit Rangonius cum Octavia, Tullia magistra (Aloisia Sigæa, Colloq. VI) :

Rangonius. *Vide ut arrigo. Sed volo nova via ad rem ire.*

Tullia. *Nova via ? non, per pruriginem meam ! non ibis nova via.*

Rangonius. *Peccavi lingua. Volui dicere, nova figura.*

Tullia. *Quæ tandem erit ? Occurrit ultro : vocant Hectoreum equum. Extende te supinum, Rangoni hastaque illa fulminatrix hostem quærat intenta, quem confodiat. Apte !*

Octavia. *Quid facere vis, me, Tullia ?*

Tullia. *Surge, et aversa intra femina tua Rangonium subjice. Ejus machæra jacentis vaginæ respondeat imminentis. Apte collocasti te. Bene est.*

Rangonius. *O dorsum Dionæum ! o lumbos eburneos! o incendiarias nates !*

till both of us exhausted, powerless and with useless limbs, sunk down, exhaling our souls in mutual embraces » (*Metamorph.*, II, ch. ii).

The next figure, — the man lying supine and the woman turning her back to him, is executed by Rangoni with Ottavia, nnder the direction of Tullia :

RANGONI : Look how stiff I stand ! But I want to try the bliss in a new way.

TULLIA : In a new way ? No! I swear by my wanton soul you shall not. You shall not take a new way.

RANGONI : It was a slip of the tongue ; I meant to say a new posture.

TULLIA : And what sort of one ? I have an idea... what they call the horse of Hector. Lie down on your back, Rangoni; let your puissant spear stand firm to the enemy, who is to be pierced, Well done !

OTTAVIA : What must I do, Tullia ?

TULLIA : Clip Rangoni between your thighs, mounting him a-straddle. His cutlass as he lies should meet your sheath poised over it. Why ! you' ve taken the position admirably. Excellent !

RANGONI : Oh ! what a back, worthy of Venus ! Oh ! the ivory sides ! Oh ! the inviting buttocks !

Tullia. Ab his abstine maledictis. Cunno maledicit, qui natibus cum laude benedicit. At enim sapis, Octavia. Voravit tibi rudem mentulam, Rangoni, heluo cunnus.

Octavia. *Ades, Rangoni. En, en ades, Rangoni, mihi opi.*

Rangonius. *Adsum, Octavia. adsum. Ades tu? ades tu?*

Tullia. *Tam cito defecistis ambo?* »

Pygiaca etiam sacra, ad quæ Eumolpus puellam quandam invitavit apud Petronium, cap. CXL, *accipienda videntur de schemate supini cum aversa :*

« *Eumolpus non distulit puellam invitare ad pygiaca sacra. Pullam: quidem exoravit, ut sederet supra commendatam bonitatem* » (*supra ipsum, cujus bonitat mater filiam commendaverat*), « *Coraci autem imperavit, ut lectum, in quo ipse jacebat, subiret; positisque in pavimento manibus, dominum lumbis suis commoveret. Ille lente parebat imperio, puellæque artificium*

TULLIA : No naughty words ! He who praises the buttocks, slanders the vulva ! You know better, Ottavia ! Her greedy vulva has swallowed your bristling member whole, Rangoni.

OTTAVIA: Quick, Rangoni, it is coming !... quick, quick, help me !

RANGONI : I am coming, Ottavia, — I am come ! Are you ? — Are you, darling !

TULLIA : How now ? Are you so quickly done up, you two ? (Aloysia Sigaea, Dial. VI).

The pygiacic (12) mysteries, to which Eumolpus in Petronius (Satires, ch. CXL), invites a young girl, refer to the posture practised by the man lying on his back, with the woman upon him, her back turned towards him.

« Eumolpus did not hesitate to invite the young girl to the pygiacic mysteries, but begged of her to seat herself upon the goodness known to her (that being himself, to whose goodness the mother had recommended her daughter), and ordered Corax to get on his stomach under the bed on which he was, so that with his hands pressed against the floor, he might assist with his movements those of his master. Corax obeyed, beginning with slow undulations responding to

---

(12) From πυγή — buttock.

pari motu remunerabat. Cum ergo res ad effectum spectaret, clara Eumolpus voce exhortabatur Coraca, ut spissaret officium. Sic inter mercenarium amicamque positus senex veluti oscillatione ludebat. ».

Quid mirum, si in pygiacis istis sacris forte solœcismum fecit Eumolpi mentula, aberrando ab una caverna ad alteram?

Imaginem hujus figuræ in æs incisam reperies in elegantissimo opere Hancarvilliano inscripto : Monuments du culte secret des dames romaines, *capiti* xxv *adjectam, neque te pigebit accepisse verba doctissimi interpretis ;*

« *Cette attitude est du goût de beaucoup de gens, et les dames mêmes y trouvent plus de plaisir. On prétend que Priape va plus au fond, et que la belle, par ses mouvements, se procure une volupté plus vive et une libation plus abondante.* »

Num fieri possit, ut aversus commode futuat supinam, viderint experti. Recte enim Aloisia. Colloq. VI :

those of the young girl. When the crisis was approaching, Eumolpus exhorted Corax with a loud voice to quicken up his movements. Thus placed between his servant and his mistress, the old man took his pleasure as in a swing. »

Would it be surprising, if in these posterior mysteries, Eumolpus' member had perchance gone wrong, and taken by mistake one orifice for the other ?

You will find this figure represented in a copper-plate engraving in the very elegant book of d'Hancarville, *Monuments du culte secret des dames romaines*, ch. xxv, and you will be glad to know the note, with which the learned annotator accompanies the same.

« This attitude is to the taste of many men, and even the ladies find an increase of pleasure in practising it. It is supposed, that Priapus penetrates farther in, and that the fair one by her movements procures for herself a more voluptuous delight, and a more abundant libation. »

Is it possible for the man, conveniently, to manage the business while turning his back to the woman lying on her back ? Experts must decide. Aloysia Sigaea says with good common sense :

« *Multæ sunt,* » *inquit,* « *quæ ad effectum venire nequeant, licet supra quam excogitari possit flexibiles sint coeuntium in Veneris sacra artus et lumbi. Profecto plura in mentem meditando et commentando solent cadere quam vere fieri possint. Ut impotentis animi desideriis nihil impervium, sic nihil cogitationi exsultabundæ et intemperanti difficile. Quo vult, et qua tentat viam, insinuat se; vel in abruptis invenit planam. Non ita corporibus facilia factu omnia, quæ mens aut bona aut mala suadet.* »

Sedentes viros opus peragentes cum fœminis adversis spectare est in altero opere Hancarvilliano, cui index : Monuments de la vie privée des douze Césars, *tabula XXVII, ejusdemque operis tabula XV ostendet curiositati tuæ figuram sedentis aversam futuentis. Augustus ibi sedet, Terentiam* (13)*, Mæ-*

---

(13) *Dio Cass. LIV, 19 :* Οὔτω γὰρ οὖν πάνυ αὐτῆς ἤρα, ὥστε καὶ ἀγωνίσασθαί ποτε αὐτὴν περὶ τοῦ κάλλου, πρὸς τὴν Λιουίαν ποιῆσαι. *Haud inepte instituit certamen de forma :*

« There are many postures it is impossible to execute, even supposing the joints and loins of the candidates for the sacred joys of Venus more flexible than can be believed. By dint of pondering and reflection more ideas occur to the fancy than it is practicable to realize. Nothing is inconceivable to the longings of an unbridled will; nothing difficult to a furious and unregulated imagination. Love will find out a way ; and an ardent fancy level mountains. Only the body is unable to comply with everything the mind, good or bad, suggests.»

In another work of d'Hancarville's, *Monuments de la vie privée des douze Césars*, plate XXVII, you find represented men seated and copulating with women, who are facing them ; plate XV, in the same book presents to your curiosity a man sitting and working a woman, who turns her back on him. Augustus is seated : he is attacking backwards, with true imperial audacity, Terentia (13), the wife of Maecenas, after drawing

---

(13) Dio Cassius, LIV, 19 : « He was so fond of her, that one day he matched her against Livia, as to which of them was the most beautiful. » It was no bad idea to engage them in such a match, but think you he suffered them to fight this out in any costume but that in

cenalis, præsentis illius quidem, sed dormientis, nempe imperatori dormientis, uxorem gremio accep-tam pone fodiens imperatoria licentia. Similem figu-ram quæras in Contes et Nouvelles en vers par Jean de la Fontaine, *tabula fabellæ* le Tableau *adjecta, pagina 223 tomi II exempli Amstelodami anno 1762 excusi.*

Nihil frequentius coitu stantis cum adversa, qui cum unoquoque fere loco peragi facillimo negotio potest, tunica modo amicæ sublata teloque virili educto, tum maxime accommodus videtur rationibus eorum, si qui opportunitate raptim oblata uti velint, præsertim ubi opus est, ut fere fit in rebus furtivis, properato. Ita stabant vicinæ illæ sine fine prurientes, quarum salacitatem queritur Priapus Priapeio *XXV :*

> *Aut præcidite seminale membrum,*
> *Quod totis mihi noctibus fatigant*
> *Vicinæ sine fine prurientes,*
> *Vernis passeribus salaciores,*
> *Aut rumpar '...*

---

an putas, alio cultu certantes tulisse, atque eo, quo spectandas se præbuerunt Deæ devorantibus oculis Paridis ?

her onto his lap ; Maecenas is present, asleep — asleep of course only for the Emperor. You may see a similar posture in the *Contes et Nouvelles en vers* by Jean de la Fontaine ; it is on the plate appended to the tale, called *Le Tableau*, p. 223, vol. II, Amsterdam, 1762.

Nothing is more frequent than conjunction whilst standing, the woman with her back to the man ; it is indeed very easy to do it that way in any place, as you have only to lift up the fair one's petticoats, and out with your weapon ; it is, therefore, the best manner for those who have to make instantaneous use of an opportunity, when it is important to be sharp about it, as may happen, when you take your pleasure in secret. Thus Priapus complains of the wives and daughters of his neighbours, who came incessantly to him burning with ticklish desires.

« Cut off my genital member, which every night and all night long my neighbours' wives and daughters, for ever and for ever in heat, more wanton than sparrows in springtide, tire to death, — or I shall burst !... » (*Priapeia*, XXV).

---

which the Goddesses three presented themselves before the dazed eyes of Paris?

*Nostra ætate memini artis medicæ magistrum
celeberrimum (pæne nomen adjeci), arcessita, ut rei
fidem faceret, erubescente filia, auditoribusque sub-
ridentibus digito commonstrata, exclamare :* « *Hanc
stando feci.* » *Imaginem figuræ petas ex* Monuments de la vie privée des douze Césars, *tabula
XLVI, et similem ex* Monuments du culte secret
des dames romaines, *XIII.*

*Sed potest etiam stans coire tum adversa sublata,
ita quidem, ut aut totum corpus tollatur, cruribus
fœminæ lumbis viri impositis, aut inferior tantum
pars corporis sursum levetur, superior jaceat supina.
Vis tu figuræ utriusque non illepidæ adspectu pascere oculos? evolvas, nec pœnitebit, tabulam XXIV in*
Monuments du culte secret des dames romaines,
ac tabulam XL in Monuments de la vie privée
des douze Césars. *Alterutra species, nisi quid me
fallit, obversabatur ante oculos Nasoni* (De Arte,
III, 775, 76) :

> *Milanion humeris Atalantes crura ferebat ;
> Si bona sunt, hoc sunt accipienda modo.*

I remember a medical man of our time, one of
the most celebrated professors, (I had nearly ut-
tered his name), who to emphasize this, called
his daughter, and pointing to the blushing girl,
while his hearers could not help smiling said :
« This girl I fabricated standing. » A representation of this position is to be found in the *Monuments de la vie privée des douze Césars*, pl. XLVI,
and another in the *Monuments du culte secret des
dames romaines*, pl. XIII.

But further, a man may join himself to a woman standing face to face by supporting her in
such a way, that her whole body is lifted up, her
thighs resting on the man's hips, or else by lifting up the lower part of her body, whilst the
upper part is resting on a couch. Will you feast
your eyes with a representation of this not un-
graceful position ? If so you will not omit to look
at plate XXIV of the *Monuments du culte secret
des dames romaines*, and plate XL of the *Monuments de la vie privée des douze Césars*; Ovid,
if I am not mistaken, had his eyes on one or the
other of these figures :

« Milanion was supporting Atalanta's legs on
his shoulders; if they are fine legs this is how

*Certe priorem speciem depinxit nequitiarum Ma-
gistra, Aloisia Sigæa, ita quidem vivide, lepide,
laute, ut nihil posset supra, Colloq. VI :*

« *Proximus successit Turrianus... Surrexeram* »
(*Tullia loquitur*) » *e lecto ; nuda eram : arrigebat.
Nec mora. Mammam manu utraque prehendit utramque, et intorquens intra femina spiculum fervidum et
durum :* « *En,* » *inquit,* « *domina, ut te appetit hoc*
« *telum, non quo letum, sed læta omnia inferam tibi.*
« *Sis precor dux ipsa cæcutienti mer:tulæ hoc in cæco*
« *itinere, ne aberret a scopo : nam manus meas ab hac*
« *felicitate, qua fruuntur, haud dimoverim.* » *Facio
ut fieri volebat. Appuli ego igneum telum ad igneum ostium. Sensit, impellit et infigit... Momento, et ad
alterum alterumve concussum resoluta sum incredibili
cum titillatione, ita ut parum abfuerit, quin deficerent
poplites mihi.* « *Siste,* » *aio,* « *fugientem animam* ».
— « *Scio qua fugit,* » *refert subridens.* « *Tibi scilicet
elapsuram per id infimum putas ostium, quod teneo :
sed ecce occlusum id est aptissime.* » *Dicens conten-
tione quadam spiritus summa faciebat, ut incresceret
moles turgentis mentulæ, et :* « *Retro repellam fugi-*

they should be held » (*Art of Love*, III, vv. 775, 776). The former of these modes is no doubt that described by Aloysia Sigaea, Past Mistress of these naughtinesses, and with a vivacity, a grace, and elegance that leaves nothing to be desired :

« La Tour came forward instantly..... I had thrown myself on the foot of the bed » — (Tullia is speaking) — « I was naked; his member was erect. Without more ado he grasps in either hand one of my breasts, and brandishing his hard and inflamed lance between my thighs, exclaims « Look Madam, how this weapon is darting at « you, not to kill you, but to give you the greatest « possible pleasure. Pray, guide this blind appli- « cant into the dark recess, so that it may not miss « its destination; I will not remove my hands « from where they are, I would not deprive them « of the bliss they enjoy. » I do as he wishes, I introduce myself the flaming dart into the burning centre; he feels it, drives in, pushes home... After one or two strokes I felt myself melting away with incredible titillation, and my knees all but gave way. « Stop », I cried — « stop my « soul, it is escaping! » « I know », he replied, « laughing, from where. No doubt your soul « wants to escape through this lower orifice, of

tivam animam, » *adjiciebat, acerrimos etiam motus ciebat. Altius ad vivum persedit mucro. Ea vi sursum dulces ingerebat impetus, deliciosos penetrabat furores, ut, quando certe omne non poterat corpus, saltem cupiditates omnes, desideria, libidines, cogitationes animunque amemtem in corpus meum effunderet libidinoso nisu. Demum cum sensit liquidi æstus adventantem vesaniam, manus natibus meis subjicit, sublevat in acra. Ego furentis artus arctissimis brachiorum alligo complexibus, et femorum tibiarumque alterno volumine femora natesque, ika ut ejus ab collo penderem vibrata ex humo. Sic pendebam quasi clavo affixa. Dum in longum labor trahitur, iterum non segnem me solvit Venus in Venerem. Temberare mihi non potui, quin exclamarem acriori amoris œstro percita : « Sentio omnes, sentio Junonis cum Jove concumbentis delicias omnes; feror in cœlum! »... Eodem temporis puncto exundantis seminis humescenti igne genitale arvum conspersit Turrianus, quem Venus et Amor*

« which I have possession; but I keep it well stop-
« pered. » Whilst speaking he endeavoured, by
holding his breath, still further to increase the
already enormous size of his swollen member.
« I am going to thrust back your escaping soul »,
he added, poking me more and more violently.
His sword pierced yet deeper into the quick. Re-
doubling his delicious blows, he filled me with
transports of pleasure, — working so forcefully
that, albeit he could not get his whole body into
me, he impregnated me with all his passion, all
his lascivious desires, his very thoughts, his
whole delirious soul, by his voluptuous embraces.
At last feeling the approach of the ecstasy and
the boiling over of the liquid, he slips his hands
under my buttocks, and lifts me up bodily. I do
my part; I twine my arms closely round his
form, my thighs and legs being at the same
time intertwisted and entangled with his, so
that I found myself suspended on his neck in the
air, lifted clean off the ground; I was thus hanging,
as it were, fixed on a peg. I had not the patience
to wait for him, as he was going on, and again
I swooned with pleasure. In the most violent
raptures I could not help crying out — « I feel
« all... I feel all the delights of Juno lying with
« Jupiter. I am in heaven. » At this moment La
Tour, pushed by Venus and Cupido to the acmé

omnibus suis agebant furoribus in libidinem. Hedera
non ita nuci hæret circumvoluta, ut hærebam Turriano
brachiorum femorumque amplexu conjuncta. »

Speciem vero posteriorem, qua fingi posse diximus
coitum stantis cum sublata, etsi paululum immu-
tatam, repræsentavit Conradus cum Tullia (Aloisia,
Colloq. VI) :

« *Mihi femina* » (*Tulliæ verba audis*) « *aperuit.*
Non displicebat Conradus, nec admodum placebat : nec
negavi, nec dedi... Ille vero novum molitur modum,
nec ineptum. In sinistrum sibi humerum tollit dextrum
supinæ femur : post transfigit ictum exspectantem, non
optantem. Femori dextro suo supinæ injecerat sinistrum.
Adacto in intima telo concutere, subagitare, urgere.
Quid plura ? »

Verum enimvero potest etiam stans inire aversam,
quadrupedum more, quorum coitus fieri solet mare

of voluptuousnes, poured a plenteous flood of his well into the genial hold, burning like fire. The creeper does not cling more closely round the walnut tree than I held fast to La Tour with my arms and legs » (Dial. VI).

As to the last manner by means of which copulation may be achieved, the man standing with the woman half lifted up, Conrad practises it with slight modifications.

(TULLIA speaking) : « He opened my thighs — I do not dislike Conrad, though I am not particularly partial to him. I neither consented, nor refused. As to him, he fancied a novel posture, and not at all a bad one. I was lying on my back; he raised my right thigh on his shoulder, and in this position he transfixed me, while I was awaiting the event, without greatly desiring it. He had at the same time extended my left thigh along his right thigh. His tool plunged in to the root, he began to push and poke, quicker and quicker. What need to say more? Picture the conclusion for yourself » (Dial. VI).

Last of all, a man can get into a woman turning her back to him after the manner of the quadrupeds, who can have no connection with their females otherwise than by mounting upon

fœminam aversam inscendente (14). *Fuerunt qui fœminas pone dedolatas fœcundius parere crederent.* Lucretius (De Rerum Natura, *IV*, 1259-1262)

> *... Nam more ferarum*
> *Quadrupedumque magis ritu plerumque putantur*
> *Concipere uxores, quia sic loca sumere possunt*
> *Pectoribus positis sublatis semina lumbis.*

Aloisia Sigæa, Colloq. VI :

« *Viam Veneris esse dicunt alli ex Naturæ præscripto, si quadrupedum more prona et projectis lumbis ineatur mulier : nam sic promtius virilem invehi in muliebrem sulcum et seminis fluctus in arvum genitale... Sed negant medici pronæ concubitum naturæ convenire, qui partium generationi insudantium conformationi, ut probant, non convenit.* »

Quicquid id est, sæpe fit ut nequeant mulieres iniri secus atque aversæ. Quo enim alio modo obesus venter ventri obeso aut gravido commissus rei finem reperiat? Hanc ob causam Augustus fertur Liviam

---

(14) *Uberius hunc locum tractavit Plinius, capite 63 libri* X Historiæ Naturalis.

them from behind (14). Some authorities have held that a woman conceives easier while on all fours. Lucretius says :

« .... Women are said to conceive more readily when down after the manner of beasts, as the organs can absorb the seed best so, when the bosom is depressed and the loins lifted » (*Of the Nature of Things*, IV, vv. 1259-1262).

Also Aloysia Sigaea :]

« Some people pretend that the fashion to make love indicated by Nature is that one where the woman offers herself for copulation after the manner of the animals, bent down with the hips raised; the virile ploughshare penetrates thus more conveniently into the female furrow, and the seminal flow waters the field of love... The doctors, however, are against this posture; they say it is incompatible with tne conformation of the parts destined for generation ». (Dial. VI.)

However this may be, it happens frequently, that women cannot be managed in any other way. Given an obese man and a woman likewise obese or with child, how are they to do

---

(14) Pliny has treated this at great length in his *Natural History* (Book X, ch. 63).

Drusillam, cum Tiberii Neronis matrimonio sextum jam mensem gravidam abduxisset, pecudum more compressisse, cujus compressus jucundam imaginem tibi præbebunt Monuments de la vie privée des douze Césars, *tabula VII; at cur fraudari te patiamur iis, quæ luculentus editor ad illustrandam tabulam adnotavit? Sic fere habent :*

« Cette Drusille est la fameuse Livie, femme de Tibère Néron, qui avoit été un des amis d'Antoine : Auguste en devint passionnément amoureux, et Tibère la lui céda, quoiqu'elle fût grosse de six mois. L'on plaisanta beaucoup sur cet empressement de l'empereur, et un jour qu'ils étoient tous à table, et que Livie étoit couchée près d'Auguste, un de ces enfants nus, que les matrones élevoient pour servir à leurs plaisirs, s'approchant de Livie : « *Quid agis hic, domina,* » lui dit-il, « *ecce enim maritus tuus* » (*Neronem monstrabat*) ; « *illic est* (15). » Livie accoucha peu de temps après, et l'on disoit publiquement à Rome que les

---

(15) *Conferas caput 44 libri XLVIII Dionis Cassii.*

the thing otherwise ? This is the reason why, so they say, Augustus having married Livia Drusilla, divorced wife of Tiberius Nero and already six months gone in pregnancy, had connection with her after the manner of animals. Plate VII of the *Monuments de la vie privée des douze Césars* will give you an idea of the posture assumed by both of them. But why should we not give you the annotations whereby the learned editor has elucidated the plate ? Here they are :

« This Drusilla was the famous Livia, the wife of Tiberius Nero, who had been one of Anthony's friends. Augustus fell violently in love with her, and Tiberius gave her up to him, although she was at the time six months with child. A good many jokes were made about the eagerness of the Emperor, and one day, while they were all at table, and Livia was reclining by Augustus, one of those naked children, whom matrons used to educate for their pleasures, going up to Livia said : « What are you doing « here ? yonder is your husband », pointing to Nero, «there he is » (15). Soon afterwards Livia was confined, and the Romans said openly, that lucky people get children three months after

---

(15) Compare Dio Cassius, bk. XLVIII, ch. 44.

gens heureux avoient des enfants après trois mois
de mariage, ce qui passa même en proverbe. Un
historien dit qu'Auguste fut obligé de caresser sa
femme *more pecundum*, à cause de sa grossesse ; et
c'est à cette luxurieuse attitude que fait allusion
le camée d'Apollonius, graveur célèbre du temps
d'Auguste. L'état où étoit Livie peut, il est vrai,
avoir rendu cette posture nécessaire, mais il paroît
qu'elle étoit en tout temps du goût des Anciens,
soit qu'ils crussent, ainsi que l'indique Lucrèce,
que cette attitude étoit favorable à la génération,
soit plutôt qu'ils la préférassent par un raffinement
de volupté. Les postures les plus recherchées,
les moins naturelles souvent, ont paru en tout
temps à quelques débauchés augmenter le plaisir
de la jouissance. Mais il faut convenir que l'imagination va encore au delà de la possibilité réelle. »

*Singularem causam, cur necesse sit coire cum
aversa, commenta est Aloisiæ sagacitas, Colloq.
VII :*

« *Commendant Veneres* » (cunnum) « *qui non omnino inter femina delitescat conditus : novem decemve
distet tantum pollices ab umbilico. Demissa plerisque
puellis itu fugit pubes, ut aversa videatur ad Venerem
via. Difficilis cum istis concubitus. Non potuit Theodora*

being married, which passed into a proverb. One historian says that Augustus was obliged to caress his wife « after the manner of beasts » on account of her pregnancy, and it was to this luxurious attitude that the cameo of Apollonius, the celebrated gem-cutter of the time of Augustus, makes allusion. True that the state in which Livia was may have made this posture necessary : but it seems that it was at all times to the taste of the Ancients, either because they considered this attitude favourable for procreation, as Lucretius maintains, or because they found it to be a refinement of voluptuousness. The most extraordinary and least natural postures have always appeared to rakes as enhancing the pleasure of the conjunction. But it must be admitted that imagination still outruns actual possibilities. »

A singular reason for the necessity of encountering a woman backwards is given by Aloysia Sigaea, with her usual sagacity :

« For pleasure, one likes a vulva which is not placed too far back, so as to be entirely hidden by the thighs; it should not be more than nine or ten inches from the navel. With the greater number of girls the pubis goes so far down, that it may easily be taken as the other way of pleasure. With such coition is difficult. Theo-

Aspilcueta nisi posito pectore et sublatis genua lumbis devirginari. Frustra supinæ vir insudarat superfusus : oleum perdiderat. »

Jubet Ovidius eas potissimum quærere coitum aversum, quibus jam venire cœperint rugæ corpus arantes (De Arte, *III,* 785, 86) :

> *Tu quoque cui rugis uterum Lucina notavit,*
> *Ut celer aversis utere Parthus equis.*

Eodem spectare videtur præceptum paulo ante versu 774 *datum :*

> *Spectentur tergo quis sua terga placent.*

Sed missa necessitate sæpenumero constat fœminas pone futui libidinis gratia, cum summa sit voluptas voluptatem variare. Nec alia de causa Fabricium Tullia passa est aversa apud Aloisiam Sigæam, Colloq. *VI :*

« *Surgente Aloisio* » (Tullia loquitur), « *novam se Fabricius accingit ad pugnam. Rubicunda illi et minitabunda turgebat mentula.* — « *Amabo, domina ob*

dora Aspilqueta could not be deflowered, till she placed herself prone on her stomach, with her knees drawn up to her sides. Vainly had her husband tried to manage her, while lying on her back, he only lost his oil » (Dialogue VII).

Ovid recommends this way with women who begin to be wrinkled :

« Likewise you, whose stomach Lucina has marked with wrinkles, mount from behind, like the flying Parthian with his steed » (*Art of Love*, III, v. 785, 86).

The same advice also seems to be given by him a little before :

« Let them be seen from behind whose backs are sightly » (v. 774).

But besides necessity, it is a fact that women are worked in this way out of mere caprice, variety offering the greatest pleasure. It is simply for this reason that Tullia suffers Fabrizio to do her that way, in Aloysia Sigaea :

« As Aloisio got up » (Tullia speaks) « Fabrizio makes ready for another attack. His member is swollen up, red and threatening. « I beg of you « Madam », he says, « turn over on your face. » I did as he wished. When he saw my buttocks,

verte te in faciem, » ait. *Obverto, ut volebat... At
enim ut nates vidit, quæ candore suo ebur et nivem
obscurarent :* « *O te pulchram!* » ait. « *Sed erige te in*
« *genua, demisso superioris corporis trunco.* »... *De-
mitto caput et pectus tollo nates... Trusit in intimam
vulvam rapidum et igneum telum. Mammam utramque cepit manu utraque. Post agitare cœpit, et momento
dulcis profluere rivus in mollem Veneris sinum, et ego
etiam miris deliniri deliciis. Præ voluptate parum ab-
fuit, quin deficerem. Ea me seminis copia excreti ex Fa-
bricii lumbis implevit et demulsit, ea copia excreti e
meis exhausit mihi vires. Hoc uno concubitu plus amisi
virium, quam prioribus tribus* (16). »

*Nova nec infaceta ratione peractus est coitus ille
àversus, cujus bella imago conspicitur in* Monuments du culte secret des dames romaines, *ta-*

---

(16) *Res inventionis est satis antiquæ.* Huc spectant
Aristophanea illa in Pace *v. 896* :

Ἐπὶ γῆς παλαίειν, τετραποδηδὸν ἑστάναι,

et in Lysistrata, *v. 231* :

Οὐ στήσομαι λέαιν' ἐπὶ τυροκνήστιδος,

whiter than ivory and snow, « How beautiful
« you are! » he cried. « But raise yourself on your
« knees, and bend your head down. » I bow my
head and bosom, and lift my buttocks. He thrust
his swift-moving and fiery dart to the bottom of
my vulva, and took one of my nipples in either
hand. Then he began to work in and out, and
soon sent a sweet rivulet into the cavity of Venus. I also felt unspeakable delight, and had
nearly fainted with lust. A surprising quantity of
seed secreted by Fabrizio's loins filled and delight-
ed me; a similar flow of my own exhausted
my forces. In that single assault I lost more vigour than in the three preceding ones » (Dialogue VI) (16).

This copulation from the back is practicable
in another very pleasant fashion, an excellent
reproduction of which can be seen in the *Monu-
ment du culte secret des dames romaines*, plate
XXVIII. A woman is represented with her

---

(16) The thing itself is very old; Aristophanes alludes
to it in the *Peace* :
« To wrestle on the ground, to stand on all fours »
(v. 896).
And in the *Lysistrata* :
« I will not squat down like a lioness carved on a
knife-handle » (v. 231).

bula XXVIII. In manus illic procumbit fœmina, inferiore corporis parte funiculis sublata, et stanti fututori obversa. Neque valde diversam figuram exhibuisse videtur uxor illa fabri, quam, narrante **Apuleio** Metamorph. *libro IX,* « *inclinatam dolio pronam superincurvatus, secure dedolabat* » (*adulter*). *Lepidi facinoris imago adjuncta est fabulæ* le Cuvier *in* Contes et Nouvelles par Jean de La Fontaine, *tomo II, pagina* 215.

hands placed on the ground, while the lower part of the body is lifted up and suspended by cords; she is turning her back to the man who stands. This seems to be much the same position as was taken up by the wife of the artisan Apuleius speaks of in his *Metamorphoses* (book IX), whom « bending over her, the lover planed with his adze, while she leant forward over a cask ». An engraving showing this ingenious attitude is appended to the story of *The Tub* in the *Contes et Nouvelles en vers* of Jean de La Fontaine, vol. II, p. 215.

CAPUT II

DE PÆDICANDO

ÆC habuimus de fututione quæ diceremus.
Jam sequitur ut exponamus de alterius Veneris genere, quod quidem mentula perficit
ope culi. Si quis opus peragit mentula culo, sive maris,
sive fœminæ, immissa, pædicat. Qui pædicat dicitur
pædicator, pædico, draucus (17) : qui pædicatur
pathicus, cinædus, catamitus (18), mollis delica-

---

(17) Draucus, patrans, a δράω, pro dravicus, ut cautus
pro cavitus, lautus pro lavitus.

(18) Catamitum, Festo auctore, pro Ganymede dixerunt,
qui fuit Jovis concubinus. Simili modo corrupte pronuntiabant
Proserpinam pro Persephone, Æsculapium pro Asclepio, Car-
thaginem pro Carchedone. Pollucem pro Polydeuce, Sibyllam
pro Siobula, masturbare pro manu stuprare.

CHAPTER II

ON PEDICATION

S o much for copulation in the normal way. We will now discuss another mode of pleasure, — that due to introduction of the member into the anus. A man who exercises his member in the anus, be it of a man or a woman, pedicates; he is called a pederast, pedicon, drawk (17), and the other party, who allows himself to be invaded in that way, is called the patient, cinaedus, catamite (18), minion, effe-

---

(17) *Drawk*, from δράω, I work, execute; for *dravicus*, as *cautus* for *cavitus*, *lautus* for *lavitus*.

(18) Catamite, according to Festus, is the same thing as Ganymede, the minion of Jupiter; the Latins, by similar corruption of words, pronounced *Proserpina* for *Persephone*, *Aesculapius* for *Asclepios*, *Carthago* for *Carchedo*, *Pollux* for *Polydeukes*, *Sybilla* for *Siobulé*, *masturbare* for *manu stuprare*.

tus : pathicus adultior vel emeritus, exoletus. Mas-
culæ Veneris (nam cum multo rarius fiat, ut pædi-
centur fœminæ quam mares, mascula solet dici ab
eo quod plerumque fit), masculæ igitur Veneris
fructu satiatur libido aut agendo, quod est pædico-
num, aut patiendo, quod est pathicorum. Et volup-
tas quidem pædiconis facile intelligitur, cum omnis
voluptas mentulæ pendeat ex frictione; qui autem
fieri possit, ut pathicus voluptatem capiat alieno pene
intra viscera acto, difficilius videtur ad intelligen-
dum, mei quidem ingenii exiguitati, qui sim talium
artium plane rudis atque hospes. Cave enim existi-
mes, voluptatem pathici tantum esse secundariam,
neque pathicum substernere pudicitiam pædiconi nisi
eo, ut legitimum Veneris lusum pædicando sibi præ-
ludat, ignaviæque mentulæ, quoad ejus possit, me-
deatur, vel adspectu virtutis alieni nervi, vel podicis
quadam titillatione, quemadmodum eandem vim non
modo digitis inesse in anum (19) *trusis docet Anto-*

---

(19) *Similiter scorteum penem ano Encolpii inseruit Œno-*
thea ad languentem nervum pueri excitandum; Petronius, c.
138 : « *Profert Œnothea scorteum fascinum, quod, ut oleo et*

minate ; if adult or worn out, he is named exo-
lete. The masculine pleasure (so called because
women allowed themselves much more rarely
to be pedicated than men) is appreciated equally
by the active party, the pedicon, as by the passive party, the patient. The pleasure of the pedicon is easy to understand, as the enjoyment
of the virile member consists in the intensity of
the friction ; the pleasure felt by the patient by
the introduction of the member in his entrails is
more difficult to make out, — a least for my
feeble intelligence, for such practices are quite
strange to me. Do not believe, however, that the
pleasure of the patient is only secondary, nor
yet that he prostitutes himself only in order to
do the same afterwards himself, nor that he re-
medies in this way the sluggishness of his own
member by the vigorous working of another
man's nerve causing a pleasurable titillation of
the posterior, analogous to that which Antonius
Panormitanus (*Hermaphroditus*, I, 20), tells us
may be produced by inserting the fingers in the
anus (19), or still better, by beating the same

---

(19) Thus Oenothea, to excite the lad's feeble nerve,
pushes a leathern mentula (member) into Eucolpius'
anus (Petronius, 138) : « Oenothea fetches a leathern con-

nius epigrammate XX libri prioris Hermaphroditi, *sed et verberibus podici inflictis Aloisia Sigæa,
Colloq. V :*

« *Audio esse nostros inter homines Alphonsum mar-
chionem, quem verbera excitant ad pugnam, alioquin
imbellem et ignavum. Virgis cædi sibi nate⁵ jubet, vapulat egregie : prostat interim illi uxor resupina in lecto. Dum vapulat, arrigit, et quo acriores ictus, eo tentigo vehementior.Cum parata sibi videt arma, aggreditur
jacentem, et rapidissimos ciens in substratam motus
perfundit in subantem cælestia Veneris dona, et omnes,
quæ ex Venere capi possunt, capit voluptates* (20). »

*Et quid aliud commenta est ingeniosa mentula
Russavii Genevensis, qui Lamberceriæ virgini, summum pueri femur exclamare cogenti, pœnas illas
per omnem vitam efflictim exoptatas dedit*? *Audias*

---

minuto pipere atque urticæ trito circumdedit semine, paulatim
cœpit inserere ano meo. » De alio usu scortei fascini infra
capite sexto dicendum veniet.

(20) Etiamnum in lupanaribus Londinensibus non deesse,
qui verbera præstent desiderantibus, narrat auctor Gynæologiæ Germanice conscriptæ, tomo III, p. 392.

locality with rods, according to Aloysia Sigaea :

« Amongst the men of our acquaintance, I have
heard the Marquis Alfonso say that rods act as
spurs to the amorous battle ; without them he
would be sluggish and impotent. He has his buttocks flogged with rods vigorously, his wife being
present lying ready on the bed. During the flag-
ellation his tool begins to stiffen, and the more
violent the strokes are, the stronger is the ten-
sion. When he feels himself in proper condition,
he precipitates himself upon his wife, works
her with rapid movement, and inundates her
with the heavenly gifts of Venus, and wins all
the delights a man may find in Love » (20) (Dialogue V).

What else was it but this that so stirred Rous-
seau, the precocious genius of Geneva, and his
boyish member, and brought such ideas into his
head, when on one occasion Mlle. Lambercier,

---

trivance; this she first oiled and sprinkled with pepper
and crushed nettle-seeds, and then proceeded to push
little by little up my anus. » We shall have to speak in
chapter vi. of another use of these leathern tools.

(20) According to the author of the *Gynaeology* (German
edition, vol. III, p. 392) there are to be found at this
day in the London brothels women who make it their
business to flagellate customers who desire it.

ipsum rem festive gestam qua solet elegantia narran-
tem libro primo Confessionum *Francogallice scrip-*
tarum, inde a pagina 22 exempli Genevæ 1782 *ty-*
pis impressi, missis tamen nonnullis, quæ modo ad
amplificandum et exornandum addidit auctor im-
mortalis :

« Comme Mlle Lambercier avoit pour nous l'affection d'une mère, elle en avoit aussi l'autorité, et la
portoit quelquefois jusqu'à nous infliger la punition
des enfants, quand nous l'avions méritée. Assez
longtemps elle s'en tint à la menace, et cette menace d'un châtiment tout nouveau pour moi me
sembloit très effrayante : mais après l'exécution je
la trouvai moins terrible à l'épreuve que l'attente ne
l'avoit été, et ce qu'il y a de plus bizarre est que ce
châtiment m'affectionna davantage encore à celle
qui me l'avoit imposé. Il falloit même toute la vé-
rité de cette affection et toute ma douceur naturelle
pour m'empêcher de chercher le retour du même
traitement en le méritant : car j'avois trouvé dans
la douleur, dans la honte même, un mélange de
sensualité qui m'avoit laissé plus de désir que de
crainte de l'éprouver derechef par la même main.
Qui croirait que ce châtiment d'un enfant reçu à
huit ans par la main d'une fille de trente a décidé

cracking the whip upon the buttocks of the child, inflicted that punishment, which he afterwards was longing for all the rest of his life? Hear him relate the circumstance himself in his merry way and with his habitual charm of style, in the first book of the *Confessions*; we only omit small matters, added by the immortal author for the amplification of the narrative :

« As Mlle. Lambercier had for us the affection of a mother, so she had the authority of one, and she carried the latter so far as to inflict upon us the punishment of children when we had deserved it. For a long time she only used threats, and such a threat of a novel punishment seemed very dreadful to me; but after the execution I found the experience less terrible than the expectation, and the oddest thing was, that the punishment made me more partial to her, who had inflicted it, than I had been previously. I stood in fact in need of all this affection for her and of all my natural mildness, in order to hold back from provoking the same punishment by acting so as to deserve it, for I had found in the pain, and even in the shame, a mixed feeling, in which sensuality predominated, and which left me with more desire than apprehension of experiencing the same treatment over again from

de mes goûts, de mes désirs, de mes passions, de moi pour le reste de ma vie ? Tourmenté longtemps sans savoir de quoi, je dévorois d'un œil ardent les belles personnes ; mon imagination me les rappeloit sans cesse, uniquement pour les mettre en œuvre à ma mode, et en faire autant de demoiselles Lambercier. N'imaginant que ce que j'avois senti, je ne savois porter mes désirs que vers l'espèce de volupté qui m'étoit connue. Dans mes sottes fantaisies, dans mes érotiques fureurs, dans les actes extravagants auxquels elles me portoient quelquefois, j'empruntois imaginairement le secours de l'autre sexe, sans penser jamais qu'il fût propre à nul autre usage qu'à celui que je brûlois d'en tirer. Mais quand enfin le progrès des ans m'eut fait homme, mon ancien goût d'enfant s'associa tellement à l'autre, que je ne pus jamais l'écarter des désirs allumés par mes sens, et cette folie, jointe à ma timidité naturelle, m'a toujours rendu très peu entreprenant près des femmes, faute d'oser tout dire ou de pouvoir tout faire : l'espèce de jouissance dont l'autre n'étoit pour moi que le dernier terme, ne pouvant être usurpée par celui qui la désire, ni devinée par celle qui peut l'accorder. J'ai ainsi passé ma vie à convoiter et me taire auprès des personnes que j'aimois le plus. N'osant jamais déclarer mon goût, je l'amusois du moins par des rapports qui m'en conservoient l'idée. On peut juger de ce

the same hand. Who would believe that this chastisement of a child eight years old by the hand of a maiden of thirty should have influenced my tastes, my longings, my passions for the remainder of my life? Tormented by I know not what, my eye feasted ardently upon good-looking females; they constantly came into my mind doing to me as Mlle. Lambercier had done. Imagining only what I had experienced, my desires did not pass beyond the sort of voluptuous feeling I had known already. In my foolish fancies, in my erotic fury, in the extravagant acts to which they incited me sometimes, I borrowed in imagination the help of the other sex, without ever dreaming it was good for any other use than that which I wanted to make of it. When in the course of time I had grown up to manhood, my old taste of childhood associated itself so much with the other, that I never could divert the desires which fired my senses; and this absurdity, joined to my natural timidity, made me always anything but enterprising with women, as I dared not say all or could not do all I wanted; the sort of enjoyment, of which the other was for me but the last stage, could neither be initiated by the one who longed for it, nor guessed at by the other who might have granted it. Thus I have passed through life coveting, yet not daring

qu'ont pu me coûter de semblables aveux, sur ce que
dans tout le cours de ma vie, emporté quelquefois
près de celles que j'aimois par les fureurs d'une passion qui m'ôtoit la faculté de voir, d'entendre, hors
de sens, et saisi d'un tremblement convulsif dans
tout mon corps, jamais je n'ai pu prendre sur moi
de leur déclarer ma folie, et d'implorer d'elles dans
la plus intime familiarité la seule faveur qui man-
quoit aux autres. Cela ne m'est jamais arrivé qu'une
fois dans l'enfance, avec une enfant de mon âge :
encore fut-ce elle qui m'en fit la première propo-
sition. »

*Jam redeamus illuc unde divertimus. Si voluptas
pathica non potest ita animo concipi, ut per podicem,
velut ambage facta, eatur ad mentulam, debemus
potius sic statuere et judicare, simili pathicos laborare prurigine podicis, atque alii soleant inguinis,
et vero fontem inesse proprium voluptatis in podice,
incognitum non expertis (21). Certe pruriginem podicis sine ullo fuco testatur Martialis, VI, 37 :*

---

(21) *Ad podicis pruriginem restinguendam Siphnii
(Siphnus una ex Cycladibus) hoc moris habebant, ut podi-*

to tell the persons I loved most what it was I coveted. Never bold enough to declare my inclination, I amused it as least by ideas in connection with it. One may judge what such avowals must have cost me, considering that all through my life, seized in the presence of those I loved by the fury of a passion which bereft me of voice, hearing and sense, and made me tremble all over convulsively, I never could venture to tell them my folly, and ask them to add the one familiarity which I wanted to the other ones. I only got to it once in my childhood, with another child of my age, and the proposal came from her. »

However to return to our proper subject, from which we have strayed. If pleasure felt by the passive party cannot be conceived to be of a kind, which through the anus is communicated to the mentula (member), we must come to the conclusion that the *patient* experiences in the anus the same kind of irritation which the other party feels in his genital parts ; that, therefore, the *patient* feels in that place a real pleasure unknown to those who have not tried it (21). Mar-

---

(21) In order to appease the ardours of the anus, the Siphnians (Siphnos, one of the Cyclades) were in the hab-

Secti podicis usque ad umbilicum
Nullas reliquias habet Carinus,
Et prurit tamen usque ad umbilicum,
O quanta scabie miser laborat !
Culum non habet, est tamen cinædus.

Tulliam quoque hujusmodi pruriginis rabies in-
vasit, ipsa referente apud Aloisiam Sigæam, Col-
loq. VI :

« *Cu proficerem nihil, parui furentibus. Tunc pro-*
nus inclinat se in nates Aloisius. Pilum postico admovet,
pulsat, percutit, post summo nisu irrumpit. Ego gemi-
tum misi. Sed illico extractum ex ulcere telum condit
in vulvam, et multo semine depluit in lubricum uteri
sulcum. Aggreditur re peracta eodem modo Fabricius.
Rapido vibrat hastam puram impetu, totamque brevi
in viscera abdidit. It reditque aliquamdiu repetita via,

---

cem digito foderent, unde novum id libidinis genus proprio
verbo Græci dixerunt σιφνιάζειν. *Suidas :* Σιφνιάζειν, τὸ
ἅπτεσθαι τῆς πυγῆς δακτύλῳ.

tial at any rate speaks out without any circumlocution of this rut of the anus :

« Of his anus, split to the navel, not a vestige is left to Carinus; for all that he is in rut to the very navel. Oh! the scurvy lot of the wretch! Bottom he has none, — but he *will* be a cinede » (VI, 37).

An ardour of this strange sort even affected Tullia, as she confesses herself in the pages of Aloysia Sigaea :

« Seeing resistance was in vain, I yielded to the madmen. Aloysio bends forward over my buttocks, brings his javelin to the back-door, knocks, pushes, finally with a mighty effort bursts in. I gave a groan. Instantly he withdraws his weapon from the wound, plunges it in the vulva and spurts a flood of semen into the wanton furrow of my womb. When all was over, Fabrizio attacks me in the same fashion. With one rapid thrust he introduced his spear, and in less than no time made it disappear in my entrails ; for a little time he plays at come and go, and scarce credible as it may sound, I found

---

it of introducing a finger up the anus. The Greeks called this proceeding to *siphnianize*. Suidas : *Siphnianize*, — to finger the posterior.

et quod fieri posse non putabam, etiam invasit me nescio cujus pruriginis rabies, ut huic me assuefieri posse rei, si velim, non dubitem. »

Confirmat etiam podicis pruriginem Cœlius Rhodiginus Lectionum antiquarum *libro XV,* capite x :

« *Cinœdulos scimus summa, dum turpiter atteruntur, perfrui voluptate;* » *addita insuper causa, quæ vera sit an commentitia viderint medici :* » Quibus meatus » *(seminis genitalis)* « *habitu suo naturali privantur, vel quia occæcati sunt qui ad penem tendant, quod spadonibus hisque similibus evenit, vel etiam aliis de causis, iis talis humor in sedem confluit. Qui si admodum semine genitali abundant, excrementum illud large in eum locum se colligit. Itaque quum excitata cupiditas est, attritum pars ea desiderat, in quam confluit excrementum. Quibus itaque sedem humor ille adivit, hi pati tantummodo avent.* »

Quicquid id est, nihil certius voluptate pathica. Tanti enim erat pathicis olim Romanis, rigidum penem in clune habere, ut magnam mentulam non possent videre nisi spumantibus labellis, atque ade

myself invaded by a prurient fury to such an extent that I have no doubt, that I should get accustomed to it very well, if I chose » (Dialogue VI).

Coelius Rhodiginus confirms this pruriency of the anus in chap. 10. of XV. book of his *Lectiones antiquae.*

« We know », he says, « that the minions experience a very great pleasure in undergoing this shameful act. »

And he gives a reason for it too, whether good or bad the doctors may decide : « With people whose seminal ducts are not in normal condition, be it that those leading to the mentula are paralysed, as is the case with eunuchs and the like, or for any other reason, the seminal fluid flows back to its source. If this fluid is very abundant with them, it accumulates in great quantities, and then the part where the secretion is accumulated longs for friction. People thus situated like above everything to play the part of *patients.* »

Be this as it may, nothing is more certain than the fact of such enjoyment on the part of the *patient.* So highly did the Roman cinedes prize a stiff member between their buttocks, that they could not see a big mentula without their mouths

*vel ultimum denarium darent, ut conditionibus bene
vasatorum fruerentur.*

Juvenalis, IX, 32-36 :

> *Fata regunt homines : fatum est in partibus illis*
> *Quas sinus abscondit. Nam si tibi sidera cessant,*
> *Nil faciet longi mensura incognita nervi,*
> *Quamvis te nudum spumanti Virro labello*
> *Viderit...*

Martialis, I, 97 :

> *Rogabit, unde suspicer virum mollem ?*
> *Una lavamur : adspicit nihil sursum,*
> *Sed spectat oculis devorantibus draucos,*
> *Nec otiosis mentulas videt labris.*

Idem, II, 51 :

> *Unus saepe tibi tota denarius arca*
> *Cum sit, et hic culo tritior, Hylle, tuo,*
> *Non tamen hunc pistor, non auferet hunc tibi caupo,*
> *Sed si quis nimio pene superbus erit.*
> *Infelix venter spectat convivia culi,*
> *Et semper miser hic esurit, ille vorat.*

Quid? quod plausu resonabant balneæ, cum in·
trabant mentulatiores ; Martialis, IX, 34 :

watering; they were ready to give their last penny to enjoy the favours of a man extraordinarily gifted in that way.

Juvenal, IX, v. 32-36 :

« Destiny governs man; it influences the parts, which the toga covers. If your star pales, useless will be the length and strength of your member to you, — even though Virro shall have seen you naked with lips that water. »

Martial, I, 97 :

« He wants to know why I think he is a minion? We bathe together; he never raises his eyes, but gazes with devouring looks at the sodomites; and cannot behold their members without his lips trembling. »

And again, II, 51 :

« Oftentimes you have no more than a single penny in your box, and that penny more worn than your anus, Hyllus; yet neither baker nor wine shop will have it, but some man who sports an enormous member. Your unfortunate belly must starve for your anus; while the latter devours, the former is famished. »

It is therefore not astonishing that the public baths resounded with plaudits, when men with extraordinary members entered them.

Audieris in quo, Flacce, balnco plausum,
Morionis illic esse mentulam scito.

Juvenalis, VI, 373, 374 :

Conspicuus longe cunctisque notabilis intrat
Balnea...

Nec sine arte quadam adhibita officio jungebantur
pathici. Continebatur autem disciplina pathicorum
duobus potissimum præceptis, altero ut vellcrentur,
altero ut ceverent.

Primum igitur pathicis studiose exstirpandi erant
pili de toto corpore (22). *Depilabant labra, brachia,*
pectora, crura, virilia, ante omnia vero lævigabant
aram voluptatis pathicæ, podicem. Martialis, II,
62 :

---

(22) *Excepto quidem capillo, nam diligenter alebant co-*
mam. Horatius, Carm. X libri IV ad Ligurinum :

> Cum, quæ nunc humeris involitant,
> Deciderint comae...

Idem Epodo XI : « Alius ardor teretis pueri longam re-
nodantis comam (amore Lycisci me expediet). » Hinc
capillati audiunt a Martiale, III, 58; II, 57, et comati,
XII, 99.

Martial, IX, 34 :

« If you hear clapping of hands in the bathing hall, Flaccus, you may be sure some deformed person's enormous member is there. »

Juvenal, VI, v. 373, 374 :

« Far seen, pointed at by all men's fingers, he enters the baths. »

It was not without some art that the patients performed their functions. But their business was made up of these two chief requirements : depilation and knowing how to use the haunches.

Patients took care in the first place to remove the hair carefully from all parts of their body (22); from the lips, arms, chest, legs, the virile parts, and in particular from the altar of passive lust, the anus: Martial, II, 62 :

---

(22) Always, however, excepting the head, for they took great care of their head of hair. Horace, Ode X, book IV., says to Ligurinus :

« When those curls are gone, that now descend to your shoulders... ».

And (Epode XI, v. 40 43) : « Nothing », he says, « will take away his love for Lyciscus, save another love for a plump youth, tying up his long hair. » In the same sense Martial speaks of *Capillati* (III, 58; II, 57), and of *Comati* (XII, 99).

Quod pectus, quod crura tibi, quod bracchia vellis,
 Quod cincta est brevibus mentula tonsa pilis,
Hoc præstas, Labiene, tuæ, quis nescit ? amicæ,
 Cui præstas culum, quem, Labiene, pilas ?

 Idem, IX, 28 :

  Cum depilatos, Chreste, coleos portes,
  Et vulturino mentulam parem collo,
  Et prostilutis lævius caput culis,
  Nec vivat ullus in tuo pilus crure,
  Purgentque crebræ cana labra volsellæ,
  Curios, Camillos, Quinctios, Numos, Ancos,
  Et quidquid usquam legimus philosophorum
  Loqueris, sonasque grandibus minax verbis,
  Et cum theatris sæculoque rixaris.
  Occurrit aliquis inter ista si draucus,
  Nutu vocatum ducis...

 Idem, IX, 58 :

  Nil est tritius Hedyli lacernis :
  Res una est tamen, ipse non negabit,
  Culus, tritior Hedyli lacernis.

 Huc spectat culus Hylli, tritior ultimo hominis denario, apud eundem, II, 51 : *huc vulsum corpus pathici Othonis, apud Suetonium in* Othone, *cap.*

« Pluck out the hair from breast and legs and arms; keep your member cropped and ringed with short hair; all this, we know, you do for your mistress' sake, Labienus. But for whom do you depilate your posteriors? »

And IX, 28 :

« While you, Chrestus, appear thus with your parts all hairless, with a mentula like a vulture's neck, and a head as shining as a prostitute's buttocks with never a hair appearing on your leg, and with your pallid lips all shorn and bare, you talk of Curius, Camillus, Numa, Ancus, of all the hairy heroes we have ever read of in history, and spout big words and threatenings against theatres and the times. Let but some big-limbed man come into sight, you call him with a nod, and take him off... »

And he says, IX, 58 :

« Nought is worse worn than Hedylus' rags, save one thing only (he cannot deny it himself), his anus; — this is worse worn than his rags. »

In a similar way he has spoken before of the anus of Hyllus as more worn by friction than a poor man's last penny (II, 51), and Suetonius (*Life of Otho*, ch. XII) speaks similarly of

XII; *huc illud Catulli carmine* 33 *in Vibennium juniorem :* « *Nates pilosas non potes asse venditare.* »

Idcirco Icelum oravit Galba, ut prius velleretur quam seduceret; Suetonius in Galba, *cap.* XXII :

« *Libidinis in mares pronior, eos non nisi præduros exoletosque. Ferebant in Hispania Icelum e veteribus concubinis, de Neronis exitu nuntiantem, non modo arctissimis osculis palam exceptum ab eo, sed ut sine mora velleretur oratum, atque seductum.* »

Podicem lævigabant vel illi, quibus alias curæ erat, ut fronte hirsuta barbaque promissa priscorum philosophorum gravitatem præ se ferrent. Martialis, IX, 48 :

*Democritos, Zenonas inexplicitosque Platonas,
    Quidquid et hirsutis squalet imaginibus,
Sic quasi Pythagoræ loqueris successor et hæres;
    Præpendet mento nec tibi barba minor.
Sed quod et hircosis serum est, et turpe pilosis,
    In molli rigidum clune libenter habes.*

the body of Otho, given to the habits of a catamite, and Catullus (Carm. 33) reproaches the
younger Vibennius : «You could not sell your
hairy buttocks for a doit ».

For the same reason Galba requested Icelus to
get depilated before he was to take him aside.
Suetonius, *Galba*, ch. xxii :

« He was very much given to the intercourse
between men, and amongst such he preferred
men of ripe age, exoletes. It is said that when
Icelus, one of his old bedfellows, came to Spain,
to inform him of Nero's death, he, not content
with kissing him closely before everyone present, asked him to get at once depilated, and
then took him aside with him quite alone. »

Moreover even those depilated their anus, who
by dint of a rough head of hair and a bristly
beard, tried hard to simulate the gravity of the
ancient Philosophers. Martial, IX, 48 :

« Democritus and Zeno and ambiguous Plato,
— all the sages whose portraits we see decked
with bristling hair, — you prate of ; you might
well be Pythagoras' heir and successor ; while
from your own chin hangs no less imposing a
beard. But as bearded man it is a shame for you
to receive a rigid member between your smooth
posteriors. »

Juvenalis, II, 8-13 :

> *Fronti nulla fides : quis enim non vicus abundat*
> *Tristibus obcenis ? castigas turpia, cum sis*
> *Inter Socraticos notissima fossa cinædos ?*
> *Hispida membra quidem, et duræ per brachia setæ*
> *Promittunt atrocem animum, sed podice lævi*
> *Cæduntur tumidæ, medico ridente, mariscæ.*

Persius, IV, 37, 38 :

> *Tu cum maxillis balanatum gausape pectas,*
> *Inguinibus quare detonsus gurgulio extat?*

Inde est quod Martialis Charidemum jubet nates pilare, ut videatur pathicus magis quam fellator (VI, 56) :

> *Quod tibi crura rigent setis et pectora villis,*
> > *Verba putas famæ te, Charideme, dare.*
> *Exstirpa, mihi crede, pilos de corpore toto,*
> > *Teque pilare tuas testificare nates.*
> *Quæ ratio est ? inquis. Scis multos dicere multa.*
> > *Fac pædicari te, Charideme, putent.*

Neque vero pathicorum tantum erat depilari, sed

Juvenal, II, v. 8-13 :

« Put not your trust in faces; everywhere is debauchery rampant! Thou wouldst whip the vicious; Thou! thou! — the most notorious of all Socratic minions ! Hair-covered limbs and coarse hair along the arms bespeak a fiery soul ; but on your smooth anus the surgeon cuts away the swollen tumours, a grin on his face the while. »

Persius, IV, v. 37, 38 :

« Tell me, when you comb a scented beard upon your cheeks, why does a shaven member stand forth from your groin ? »

This is why Martial (VI, 56) advised Charidemus to get his buttocks depilated, so that he might be taken for a *patient* rather than for a *fellator* :

Because your thighs bristle with coarse hair, and your chest is shaggy, your think, Charidemus, to leave your words to posterity.

Take my word, and pluck out the hairs all over your body, and get it certified you depilate your buttocks. What for? you ask. You know they tell many tales about you ; make them believe, Charidemus, that you are acting the *patient*. »

It was not *patients* only that had themselves

omnino hominum vitam umbratilem ac delicatam
ducere suetorum (23) *Quintilianus*, Instit. orat.
I, 6 :

« *Igitur ut velli et comam in gradus frangere et*
in balneis perpotare, quamlibet hæc invaserint civitatem,
non erit consuetudo, quia nihil horum caret reprehen-
siore. »

Mirum, quod cui coma in gradus fracta bilem
movit, idem ille Quintilianus lenissime ferendas
putavit mulieres cum viris lavantes (V, 9) :

« *Nam si est signum adulteræ lavare cum viris, erit*
et convivere cum adolescentibus, deinde etiam familiari-
ter alicujus amicitia uti; ut fortasse corpus vulsum,
fractum incessum, vestem muliebrem dixerit mollis et
parum viri signa, si cui illa ex impudicitia fluere vi-
deantur. »

Hujusmodi munditiarum fere muliebrium homi-

---

(23) *Alas autem vellere necessarium videbatur ad curam*
corporis : Seneca, Epist. 114. « *Alter se justo plus colit,*
alter se justo plus negligit : ille et crura, hic nec alas qui-
dem vellit ! »

depilated; men leading an idle, careless life followed the same practice (23).

« To be depilated, to have the hair dressed in
tiers of ringlets, to tipple to excess in the baths,
— these practices prevail in the city; still they
cannot be said to be customary, for nothing of
all this is exempt from blame » (Quintilian, *Instit.
orat.*, I, 6).

It is rather surprising that the same Quintilian, whose bile is stirred by curled hair, has let
it pass by patiently, that women should bathe
together with men :

« If it is a sure sign of adultery for a woman
to bathe with men, why ! it will be adultery to
dine with young friends of the male sex, to have
a male friend. You might as reasonably say a
depilated body, a languid gait, a womanish
robe, are certain signs of effeminacy, of want of
virility : for such will seem to many to reveal im-
morality of character » (*Ibid.*, V, 9).

Martial (II, 39) has also noticed, and not once

---

(23) To depilate one's armpits was, however considered
as being necessary to the cleanliness of the body : « One
man keeps himself tidy, another neglects himself more than
is right; one man depilates his legs, another does not
depilate even his armpits. » (Seneca, letter CXIV.)

*nes, de capsula totos, non uno loco notavit Martia-
lis, II, 39 :*

> *Rufe, vides illum subsellia prima terentem,*

. . . .

> *Cujus olet toto pinguis coma Marceliano,*
> *Et splendent vulso brachia trita pilo?*

Item, V, 62 :

> *... Crispulus iste quis est*
> *Crura gerit nullo qui violata pilo ?*

*Nec talia sprevit ingens animus Julii Cæsaris :
Suetonius, cap. 45 :*

> « *Circa corporis cu ram morosior, ut non solum ton-
> deretur (forcipe) diligenter ac raderetur (novacula), sed
> velleretur etiam, ut quidam exprobraverunt.* »

*Eo pertinent vasa Samnitica, calefactandæ re-
sinæ ac pici devellendis hominibus ac lævigandis,
quæ in rebus Commodi Pertinacis jussu, auctione
facta, palam divenditis numerat Julius Capitolinus
in* Pertinace, *capite octavo. Nam utebantur ad pi-*

only, the habits of those men who practised feminine arts of the toilette, and looked just as if they had come out of a band-box :

« Rufus, see you that man there on the first benches .... whose oiled curls exhale the whole shop of Marcelianus, and whose polished arms shine without a hair to be seen? »

Again, he says, V, 62 :

« ..... Who is this Crispulus, who has legs undisfigured by a single hair ? »

Even the great Caesar did not disdain this coquetry, Suetonius, ch. 45 :

« He took too much care of his appearance, to the point of not only having his beard removed with nippers, and shaved with a razor, but even of being depilated, for which things he was blamed. »

This custom is connected with those Samnite vases, filled with rosin and pitch to be heated for depilation, and for softening the pitch, found amongst the properties of Commodus, and which by the orders of Pertinax were sold by public auction. Julius Capitolinus speaks of them (*Pertinax*, 8). For removing the hair there

los exstirpandos aut volsella, aut dropace sive psilo-
thro. Volsellam commemorat Martialis, IX, 28,
quem locum paulo ante laudavimus. De dropace sive
psilothro ab eodem fit mentio, III, 74 :

> Psilothro faciem lævas et dropace calvam;

Item, VI, 93 :

> Psilothro viret;

Item, X, 65 :

> Lævis dropace tu quotidiano.

Fiebat dropax sive psilothrum ex resina oleo li-
quata. Plinius, Hist. nat. XIV, 20 :

« *Resina omnis dissolvitur oleo, pudetque confiteri,*
maximum jam honorem ejus esse in evellendis virorum
corpori pilis. »

Aetius libro III, cap. CXC, *Operis medici :*

Ὁ μὲν οὖν ἁπλούστερος δρώπαξ ἐστὶν ἡ πίττωσις
λεγομένη. Πίττα δὲ ξηρὰ τήκεται μετὰ ἐλαίου πάνυ
βραχυτάτου. Ἔπειτα θερμὴ οὖσα ἐπιχρίεται δέρματι
καὶ προξυρηθέντων τῶν τόπων προσκολλᾶται, καὶ πρὶν

were used in fact either tweezers or an unguent called dropax or psilothrum. Martial mentions the use of the tweezers in the Epigram (IX, 28) quoted before; of dropax or psilothrum he speaks in Book III, 74 :

« You depilate your face with psilothrum and your head with dropax. »

And again VI, 93 :

« She revives her youth with psilothrum. »

And X, 65 :

« You rub yourself every day with dropax. »

The dropax or psilothrum was obtained by melting rosin in oil (Pliny, *Natural History*, XIV 20) :

« Rosin dissolves in oil, and I am ashamed to say, that the most honest use made of this mixture is to serve people as a depilatory. »

Aëtius also mentions it in Book III, ch. cxc, of his *Opus Medicum* :

« The simplest dropax is the one called pitch-plaster. Dry pitch is diluted with oil; it is applied hot to the skin, which must first be cleanly shaved, under which circumstances it adheres closely. Before the plaster is quite cold, it is taken off,

τελέως ψυγῆναι ἀποσπᾶται. Καὶ πάλιν θερμαθέντος
τοῦ ἐμπλάσμχτος παρὰ πυρὶ προσκολλᾶται, καὶ ὁμοίως
πρὶν ψυγῆναι ἀποσπᾶται, καὶ τοῦτο γίνεται πολλάκις.

Hinc « resinata juventus » Juvenalis, VIII,
114; *hinc :*

...*Fructicante pilo neglecta et squalida crura*

Nævoli, cujus

...*Nullus tota nitor in cute, qualem*
Præstabat calidi circumlita fascia visci,

apud eundem, IX, 13-15. *Quid aliud sibi volunt*
ungues Gargiliani, resinanon resecandi, apud Mar-
tialem, III, 74?

Utrumque pilandi modum conjunxit, puto, Per-
sius, IV, 37-41 :

Tu cum maxillis balanatum gausape pectas,
Inguinibus quare detonsus gurgulio extat?
Quinque palæstritæ licet hæc plantaria vellant,
Elixasque nates labefactent forcipe adunca,
Non tamen ista filix ullo mansuescit aratro.

Nam forceps est volsella, et elixæ nates referri
videntur ad dropacem calidum, quo imposito sane

warmed again, and put on afresh; again it is removed before being cold, and this process is repeated several times. »

Hence Juvenal's, « Youthfulness by pitch », (VIII, 114), and

« The thighs neglected and dirty with tufts of hair » of Nævolus, to whom he says :
« Your skin has none of the gloss, that of old the well-smeared plaster of hot pitch gave it » (Sat. IX, 13-15).

What else does Martial, mean when (III, 74), he speaks of « Gargilanus' nails, — that cannot be trimmed with pitch ?

Persius (IV, 37-41) has, I presume, joined together both modes of depilation :

« Tell me, when you comb a scented beard upon your cheeks, why does a shaven member stand forth from your groin ? Though five strong men weed your plantation and work your parboiled buttocks with the hooked tweezers, I tell you there is no plough will tame that stubborn field ! »

Here *forceps* is the same thing as *volsella* (tweezers); while the « parboiled buttocks » would seem to refer to the hot *dropax*. After the applic-

*cutis non poterat, quin speciem aliquam coctæ car-
nis indueret. Hunc Persii locum ob oculos habuit
Ausonius epigrammate* 131 :

> *Inguina quod. calido lævas libi dropace, causa es
> Irritant volsas lævia membra lupas.
> Sed quod it elixo plantaria podice vellis,
> Et teris incusas pumice Clazomenas,
> Causa latet, bimarem nisi quod patentia morbum
> Appetet, et tergo femina, pube vir es.*

*Clazomenæ quidem haud dubie sunt nates fractæ,
ruptæ, fissæ, quales solent esse pathicorum, uti
Carini, cujus sectum podicem notavit Martialis,
VI,* 37 ; *ita dictæ Græco vocabulo, nam* κλάζω *sonat « frango », ut ludatur in ambiguo urbis nomine:
quemadmodum lusisse fertur Gonsalvus Cordubensis, qui cum pædicare cupiebat, dixit ire se velle
Aversam; cum ori illudere, in Orientem; cum lingere cunnum, in Liguriam. Quod Clazomenæ dicuntur incusæ, vult Ausonius, Clazomenas corporii
hominis pro natibus quasi cudendo esse impressas;*

cation of such a plaster the skin could not but
have a boiled look.

Ausonius (*Epigr*. CXXXI.) alludes to this
passage of Persius :

« The reason you smooth your groin with hot
dropax is that a skin soft and smooth entices
the whores, plucked smooth themselves. But
that you pluck out the herbage from your parboiled bottom, and polish up with pumice your
battered Clazomenae, what means this, — if
not that the vice of man with man works in you,
and you are a woman behind, a man in front. »

The *Clazomenae* are without a doubt the man's
buttock, limp and cracked, as those of *patients*
will be, as those of Carinus were, whom Martial
(XI, 37) blames for « his lacerated anus ». Ausonius calls them so from the Greek κλάζω, in
Latin « frango » (I break), thus playing with
the name of a city. Gonzalvo the Cordevan
makes a similar pun, when, desiring to pedicate,
he says, he wishes to go to Aversa; also when
he wishes to irrumate the mouth, he says : « I go
to the Orient », or when he is about to lick the
vulva, in Latin *ligurire*, « I go to Liguria ». By
calling the Clazomenae hammered (battered)
Ausonius means to imply that they were as if

velut si quis nostratium de calvo joculariter diceret :
scalpit Calam incusam. Quo quid planius? quid
elegantius? Non erat igitur, quod sensum loci la-
tere pronuntiaret Forcellinus. Alii pro incusas edi-
derunt inclusas, ut fissura esset intelligenda, na-
tium tumore utrinque inclusa. Sed primum Clazo-
menæ commode illæ quidem dici possunt fissæ nates,
nequaquam autem fissuræ ipsæ : deinde quis est,
qui lævigare miserum fissuram potius quam nates
inepte voluisse sibi persuadeat?

Fuerunt qui mulierum ope ingeniose uterentur ad
depilandum : dictæ officiosæ illæ ustriculæ, *quod*
dropace calente cruribus aliisve partibus corporis
adglutinato pilos ustularent. Tertullianus, de Pallio, *cap.* 4 : « *Patiens jam ustriculas* », *jocante*
Salmasio ad hunc locum, pagina 284 : *Olim us-*
triculæ vellendis cruribus repertæ, hodie torquendis
ingeniis videntur esse. » *Num dubitas Augusto,*

polished with a hammer, by having served as
an anvil. It is as if my fellow-countrymen were
to say in joke of a bald man (in German *Kahl*),
« he scratches his polished Kehl ». What could
be clearer or wittier? Forcellini is therefore wrong
in saying this passage of Ausonius has no sense.
Other editors have *inclusas* instead of *incusas*,
indicating the fissure which separates the buttocks, by the rotundities of which it is on both
sides closed in. But in the first place the Clazomenae may well be the buttocks, they being
cleft, though not indeed themselves a cleft; in
the second place, who could imagine this miserable man depilated the cleft of the buttocks
rather than the buttocks themselves?

Some persons, by a refinement of luxury,
employed women to depilate them. Such women
called themselves *ustriculae* (from *urere*, to
burn), as they made use of a sticky plaster of
boiling dropax to burn the hair on the legs and
other parts of the body. Tertullian (*De Pallio*,
ch. 4), says : « So effeminate as to employ *ustriculae* »; while Salmasius, commenting playfully
on the passage, p. 284, declares : Once upon a
time *ustriculae* served to depilate the legs; now
they serve to harass our minds. » Augustus, who

Suetonio teste, cap. 68 : « *crura solito suburere nuce ardenti, quo mollior pilus surgeret* », *hanc quoque operam suavem commodasse ustriculas?*

Deinde mulieres et ipsæ lanuginem pubis indigne ferentes pilabantur (24); *Martialis, XII,* 32 :

---

(24) *Neque tamen mulieres Græcæ hunc morem dedignatæ sunt :* Aristophanes in Lysistrata, *v.* 89 :

Κομψότατα τὴν βληχώ γε παρατετιλμένη.

Item in Ranis, *v.* 519. Ὀρχηστρίδες ἡβυλλιῶσαι, κἄρτι παρατετιλμέναι. *Item in* Concionantibus, *v.* 719, τὸν χοῖρον ἀποτετιλμένας. *Habuisse vero etiam viros Græcos vulsum cunnum magis in deliciis quam pubem, etsi nostratibus id forsan secus videatur, patet ex loco Aristophanis in* Lysistrata, *v.* 151, 52, *quo vulsus cunnus in causis ponitur, quod viri arrigant et coire cupiant :*

. . . . (εἰ)
Γυμναὶ παρίοιμεν δέλτα παρατετιλμέναι,
Στύοιντ' ἂν ἄνδρες, κἀπιθυμοῖεν πλεκοῦν.

Sed et vetularum erat, cunnum pilis nimium horrentem vellere, ut minus viderentur annosæ. Martialis, X, 90 :

Quid vellis vetulum, Ligella, cunnum?
Quid busti cineres tui lacessis?
Tales munditiae decent puellas.
Erras, si tibi cunnus hic videtur,
Ad quem mentula pertinere desit.

according to Suetonius, « was in the habit of singe-
ing his legs with burning nutshells, to make
the hair grow more silky » (*Augustus,* ch. 68),
no doubt made use of the nimble hands of these
ustriculae.

Women likewise resorted to depilation (24),

---

(24) The Greeks did not disdain this strange pratice
any more than the Romans. Aristophanes, in the *Lysistrata* (v. 89).

« My affair will be tidy with the couchgrass pluck'd
off. » In the « Frogs » he speaks of dancing girls barely
arrived at puberty beginning to tear off the fur » (v. 519);
in the *Thesmophoria₂usae* again the reis mentioned « a
mons Veneris plucked clean » (v. 719). That the Greeks
preferred a bare pubis to a furred one, though we may
be of a different opinion, is apparent from another passage of Aristophanes, in the *Lysistrata,* v. 151, 2, where
a smooth pubis is represented as a chief incitement to
virile ardour :

« If we were to go naked with a smooth pubis, our
husbands' members would stand, and they would be
fain to have us. »

As to old women, they likewise denuded their pubis
of the bristles in order to appear less decrepit. Martial,
X, 90.

« Ligella, do you pluck your old affair, and stir the
ashes of your burnt-out fire?

Refinements such as those are for young maidens;
you are in error if you think that thing a vulva that a
man's member will no longer recognize ».

The depilation of the vulva was also used as a punishment.

Nec plena turpi matris olla resina.
Summœnianæ qua pilantur uxores.

*Uti viri mulieribus, ita mulieres callidæ vicis-
sim viris pectines tradebant pilandos, stomachante
Plinio,* Hist. nat., *XXIX,* 8 :

« *Pectines in fœminis quidem publicati. Ita est profecto : lues morum nec aliunde major quam e medicina.* »

---

*Interdum et ignominiæ causa cunni vellebantur. Aristo-
phanes in* Thesmophoriis, *v.* 545-46 :

Ταύτης ἀποψιλώσομεν τὸν χοῖρον, ἵνα διδαχθῇ
Γυνὴ γυναῖκας οὖσα μὴ κακῶς λέγειν τὸ λοιπόν.

*Sic etiam mœchos deprensos hæc pœna manebat, ut
podex raphano aut mugili faciendus, adsperso cinere
calido, cum inguine depilaretur. Aristophanes in* Nubibus,
v. 1079 :

Τί δ', ἢν ῥαφανιδωθῇ πιθόμενός σοι,
Τέφρᾳ τε τιλθῇ ;

Suidas sub Ῥαφανίς · Οὕτω γὰρ τοὺς ἁλόντας μοιχοὺς
ἠκίζοντο · ῥαφανίδας λαμβάνοντες καθίεσαν ἐπὶ τοὺς πρωκ-
τοὺς τούτων, καὶ παρατίλλοντες αὐτοὺς θερμὴν τέφραν ἐπέ-
παττον.

looking upon the fleece of the pubis as something disgusting. Martial :

« ... Nor yet one of your mother's pots full of foul rosin, such as the women of the outer suburbs use to depilate themselves withal » (XII, 32).

As men employed women to free them of hair, so women offered their pubis without shame to men for the same office. Pliny's bile rises at this (*Nat. Hist.*, XXIX, 8) : « Women are not afraid to show their pubis. It is but too true, nothing corrupts manners more than the art of the medical man. »

Aristophanes, *Tesmophoriazusae*, 545, 6.
« We will pluck her pubis, and teach her so, woman as she is, not to speak ill of women. »
The same punishment was inflicted upon adulterous women taken in the act; a black radish or a mullet was introduced into her anus, which was then depilated, as well as her pubis, with burning cinders. Aristophanes, *Clouds*, 1079 :
« What, must you suffer the empalement with the radish, and the hot cinders? »
Suetonius, under the word 'Ραφανίς : « Thus they treated adulteresses who had been caught in the act : they took black radishes and planted them in their anus, which they rubbed with hot cinders, after having torn out the hair. »

Ne ipsi quidem Imperatores dedignabantur, officium devellendi concubinis præstandum : Suetonius de Domitiano, *cap.* 22 :

« *Erat fama quasi concubinas ipse develleret, nataretque inter vulgatissimas meretrices.* »

Lampridius, de Heliogabalo, *cap.* 31 :

« *In balneis semper cum mulieribus fuit, ita ut eas ipse psilothro curaret, ipse quoque barbam psilothro, accurans, quodque pudendum dictu est, eodem quo mulieres accurabantur, et eadem hora. Rasit et virilia subactoribus suis ad novaculam manu sua, qua postea barbam fecit.* »

Quippe pudendum dictu Lampridio visum est, quod illum ipsum dropacem, quem modo mulieres, pectinibus pilandis emplastri instar adplicuissent, statim et eadem hora, ante quam fœtorem redolere desiisset, barbæ adglutinare non dubitaret imperator.

Sed, ut ad pathicos revertamur, nec eos devellendos curam illustrium amatorum defecisse, docet exemplum Hadriani, quem, Spartiano auctore cap. 4 :

The emperors themselves condescended to undertake this office for their concubines.

Suetonius, *Domitian*, ch. 22 :

« It was rumoured, that he was fond of depilating his concubines himself, and would bathe amid a crowd of the most infamous courtezans. »

Lampridius, *Heliogabalus*, chap. 31 :

« In his baths he was always together with the women, and he made their toilets with psilothrum : he used psilothrum likewise for his beard, and, disgusting to relate, the same which the women had just been using. With his own hand he shaved off the fleece from the virile part of his pedicons, and then shaved his own beard. »

What Lampridius finds so repugnant, is that the emperor did not hesitate to use upon his beard the same ointment, which the women had just been applying as a plaster upon the pubis, and which he used at once and before the bad smell had evaporated.

But to return to our *patients*, they also were not in want of illustrious lovers, who took care to depilate them ; an example of this we find in the emperor Hadrian, according to Spartianus, who says, ch. 4 :

« *Corrupisse Trajani libertos, curasse delicatos, eos-
demque sæpe levisse per ea tempora, quibus in aula fa-
miliarior fuit, opinio multa firmavit.* »

*Quo enim alio modo Hadrianum putemus cu-
rasse delicatos, quam quo Heliogabalum curasse
mulieres mox vidimus, psilothro? præsertim cum
illos statim dicatur etiam sæpe levisse, quod sine
dubio ita fecisse erit existimandus, ut pane madido
lineret faciem pathicorum, vel ad candorem nito-
remque cuti conciliandum, vel ne citius barbati essent. Suetonius in* Othone, *cap.* 12 :

« *Quin et faciem quotidie rasitare, ac pane madido
linere consuetum* » (*fuisse Othoni traditur*), « *idque
instituisse a prima lanugine, ne barbatus unquam esset.* »

Inde in eundem Othonem aculeus Juvenalis, II,
107 :

Nimirum summi ducis est . . . .
. . . . *curare cutem* . . . .
Et pressum in faciem digitis extendere panem.

Quid mirum, si ejusdem disciplinæ usus et mu-

« That he corrupted the freedmen of Trajan,
made the toilet of his minions, and often depilated them, while he was attached to the Court,
is generally believed. »

In what other way can we believe Hadrian to
have made the toilet of these minions, if not in
the same way in which Heliogabalus made the
toilet of his females, with psilothrum, particularly as it is added that he depilated them frequently? We may take it for granted that he
used that ointment, or that he rubbed their faces
with moistened bread, either to improve their
skin or to hinder the beard growing too soon.
Suetonius, *Otho*, ch. 12 :

« He shaved his face every day, and rubbed
it with damp bread, a habit which he had contracted when the first down began to appear, so
as not to get bearded. »

Juvenal (II, 107), has aimed an arrow of the
same sort at Otho :

« It surely is the duty of a mighty Captain . .
. . . . to keep his skin right smooth . . . and
knead bread with his fingers to make a plaster
for his face. »

What wonder then if the women cherished

lieribus in deliciis fuit? Quis est, cujus in memoria non penitus insederit mulier ista ab Juvenale mira arte depicta, versiculis 460-472 Satiræ illius, Salmasio quidem judice divinæ, sextæ? « Multo pane tumet facies, » unde « miseri viscantur labra mariti », ut dubites.

> *... Quæ mutatis inducitur atque fovetur*
> *Tot medicaminibus, coctæque siliginis offas*
> *Accipit et madidæ, facies dicatur, an ulcus...*
> *Tandem aperit vultum, et tectoria prima reponit.*
> *Incipit agnosci, atque illo lacte fovetur,*
> *Propter quod secum comites educit asellas,*
> *Exul Hyperboreum si dimittatur ad axem.*

Videntur ad infucandam faciem interdum et adhibuisse tectoria ex creta facta, ut cinædus ille Petronii, cap. 23, qui super inguina Eucolpii diu multumque frustra moluit :

« Perfluebant per frontem sudantis acaciæ rivi, et inter rugas malarum tantum erat cretæ, ut putares detectum parietum nimbo laborare.

similar artifices? Who can help thinking of the woman depicted with such marvellous art by Juvenal, from verse 460 to verse 472 of that Sixth Satire, to which Salmasius gave the epithet, of « divine » ? « Her face is all puffy with bread crumbs, where the lips of the poor husband keep sticking », to such an extent, that one doubts :

« ... Whether her countenance, plastered and *massaged* with so many preparations, overlaid with poultices of boiled and moistened flour, should be called a face at all, — or a sore... At last she peels her face, removes the outermost layers. For the first time she may be recognized for herself. Then she treats her skin with asses' milk, for which she drags about in her train a herd of asses, — and would take them with her, if she were exiled to the North Pole. »

For painting the face it seems that a coating of chalk was used, as in the case of the Pederast mentioned in Petronius, who perspired so violently in working vainly the groin of Eucolpus :

« From his perspiring forehead flowed rivulets of acacia juice, and in the wrinkles of his cheeks there was such a mass of chalk that you might have believ edyo suaw a wall exposed to

At mittamus tandem hunc viscum, ne plane inhærescere videamur.

Alteram partem disciplinæ pathicæ versari diximus in cevendo. Cevet qui clunes subsultim movet agitatque in opere, ut Venus concinnior et sibi sit, et pædiconi. Idem cum faciunt fœminæ in fututione, dicuntur crissare. Martialis, III, 95 :

Sed pædicaris, sed pulchre, Nævole, ceves.

Juvenalis, II, 20-23 :

... Et de virtute locuti
Clunem agitant. — « Ego te ceventem, Sexte, verebor ? »
Infamis Varillus ait...

Idem, IX, 40 :

Computat et cevet...

Plautus in Pseudolo, III, v. 75 :

Sic conquiniscet istic, ceveto simul.

the wind and washed by the rain » (*Satyricon*, ch. 23).

But let us leave all these nasty preparations, before we find ourselves stuck fast in them.

We have said that another branch of this bus·iness, on the part of the *patient*, consists in *cevere*. A *patient cevet*, who during the action wriggles and moves his haunches up and down, so as to enjoy more pleasure himself and give more pleasure to the pedicon. Women, doing the same in copulation, are said to *crissare*. Martial, III, 95 :

« Nay! you pedicate finely, Naevolus; you ply your haunches right well. »

Juvenal, II, 20-23 :

« ... Virtue on their lips, they ply their buttocks. — 'Shall I honour you, in the act of your back-play, Sextus?' says the infamous Varillus... »

The same author, IX, 40 :

« With calculated art moves his haunches. »

Plautus, in the *Pseudolus*, III, 75 :

« Soon as ever the fellow cowers down, ply your haunches in time to him. »

Quare nonnullis, haud scio an recte, visum est cinædorum nomen inde ductum, quod soleant κινεῖν τὰ αἰδοῖα. *Certe femoris facilitas cluniumque agilitas numerantur in virtutibus pathicorum apud Petronium, cap. 23. Intrat cinædus, qui ejusmodi carmina effudit :*

Huc huc convenite nunc, spatalocinædi,
Pede tendite, cursum addite, convolate planta,
Femore facili, clune agili, et manu procaces,
Molles, veteres, Deliaci manu recisi.

Huc redit epigramma XXXVI libri prioris Hermaphroditi *nostri, quod conferas, si tanti. Cum qui cevet alteri morigeretur, ad adulationem transfertur : Persius, I, 87 : « An Romule ceves? » quemadmodum versa vice irrumare ad contumeliam.*

Fœminas pariter posse pædicari ac mares, natura ipsa docet : voluisse vero etiam, monumenta vetus-

For this reason some authorities hold, I do not know whether rightly or wrongly, the word *cinede* to come from the fact that the wretches known by that name are in the habit of *wriggling the private parts* (in Greek, κινεῖν τὰ αἰδοῖα). Undoubtedly the suppleness of the thighs, the agility of the buttocks are counted amongst the particular talents of cinedes in Petronius, ch. 23 :

Enter a Cinede reciting these verses :

« Hither, come hither, cinede wantons, — stretch the foot and take your course, fly with soles in the air, with supple thighs, and nimble buttocks, and libertine hands, — all ye old, emasculated minions of Delos, come ! »

To this subject also refers Epigram XXXVI of the Ist. Book of the *Hermaphroditus*, edited by us; which consult, reader, if worth your while. As he who wriggles with his haunches does it to please somebody, people use the word *cevere* also to convey the meaning of sycophancy or adulation. Thus : « An, Romule, ceves » (What Romulus, you fawn too?) in Persius (I, 87); in the same way *irrumate* is used in the sense of an outrage, affront.

That women *can* be pedicated, exactly the same as men, is indicated by nature; that they

tatis haud pauca loquuntur. Apulejus Metamorphoseon *libro III, p.* 138 :

« *Sic nobis gannientibus libido mutua et animos
simul et membra suscitat, et omnibus abjectis amiculis
hactenus denique intecti bacchamur in Venerem, cum
quidem mihi jam fatigato de propria liberalitate Fotis
puerile obtulit corollarium.* »

Martialis, IX, 68 :

*Lascivam tota possedi nocte puellam,
    Cujus nequitias vincere nemo potest.
Fessus mille modis, illud puerile poposci :
    Ante preces totas primaque verba dedit.*

Idem, XI, 105, *ad uxorem* :

*Pædicare negas : dabat hoc Cornelia Graccho,
    Julia Pompeio, Portia, Brute, tibi.
Dulcia Dardanio nondum miscente ministro
    Pocula, Juno fuit pro Ganymede Jovi.*

*Sic et Aloisium et Fabricium experta est Tullia
apud Aloisiam Sigæam, loco supra jam allato.*

have consented, is proved by numerous testimonies in Antiquity. — Apuleius, *Metamorphoses*, III, p. 138 :

« While we were thus prattling, a mutual desire invaded our minds and roused our limbs; having undressed entirely we gave ourselves up to the transports of Venus. I soon felt tired. Fotis of her own good will offered me the catamite corollary. »

Martial, IX, 68:

« All night long I possessed a lewd young maiden, whose complaisant demeanour it were impossible to excel. Exhausted with a thousand modes of love. I asked for the puerile service, which she granted at once before I had finished my asking. »

The same, XI, 105, reproaches his wife as follows :

« You refuse to pedicate ; yet Cornelia allowed it to Gracchus, Julia to Pompey, and Portia did it for Brutus. Ere the Derdanian Cupbearer served the wine, Juno herself acted Ganymede for Jupiter. »

Tullia permitted the same to Aloysio and Fabrizio, in *Aloysia Sigaea*; we have quoted the

*Non aliter Venerem variavit Crispa apud Auso-
nium epigrammate* 71 :

... *Molitur per utramque cavernam.*

*Mirifice autem Græci veteres postico usu fœmina-
rum delectabantur.* Nam dici non potest, quanti
fuerint miratores pulchrarum natium, ita ut puellæ de præstantia natium publice contenderent, Pa-
ridibus ad sententiam dicendam electis. In agro
quidem Syracusano, quemadmodum auctor est
Athenæus, XII, 80, rustico duæ erant filiæ formosæ, quæ, cum de clunium pulchritudine sæpius am-
bitiose inter se certavissent, tandem in viam publi-
cam egressæ adolescenti Syracusano forte prætereunti
spectandas se præbuerunt, qui judicato natu majo-
ris clunes pulchriores esse, ejus amore flagrare cœpit, reversusque in urbem juniori fratri exposuit,
quid accidisset. Rus ille profectus, puellis nudis
spectatis, alteram amavit. Hæ igitur puellæ adolescentibus suis, iisque locupletibus, matrimonio
mox junctæ a civibus καλλίπυγοι vocatæ sunt, quod

passage Crispa tastes the same variety of pleasure, in Epigram LXXI of Ausonius :

« She lets herself be done in either orifice. »

The ancient Greeks took great delight in the
posterior Venus. One can scarcely express what
fervent admirers they were of beautiful buttocks;
it went so far, that young girls competed in public, before an assemblage sitting as it were in
another » Judgement of Paris » to pronounce
which of them was the most gifted in that respect. Athenaeus (XII, 80) informs us that in
the environs of Syracuse a villager had two
daughters who often quarrelled as to which of
them had the finest posteriors ; one day they showed them on the highway to a young man from
Syracuse, who chanced to be passing, and asked him to adjudicate between them. He decided in favour of the elder sister, fell at once
violently in love with her, and on his return
home he told his younger brother what had be-
fallen him. The latter went forthwith to see the
two girls, and became enamoured of the younger. Soon they got married to the two youths,
who were opulent, and they were called by their
fellow-citizens the *Callipygi*, because, although

infimo loco natis nates pro dote fuissent, et gratæ templum Veneri dedicaverunt, καλέσασαι Καλλί-πυγον τὴν θέον. *Quæ cum ita sint, non mireris, ut quæque puella pulchrarum clunium laude esset florentissima, ita ad officium puerile præstandum et ex optatissimam fuisse et paratissimam. Tale officium Mania præstitit Demetriv, teste Machone apud Athenæum, XIII, 42, ita ut regi nates poscenti, præmio accepto diceret :*

Ἀγαμέμνονος παῖ, νῦν ἐκεῖν' ἔξεστί σοι.

Tale corollarium rogavit adolescentulus quidam Ponticus Gnathænam quam tota nocte possederat, mane, eodem Machone narrante, ibidem, XIII, 43. Nihil aliud petiit Demophon, delicatus ille Sopho-

of lowly birth, their posteriors served them for a dowry. Full of gratitude, they dedicated a temple to Venus, under the title of Venus Calli-pygos (Venus of the beauteous buttocks).

It will not surprise you, that any young girl remarkable for her beautiful posteriors amongst her companions was all the more in request for the puerile office, and all the more disposed to lend herself to it. Mania consented to it in favour of Demetrius, as testified by Machon, in Athenaeus (XIII, 42), when the king wanting to enjoy her buttocks, she accepts his gift, and says :

« Son of Agamemnon, it is now *your* turn to have them (25). »

A certain young man, Ponticus by name, exacted the same corollary in the morning from Gnathena, whom he had possessed all night; it is again Machon who tells us the story (*ibid.*, XIII, 43). Demophon, the minion of Sophocles, asked

---

(25) To understand this, the sentence must be complete; the worthy Forberg takes his readers for too learned ; Mania, in the poem of Machon, says to Demetrius, offer-ing her buttoks :

« Son of Agamemnon, it is now *your* turn to have them, — you who have ever been so liberal with your own. » (Note of the translator.)

clis, a Nico timente, en quid de suis clunibus, qua-
rum quidem laude celebrabatur (λέγεται ἐσχηκέναι
πυγὴν πάνυ καλὴν). *Sophocli commodaret: ibidem,*
XIII, 45. Ingeniose autem deprecata est hanc patien-
tiam Gnathænium, ibidem, XIII, 44. Nam cum
faber quidam ærarius illiberaliter inter suos glo-
riatus esset, se meretricula illa quinquies deinceps
equitem vectatum fuisse (ἑξῆς καθιππάσκι ἐπ' αὐτῆς
πεντάκις), *Andronico, quem alias unice in deliciis*
habebat, re cognita graviter cum illa querenti, quod
quo schemate furciferum istum abunde frui passa
esset, id ne precibus quidem impetrare ipsi contigis-
set, respondit Gnathænium, tangi se noluisse mam-
mas ab homine squaloreque et fuligine obsito, et
propter hanc causam schema se illud callide excogi-
tavisse, nihil ut nisi et extremam et minimam
miser partem caperet. Imaginem viri pædicantis

the same favour of Nico (26) who being fam-
ed for the beauty of her buttocks, — « she is said
to have had an exceedingly beautiful bottom »
— was afraid he might lend them to Sophocles
(*ibid.*, XII. 45). Gnathaenion (*ibid.*, XIII, 44)
made an ingenious excuse for having been similarly complaisant. A certain tinker having
ungenerously boasted he had five times running
mounted that little courtezan in that way, An-
dronicus, whom she preferred to everybody
else, got to hear it, and reproached her bitterly
for having allowed such a blackguard to enjoy
her so abundantly in a posture which his prayers
never obtained from her. Gnathaenion replied
that, not caring to have her breasts handled by
a fellow black with dirt and soot, it had appeared to her better to take that posture, so as to
receive the least possible fraction of the wretch-

---

(26) The following is the passage from Machon, as quoted by Athenaeus; without a knowledge of it Forberg's
allusion remains obscure :

« ... Demophon, Sophocles' minion, when still a youth
had Nico, already old and surnamed the she-goat; they
say she had very fine buttocks. One day, he begged of
her to lend them to him. 'Very well', she said with a
smile, — 'Take from me, dear, what you give to Sophocles.' » (Note of the translator.)

fœminam dat tabula XXVII in Monuments du culte secret des dames romaines.

Neque tamen sine aliquo incommodo atque adeo periculo officium præstari pathicum, docet Magistra voluptatum Aloisia (Colloq. VI) :

« *Acerrimi incutiuntur oppresso cruciatus, ac ple-rumque, si crassior infindat contus, teterrimi ex ea morbi petulantia enascuntur, quos nulla Æsculapii curet industria. Disruptis musculorum vinculis con-tingit postea excrementa effluere etiam invitis. Quo quid turpius? Novi tam diris inde afflictatas fœminas nobiles ægritudinibus enatorum et pullulantium ulcerum ut sanitati post duos tresve annos vix sint restitutæ. Ego quidem* » (Tulliam audis) « *ex Aloisii Fabriciique sacris amplexibus non evasi omnino sana. Primum dum pila infigunt, vehementem tuli cruciatum : mox levis ægram solata est titillationis umbra... Postquam vero domum redii, ardentissimus rursus me dolor cepit in ea parte, quam laceraverant. Incendio torrebar pru-*

ed creature's body. Plate XXVII of the *Monu-menis du culte secret des dames romaines* presents the picture or a man pedicating a woman.

It is, however, not without some inconvenience, or even danger, that one lends oneself to the passive part. Aloysia Sigaea, Past-Mistress in the Sciences of Love, enlightens us on this point :

« In the first place intolerable sufferings are inflicted upon the *patient*, for in most cases he is invaded by too large a stake; hence frightful infirmities, incurable by all the art of Aesculapius. The confining muscles are ruptured, and consequently the excrements cannot be held back and escape. What could be more disgusting ? I have known noble ladies afflicted with cruel maladies to such a degree by eruptions and ulcers, that it took them two or three years to recover their health. I myself (Tullia) have not escaped scot free from the accursed embraces of Aloysio and Fabrizio. When they first forced their darts in, I endured atrocious pain, but soon the feeling of slight titillation consoled me... When however I reached home again, I felt a burning pain at the place they had lacerated ; I felt myself consumed by an itching as if I were on fire, and in spite of the nursing of Donna Orsini, it

*rienti. Et sane Ursinæ ope ignis hic sacer vix restinc-
tus est, Pereundum erat miseræ neglectis vulneribus.* »

*Jam intelliges, cur puero Nævoli doluerit culus,
apud Martialem, III, 71 : cur idem, VI, 37, podicem Carini dixerit sectum ; quid sibi velit morsus
ejusdem, IX, 48 :*

> *Tu qui sectarum causas et pondera nosti,
>   Dic mihi, percidi, Pannice, dogma quod est ?*

*Debebat enim mollis iste philosophus, quasi Py-
thagoræ successor et hæres loqui solitus, sectarum
etiam natium causas et mentularum pondera nosse.
Pathicorum morbo laboravit is quoque, cui incusas
pro natibus Clazomenas risisse Ausonium supra
vidimus.*

*Maluerunt pædicones videri quam pathici. Hinc
festivum illud epigramma Martialis, XI, 89 :*

> *Multis jam, Lupe, posse se diebus
> Pædicare negat Charisianus.*

cost much trouble to extinguish that confounded fire. If my lacerations had been neglected, I should have died a miserable death » (Dial. VI).

You understand now why the young slave of Naevolus (Martial (III, 71) had pain at the anus; why the same Martial (VI, 37) says Carinus' posteriors had to be cut; and where the sting lies in the following distich :

« You, who know all the reasons and weighty arguments of the sects, — come tell me, what dogma is it bids you be perforated » (IX, 48).

This effeminate philosopher, who affected to speak as though he had been the successor and heir of Pythagoras, was indeed bound, if anyone was, to know the reasons of lacerations (27) of the anus, and the weights of men's members. He was accustomed to the passive part, of whom Ausonius says in mockery, as we saw a little above, that his *clazomenae* served as an anvil :

Men preferred to be supposed *pedicators* rather than *patients*; hence Martial's witty epigram:

« It is now many a long day, Lupus, that

---

(27) *Secta*, sect (from *sequor*) may also be derived from *secare*, to cut, and thus mean : laceration. (Note of the translator.)

Causam cum modo quærerent sodales,
Ventrem dixit habere se solutum.

Visne cernere pictam pædicantis imaginem, opere
quidem importune interrupto, sed nihil minus festi-
vam? Præbebit tabula capiti tertio partis tertiæ
Feliciæ *adjuncta.*

Et Græcos et Romanos fuisse tam acerrimos pæ-
dicones, qnam fortissimos cinædos, quis est quin
sciat? cum in auctoribus Græcis Romanisque, indi-
gnantibus scholarum magistris, utramque paginam
faciat mascula Venus:

« *Eodem omnes furore* » *(verba sunt Aloisiæ Si-*
gææ, Colloq. *VI, quibus non potuimus aut aptiora aut*
elegantiora dare, adnotationibus tamen nostris illus-
trata) « *ardebant plebs, magnates et reges. Philippum,*
Macedonum regem (28), *hæc insania confodit Pausa-*

---

(28) *Paulo secus Justinus, IX, 6 : « Hic Pausanius pri-*
mis pubertatis annis stuprum per injuriam passus ab At-
talo fuerat, cujus indignitati hæc etiam fœditas accesserat :
nam perductum in convivium solutumque mero Attalus non
suæ tantum, verum et convivarum libidini, velut **scortum**

Charisianus has been saying he cannot pedicate. But whenever his friends asked him why, he said his bowels were relaxed » (XI, 89).

Would you see the picture of a man engaged in pedication? he is being interrupted in the midst of his business, but the drawing is not the less pleasant for that. The engraving belonging to chapter III. of the third part of *Felicia*, presents this position.

Who does not know that the Greeks and Roman were intrepid pedicons and determined cinedes? In the Greek and Latin authors, to the indignation of the pedagogues, the male Venus parades on every page :

« All burnt with the same fire » — we are quoting Aloisia Sigaea, and we could not express ourselves better or more elegantly. We are, however, going to make annotation to this extract, — « all burnt with the same fire, the common people, the higher classes, the King. This depravity cost Philip, King of Macedon, his life (28);

---

(28) Justinus tells the tale somewhat differently : « Pausanias had had to undergo since his puberty the violence of Attalus, who added to this indignity a crying outrage : having invited him to a feast and made him drunk, he not only satisfied upon him, when full of wine, his brutal lust.

niæ manu, quem compresserat. Hæc Julium Cæsarem
(29) Nicomedi regi subjecit, omnibus hominibus in fœmi-

---

vile, subjecerat, ludibriumque omnium inter æquales reddi-
derat. Hanc rem ægre ferens Pausanias querelam Phi-
lippo sæpe detulerat. Cum variis frustrationibus, con
sine risu, differretur, et honoratum insuper ducatu ad-
versarium cerneret, iram in ipsum Philippum vertit, ultio-
nemque, quæm ab adversario non poterat, ab iniquo judice
exegit. »

(29) *Suetonius in* Julio Cæsare, *cap. 49 :* « *Cicero non*
contentus in quibusdam Epistolis scripsisse, a satellitibus
eum in cubiculum regium eductum, in aureo lecto, veste
purpurea decubuisse, floremque ætatis in Bithynia contami-
natum, quondam etiam in Senatu defendenti Nysæ causam,
filiæ Nicomedis, beneficiaque regis in se commemoranti :
« Remove », *inquit,* « isthæc oro te, quando notum est, et*
quid ille tibi, et quid illi tu dederis ». Gallico denique trium-
pho milites ejus inter cetera carmina, qualiter currum pro-
sequentes jocularitei canunt, etiam vulgatissimum illud pro-
nuntiaverunt :

> *Gallias Caesar subegit, Nicomedes Caesarem.*
> *Ecce Caesar nunc triumphat, qui subegit Gallias,*
> *Nicomedes non triumphat, qui subegit Caesarem.*

he died by the hand of Pausanias, whom he had outraged. It subjected Julius Caesar to the passion of King Nicomedes (29), — Caesar, « wife

---

but allowed him to be used by all the guests like a vile courtezan, and made him the laughing stock of his equals. Unable to bear this infamy Pausanias carried his complaint before Philip many and many a time, but the King always put him off with illusory promises. When Pausanias however saw Attalus elevated to the rank of the Chief of the Army, his fury turned against Philip, and the vengeance which he could not take upon his enemy, he took upon the iniquitous judge » (IX, 6).

(29) Suetonius, *Julius Cæsar*, ch. 48 : « Not content with having written in some of his letters that Cæsar was conducted by the guards to the bed-chamber of the King, slept there in a golden bed hung with purple, and that he allowed the bloom of his youth to be blighted in Bithynia, Cicero said to him one day in the midst of the Senate, where Cæsar was defending the case of Nysa, the daughter of King Nicomedes, and spoke of his obligations to that King : Pray, let us pass over all this ; it is only too well known what you have received, and what you have given. »

On the day of his triumph over the Gauls, the soldiers sung the following verses, amongst those which are usually sung behind the triumphal car, and they are well known.

« Cæsar has subdued the Gauls, and Nicomedes Cæsar : this day is Cæsar triumphant for having subdued the Gauls, and Nicomedes, who subdued Cæsar, has no triumph. »

Catullus (*carm.* 57) :

11

*nam vertit ut omnibus mulieribus (30) erat. Augustus
(31) id dedecus non fugit. Tiberio (32) et Neroni pro laude*

Catullus, carmine 57 :

> Pulchre convenit impiobit cinaedis
> Mamurrae pathicoque Caesarique.

(30) *Suetonius in* J. C. *c. 51.* « *Ne provincialibus quidem matrimoniis abstinuisse, vel hoc disticho apparet, jactato
æque a militibus per Gallicum triumphum :*

> Urbani, servate uxores, moechum calvum adducimus.
> Aurum in Gallia effutuisti · hic sumsisti mutuum. »

Idem c. 52. « *Helvius Cinna tribunus plebis plerisque con-
fessus est, habuisse se scriptam paratamque legem, quam
Cæsar ferre jussisset, quum ipse abesset, uti uxores, libero-
rum quærendorum causa, quas et quot ducere vellet, liceret.
Ac ne cui dubium omnino sit, et impudicitiæ eum, et adulte-
riorum flagrasse infamia, Curio pater quadam eum oratione
omnium mulierum virum, et omnium virorum mulierem ap-
pellat.* »

(31) *Suetonius, in* Augusto, *cap. 68.* « *Sextus Pompe-
jus eum ut effeminatum insectatus est, Marcus Antonius,
adoptionem avunculi* » (*immo magni avunculi*) « *stupro
meritum. Sed et populus quondam universus ludorum die et
accepit in contumeliam ejus, et assensu maximo comprobavit
versum in scena pronunciatum de Gallo matris Deum tym-
panizante :*

> « Videsne ut cinaedus orbem digito temteret »

Imaginem Augusti Cæsari substrati spectes in Monu-

of all men, and husband of all women » (30).
Augustus did not escape this shame (31), Tiber-

« How well they go together, those shameless cinedes,
Mamurra the *patient*, and Cæsar. »

(30) Suetonius, *Julius Cæsar*, ch. 51 : Nor yet did he respect the conjugal bed in the provinces; this appears from
the distich, also sung by the soldiers at the triumphal
entry :

« Citizens mind your wives; we bring you the bald-
headed adulterer. You expended gold in Gaul; here you
are taking your change. »

The same author (*Julius Cæsar*, ch. 52) says : « Helvius Cinna, tribune of the people, admitted to many
people, that he had drawn up and kept ready a law by
the instructions of Cæsar, to bring it forward during his
absence, by which he would be at liberty, with a view
to leaving offspring, to marry whom he would and as
many wives as he wished. So that nobody should be in
any doubt about the notoriety of his lewdness and infamy, Curio, the elder, in one of his pleadings, calls
him the husband of all women, and the wife of all husbands. »

(31) « Sextus Pompeius reproached him for being effeminate, and Marc Anthony says he bought his adoption
from his uncle (or rather his great-uncle) by prostituting
himself to him. On a day of public games all the world
understood and applied to him very demonstratively the
following verses, spoken of a Priest of Cybelé, Mother
of the Gods, playing the tambourine » :

« See you how a cinede governs the world with a
finger? » (Suetonius, *Augustus*, ch. 68.)

A picture representing Augustus playing the part of

fuit. Tigellino (33) *nupsit Nero, Sporus* (34) *Neroni.*

---

ments de la vie privée des douze Césars, *tabula VI, Cæsarisque Nicomedi ibidem tabula I.*

(32) *Suetonius, in* Tiberio, *c. 44.* « *Fertur etiam in sacrificando quondam captus facie ministri acerram præferentis nequisse abstinere, quin pœne vixdum re divina peracta ibidem statim seductum constupraret, simulque fratrem ejus tibicinem atque utrique mox, quod mutuo flagitium exprobrarant, crura fregisse.* » *Impotentis hominis facinus pictum adspicias tabula XX operis Hancarvilliani modo laudati.*

(33) *Immo Pythagoræ. Tacitus,* Annal., *XV, 37.* « *Nihil flagitii reliquerat, quo corruptior ageret, nisi paucos post dies uni ex illo contaminatorum grege, cui nomen Pythagoræ fuit, in modum solemnium conjugiorum denupsisset. Inditum Imperatori flammeum, visi auspices, dos et genialis torus, et faces nuptiales : cuncta denique spectata, quæ etiam in fœmina nox operit.* » *Quem Tacitus Pythagoram dixit, idem videtur, cui Doryphori nomen, sive ab officio, sive per errorem, imposuit Suetonius in* Nerone, *cap. 29.* « *Doryphoro liberto etiam, sicut ipsi Sporus, ita ipse denupsit : voces quoque et ejulatus vim patientium virginum imitatus.* » *Imaginem præbet tabula XXXVIII operis citati.*

(34) *Suetonius, in* Nerone, *c. 28.* « *Puerum Sporum,*

ius (32) and Nero gloried in it. Nero married
Tigellinus (33), and was himself espoused by

---

a *patient*, is in the *Monuments de la vie privée des douze
Césars*, pl. VI., and another of Cæsar and Nicomedes,
pl. I.

(32) « It is even said, that during a sacrifice, he could not
restrain himself, smitten with the pretty face of the in-
cense-bearer; the divine service barely finished, he took
the youth aside, and debauched him, and then did as
much for his brother, who played the flute. Soon afterwards he ordered their legs to be broken, because they
reproached each other with their infamy (Suetonius,
Tiberius, ch. 44). The act of this madman is represented
on pl. XX. in the work of d'Hancarville, cited on a pre-
vious page.

(33) And also Pythagoras. « One would have thought
that nothing was left for him in the way of debauchery,
and that he had reached the limits of depravity, if he
had not a few days later chosen out of this infamous
herd a certain Pythogoras, whom he took for his husband
with all the solemnity of a marriage. The *flammeum*
was put on the Emperor's head, the auspices were con-
sulted, neither dowry nor nuptial torches were forgotten;
all was done openly, even those things, which, if done
with a woman, are hidden by the night (Tacitus, *Annals*, XV, 37). The man called Pythagoras by Tacitus,
appears to be the same to whom Suetonius (*Nero*, ch. 29),
gives the name of Doryphorus, either on account of his
services, or by mistake. « He took for husband the freed-
man Doryphorus in the same way in which Sporus had
taken him himself for husband, and he counterfeited
the cries and sobbings of virgins when losing their maid-

*Trajanum (35) optimum principem pædagogium co-
mitabatur, Orientem totum victoriis peragrantem.
Venustorum et formosorum turmam puerorum, quos
in complexus suos dies noctesque ciebat, pædagogium*

---

*exsectis testibus etiam in muliebrem naturam transfigu-
rare conatus, cum dote et flammeo persolemni nuptia-
rum celeberrimo officio deductum ad se pro uxore habuit.
Exstatque cujusdam non inscitus jocus, bene agi potuisse
cum rebus humanis, si Domitius pater talem habuisset
uxorem. Hunc Sporum, Augustarum ornamentis excul-
tum lecticaque vectum, et circa conventus mercatusque Græ-
ciæ ac mox Romæ circa Sigillaria comitatus est identidem exosculans. » Pictas exhibet prodigiosas nuptias tabula XXXIV operis Francogallici, toties a nobis in partem
vocati.*

(35) *Spartianus, in* Hadriano, *cap.* 2. « *Fuit* » *(Hadrianus)* « *in amore Trajani, nec tamen ei per pædagogos puerorum, quos Trajanus impensius diligebat, malefaventia defuit.* »

Sporus (34). Trajan (35), the best of rulers, was accompanied by a *paedagogium*, while he marched from victory to victory through the Orient. What he named his *paedagogium* was a troop of pretty lads, well developed, whom he called day and night to come to his arms. Antinous served as mistress to Hadrian, — a rival to Plotina, but

---

enhead. » Plate XXXVIII of the above quoted work shows an illustration of this anecdote.

(34) « He went so far as to try to change a young man into a woman; his name was Sporus, and he had him castrated; having given him a dowry, he caused him to be brought to him with the *flammeum* on his head, and married him with all the nuptial solemnities. There has come down to us an appropriate saying on somebody's part, namely, whether it might not have been better for human kind if Domitian, his father, had married a woman of that sort. He made Sporus dress himself in the costume of the Empresses, and had him carried in his litter; he travelled with him in that way, taking him through the meetings and markets in Greece, and soon after in Rome, about the time of the Sigillarian festivities, kissing him from time to time » (Suetonius, *Nero*, chap. 28). Plate XXXIV in the repeatedly quoted French work, gives a representation of the abominable wedding.

(35) « He (Hadrian) enjoyed the affection of Trajan, but this did not save him from the malevolence of the pedagogues of the young boys Trajan loved so ardently » (Spartianus, *Hadrian*, ch. 2).

vocabat. Antinous Hadriano (36) *pro domina fuit,
Plotinæ rivalis, sed felicior. Mortuum luxit imperator,
et qui in vivis esse desierat, retulit in Deos, aris et
sacellis consecratis. Antoninum Heliogabalum, Severi
nepotem, per omnia cava corporis* (37) *ut loquitur vetus*

---

(36) *Spartianus, in* Hadriano, *cap. 14. « Antinoum
suum, dum per Nilum navigat, perdidit, quem muliebriter
flevit; de quo varia fama est, aliis eum devotum pro Hadriano asserentibus, aliis quod et forma ejus ostentat, et nimia voluptas Hadriani. Et Græci quidem volente Hadriano
eum consecraverunt, oracula per eum dari asserentes, quæ
Hadrianus ipse composuisse jactatur. » Hieronymus in* He-
gesippo : *« Antinous servus Hadriani Cæsaris, cujus et
gymnicus agon exercetur Antinoius, civitatemque » (Anti-
noiam) « ex ejus nomine condidit, et statuit prophetas in
templo ».*

(37) *Lampridius in* Heliogabalo, *c. 5. « Quis enim ferre
posset principem, per cuncta cava corporis libidinem recipientem, quum ne belluam quidem talem quisquam ferat?
Romæ denique nihil egit aliud, nisi ut emissarios haberet,
qui ei bene vasatos perquirerent, eosque ad aulam perduce-
rent, ut eorum conditionibus frui posset. Agebat præterea
domi fabulam Paridis, ipse Veneris personam subiens, ita ut
subito vestes ad pedes defluerent, nudusque una manu ad*

more fortunate than she was (36). The emperor mourned over his death, and placing the
dead man amongst the Gods, he raised altars
and temples in his honour. Antoninus Heliogabalus, nephew of Severus, was accustomed, an
old author says (37), to have pleasures adminis-

---

(36) « He lost,during his navigation of the Nile,his dear
Antinous, and wept for him like a woman. There are
sundry allegations about this Antinous; some say he was
devoted to Hadrian, others point to the beauty of his
shape,and to the pleasure Hadrian experienced with him.
At the instance of Hadrian the Greeks placed him in the
ranks of the Gods, and affirmed that he gave oracular
decisions; those oracles, it is said, were composed by
Hadrian himself » (Spartianus, *Hadrian*, ch. 14). St. Jerome says in the *Hegesippus* : « Antinous, a slave of the
Emperor Hadrian, after whom a circus was named the
Antinoian, founded also a town bearing his name (An-
tinoia), and established an Oracle in the temple. »

(37) « Who, indeed, could put up with a ruler who imbibed pleasure through all the cavities in his body? Not
even a beast would be suffered to do so. At Rome his
only care was to send out emissaries, who had to look
out for and to bring to the court the best shaped men
for his enjoyment. He had a performance of the comedy
of « Paris » in his palace, played the part of Venus himself, and suddenly dropping his clothes, he appeared naked with one hand on his chest and the other covering
his pudenda ; he then knelt down and offered his raised
buttocks to his pedicon » (Lampridius, *Heliogabalus*, ch. 5).
And a little farther on : « He loved Hierocles to such

scriptor, Venerem excipere solitum, sua tempora pro monstro habuere. Huic etiam Veneri severa Philosophiæ gravitas saltavit, pæderastiæ choro mista. Alcibiades et Phædon cum Socrate (38) *dormiebant, si quando*

---

*mammam, altera pudendis adhibita, ingenicul
aret, posterioribus eminentibus in subactorem rejectis et oppositis. » Et mox cap. 6. « Hieroclem vero sic amavit, ut eidem inguina oscularetur, quod dictu etiam verecundum est, Floralia sacra se asserens celebrare. » Non dubitavit repetere propudiosas nuptias Neronis et Pythagoræ. Lampridius, cap. 10 : « Zoticus sub eo tantum valuit, ut ab omnibus officiorum principibus sic haberetur, quasi domini maritus esset. Nupsit et coiit, ut et pronubum haberet, clamaretque : « Concide, Magire! » et eo quidem tempore, quo Zoticus ægrotabat. » Magirus dictus Zoticus ab artificio patris coqui.*

(38) *Neque tamen defuisse Socrati defensores strenuos, quis est, quem fugiat? Sit tibi instar omnium unus Bruckerus, Hist. crit. philos. I, 539, 40. Certe Alcibiadem Plato* in Symposio, *ut verbis utar Nepotis in* Alcibiade, c. 2. « induxit commemorantem, se pernoctasse cum Socrate, neque aliter ab eo surrexisse. ac filius a parente debuerit. » Xanthippen quidem, an mirum? graviter tulisse maritum tam familiariter uti formoso Alcibiade, refert Ælianus* Variæ historiæ, XI, *12, ita ut placentam Socrati ab Alci-*

tered to him through all the orifices in his body;
his contemporaries looked upon him as a monster. Before this Venus grave philosophers danced in company with pederasts. Alcibiades and
Phaedo slept with Socrates (38), when they want-

---

a degree as to kiss his virile parts, a thing I blush to report; he said that he thus celebrated the Floralia « (*Ibid.*,
ch. 6). He did not hesitate to repeat the infamous wedding of Nero with Pythagoras : « Zoticus had such power
over him that the principal officials of the state treated
him as though he really were the husband of the Emperor.
He married him, and made him consummate the marriage in the presence of the giver away of the bride, telling him, « Push in, Magira! » And this was done at a
time when Zoticus was ill » (Lampridius, ch. 10). Zoticus was called Magira on account of the profession of
his father, who had been a cook.

(38) Socrates, as is well known, has not been in want of
warm defenders; Brucker (*Critical History of Philosophy*,
I, pp. 539, 540), may stand for all of them. Undoubtedly
Plato, in the *Symposium*, brought in Alcibiades, who says
he recollects, to use the expression of Cornelius Nepos
(*Alcibiades*, ch. 2.) « to have passed a night with Socrates, but not otherwise than a son might with his father. » But Xantippe, and it is not surprising, was indi-
gnant that her husband should be on such familiar terms
with a good-looking youth like Alcibiades; and Aelian (*Va-
riae Historiae*, XI, 12), relates that she stamped upon a cake
sent by Alcibiades, which made Socrates laugh and cry
out : « What are you doing? You cannot eat it now. I
do not care for it at all! » But, Socrates! good morals

alacrem vellent præceptorum. Ab tam sancti viri amo-
ribus duxit originem hæc dicendi in Venereis formula :
Socratica fide diligere Omnia Socratis facta dictave
omnibus philosophorum sectis sacra : illi sacellum con-
ditum et ara erecta; facta legis vim, dicta oraculi
auctoritatem habuere. Philosophi ab Herois (nam inter
Heroes relatus Socrates) indigetisque sui exemplo non
descivere. Lycurgus, qui Laconum legislator aliquot
ante Socratem sæculis bonum et utilem esse posse civem
negavit, cui non esset concubinus amicus, volebat nudas
virgines in theatro palam exerceri, ut liberior hic
adspectus amoris aciem, quo natura ferente rapiuntur
ad illas homines, abtunderet, et in amasios et sodales
ardentiorem converteret. Nam non ita tangunt adsueta.

---

biade dono missam pedibus conculcaret, dicente Socrate risu
sublato : « Neque tu igitur quidquam ex eo habebis! Quid
autem tu quæris? Non assis facio. » Sed habere, Socrate,
mores vix poteras hos, et hos amicos. De Socraticis nomi-
nasse suffecerit Platonem, quem Diogenes Laertius, III, 23,
amasse tradit Asterem, Phædrum, Alexin, imprimis Dio-
nem, adjecto epigrammate Platonis in Dionem, ita desi-
nente :

Ὦ ἐμὸν ἐκμήνας θυμὸν ἔρωτι Δίων.

ed to get their tutor into good humour. It is
from this kind of amours practised by the vener-
able man, that is derived the erotic phrase : to
love *Socratically*. Every action and every word
of Socrates were held as sacred by all sects of
philosophers; they built a temple and erected
an altar in his honour; all his actions had legal
force, and his words the authority of an oracle.
The philosophers did not turn away from the
example set by their Hero (for Socrates took
rank with the Heroes) and new national divinity. Lycurgus, the Spartan legislator, living
some centuries before Socrates, refused the title
of a good and deserving citizen to any man who
had not a friend that served him as a concubine.
He willed it that virgins should perform naked
on the stage, so that the view of their charms
freely exposed, should dull in men that sensual
longing which by the aid of nature draws them

---

and such friends are incompatible. Enough to name
amongst the disciples of Socrates Plato, whom Diogenes
Laërtius (III, 23), declares to have loved Aster, Phae-
drus, Alexis, and before all Dion; he quotes an epigram
of Plato on Dion, ending thus :
  « O you, who have so fiercely burnt my heart with
love, you Dion! »

De poetis quid loquar (39)? *Anacreonta* (40) *urebat Bathyllus pleræque omnes facetiæ versantur circa hæc. Hujus sunt generis :*

———————

(39) *De Pindaro Valerius Maximus, IX, 12.* « *At Pindarus quum in gymnasio super gremium pueri* » *(Theoxeni, Suida teste)* « *quo unice delectabatur, capite posito quieti se dedisset, non prius decessisse cognitus est, quam, gymnasiarcha claudere jam eum locum volente, nequicquam excitaretur.* » *De Sophocle Athenæus XIII, 81,* φιλομείραξ ἦν ὁ Σοφοκλῆς, ὡς Εὐριπίδης φιλογύνης, *lepida mox cap. 82, addita narratiuncula de puero a Sophocle jactura lænæ compresso, qua rapta puer aufugerit, quod ut cognoverit Euripides, irriso decepto poeta, dixisse : se et ipsum aliquando usum esse puero illo, sed nihil amplius addidisse : quo Athenæi loco miror verbum* προσθεῖναι *suspectum visum esse magno Casaubono, quo nihil verius, nihil aptius. Uterque puero dedit album virus, sed alter addidit lænam, alter non addidit.*

(40) *Horat.* Epodo *XIV, 9, 10 :*

> *Non aliter Samio dicunt arsisse Bathyllo*
> *Anacreonta Teium.*

to women, that they might thus reserve all their
passion for their friends and companions. For
what men see every day loses half its effect.

Again, why speak of the Poets (39)? Anacreon (40), was hotly in love with Bathyllus ; almost all pleasantries of Plautus have this
subject for their aim ; they are of this kind :

---

(39) Valerius Maximus (IX, 12) relates of Pindar : « One
day, at the Gymnasium, Pindar, leaning his head against
the breast of a young lad, whom he loved above all
(Suidas says his name was Theoxenes), fell asleep ; no
sooner had the head of the establishment seen him a-
sleep than he ordered all the doors to be closed, for fear
of the poet being awakened. » Athenaeus on his part
(XIII, 81) tells us of Sophocles : « Sophocles loved boys
to the same degree as Euripides loved women » ; and a
little farther on (ch. 82) he relates the story of a youth
whom Sophocles enjoyed, but at the price of his mantle,
which the rogue abstracted. Euripides, having been informed of this adventure. mocked the poet for having
been thus done : « I also », he said, « have had him,
but he got noting else out of me. » I am surprised that
this passage of Athenaeus should have appeared doubtful
to the celebrated Casaubon, on account of the expression
« got out of me » which is quite correct and applicable.
Sophocles and Euripides had both lavished their white
fluids upon the little rogue; but from one of them he got
besides a mantle, from the other nothing else.

(40) « No less fiercely burned the love of Anacreon of
Teos, they say, for the Samian youth Bathyllus « (Horace, *Epodes*, XIV, 9, 10).

162   THE MANUAL

Faciam (41) *quod pueri solent, conquiniscam ad cistulam;*

---

(41) *Immo Plauti verba,* Cistellaria, *IV, 1, 5, hæc sunt:*

Faciundum est puerile officium; conquiniscam ad cistulam,

id est, incurvabo me ad cistulam humo tollendam, eorum more, qui culo obverso pædiconibus obsequuntur. Nam puerile officium idem est, quod Apulejus Metamorph. *III, p. 138, puerile dixit corollarium, et Martialis IX, 68 puerile simpliciter : conquiniscere autem, Nonio teste, p. 531. Gothofredi, est inclinari, et peculiariter dictum videtur de gestu pathico, ut in* Pseudolo :

Si conquiniscet istic, ceveto simul.

Dixerunt etiam, aliquanto fere significantius, ocquiniscere. Nonius, *p. 567. « Ocquiniscere est proprie inclinari.* Pomponius Prostibulo : *Ut nullum civem pædicavi per dolum, nisi ipsus orans ultroque ocquinisceret.* Idem Pistore : *Nisi nunc aliquis subito obviam occurrit mihi, qui ocquiniscat, quo compingam terminum in tutum locum. » A gestu ocquiniscentis non multum abludit, sed aliquantulum tamen, gestus ingeniculantis, quo Heliogabalus, Lampridio teste cap. 5. usus est, « posterioribus eminentibus in subactorem rejectis et oppositis. » Ingeniculabat, non conquiniscebat, Timarchus ille Luciani in* Apophrade, *p. 152, tomi VII Operum a Jo. Petro Schmidio editorum :* Καὶ μέμνηνται οἱ τότε ὑμῖν ἐπιστάντες, καὶ σὲ μὲν ἐς γόνυ συγκαθήμενον ἰδόντες, ἐκεῖνον δὲ οἶσθα ὅ, τι καὶ ποιοῦντα, εἰ μὴ παντάπασιν ἐπι-

« I shall do like the lads, I will cower down over a hamper (41). »

---

(41) The actual words of Plautus are :
« I must do the puerile service ; I will cower down over a hamper » (*Cistellaria.* IV, sc. I, v. 5), — which means, I will bend down to the hamper, raising the buttocks, and thus present them to the pedicon. This is, in fact, what is called, the « puerile office », and which Apuleius (*Metam.* III, ch. 2), calls « the puerile corollary ». Martial (IX, 68) says simply, « *illud puerile.* » *Conquinescere* is according to Nonius, p. 531, Gottfried's edition, to curve the spine, an expression designating in particular the passive posture as we have seen in the *Pseudolus* :

« When he curves the spine, then simultaneously wriggle your buttocks. »

Some authors have also used a still more forcible expression, « *Ocquinescere,* » viz., « to cower low down » (Nonius, p. 567). Pomponius, on word « *Prostibulum* » : « I have never forced pedication upon any citizen; I have always abstained, unless the patient had asked me and cowered down of his own free will. » And on word « *Pistor* » : « Unless somebody anticipated my desires, willingly crouching down so that I could do the thing securely. » This position of the patient cowering down is very rarely alluded to; the question generally turns upon his kneeling. « Thus, » says Lampridus of Heliogabalus, he offered himself with the buttocks raised to the pedicon » (ch. 5). Heliogabalus was kneeling, and not crouching. The same is the case with Timarchus in Lucian : « All that were near you remember it; they have seen you on your knees, while your accomplice did you know what « (*Apophras,* p. 152, vol. VII. — Works of Lucian edit. by J.-P.

Et :

Conveniebatne machæra militis in vaginam tuam (42)?
*Ille immo poeticæ artis apex, Maro, qui Parthenias
appellatus ab ingenuo et ingenito pudore, Alexandrum
dono sibi a Pollione datum amabat et sub Alexis nomine
laudavit* (43). *Ovidium idem morbus tentavit, prætulit*

λήσμων τις εἶ. *Vis tu spectare utrumque gestum ?* in Monuments de la vie privée des douze Césars, *habebis tabula
XXVII conquiniscentem, tabula XXXVIII ingeniculantem.
Cum rure cacaturientes soleant conquiniscere, factum est, ut
etiam ii, qui pædicarentur, cacare dicerentur et cacare quidem
mentulam, quam alternis ineuntem et exeuntem pathicus sane
videri potest cacare. Hinc illud in* Priapeio *LXX :*

> Ad me respice, fur, et aestimato
> Quot pondo tibi mentula est cacanda.

Eodem spectat epigramma 70 libri IX, apud Martialem :

> Cum futuis, Policharme, soles in fine cacare :
> Cum paedicaris, quid, Policharme facis ?

(42) *Pseudolo, IV,* 7, *85.*

(43) *Et poteras, Aloisia, et vero debebas Horatium addere,*
Epodo *XI :*

> Nunc amor Lycisci me tenet,
> Unde expedire non amicorum queant
> Libera consilia, non contumeliae graves.

Satir. I, II, *116-119.*

Or again :

« The soldier's poniard did it fit your sheath (42)? »

That grand master of the art of poetry, Maro, who won the surname of Parthenias by his ingenuousness and innate modesty, cherished a certain Alexander, whom Pollio had given to him as a present, and he has celebrated him under the name af Alexis (43). Ovid suffered from

---

Schmid). If you would like to see these two postures, you will find them in the *Monuments de la vie privée des douze Césars*, pl. XXVII., a *patient* crouching, and pl. XXXVIII, a *patient* kneeling.

From the fact that men wanting to void their excrement when out of doors cower down, it has come about that passive pederasts were said to sh...t, — in fact to sh...t the active party's member as it goes in and out of the anus. Hence in the *Priapeia*, LXX :

« Look at me, thief, and realize the weight of the member you will have to sh...t. » Martial (IX, 70) also plays on the word :

« When you love a woman, Polycharmus, you always sh...t before you have done. Tell me, Polycharmus, what you do, when you pedicate? »

(42) *Pseudolus*, IV, sc. VII, 85.

(43) You might very well, Aloysia have quoted Horace too (*Epodes*, XI) :

« ... Now Lyciscus holds me in love-bonds, from which neither friendly advice, nor humiliating affronts avail to liberate me.

And *Satires*, I, ii, v. 116-119.

tamen puellas pueris, quod voluptatem his in lusibus vellet
communem, non sibi propriam. Amare se Venerem
ait (44), *quæ utrimque resolvat. Hinc fieri, quod pueri*
amore minus tangatur. Quum se negligi viderent
puellæ ab iis quos amarent, et uxores ab iis, in quorum
sacra per nuptias venerant, si muliebri tantum mere-
rent stipendio, ad puerile deflexere officium. Eo res ad-
ducta vecordiæ, id etiam novis ut prius nuptis extor-
queretur, dehinc per puerum ad puellam iretur, uter-
que utrique uno in corpore sexus confunderetur. Priapus
in Veterum lusu, qui accesserit ad stipitem suum olerum
ur, hnnc daturum minatur (45), *quod virgo prima*
dat nocte cupido marito, alterius loci dum inepta vul-
nus timet.

..... *Tument tibi cum inguina, num, si*
Ancilla, aut verna est praesto puer, impetus in quem
Continuo fiat, malis tentigine rumpi?
Non ego!

(44) *De Arte amatoria, II, 683, 84.*
(45) *Priapeio secundo.*

the same malady; he however preferred young girls to lads, because in his amusement he wanted reciprocal pleasure, and not a selfish enjoyment. He said he loved the pleasure « of the simultaneous ejaculation of both parties » (44), and for this reason he was less given to the love of boys.

Young girls and wives finding themselves neglected, the first by those they loved, the other ones by their husbands, instead of offering their services only as females, resolved to play the part of the lads. The depravity became so great that this complaisance was actually extorted from brides, as it was before from married women; in fact the husband went at the young wife pederastically, and the two sexes were joined in one and the same body. In the facetious poems of the ancients, Priapus (45) threatens every thief of vegetables from his garden that comes

---

« When your privates are swelling, if some maid-servant or slave-boy is at hand for you to assail forthwith, do you choose rather to burst with desire ? Nay! not I! »
(44) Art of Love, II, 683, 684.
(45) Priapeia, II.

« *Fingit, nam quidlibet audendi æqua fuit semper potestas pictoribus et poetis, Valerius Martialis* (46) *sibi uxorem obmurmurantem nates etiam esse, quod deterreret a puerorum amore amentem. Junonem hac ait parte placere Jovi; nec tamen se suaderi : aliam esse pueri partem, aliam fœminæ. Utatur uxor parte*

---

(46) *Epigr. 44 libri XI :*

> Odi concubitus, qui non utrimque resolvant :
>   Hoc est cur pueri tangar amore minus.
> Deprensum in puero tetricis me vocibus uxor
>   Corripis : et culum te quoque habere refers.
> Dixit idem quoties lascivo Juno Tonanti ?
>   Ille tamen gracıli cum Ganymede jacet.
> Incurvabat Hylam posito Tyrinthius arcu :
>   Tu Megaram credis non habuisse nates ?
> Torquebat Phoebum Daphne fugitiva, sed illas
>   Oebalius flammas jussit arbire puer.
> Briseis multum quamvis aversa jaceret,
>   Aeacidae proprior laevis amicus erat.
> Parce tuis igitur dare mascula nomina rebus.
>   Teque puta cunnos uxor habere duos.

Simile illud ejusdem, XII, 98 :

> Cum tibi nota tui sit vita fidesque mariti,
>   Nec premat ulla tuos solicitetque toros ;
> Quid quası pellicibus torqueris ınepta ministris ,
>   In quibus et brevis est et fugitiva Venus ?
> Plus tıbi quam domini pueros praestare probabo .
>   Hi faciunt, ut sis foemina sola viro.
> Hi dant, quod non vis uxor dare. « Do tamen, » inquis,
>   « Ne vagus a thalamis conjugis erret amor. »
> Non eadem res ęş : Chiam volo, nolo mariscam ;
>   Ne dubites quae sit Chia, marisca tua est.

near his weapon, to make him sacrifice what in
the first night the bride accords to her ardent
husband, for fear that he may wound another
part.

Making use of his imagination with the licence
ever granted both to painters and poets, Valerius Martial (46) pretends to hear his wife grum-
ble that she also had buttocks, and that he had

---

(46) Epigr. 44, book IX :
« Catching me with a boy, you harass me with your
cries, and you tell me, my wife, that you have posteriors
too.

Many and many a time did Juno say the same to Jupiter the Thunderer ; yet he continued to sleep with slender
Ganymede.

He of Tyrius, laying his bow aside, bent Hylas under
him : think you therefore that Megara was without buttocks? Daphné, by her flight, vexed Phœbus, but his
love's ardour found relief in the end in the boy Oeba-
lius. Although Briseis slept, often with her back turned
upon him, his smooth-skinned friend Patroclus was
more to the taste of the son of Aeacus.

Cease then, wife, to call your affairs by masculine
names ; better consider you have two vulvas.

His Epigram XII, 98, treats of the same matter :

Knowing as you do the honest walk and fidelity of
your husband, and that he never misuses your bed with
concubines, why, foolish woman, torment yourself about
those venal boy lovers, — brief and fugitive is the pleasure from their complaisance !

They are more useful to you than to their master, I

sua jubet. Sed sedebant (47) *in fornicibus pueri puel-*
læve sub titulis (48) *et lychnis* (49), *illi fœmineo*

Scire suos fines matrona et fœmina debet :
Cede suam pueris, utere parte tua.

(47) *Sedebant prosedæ Plauti in* Pœnulo, *I,* 2, 54; *aliæ*
stabant : Horat. Sat. I, II, 30 : « *Alius* (vult) *nullam,*
nisi olente in fornice stantem. »

(48) *Juvenalis, VI, 123 :* « *Titulum mentita Lyciscæ* »
(Messalina). *Petronius c.* 7. « *Video quosdam inter titulos*
nudasque meretrices furtim conspatiantes. Tarde, immo jam
sero, intellexi, me in fornicem esse deductum. » *Martialis,*
XI, 46 :

Intrasti quoties inscriptae limina cellae,
Seu puer arrisit, sive puella tibi...

Meretrices autem nomen mutasse constat ex loco Plauti in
Pœnulo, *V,* 3, 20, 21.

Namque hodie earum mutarentur nomina,
Facerentque indignum genere quaestum corpore,

no need of boys. « Juno », she says, « also pleased Jupiter from that side. » Tho poet is not to
be convinced, he answers her that the part
taken by a boy is one thing, and that of the wife
another, and that she ought to be satisfied with
hers.

Under the name-boards (47) and the lamps
(48) in the brothels sat (49) boys as well as girls,
the first dressed in the feminine stola, the latter
in the manly tunic, and with their hair dressed
like boys. Under the guise of one sex was found

---

tell you, for they make him think that one wife is better
than they all. They give what you will not give; — But
I will, you say, so that the volatile husband stray not from
the conjugal bed.

But it is not the same thing, I want a fig not an orange,
and you must know theirs is a fig, yours an orange;
Look! a matron, a woman like you, must know what belongs to her. Leave to boys what is theirs, and do you
make the best of what is yours. »

(47) Some prostitutes sat (Plautus, *Poenulus*, I., ii.,
v. 54), others stood : « Another man will only have
the harlot that stands upright in the unclean brothel. »
(Horace, Sat. I., ii., v. 30.)

(48) Juvenal's Messalina (VI., v. 123) prostitutes herself
« under the fictitious name-board of Lycisca. » Petronius : « I see men gliding in stealthily between the

*comti mundo sub stola, hæ parum comtæ sub puerorum
veste, ore ad puerilem formam composito. Alter veni-
bat sexus sub altero sexu.* Prima mali sedes Asia (50),

---

(49) *Horat. Sat. II, 7, 48, 49.*

*... Sub clara nuda lucerna
Quaecunque excepit turgentis verbera caudae...*

Juvenalis, VI, 130, 131.

*... Fumoque lucernae
Foeda lupanaris tulit ad pulvinar odorem.*

(50) *Variant auctores. Herodotus, I, 135* : Πέρσαι ἀπ'
Ἑλλήνων μαθόντες παισὶ μίσγονται. *Plutarchus*, de Maligni-
tate Herodoti, *p. 857, t. II, Operum Francofurti anno 1620,
typis impressorum* : Καίτοι πῶς Ἕλλησι Πέρσαι διδασκάλια
ταύτης ὀφείλουσι τῆς ἀκολασίας παρ' οἷς ὀλίγου δεῖν ὑπὸ
πάντων ὁμολογεῖται παῖδας ἐκτετμῆσθαι πρὶν Ἑλληνικὴν
ἰδεῖν θάλασσαν; *Athenæus, XIII, 79* : Τοῦ παιδεραστεῖν
παρὰ πρώτων Κρητῶν εἰς τοὺς Ἕλληνας παρελθόντος, ὡς
ἱστορεῖ Τίμαιος. Ἄλλοι δέ φασί τῶν τοιούτων ἐρώτων
κατάρξασθαι Λάϊον, ξενωθέντα παρὰ Πέλοπι, καὶ ἐρασθέντα
τοῦ υἱοῦ αὐτοῦ Χρυσίππου ὃν καὶ ἁρπάσαντα καὶ ἀναθέμενον
εἰς ἅρμα εἰς Θήβας φυγεῖν. *Et cui non est audita Sodomita-
rum antiquissima intemperantia ?*

the other. Asia (50) was the original home of

---

name-boards and the naked prostitutes; I understood, alas, too late, that I had been introduced into a bad place. (*Satyr.* ch. 7.) Martial (XI., 46) :

« When you pass the threshold of a chamber with name-board over the door, whether it be a boy or a girl that greeted you with a smile ».....

That the prostitutes changed their names is apparent from a passage in Plautus (*Poenulus*, V, iii, 20, 21 :

« For to-day they were to change their names, and will lend their bodies for infamous traffic. »

(49) Horace, Sat. II, vii, 48, 49 :

« ..... Every woman that naked beneath the bright lamplight endured the thrusts of a swollen member. »

Juvenal, VI, 130, 131.

« Foul with the reek of the lamp, she bore to the Imperial couch the stink of the brothel. »

(50) Authors vary on this point. Herodotus : « The Persians pollute young boys; they have learned it from the Greeks (I, 135). Plutarch refutes the asssertion : « How can the Persians be indebted to the Greeks for these impurities, when all historians are agreed upon the fact that they had eunuchs before they had ever come near to the Grecian seas? » (Of the Maliciousness of Herodotus, p. 857, vol. II of Frankfort edition of 1620). Athenaeus : « Pederastia was first introduced in Greece by the Cretans, as is related by Timaeus; other authors however have asserted that the man who first imported that sort of love was Laius, who, having been hospitably received by Pelops, fell in love with Chrysippus, the son of his host, carried him off in his chariot, and fled to Thebes. » (XIII, 79.) And who has not heard of the incontinence of the inhabitants of Sodom ?

*nec tamen Africa ab hac peste pura, quæ per conta-
gium mox Græciam et contiguas Europæ partes* (51)
pervasit. Orpheum, *in Thracia fœtulenti ludi inven-
torem et suasorem, spretæ Ciconum matres*

*Inter sacra Deum nocturnaque orgia Bacchi,
Discerptum latos juvenem sparsere per agros,*
　　　　　　　　　　　　　　　　(*Virgilius,* Georg. *IV,* 521, 22.)

Celtas narrant (52) *vetustis illis temporibus, si qui
se hoc a morbo præstarent incolumes, ludibrio habuisse :*

---

(51) *Nominatim Eubœam, unde* χαλκιδίζειν, *Hesychio auctore ponitur* ἐπὶ τῶν παιδεραστούντων, *quoniam apud Chal-
cidenses* ἐπλεόναζον οἱ παιδικοὶ ἔρωτες. *Dixerunt etiam*
φιχιδίζειν, *ab ignota civitate; Suidas :* Καὶ φιχιδίζειν ἐπὶ τοῦ
παιδεραστεῖν. *Similiter* σιφνιάζειν, *a Siphno insula maris
Ægei ; Hesychius :* Σιφνιάζειν καταδακτυλίζειν · διαβέβληνται
γὰρ οἱ Σίφνιοι ὡς παιδικοῖς χρώμενοι. *Alio quoque detorqueri
verbum* σιφνιάζειν, *supra vidimus.*

(52) *Athenæus, XIII,* 79 : Καὶ Κελτοὶ δὲ, τῶν βαρβάρων
καίτοι καλλίστας ἔχοντες γυναῖκας (*quid mirum, miratorem
albi cunni tam omnivolum, quam Julium Cæsarem fuisse
constat, non abstinuisse provincialibus matrimoniis in Gallia ?*)
πχιδικοῖς μᾶλλον χαίρουσιν · ὡς πολλάκις ἐνίους ἐπὶ ταῖς
δοραῖς μετὰ δύο ἐρωμένων ἀναπαύεσθαι.

this pest, then Africa got infected, and soon the
scourge invaded Greece and the adjoining countries of Europe (51). In Thrace Orpheus was the
importer and supporter of this unclean pleasure.
The Thracian women, finding themselves held in
contempt,......

« During the sacred feasts and the nocturnal
orgies of Bacchus, tore the youth to pieces, and
bestrewed the wide plains with his limbs. (Virgil, *Georg*. IV, 521, 522.)

It is alleged that in those ancient times the
Celts (52) ridiculed those amongst them who kept

---

(51) Particularly in Euboea, whence the expression,
« Chalcidize », meaning, according to Hesychius, to
pedicate, because masculine loves flourished among the
Chalcidians. « Phicidize » is another expression for the
same thing from the name of a town now unknown ;
Suidas : « Phicidize, to be a Pederast », and similarly,
« Siphnianize » from Siphnos, an island in the Ægean ;
Hesychius says : « Siphnianize, that is to finger the anus :
the inhabitants of Siphnos are, in fact, given to the
practice of pederastia. » We have seen above that the
meaning of Siphnianize has been perverted.

(52) Athenaeus, XIII, 79 : « Of all the barbarians the
Celts, although their women are most beautiful — it is,
therefore, not surprising that an ardent amateur of
« fine women, » such as Julius Caesar is described to us,
should in the Gallic Provinces have been not over respectful
to the conjugal bed — the Celts take more pleasure in

*nec munerum, nec honorum participes erant. Qui pu-
ros sibi servarent mores, effugiebantur ut impurati.
Non juvat in publica totius civitatis dementia esse solum
sapientem, et qua non juvat nec etiam decet.* »

Habes Aloisiæ luculentam orationem.

Neque vero etiam recentioribus temporibus (53)
*masculæ Veneris amorem evanuisse argumento sunt
Persæ, quos huic voluptatis generi deditissimos esse*

---

(53) *Veniam dabis, medioxime Marce Pullarie, quod te
propemodum præterivimus. Ausonius, Epigrammate 70 :*

> Quis Marcus Feles nuper pullaria dictus,
> Corrupit totum qui puerile decus,
> Perversae Veneris postico vulnere fossor,
> Lucili vatis subulo, pullipremo.

*Pullariam felem dicit, qui, ut felis (nam feles idem quod
felis) aves, ita ipse pueros captaret, ac Lucilii verbis (cujus
ergo Satiras ut adhuc legeret tam felici esse contigit Ausonio)
subulonem, podices cinædorum pene quasi subula sutoria per-
cidentem, et pullipremonem, puellos comprimentem et subigen-
tem.*

aloof from this pratice; such could expect neither civil employment nor honours. Those, that
preserved the purity of their morals were shunn-
ed as impure. « In a town where everyone is
mad, it is not good to be alone sane, and by reason of its not being good it is not advisable. »
(Dialogue VI.)

This ends our brilliant extract from Aloysia
Sigaea.

Even in our own days (53) the taste for the male
Venus has not disappeared, witness the Persians,

---

pederastia than any other Nation, to such a degree that
amongst them it is no rarity to find a man lying between two minions.

(53) Pardon me, illustrious Marcus Pullarius, for having
almost forgotten you. Ausonius, Epigr. LXX. :

« Which Marcus? The one they call the « cat that
catches boys », he who tarnishes all the purity of childhood, who plies with his back-door tool the rearward
Venus, the poet Lucilius' *subulo*, his *pullipremo*. »

Ausonius calls him the pullarian cat, because he hun-
ted after young lads (puelli) as the cat gives chase to
brids; he calls him, applying to him the same epithets
as Lucilius, whose Satires he had the opportunity of
reading, — more fortunate in this than we, — a *subulo*
(from *subula*, an awl), wanting to make it understood
that with his member he transfixed, like a cobbler with
his awl, the anus of cinedes; and *pullipremo*, from his
compressing in his work young lads.

ii referunt, qui illas regiones peragraverunt, ut Adamus Olearius libro V, cap 15. *Itinerarii: Itali atque Hispani, si fides Aloisiæ: Batavi, apud quos medio circiter sæculo XVIII hanc consuetudinem ita invaluisse narrat Jo. Davides Michaelides in* Jure Mosaiso, *patria lingua edito, paragrapho* 258, *ut non nisi capitis pœnis coerceri posset: Parisienses, memorante* Gynæologiæ Germanica lingua *conscriptæ auctore, a multiplici scientia instructo, tomo II, p.* 427, *insuper addente, in omnibus fere magnis Europæ urbibus etiamnum reperiri, qui, sive gaudiorum consuetorum satietate, sive morbi turpis metu, posticam Venerem anticæ præferendam ducant, exceptis Anglis, quibus ea res execrandissimum nefas videatur: et ne generatim tantum atque universe loquamur, Gonsalvi* (54) *Cordubensis et Vendomii* (55), *belli ducum præstantissimorum*

---

(54) *Aloisia, III, 48 :* « *Si puerum, nam et pædico erat acerrimus* » (*Gonsalvus Cordubensis*) « *prurienti cuperet peni, dicebat Aversam se cogitare, celebrem urbem.* »

(55) *Vide sæculi XVIII historiam a Christiano Dan. Vos-*

who are very much addicted to this kind of pleasure, as is related by those who have travelled in
their country. Amongst others there is Adam
Lhuilier, chapter 15, book V, of his *Itinerary*.
If we may trust to Aloysia Sigaea, the Italians and
Spaniards did it; also the Dutchmen, with whom
towards the middle of the XVIIIth. Century,
as J. David Michaëlides tells us in his *Treatise
on the Law of Moses* (in Dutch), § 258, this habit
was so much in vogue, that the punishment of
death was hardly of avail against it; also the Pari-
sians, according to the Author of the *Gynaeology*
(in German, vol. II., p. 427), a fully com-
petent authority, who adds that in almost all
the great cities of Europe there are to be found
plenty of people who, either being satiated with
the ordinary pleasure, or afraid of infectious dis-
eases, prefer the posterior to the anterior Venus,
— the English always excepted, who abominate
this practice. Not to be for ever talking generalities
and never giving definite instances, the cases of
Gonzalvo of Cordova (54) and of Vendôme (55),

---

(54) « Menacing with his couched lance some youth (he
was a determined pedicon), he would say he intended
to go to Aversa, a famous town » (Aloysia Sigaea, Dialogue VII).
(55) See the « History of the Eighteenth Century », by

exempla, annalium monumentis satis vulgata, qui-
bus etiam illustriora quædam nostræ ætatis, fama
audaci ferente, adjungere possemus : scriptores ma-
gni, regis maximi, p. o. ejusque cum ingenii acu-
mine, tum dicendi copia, tum plurimarum litera-
rum, nec earum vulgarium, sed interiorum et
reconditarum laude unius omnium, quoad vixit,
florentissimi(56), ita ut vel illi viro, in quo tantam
Ciceronianæ eloquentiæ vim hodie et lætamur et
admiramur enitere, quantam post magni Ernestidis
excessum non vidit Germania, Sphingiacum propo-
neret ænigma, nisi vereremur, ne quid invidiæ

---

sio Germanice scriptam, parte V, p. 364. Nam pædicones
minorum gentium, de quidus mentio facta est ab vidua Phi-
lippi, primi Aurelianensis ducis, festivissimis literis ante
hæc septem lustra demum in lucem editis, pp. 74, 284, 350,
purpuratus Bullionensis, eques Lotharingicus, comes Marsa-
nensis, Franciscus Ludovicus, princeps Contiacensis, cum co-
mite Veromanduensi cinædo, inferiori hocce loco contenti sunto.

(56) *Absit malignus interpres ! Improbe facit, qui in alieno*
libro ingeniosus est.

both of them excellent Generals, have been made notorious enough by historical documents; to these we could add other still more illustrious examples, taken from our own time and made known by a heedless fame; that of a great author, of a great king, the father of his country, and of a man, who during his life gained general admiration by the penetration of his intellect, and the splendour of his language, and whose knowledge embraces all branches of knowledge, not only the ordinary ones, but the profoundest and most abstruse (56), — a man that might well propose the riddle of the Sphinx to his eminent confrère in whom we delight to admire the power of a truly Ciceronian eloquence, unknown in Germany since the death of the

---

Christ. Dan. Voss (in German, Part. V, p 364). As to pedicons ol less exalted position, of whom mention is made by the widow of Philip, first Duke of Orleans, in her amusing letters (pp. 74, 284, 350), which appeared about thirty years ago, there are: the Cardinal de Bouillon, the Chevalier de Lorraine, the Comte de Marsan, François Louis, Prince de Conti. These together with the Comte de Vermandois, a cinede this last, must rest content to appear in a mere foot-note.

(56) Do not misunderstand what I say. It is not for an honest man to sharpen his wits at the expense of another's book.

nostra aliqua culpa, quanquam citra omnem vo-
luntatem nostram atque sententiam, accederet sanctæ
memoriæ virorum excellentissimorum.

Novos vero desideras ? Multus est in utroque ge-
nere Pacificus Maximus. Elegia I, pag. Parisiensi
107 :

> *Causa mei moris solus fuit ipse magister,*
>   *Cui pater et mater me male cauta dedit.*
> *Rex pædiconum fuit hic : non unus ab hujus*
>   *Effugit manibus, talis in arte fuit.*
> *Multa quidem didici, quæ non didicisse juvaret*
>   *Plurima per culum, multa per ora bibi.*

Idem Elegia II ad Ptolemæum, p. 110 :

> *Jam tibi servantur, quascunque, ingrate, paravi,*
>   *Et nisi tu, nostras nullus habebit opes.*
> *Illa etiam major multo est mea mentula : septem*
>   *Tunc habuit digitos, nunc habet illa decem.*

Idem Elegia IV ad Marcum, p. 113 :

> *Non meliore mihi poteris occurrere, Marce,*
>   *Quam nunc, non ullo commodiore loco.*
> *Arbiter omnis abest, locus est sine judice tutus,*
>   *Fœmina nil boterit, masque referre nihil.*

great Ernesti. These examples, I say, we could easily allege, were we not apprehensive of raising, quite contrary to our purpose and intention, a feeling of odium against the pious memory of most distinguished men.

Do you wish for any more? Pacificus Maximus offers a goodly number, both of the active and the passive parties. *Elegy* I, p. 107, of the Paris edition :

« The sole cause of my badness was my master, — the man my father and mother incautiously entrusted me to. He was the king of pedicons; not one escaped his lust, so artful and winning was he. Many a thing I learned, I had better have left unknown ; much did I absorb through my rectum, much through my lips. »

Elegy II, to Ptolemy (p. 110) :

« For you, ungrateful boy, I keep my treasures all, and no one shall enjoy them but yourself; my mentula is growing : while it used to measure seven inches, now it measures ten. »

Elegy IV, to Marcus (p. 113) :

« You could not, Marcus, find a better, a more convenient, place, in which to meet me ; not a spy is here nor witness, neither man nor woman

Hic inter salices et prata virentia fiet,
  Frondibus immixtos arbor opaca teget.
Rivulus hic dulci suadebit murmure somnos,
  Multaque de ramis quæ bene cantat avis.
Huc ades, atque sinus paulatim inlabere nostros,
  O desiderii cura laborque mei!

Idem Elegia XIV, p. 128 :

Ad me cum puerum talem duxisset Etruscus
  Qualem rara solet mensa videre Jovis,
« Hunc », ait, « apprensa tota tibi tradimus aure
  « Hæreat ut lateri nocte dieque tuo.
« Dique Deæque velint isto tenearis amore!
  « Si pædicabis, non nisi doctus erit. »
Tunc ego : — « Libertas placet hæc concessa pudori
  « Cogar et officio parcior esse tuo.
« Ne dubita, bonus est, melior jam fiet, ab omni
  « Doctrinam dices parte bibisse meam. »
Lætus abit, capio lætus mea gaudia, longam
  Omne mihi visum est tempus habere moram
O macta virtute patrem solumque probandum,
  Et qui tam magna solus in urbe sapit !
Hic puero culum, penem ligat ille magistro :
  Creditis hoc, stulti, discere posse modo ?
O fortunatum cui me fecere magistrum,
  Grataque cui talem fata dedere patrem !

can tell tales. Let's do it under the willows in this verdant meadow; the drooping boughs will hide us with their foliage. The rivulet will lull us to sleep with its pleasant murmur, and the bird that warbles mid the boughs. Hither come, and glide into my lap, thou that art torment at once and remedy of my desires! »

Elegy XIV (p. 128) :

« One day Etruscus brought to me a youth, so fair as is seldon seen at Jupiter's board : « I give « him up to you », he said, « lay hold of him, « that he may cling to you both day and night. « May the gods grant you love him well; he will « be wise if you but pedicate him. »

And I : « I like this liberty conceded to my « passion; I shall always be obliged to you. Be « sure this child, good as he is, will be better « still in future; he will suck my wisdom in « through many places. »

Joyful he goes, joyful I seize hold of my prey; delay, however short, seems long to me. Oh, father proved in virtue! the one blameless man, the one sage in this great town! The master lays hands upon the lad's posteriors, the lad grasps the master's member. Think you, ye unlearned, he will learn in this fashion? Oh, lucky boy, to have

Idem Elegia XV, p. 131 :

Mentula si moritur, moritur non ulla voluptas
Pædicare senex si nequit, usque cupit.

Idem Elegea XX, p. 139 :

Mentula tam parva est, tam pars mihi deficit illa
 Ut mihi non natam vel cecidisse rear.
Tangere non digitis, oculis nec cernere possum,
 Hisque bonis nimium sors mea lenta fuit.
Teque sequi possem, Cybele, non inguine secto,
 Nil opus est testa, jam tibi Gallus eram.
Turpe quidem dictu, liceat sed vera fateri,
 Nullus me pejor vixit in orbe puer.
Dum potui, fœdæ Veneri servire paravi :
 Hanc pædiconum duxerat usque manus.
Viscera versarunt magnique et mille mutones,
 Calcatusque die nocteque culus erat.
Si pædicari quicquam valuisset in illa,
 Tenta caput posset tangere, pressa pedes.
Nil mihi profecit, nil hæc mihi crevit, et usu
 Consumta est nimio forsitan illa suo.

me for a teacher! oh lucky fate, that gave you such a father! »

Elegy XV (p. 131) :

« If the member is dead, the voluptuous wish is still alive; if the old man can no longer pedicate, he still wants to. »

Elegy XX (p. 139) :

« My member is so little, this part of me so dwindled, I almost think I never had one, or that it has disappeared; my finger cannot feel, my eye cannot see it, — fate has been but niggardly to me. I could be your attendant, Cybelé, without operation, I need no shard of glass, I am a castrated priest already. And still — it is a shame, but must be confessed; there is no worser lad than I in all the world. As soon as ever I could, I served the filthy Venus, for the hand of Pederasts had drawn me to it; a thousand members and big ones, churned in my inside, and day and night my anus was in quest. If only my passive action could have profited my member, when erect it would have touched my head, when limp my feet ; but nothing did it good, it never grow. And what I did, perhaps only made it worse. Every boy likes to see his member grow, get big enough to amply fill his hand. »

Quilibet hoc unum puer, ut sua mentula crescat
Optat, et ut magna compleat illa manum.

Jam satis pædicavimus. Nunc irrumandum est

But enough of pedication ; irrumation is our next business.

CAPUT III

DE IRRUMANDO (57)

ENEM in os arrigere dicitur irrumare, quod proprie est mammam præbere : nam rumam, Nonio teste, pagina 579 Gothofredina, Veteres mammam dixerunt. Penis ori immissus perfricari vult vel labris vel lingua, atque exsugi. Id si quis officii peni præstat, fellat : nam sugit : et fellare priscis erat sugere, eodem Nonio auctore p. 547. Convenit Græcum θηλάζω, *quemadmodum conveniunt* θήρ *et* φήρ, *fera,* θύλλις *et*

---

(57) *Ecce tibi eadem computatio, quæ in Priapeio XII.*

Percidere puer moneo, futuere puella,
Barbatum furem tertia poena manet.

CHAPTER III

OF IRRUMATION (57)

To put the member in erection into another's mouth is called to *irrumate*, a word, which in its proper sense means to give the breast; in fact, according to *Nonius*, p. 579 (Gottfried's edition), the Ancients called the bosom *ruma*. The verge, introduced into the mouth, wants to be tickled either by the lips or the tongue, and sucked; the party who does this service to the penis is a fellator or sucker, for with the Ancients *fellare* meant to suck, also according to *Nonius*, p. 547. The equivalent to

---

(57) You see we follow the same general order as in the *Priapeia*, XII.

« *I* warn you, boy, I mean to pedicate you; with you, my girl, I will copulate. The *third* penalty is kept for the bearded ruffian. »

φύλλις, *follis*, θερμὸς *et* φερμός, *formus (warm)*, θλίβω *et* φλίβω, θλάω *et* φλάω.

Inventores spurcitiei feruntur Lesbii. Scholiastes ad versum 1337 Vesparum *Aristophanis testem citat Theopompum.*

Hinc λεσβιάζειν *sive* λεσβίζειν *dixerunt eos, qui Lesbiorum morem vet irrumando vel fellando imitarentur. Suidas :* Λεσβίσαι, μολῦναι τὸ στόμα. Λέσβιοι γὰρ διεβάλλοντο ἐπὶ αἰσχρότητι. *Idem sub* σιφνιάζειν. Λεσβιάζειν, τὸ τῷ στόματι παρανομεῖν (58). *Ac de fellando quidem verbo usus est Aristophanes in* Vespis *versu* 1337 :

Ὁρᾷς, ἐγώ σ' ὡς δεξιῶς ὑφειλόμην
Μέλλουσαν ἤδη λεσβιεῖν τοὺς ξυμπότας.

item in Ranis *v.* 1343 :

Αὕτη ποθ' ἡ μοῦς' οὐκ ἐλεσβίαζεν (59);

---

(58) *Prorsus ambigue Eustathius, p. 741 :* Λεσβιάζειν, τὸ αἰσχροποιεῖν.

(59) *Quo haud scio an pertineat illud in* Concionantibus, *v. 915.*

Ἤδη τὸν ἀπ' Ἰωνίας

fellare in Greek is θηλάζω, just as θὴρ, and φὴρ *fera* correspond; θύλλις and φύλλις, *follis*; θερμὸς and φερμός, *formus*, and English « warm »; θλίβω and φλίβω; θλάω and φλάω.

The Lesbians are believed to be the inventors of this particular nastiness. The Scholiast, in verse 1337 of the *Wasps* of Aristophanes, cites Theopompus as vouching for the fact.

This is the reason why the Greeks apply the expression « Lesbianize » or « Lesbize » to those who imitated the Lesbian usages, either as *irrumants,* or as *fellators.* Suidas : « Lesbianize — to defile the mouth; the Lesbians are in fact believed to give themselves to these shameful acts. » The same author says under the word, « *Siphnianize,* — to *Lesbianize,* that is to use the mouth abominably (58) » Aristophanes has employed the word in the sense of *sucking* (*Wasps,* 1337).

« Look, how cleverly I kept you away, when you wanted to Lesbianize the guests ».

And again in the *Frogs* 1343 :

« Has this Muse never used the Lesbian mode? (59) »

---

(58) Eustathius, p. 741, is very ambiguous : « Lesbianize, — to commit a shameful action. »

(59) I do not quite know whether the following pas-

de irrumando autem Hesychius: Λεσβιάζειν πρὸς ἀνδρὸς στόμα στύειν.

Junguntur interdum λεσβιάζειν *et* φοινικίζειν, *quasi et Phœnicum* σόφισμα *esset. Lucianus in* Apophrade, *p. 165 tomi VII Operum :*

Πρὸς θεῶν εἰπέ μοι τί πάσχεις, ἐπειδὰν κἀκεῖνα λέγωσιν οἱ πολλοί λεσβιάζειν σε καὶ φοινικίζειν.

Quomodo autem differant inter se λεσβιάζειν *et* φοινικίζειν, *inde non cognoscitur. Certe Timarchus, contra quem tam acriter disputat Lucianus, fellabat. Id docent proxime sequentia ; nam cum ad cœ-*

Τρόπον τάλαινα κνησιᾶς.
Δοχεῖς δ᾽ ἐμοὶ καὶ λάβδα κατὰ τοὺς Λεσβίους.

Videtur fellatrix Labda dici a prima litera in λεσβιάζειν, *sed locus est persolus, nam in Varroniano, quem Nonius (p. 523 Gothofredi, collato tamen Josephi Scaligeri adnotamento ad Priapeium LXXVIII) servavit,*

Depsistis, dicite Labdae,

neque lectio est indubia, neque sententia satis dilucida, versiculum autem Ausonii, Epigrammate 128 :

Cui ipse linguam cum dedit suam, Labda est,

plane alienum esse, infra aperiemus.

But Hesychius has employed it for *irrumate* :
« Lesbianize, to defile a man's mouth ».

Lesbianize and Phoenicianize are generally
used conjointly, as though this practice had been
equally common among the Phoenicians. Lucian
says in his *Apophras* (ch. 26) :

« In the name of the Gods tell me what you
are thinking of, when it is bruited about publicly that you Lesbianize and Phoenicianize? »

What the difference between the two may be
is not known. At any rate Timarchus, who is
so bitterly attacked by Lucian, was a *fellator*, as
may be readily gathered from the following.

sage from the *Thesmophoriazusae* (915-917) refers to this
or no :
« Now, unhappy girl, you long for pleasure after the
Ionian mode. Besides I think you are a Labda, as is the
way of the Lesbians. »
A fellatrix seems to have borne the name of Labda,
by reason of the first letter of the word Lesbianize : but
the passage stands quite isolated, for in that of Varro,
preserved by Nonius, and referring to the annotation of
Scaliger on the Priapeia LXXVIII, where we find :
« Depsistis, dicite. Labdae. »
the reading is doubtful, and the sense note clear. The
verse of Ausonius, Epigr. 128 :
« When he puts his tongue in, then he is a Lambda, »
has nothing to do with this question, as we shall show
later on.

*nam quandam nuptialem Cyzici venisset, ejectus
est, hera illi oris obscenitatem ita exprobrante:
« Non admiserim virum, qui virum ipse quærat ; » docent vero etiam, et multo magis, et pæne
plus quam satis est, antecedentia ; quod enim is,
qui p. 154 Timarchum deprehendit* ἐν γόνασι
κείμενον *pueri, aliud vidit* ἔργον, *quam fellantis ?
quid aliud prodit angina p. 162 in Ægypto con-
tracta, ubi parum abfuisse rumor aiebat, quin a
nauta suffocaretur,* ὃς ἐμπεσὼν ἀπέφραξε τὸ στόμα?
*quid aliud Cyclopis cognomen, ex eo ductum, quod
ebrium jacentem adolescens,* ὀρθὸν ἔχων τὸν μοχλὸν
εὖ μάλα ἠκονημένον, *velut alter Ulysses invasisset,
terebraturus buccam hiantis* (σὺ δὲ ὁ Κύκλωψ ἀναπε-
τάσας τὸ στόμα, καὶ ὡς ἔνι πλατύτατον κεχηνὼς
ἠνείχου τυφλούμενος ὑπ' αὐτοῦ τὴν γνάθον) *? ut ne
addam fugam osculorum p. 156, actionemque a*

Timarchus, having arrived at Cyzicus to be present at a wedding feast, was turned out of doors (*ibid.*, ch. 26), the mistress of the house upbraiding him in these words for the impurity of his mouth : « I would not have in my house a man who must have a man himself! » The passage preceding the above is still plainer and more to the point : What does the man reproach Timarchus with, who has surprised him kneeling before a young lad (*ibid.*, chap. 21), and who says farther on, « that he had seen him at work », if this does not apply to a *fellator* ? Besides, what is the meaning of that sore throat contracted by him in Egypt (*ibid.*, ch. 27), where according to rumour, he had been nearly suffocated by a sailor, who fell upon him and stopped his mouth ? Whence that nickname of the Cyclops (*ibid.*, ch. 28), which was given to him, because one day, when he was lying drunk on the ground, a young man, « with an upstanding stake exceeding well sharpened », threw himself upon him, to force it into his mouth, as Ulysses did with the eye of the Cyclops, « A new Cyclops, with the mouth open at full stretch, you let him burst your cheeks ». It is useless to add to this the passages with respect to those who

lingua institutam p. 158, *quæ dubites forsan fella-torem pungant an cunnilingum. Sed nec irrumare homine alienum fuisse, indicare videtur illud p.* 148, οὐχὶ σὺ τοιοῦτος ; *cum enim ante dixisset :* Εἴ τις ἴδοι κίναιδον καὶ ἀπόρρητα ποιοῦντα καὶ πάσχοντα, *in vitiis,* Ἰimarchi *patet etiam numerari* ἀπόρρητα ποιεῖν. *Poterat igitur Lucianus recte dicere Timarchum et* λεσβιάζειν *et* φοινικίζειν, *si alteri voci subjiciebat vim fellandi alteri irrumandi; utri autem subjecerit fellandi vim, utri irrumandi, nihilo minus est obscurum. Quid ? quod ne id quidem extra omnem dubitationis aleam positum est, voluisse Lucianum* λεσβιάζειν *et* φοινικίζειν *ita distinguere, ut alterum esset fellare, alterum irrumare. Nam* φοινικίζειν *poterat etiam dicere cunnilingum* (60), *quam verbo significationem infra*

---

(60) *Haud scio an Rododaphnes cognomine a Syris isti indito p.* 161, *tecte sugilletur cunnilingus, ita quidem, ut in rosa lateat cunnus, in lauri folio lingua lingens. Certe causa obs-*

repel his kisses (ch. 23), or as to the use to
which he puts his tongue (ch. 25), for it is
doubtful whether they are addressed to a *fellator*
or a *cunnilingue* (a licker of the vulva). That
Timarchus was no stranger to *irrumation*, seems
implied (ch. 17) by the apostrophe, « Are you
not all that ? » the more so as previously Lucian's
saying : « If any one sees a cinede do or suffer
the shameful act... » makes it apparent that
the active part was also one of the vices of Timarchus. Lucian could therefore justly say of
this Timarchus, that he Lesbianized and Phoe-
nicianized, if he wanted to imply by one of
these words, « sucking », and by the orther,
« irrumating. » But it is uncertain which ot
these words means « to suck », and which « to
irrumate ». But what does this matter ? There
is no doubt that Lucian intended to make this
distinction. Phoenicianize might even be applied to a *eunnilingue* (60), an expression which

---

(60) I do not know whether the nickname of Rododaphné (rose-laurel), given to Timarchus in Syria (ibid,
ch. 27), does not mean *cunnilingue*, as by rose is understood the female parts, while the laurel leaf means the
licking tongue, This surname had no doubt for Lucian
an obscene sense which he would not disclose : « In

*vindicatum imus, nec sane necesse erat exempla
adjungere earum, quæ cunnos lingui passæ fuissent.*

*Maxime autem memorabilis est locus Galeni
libro decimo* De vi simplicium, *quo* λεσβιάζειν *a*
φοινικίζειν *sic disjungit, ut alterum altero turpius
esse doceat:*

Καὶ μεῖζόν γε ὄνιδός ἐστιν ἀνδρώπῳ σωφρονοῦντι
κοπροφάγον ἀκούειν, ἡ αἰσχρουργὸν ἡ κίναιδον, ἀλλὰ
καὶ τῶν αἰσχρουργῶν μᾶλλον βδελυττόμεθα τοὺς φοινικίζοντας τῶν λεσβιαζόντων, ᾧ φαίνεταί μοι παφαπλήσιον
τι πάσχειν ὁ καὶ καταμηνίον πίνων (61).

———————

cenior visa est Luciano, quam ut enarraret : 'Εν Συρίᾳ μὲν
'Ροδοδάφνη κληθεὶς, ἐφ' ᾧ δὲ αἰσχύνομαι διηγεῖσθαι.

(61) *Quo planius iutelligas sententiam Galeni, antecedentia hæc sunt :* Πόσις δ' ἱδρῶτός τε καὶ οὔρου καὶ καταμηνίου γυναικὸς ἀσελγῆ καὶ βδελυρὰ, καὶ τούτων οὐδὲν ἧττον
ἡ κόπρος, ἣν καταχριομένην τε τοῖς κατὰ τὸ στόμα καὶ τὴν
φάρυγγα μορίοις, εἴς τε τὴν γαστέρα καταπινομένην ἔγραψεν
ὁ Ξενοκράτης, ὅ τι ποτὲ ποιεῖν δύναται. Γέγραφε δὲ καὶ
περὶ τοῦ κατὰ τὰ ὦτα ῥύπου καταπινομένου. 'Εγὼ μὲν οὖν
οὐδὲ τοῦτον ἄν ὑπέμεινα καταπιεῖν, ἐφ' ᾧ γε μηδέ ποτε
νοσῆσαι · πολύ δ' αὐτοῦ βδελυρώτερον ἡγοῦμαι τὴν κόπρον
εἶναι.

we shall dilate upon presently. Needless therefore in this place to give examples of women
who allowed their vulvas to be licked.

Very remarkable is a passage of Galen in book
X, *De vi simplicium*, in which he makes a distinction between Lesbianize and Phoenicianize,
demonstrating that the one is more shameful
than the other :

« It is worse for an honest man to be spoken
of as an eater of excrements than as being a de-
filer or a cinede; and amongst the defilers we
execrate such as Phoenicianize more than those
who Lesbianize. The latter I consider to be doing
what is as bad as the habit of drinking mens-
trual discharge (61). »

Syria they call you Rododaphné, why? I should blush
to say it. »

(61) Here is the preceding sentence, which will better
elucidate Galen's meaning : To drink sweat, urine or
menses is an abominable and detestable practice; human
excrements still more so, in spite of what Xenocrates has
written about their beneficial action when applied in
lieu of ointment about the mouth or throat, or when
swallowed. He has also spoken of the absorption through
the mouth of ear-wax. I myself could not make up my
mind to eat of them, though it were to cure my sickness
right off. Of all abominable things the most abominable,
I think, are human excrements.

*Vult, qui sordibus humanis pro medicamine uta-
tur, pejus eum audire vel turpi aut cinædo, et de
turpibus quidem detestabiliores haberi* φοινικίζοντας
quam λεσβιάζοντας. *Idcirco dubitare non poteris,
quin* φοινικίζειν *dixerit fellatores,* λεσβιάζειν *irrumatores. Nam cum detestabiliores indicaret eos esse,
qui proprius accederent ad* κοπροφάγους, *utique non
poterat non magis detestari eos, qui fellando os suum
inquinarent, quam qui irrumando alienum : debebat etiam pariter abominari cunnilingos,* καταμηνίου
πίνοντας, *de quibus infra.*

*Sed imitatores etiam exstiterunt moris Lesbiorum.
Eo nomine male a veteribus audiebant Nolani :
unde Ausonio epigrammate* LXXI *Crispa fellatrix
eam dicitur libidinem exercere « quam Nolanis capitalis luxus inussit. » Ecce autem totum epigramma festivum :*

*Præter legitimi genitalia fœdera cœtus
Reperit obscenas Veneres vitiosa libido,
Herculis hæredis quam Lemnia suasit egestas,
Quam toga facundi scenis agitavit Afrani,*

Galen means by this that the man who uses human excrements as medicine is considered worse than a fellator or a cinede ; that amongst the fellators the Phoenicianists are more abominable than the Lesbianists. There can therefore be no doubt that he designates the action of the *fellators* by the word Phoenicianizing, and by Lesbianizing that of the *irrumants*. In fact, as he judges those the worst who come nearest to the eaters of excrements, he could not detest less those who defile their mouths by fellation than those who defile the mouths of other people by irrumation ; similarly he could not help holding in abhorrence the *cunnilingues* and the drinkers of menses, of whom more later on.

But the Lesbians found imitators. The inhabitants of Nola were in bad repute amongst the Ancients in that respect ; in Ausonius, *Epigr.* LXXI, Crispa, a fellatrix, is said to practise the business « with which an unprecedented effeminacy inspired the people of Nola ». However, here is this spirited epigram in its entirety :

« Over and above the intimate joys of legitimate love, hateful lust has found out other foul modes of pleasure, of the sort the loneliness, of Lesbos taught Hercules' heir, of the sort smooth tongued

Et quam Nolanis capitalis luxus ınussit.
Crispa tamen cunctas exercet corpore in uno :
Deglubit, fellat, molitur per utramque cavernam
Ne quid inexpertum frusta moritura relinquat.

Quid ergo ? nempe non voluit inexpertum relin
quere Crispa. Futui : hæc sunt fœdera legitimi coitus ;
neque pædicari : hæc est libido Philoctetis, Hercu-
learem sagittarum hæredis, atque Afranii, de quo
Quintilianus, Instit. orat., *X,* I, *pagina* 913
Burmanniana : « Togatis », inquit, *« excellit*
Afranius ; utinamque non inquinasset argumenta
puerorum fœdis amoribus, mores suos fassus ! »
neque irrumari : hic est capitalis luxus Nolanis
inustus. Brevius et apertius omnia comprehenduntur
proximo versiculo a postremo ita, ut deglubit *sit*
genus, fellat, molitur per utramque cavernam
tres species.

Fuerunt qui et celebre illud ænigma Cœlii apud
Quintilianum, Inst. orat., *VIII,* 6, *p.* 747 :
« Quadrantariam Clytæmnestram, in triclinio

Afranius in his actor's gown displayed upon the stage, of the sort an unprecedented effeminacy inspired the men of Nola with. Crispa, with but one body, yet practises them all : masturbates, fellates, works by either orifice, — dreading to die in vain before she has tried every mode ».

To explain, — of course Crispa did not neglect to have herself entered in the usual way; these are « the intimate joys of legitimate love ». Then she allowed herself to be pedicated; this is the vice of Philoctetes, the inheritor of the arrows of Hercules, as also of Afranius, of whom Quintilian says : « He excelled in the Roman comedy; a pity that he polluted his plays with infamous masculine amours ! He thus bore witness against his own morals » (*Inst. Orat.*, X, 1). Further Crispa did not fail to allow herself to be *irrumated*, this is, « the vice their unprecedented effeminacy instilled into the men of Nola ». Lastly the whole is recapitulated quite plainly in the last line but one; to masturbate is the genus, while to fellate, and to work by one and the orther orifices are so many species, three altogether.

There are authors who think that the celebrated riddle of Coelius in Quintilian : *Clytæm-*

coam, in cubiculo nolam, » *huc trahendum putarent,
ut Nola esset, quæ Nolanorum more fellaret. At
magis placet interpretatio Alciati, statuentis, Clodiam, famosam istam Clodii sororem, Metelli uxorem, coam dici, quod voluerit in cubiculo. Nam
quod miratur Spaldingius infrequentem quadran-
tariæ injuriam, ut eadem sit nola, vereor, ne nodus
quæratur in scirpo. Quidni dicamus, Clodiam
Messalinæ instar facilitate adulterorum in fastidium versam ad incognitas libidines profluxisse* (62),
*ita ut nollet in tenebris sumi, vellet autem non
modo, admissa luce, quemadmodum Martialis, ipso
latente, XI,* 104:*

> *Tu tenebris gaudes, me ludere teste lucerna,
>   Et juvat admissa rumpere luce latus;*

sed admissis etiam testibus, viventibus, specta-

---

(62) *Taciti verba sunt,* Annal., *XI,* 26.

*nestram quadrantariam, in triclinio coam, in cubi-
culo nolam* (*Instit. Orat.*, VIII, 6, p. 747), refers
to a woman of the name of Nola, she being a *fellatrix* after the fashion of the Nolans. But I prefer
the interpretation of Alciatus; he believes that
the woman in question was Clodia, the notorious sister of Clodius, and wife of Metellus,
called *Coa*, because she liked coitus on the open
triclinium, and *Nola* because she refused the
same in bed. Spalding evinces surprise at the
want of exactitude, which the word *quadrantaria* would have in that case. To me that appears
like looking for knots in a rush. Why should we
not suppose Clodia, disgusted, like Messalina, by
the facility of her adulteries, to have been drawn
into extraordinary excesses (62) to such a point
that she would no longer have commerce with
men in the dark, but only in the glare of lighted
torches, as Martial confesses in speaking of himself (XI, 104) :

« You love the game in the dark, I like it by
lamp-light; my delight is to make my entry
with light to see by, » — and in the presence of
living witness, that she might be seen, if not

---

(62) Tacitus, *Annals*, XI, 26.

*tum nisi jacentem, certe euntem aut redeuntem ?
An dubitas usque eo licentiam pervenisse ? Quid
aliud ausus est Augustus, cui Marcus Antonius,* Suetonio teste in Augusto, 69, « *objecit,
et fœminam consularem e triclinio viri coram in
cubiculum abductam, rursus in convivium ru-
bentibus auriculis, incomtiore capillo reductam ?* »
Quid aliud Caligula, quem idem Suetonius in
Caligula, *cap.* 25, *tradit,* « *adhibitum cœnæ nup-
tiali, mandasse ad Pisonem contra accumbentem :* »
« *Noli uxorem meam premere, statimque e convivio
abduxisse eam secum?* » *et qui eodem auctore, cap.*
36, *illustriores fœminas* « *cum maritis ad cœnam
vocatas præterque pedes suos transeuntes diligenter
ac lente mercantium more considerabat, etiam faciem manu allevans, si quæ pudore submitterent :
quoties deinde libuisset egressus triclinio, cum
maxime placitam sevocasset, paulo post recentibus
adhuc lasciviæ notis reversus vel laudabat palam,*

actually on her back, at any rate going away for
it or just coming back afterwards. Do you think
that indecency could not possibly go so far?
What did Augustus do, whom Marc Anthony,
according to Suetonius, « reproached for having at a festival taken the wife of a Consular
from the triclinium to a bedroom, in the presence of her husband, and afterwards conducted
her back to the table with her face all on fire
and her hair in disorder? » (*Augustus*, ch. 69).
And Caligula, according to the same Suetonius,
« when a guest at a wedding-feast said to Piso,
who was sitting close by him : « Do not push
« up so close to my wife! » and immediately after
made her rise from table and took her away with
him » (*Calig.*, ch. 25). The same author, (*Calig.*,
ch. 36), speaking of the most illustrious Roman
ladies, tells us that Caligula « invited them to dinn-
er with their husbands, passing them in review
before him, he examined them with the minute
attention of a slave dealer, lifting their heads up
if any of them bowed them down with shame.
As often as he felt inclined, he left the triclinium
and took the chosen fair one aside with him;
then after returning to the room with the traces
of his doings still upon him, he would praise or

vel vituperabat, singula enumerans bona malave corporis atque concubitus ? « *Quid aliud illa, de qua* Horatius, Odarum *III*, 6, 25-32 :

> Mox juniores quærit adulteros
> Inter mariti vina, neque eligit
>   Cui donet impermissa raptim
>   Gaudia, luminibus remotis :
> Sed jussa coram non sine conscio
> Surgit marito, seu vocat institor,
>   Seu navis Hispanæ magister,
>   Dedecorum pretiosus emtor ?

Quid aliud quinquaginta meretrices in convivio illo Alexandri VI pontificis Romani, quo animum tuum ad Hermaphroditum *pavimus* (63). *Satisne est*

---

(63) *Repetamus autem locum festivum* Joannis Burchardi, *cujus quidem simplicitati memoriam rei debemus, ne alio te amandari queraris, ex ejus* Diario *a* Leibnitio *anno* 696 *edito, p.* 77 :

« *Dominica ultima mensis Octobris in sero, fecerunt cœnam cum duce Valentinensi in camera sua in Palatio Aposto-*

criticize these ladies openly, speaking of the beauties or blemishes of their bodies, and even how often he had repeated the enjoyment. » Horace again speaks of an adulterous woman (*Odes*, III, VI, 25-32) :

« Soon she looks out for fresher adulterous pleasures, while the husband is drunk ; and does not care to whom she grants the furtive forbidden pleasures, which with the torches extinguished, she is ready to give and take. Nay ! she does not care for her very husband's presence, and with his knowledge she rises to meet whosoever may call, say a merchant, say the commander of a Spanish ship in harbour, who buys her favours by tariff ! »

Again look at the feast of the Pope, Alexander VI, whom we have already mentioned for your profit and amusement in our *Hermaphroditus* (63).

---

(63) We will here reproduce the curious passage of Jean Burchard, to whom we owe this story. It is taken from his *Diarium*, edited by Leibnitz, in 1696, p. 77 :

« On the last Sunday in October the Duke of Valentinois had invited to supper in his chamber » (the chamber of Alexander VI), « in the Apostolical palace, fifty beautiful prostitutes, called courtezans, who, after supper, danced with the valets and other persons present, first in their clothes, and then naked. After this the table.

212 THE MANUAL

*Coarum in triclinio? Hoc igitur schemate coire
gestiebat Clodia : sola cum solo in cubiculo sine testibus, nolebat ; in proximo triclinio volebat : unde
per jocum coa et nola. Poterat Cœlius aliquanto
planius dicere in triclinio volam, extra triclinium
nolam.*

Neque vero Nolani tantum, sed omnino (64)
Osci Lesbiorum libidini traduntur deditissimi

---

lico, quinquaginta *meretrices honestæ,* Cortegianæ *nuncupa-
tæ, quæ post cœnam chorearunt cum servitoribus et aliis ibidem existentibus, primo in vestibus suis, deinde nudæ. Post
cœnam, posita fuerunt candelabra communia mensæ, cum
candelis ardentibus, et projectæ ante candelabra per terram
castenaa, quas meretrices ipsæ super manibus et pedibus nudæ
candelabra pertranseuntes colligebant,* Papa, Duce *et* Lucretia, *sorore sua, præsentibus et adspicientibus.* Tandem exposita dona ultimo, diploides de serico, parta caligarum, bireta
et alia, pro illis qui plures dictas meretrices carnaliter agnos-
cerent, quæ fuerunt ibidem in aula publice carnaliter tractatæ
arbitrio præsentium, et dona distributa victoribus. »

(64) Nola *enim oppidum Campaniæ, quæ* ɟ*ars Oscorum.*

Is this evidence enough to satisfy you as to these *Coae* of the triclinium? Well! it was after this fashion Clodia preferred to be had. Alone with a solitary lover in bed and no one by, she refused (*nolebat*); in public on the triclinium, she was willing enough for coition (*volebat coire*). Hence the jest; she was *Coa* and *Nola*. Coelius might have put it still more plainly; on the triclinium she was *Vola*, in bed *Nola*.

It was not the inhabitants of Nola only who were addicted to the Lesbian vice, the Oscans (64) generally were considered to be very much given

---

chandeliers were placed on the floor here and there, with lighted candles, and chesnuts were thrown about, which the courtezans collected moving on their hands and knees quite naked among the chandeliers, the Pope, the Duke and his sister Lucrezia being present and looking on. Finally presents were brought in · silk mantles, pairs of shoes, head-dresses, and other objects, to be given to those who had copulated with the greatest number of these courtesans: they were publicly enjoyed in the room there, the lookers-on acting as umpires, and awarding the prizes to the victors. »

(64) Nola was a city in the territory of the Campanians, It is for this reason that the *Campanian malady*, mentioned by Horace (Sat. I., V., 62), has been connected with debauchery, but without sufficient reason.

fuisse, ita ut quidam obscenum dictum vellent ab Oscis, qui antea Opsci vel Opici. Festus. p. 553 :

« *In omnibus fere antiquis commentariis scribitur Opicum pro Osco, a quo etiam verba impudentia et et eleta appellantur obscena quia frequentissimus fuit usus Oscis libidinum spurcarum.* »

Variant Veteres in re spurca oblique significanda. Ac pro irrumare *quidem dixerunt offendere buc-cam* (65), *corrumpere buccas* (66), *illudere capiti-*

Quare fuerunt, qui et Campanum morbum Horatii Sat. *I,* v. 62, *ad libidinem referrent, sed minus apte ad causam.*

(65) *Varro in* Marcipore, *Nonio teste, p. 687 :* « *Dein mittit virile veretrum in frumen* » (gulam); « *offendit buc-cam Volumni.* »

(66) *Martialis, III, 75 :*

Coepisti puras opibus corrumpere buccas.

Simile illud, II, 28 :

Calda Vetustillae nec tibi bucca placet.

that way, so much so that certain authors trace to them (the Osci), in earlier times called the Opsci or Opici, the etymology of the word « Obscene », Festus, p. 553 :

« In almost all the old treatises the word is written *Opicum* instead of *Oscum*; it is from the name of this people that shameless and impudent expressions are called obscene, because indulgence in filthy debauchery was very common among the Oscans. »

The Ancients employed many forms of circumlocution to convey the meaning of their filthy practices. For instance, instead of *irrumate*, they said : to offend the mouth (65), corrupt the mouth (66), to attack the head (67), to defy to the

---

(65) Varro, is his *Marcipor*, according to Nonius : « He introduced afterwards into his gullet the virile verge ; he offends the mouth of Volumnus. »

(66) Martial III, 75 :

« You make it your work to corrupt pure lips for gold. »

And Again II, 28 :

« Not even Vetustilla's warm mouth gives you more pleasure. »

(67) « How accustomed he was to assault the heads of the most illustrious women, is plainly evidenced by the adventure of Mallonia, who, debauched by him, refused to submit to him again. He caused her to be accused by

bus (67), *insultare capitibus* (68), *non parcere capiti* (69), *os percidere* (70), *summa petere* (71),

---

(67) *Suetonius in* Tiberio, *cap. 45 :* « *Fœminarum quoque et quidem illustrium capitibus quantopere solitus sit illudere, evidentissime apparuit Malloniæ cujusdam exitu, quam perductam, nec quidquam amplius pati constantissime recusantem delatoribus objecit, ac ne ream quidem interpellare desiit, ecquid pœniteret, donec ea relicto judicio domum se abripuit ferroque transegit, obscenitate oris hirsuto atque olido seni clare exprobata.* »

(68) *Suetonius in* Cæsare, *cap. 22 :* « *Quo gaudio* » (*Gallia comata accepta*) « *elatus non temperavit, quin paucos post dies frequenti Curia jactaret, invitis et gementibus adversariis adeptum se quæ concupisset, proinde ex eo insultatuJum omnium capitibus, ac negante quodam per contumeliam, facile hoc ulli fœminæ fore, responderit quasi alludens, in Assyria quoque regnasse Semiramin, magnamque Asiæ partem Amazonas tenuisse quondam.* » *Nempe quod probo sensu pro irridere dixerat Cæsar insultare capitibus, id ad improbum sensum detorsit adversarius, tacta simul infamia Bithynica.*

(69) *Lactantius,* Institut. div., *VI, 23 :* « *De istis loquor, quorum teterrima libido et execrabilis furor ne capiti quidem parcit.* » *Simile illud Juvenalis, VI, 299, 300 :*

> ... *Quid enim Venus ebria curat?*
> *Inguinis et capitis quae sint discrimina nescit.*

(70) *Martialis, II, 72 :*

> *Hesterna factum narratur. Posthume, coena,*

face (68), insult the head, not to spare the head (69), to split open the mouth (70). gain the

---

his informers, and kept asking her during her trial, whether she had anything to reproach herself with. Without waiting for the verdict, she ran home and transfixed herself with a poniard, upbraiding loudly the foul, hairy dotard for having wanted to abuse her mouth (Suetonius, *Tiberius*, ch. 45).

(68) He was so glad to have won Transalpine Gaul that he could not help announcing some days after in the Senate, that he had reached the fulfilment of his wishes, in spite of the hatred and malice of his enemies, and that he defied them to their face. Somebody having said to him offensively that this could not so easily be done with a woman, he replied jokingly, that Semiramis had gained a kingdom, and the Amazons had occupied a great part of Asia (Suetonius, *Caesar*, ch. 22). Caesar employed the expression : « defying to the face » in an honest sense, while his adversary invested it with an obscene signification, in allusion to his infamous acts in Bithynia.

(69) I speak of those whose abominable lasciviousness and execrable lust do not even spare the head. (Lactantius, *Instit. Div.* VI , 23.) Similarly Juvenal VI., v. 299, 300 :
« For what cares the drunken Venus ? She knows not the difference between groin and head. »

(70) Martial II, 72 :
« They say Posthumus, that they did to you last night, at supper, what I would not have let them do;

altiora tangere (72), *comprimere linguam* (73)

> *Quod nollem : quis enim talia facta probet?*
> *Os tibi percisum !*

Ludens in simili sono vocum rumor et irrumari addit :

> *... Auctorem criminis hujus*
> *Caecilium tota rumor in urbe sonat.*

Sic, II, 73 :

> *Sed rumor negat esse te cinaedum;*

III, 80 :

> *Rumor ait linguae te esse malae;*

Et III, 87 :

> *Narrat te rumor, Chione, nunquam esse fututam,*
> *Atque nihil cunno pvrius esse tuo.*
> *Tecta tamen non hac, qua debes, parte lavaris.*
> *Si pudor est, transfer subligar in faciem.*

Percidere simpliciter est pædicāre : videsis Mart. IV, 48
VII, 61, IX, 48, XI, 29, XII, 35. Priap. XII et XIV
Quod in his locis nonnulli libri dant præcidere pro percidere
mihi quidem plane intolerandum videtur.

(71) *Martialis, XI, 47 :*

> *Quid miseros frusta cunnos culosque lacessis ?*
> *Summa petas · illic mentula vivit anus.*

Priap. LXXV :

> *Per medios ibit pueros mediasque puellas*
> *Mentula, barbatis non nisi summa petet.*

(72) *Priap. XXVII :*

> *Pædicabere fascino pedali,*
> *Quod si tam gravis et molesta poena*
> *Non profecerit, altiora tangam.*

heights (71), mount to loftier regions (72), com-

— who could approve such doings? They split your mouth!... »

Then playing upon the words rumour and irrumate he adds :

« .... As the author of this crime, the town's rumour designates Caecilius. »

And again III, 73, ibid. :

« Rumour denies you are a Cinede ».

III, 80 :

« Rumour says, you have an evil tongue. »

And III, 87 :

« Rumour says, Chioné, that your vulva is intact, that nothing could be purer than it. Yet you bathe without covering the thing that should be covered; if you have any shame, then put your drawers upon your face. »

Percidere employed alone means to pedicate. Martial IV, 48; VII, 61; IX, 48; XI, 29; XII, 35; and Priapeia, XII, XIV. Some copies have *praecidere* for *percidere*, but this seems to be an untenable reading.

(71) Martial, XI, 47 :

« Why do you plague in vain unhappy vulvas and posteriors; gain but the heights, for there any old member revives. »

Priapeia LXXV :

« Through the middle of boys and girls travels the member; when it meets bearded chins then it aspires to the heights. »

(72) Priapeia XXVII :

« A footlong amulet will pedicate you ; if that will not cure you, I go higher. »

220 THE MANUAL

μίγνυσθαι τὴν ἄρρητον μίξιν (74); *pro* fellare *autem ore morigerari* (75), *ore adlaborare* (76), *lambere medios viros* (77), *lingere* (78), *tacere* (79).

---

(73) *Plautus in* Amphitruone, I, 1, 192 :

Ego tibi istam hodie scelestam comprimam linguam.

Comprimere igitur dixerunt irrumantem, quasi futuentem, quemadmodum percidere, quasi pædicantem.

(74) *Plutarchus in* Vita Cæsaris, p. 723. t. I, Operum : « Λέγεται δὲ (Καῖσαρ) τῇ προτέρᾳ νυκτὶ, τῆς διαβάσεως τοῦ Ῥουβίκωνος) ὄναρ ἰδεῖν ἔκθεσμον · ἐδόκει γὰρ αὐτὸς τῇ ἑαυτοῦ μητρὶ μίγνυσθαι τὴν ἄρρητον μίξιν. *Quo pertinet glossa Hesychii* : Ἀρρητουργία, αἰσχρουργία, κακουργὶα, τὸ ἄρρητα ἐξεργάζεσθαι. »

(75) *Suetonius in* Tiberio, *cap. 44.* « *Parrhasii tabulam, in qua Meleagro Atalanta ore morigeratur, legatam sibi sub conditione, ut si argumento offenderetur, decies pro ea sestertium acciperet, non modo prætulit, sed et in cubiculo dedicavit.* »

(76) *Horatius*, Epodo VIII, 17-20 :

Illiterati num minus nervi rigent,
Minusve languet fascinum?
Quod ut superbo provoces ab inguine,
Ore adlaborandum est tibi.

(77) *Martialis*, II, 61 :

Cum tibi vernarent dubia lanugine malae,
Lambebat medios improba lingua viros.

Idem, III, 81 :

Quid cum foemineo tibi, Baetice Galle, barathro?
Haec debet medios lambere lingua viros.

press the tongue (73,) to indulge in abominable intercourse (74), and instead of receiving the member into the mouth they said : to lend the mouth in kind complaisance (75), work with the mouth (76), lick men's middle parts (77), lick

---

(73) Plautus, in the *Amphytrion*, I, sc. 1, 192 :
« I shall compress to-day the wicked tongue. »
The Latins employed the verb « compress » for *irrumate*, as if it were a form of fornication; and similarly « split open », as if it were a form of pedication.

(74) Plutarch: « It is reported that in the night before the passing of the Rubicon, Caesar had a frightful dream; he dreamt that he was indulging in abominable intercourse with his mother. » (*Lives, Julius Cæsar,* XXXII.) Hesychius' interpretation refers to this : « Ἀρρητ-ουργία, αἰσχρουργία, κακουργία, — to perform abominable acts. »

(75) Suetonius: « A picture of Parrhasius, representing Atalanta in the act of complacently lending her mouth to Meleager was bequeathed to him with the alternative that he might have a million sesterces instead, if the subject offended him. He not only preferred the picture, but had it solemnly hung in his bedroom. (*Tiberius*, ch. 44.)

(76) Horace, *Epode* VIII, 17-20 :
« The member of the uneducated is it less rigid ? does it not long, like those of lettered men? To make it stand superbly from the groin, you need but to work it with your mouth. »

(77) Martial II, 62 :
« A doubtful down did scarcely deck your cheek, when

Uti Persius sibi sumsit cevere *ponere pro adul-*

Ausonius, epigrammate CXX :

> Lambere cum vellet mediorum membra virorum
>   Castor, nec posset vulgus habere domi,
> Repperit, ut nullum fellator perderet inguen :
>   Uxoris coepit lingere membra suae.

Factus igitur Castor ex fellatore cunnilingus.

(78) *Martialis, III, 88 :*

> Sunt gemini frates, diversa sed inguina lingunt.
>   Dicite, dissimiles sint magis, an similes.

Ergo alter erat fellator, alter cunnilingus. Idem, VII, 54 :

> Lingas non mihi, nam proba et pusilla est,
> Sed quae de Solymis venit perustis,
> Damnatum modo mentulam tributi.

Nescio unde Scioppius ad Priapeium X *resciverit, pulchre pensilibus peculiatum fuisse Martialem, qui hoc loco mentulam pusillam aperte profiteatur. Jubet autem Chrestum per contumeliam lingere pro sua mentulam servi ex gente Judæa, ad tributum duarum drachmarum Jovi Capitolino quotannis pendendarum nuper damnata, cujus quidem servi Judæi jam mentionem fecerat epigrammate 54 ejusdem libri :*

> ... Meus servus
> Judaeum nulla sub cute pondus habet ;

id est, penem habet circumcisum, glande aperta nec sub cute latente, uno verbo recutitum : nam sic intelligenda puto « recutitorum inguina Judæorum » apud Martialem VII,

simply (78), or lastly to be silent (79). Just as

---

your tongue already licked men's middle parts. » The
same III, 81 :

« Baeticus, you, a Gaul, what have you to do with
the female pit ? that tongue of yours should lick men's
middles. »

Ausonius, *Epigr.* CXX :

« When Castor longed in vain to lick men's middles,
but could take no one home with him, he found means
not to lose all pleasure of the sort, fellator as he was;
he started to lick his own wife's organs. » In other
words from being a *fellator* Castor became a *cunnilingue.*

(78) Martial III, 88 :

« They are twin brothers, but they suck different
teats : tell me are they more unlike or like? »

The one was a *fellator*, the other a *cunnilingue.*

« Again, VII, 54 :

« You shall suck not mine, which is honest and small,
but a member escaped from the fire of Solyma's city and
condemned to tribute. »

I do not know whence Scioppius (*Priap.* X), has it,
that Martial was well furnished; the latter avows in that
passage, that his mentula was quite small. To affront
Chrestus, he orders him to lick, not his, but the mentula
of a Jewish slave. He has mentioned this Jewish slave
already in Epig. 34 of the same book :

« My slave carries a heavy Jewish parcel without skin
to cover it. » That means, his member is circumcised,
the gland being uncovered, without prepuce, in one
word, « *recutitus.* » So, I think, is to be understood the
recutitorum inguine virorum of Martial (VII, 29): he
means, « the virile parts of circumcised men, » the skin
of whose glands is drawn back. *Recutitus* stands for *re-*

ari, ita Catullus irrumare pro contumeliose trac-

29, *ut sint inguina, a quorum glande cutis recessit, quemadmodum* recinctus, regelatus, reseratus, *et plura alia usur-
pantur significatione simplici contraria, nec poterit aliquid
dubitationis id tibi afferre, quod* « recutita colla mulæ », IX,
58, *manifesto sint colla nova cute vestita, cum similis signi-
ficationum differentia et alibi reperiatur,* ut in revincire.
Non possum mihi persuadere, ut iis assentiar, qui recutitos
dictos volunt a cute circumcisis recens nata, cum recutitum
esse in causis ponerent detestandi, uti* Petronius *c.* 68 : « *Duo
tamen vitia habet, quæ si non haberet, esset omnium numero-
rum : recutitus est et stertit.* » *Enimvero quis crediderit, fieri
potuisse, ut detestabilior videretur glans sub cute refecta,
quam sub cute nulla ?*

(79) *Qui irrumatur, non potest loqui, ore mentula pa-
trante obstructo, ergo tacet.* Martialis, III, 96, *in Gargilium
cunnilingum, cui deprenso tertiam pœnam minatur :*

> Si te prendero, Gargili, tacebis.

*Nam ut adulteros imberbes solebant mariti pædicare, ita bar-
batos irrumare. Inde est, quod Gallum, II, 47, retia famo-
sæ monet fugere mœchæ, ne deprensus irrumetur a marito :*

> Confides natibus? non est paedico maritus.
> Quae faciat, duo sunt : irrumat aut futuit?

inde vero etiam, quod ipse vult Thelesinam ducere, II, 49 :

> Uxorem nolo Thelesinam ducere. — Quare.
> — Moecha est. — Sed pueris dat Thelesina. — Volo.

Persius has employed the word *cevere*, to wriggle

---

cinctus, regelatus, reseratus. Many other words, e. g. *revincire,* similarly admit of two meanings, and thus, no
doubt should arise about Martial's expression : *recutita
colla mulae* (IX, 58), which refers to the mules having a
new skin covering their necks. I differ from those who
think that those were called *recutiti* whose prepuce began to grow again ; a *recutitus* was to the Romans an
object of contempt. Petronius : « He has two faults, else
he would be like any other man *recutitus est et sertit,* He
is circumcised and snores » (*Satyr.*, ch. 28). It is impos·
sible to suppose the *glans* could have been thought more
disgusting covered by a new prepuce than with none at all.

(79) A man that is being irrumated cannot speak, his
mouth being obstructed by the mentula, thus : he is silent. Martial (III, 96) says to Gargilius, a *cunnilingue,*
menacing him with the third punishment, if he should
catch him in the fact :

« If I should catch thee at it, Gargilius, I'll make thee
silent. »

Married men were in the habit of pedicating beardless
adults, and of irrumating the bearded ones. For which
reason Martial warns Gallus (II, 47) to shun the seduc-
tions of a famous rakish lady, as he was running the
risk, if taken by the husband in flagrante delicto, of
being irrumated by him :

« Your buttocks you rely on ? But the husband is no
pederast; he likes but two ways, either mouth or vulva. »

And for the same reason he consents to *marry* Thelesina (II, 49) :

« No Thelesina for me as my wife ! Why? — She is a
prostitute. Nay ! but she pays young lads. Then I consent. »

Then there is a complaint for having been deceived

tare (80). *Sic irrumatum semetipsum dicit a Mem-
mio, XXVIII, 9, 10 :*

---

inde quoque, quod ipsum fefellit adulter Pollæ, X, 40 :

> Semper cum mihi diceretur esse
> Secreto mea Polla cum cinaedo,
> Irrupi, Lupe : non erat cinaedus !

*Quippe pro puero, quem pædicaret, invenit perdurum aut exo-
letum, minus igitur idoneum jactura natis expiare culpam :
quanquam poterat etiam pro crudeliore aliorum more in podicem deprensi mœchi aut mugilem farcire : Juvenal, X,
317 :*

> ... Quosdam moechos et mugilis intrat ;

aut raphanum : Lucianus de Morte Peregrini, *Operum
tomi VII, p. 425 :* « Ἐν Ἀρμενίᾳ μοιχεύων ἁλοὺς διέφυγε,
ῥαφανῖδι τὴν πυγὴν βεβυσμένος. » *Catullus, XV :*

> Quem attractis pedibus patente porta
> Percurrent raphanique mugilesque.

Paulo obscurius est illud Martialis, IX, 5 :

> Aureolis futui cum possit Galla duobus,
> Et plus quam futui, si totidem addideris
> Aureolos a te cur accipit, Æschyle, denos '
> Non fellat tanti Galla. Quid ergo ' Tacet.

*Non pudorem tanti vendit Galla, sed tacendi incommodum
cum fellando conjunctum : erat enim garrulæ, nec ipso Martiale in eo dissentiente, IV, 81, « res magna tacere ». Huc
etiam pertinet XII, 35, de quo post paulo.*

(80) *Par ratio verbi* stuprum. *Festus, p. 449 :* « *Stuprum*

in the sense of flattering, so Catullus uses *irru-mate* as meaning to treat ignominiously (80).

---

with respect to the lover of Polla, his mistress (X, 40):

« Constantly was I told that my Polla was on intimate terms with an unknown cinede. Well, I surprise them, Lupus : no cinede was he. »

Instead of a lad, whom he would have pedicated, he finds a cool, experienced gallant, not at all likely to expiate his crime by means of his buttocks. Martial might, however, have punished him more cruelly by forcing into his fundament, either a mullet (Juvenal X, 317):

« There are adulterers whom the mullet pierces »;

or a radish. « In Armenia, taken in the act of adultery, he ran away plugged with a radish in his posteriors. » (Lucian, *De Morte Peregrini*, — Works, vol. VII, p. 425.) Catullus XV, 18, 19:

« Drawing your feet asunder, your postern wide open, they will insert into you radish and mullet. »

Martial also has used the expression of *being silent*, in the above stated sense but, somewhat more obscurely, IX, 5:

» If in two apertures you can work, Galla, and can do more than double work in both, why, Aeschylus, does she get tenfold pay? She fellates, but that is not a matter of such price surely. Nay ! it is because she must be silent ! »

It is not her infamy that Galla sels so dear; it is the inconvenience of having to be silent during the process, which, for a prattler, « is a very serious mutter, » as Martial says, IV, 81. Book XII, *Epigr.* 35, quoted later on, also refers to this.

(80) It is the same with the word *stuprun..* Festus : The

O Memmi, bene me ac diu supinum
Tota ista trabe ledtus irrumasti,

eo quod in Bithynia prætoris istius, comites non pili facientis, unde X, 12, « irrumator prætor », illiberalitatem et avaritiam expertus sit; atque XXXVII, 7, 8, contubernalibus, ad quos puella sua fugisset, minatur :

> *... Non putatis ausurum*
> *Me una ducentos irrumare sessores ?*

addito, ne dubitares, id se facturum ita, ut fronti tabernæ inscriberet flagitia insulsorum :

> *... Namque totius vobis*
> *Frontem tabernæ scipionibus scribam.*

Cetera loca, quæ solent afferri ex Catullo, XXI, 12,

---

pro turpitudine antiquos dixisse apparet in Nelci carmine :

> *Fœde stupreque castigor cotidie.*

Nævius : « Seseque ii perire mavolunt ibidem, quam cum stupro redire ad suos popularis. »

It is thus he complains of having been irrumated by Memmius XXVIII , 9, 10 :

« Oh, Memmius, well and long and leisurely,
laid on my back all the length of that beam, you
irrumated me. »

He had, in fact, experienced in Bithynia the
meanness and avarice of this Praetor, Memmius,
who had not cared a rap for his comrades'
honour, and who is alluded to in Epigr. X., 12,
« Praetor and irrumator ». In Epigr. XXXVII.,
he threatens his boon companions in debauchery,
with whom his mistress has taken refuge :

« ... Do you think I dare not irrumate alone,
as I stand here, two hundred pothouse-heroes ? »
And he adds that he would write on the front
of the tavern the infamy of these blackguards :

« . . . . Your names I shall chalk up all over
the tavern's front. »

Other passages of Catullus, XXI., 12, and
LXXIV., 5, are also quoted to prove the var-

___

ancients employed the word stuprum for turpitude, as
appears in the Song of Neleus.

« Foede stupreque castigor cotidie. »

(I am foully and disgracefully beaten every day.)

Naevius : « They would rather die than return to
their co-citizens *cum stupro* ».

LXXIV, 5, *ad latiorem irrumandi usum confir-
mandum, mihi quidem aliena videntur.*

*Impudicum videntur specialiter dixisse eum, qui
vel pædicari vel irrumari passus esset.* Priap.
LIX :

> *Si fur veneris, impudicus ibis.*

Cicero, De Oratore, *II*, 257 :

> *Si tu et adversus impudicus es...*

Horatius, Epist. *I*, 16, 36 :
> *Idem si clamet furem, neget esse pudicum.*

Lampridius, De Commodo, *cap.* 10 :

> « *Etiam puer et gulosus et impudicus fuit* », *col-
lato capite 5 :* « *Nec irruentium in se se juvenum carebat infamia;* » *et capite 1 :* « *A prima statim pue-
ritia turpis, improbus, crudelis, libidinosus, ore quoque
pollutus et constupratus fuit.* »

Alias pudica vocatur aut integra a viro : Priap.
XXXI :

> *Licebit ipsa sis pudicior Vesta*

ious employment of the word *irrumate*; but they do not seem to me to bear upon the question.

The epithet *shameless* was especially given to the man who allowed himself to be pedicated or irrumated. *Priapeia* LIX. :

« If you come to steal, you will return *shameless*. »

Cicero, *De Oratore*, II., 257 :

« If you are *shameless* before and behind... »

Horace, *Epistle,* I., xvi., 36 :

« If he calls me a thief, he denies that I am chaste. »

Lampridius, *Commodus*, ch. 10 :

« Already as a child he was a glutton and *shameless*, which is explained by what he says in chap. 5 : « He gave himself up to the infamous abuses of young men and to their assaults, » and chap. 1 : « From his tenderest age he was depraved, mischievous, cruel, a libertine ; he allowed his mouth to be soiled and defiled. »

On the other hand, a woman who had never submitted to a man, was called *chaste* (*Priapeia* XXXI.) :

« You are allowed to be as chaste as Vesta ; »
The same epithet was given to a wife that was

aut unica gaudens marito, ut illa, cujus elogium
scripsit Martialis, X, 63 :

> *Contigit et thalami mihi gloria rara, fuitque*
> *Una pudiciti mentula nota meæ.*

Exemplis et fellatorum et fellatricum jam occu-
patis age adstruamus ex Aloisia, Colloq. VII,
Chrysogonum, oris obsequium Semproniæ lepide
persuadentem:

« *Venit nudius tertius* » (*Octaviæ verba sunt*)
« *Chrysogonus ad matrem pomeridianis horis. Silebant*
et tuta erant omnia. Ut ludit, ut furit : « *Hodie*
« *mane.* » *inquit,* « *novum didici voluptatis genus.*
« *E proceribus nostris quidam, nec pænitens facti,*
« *dixit, nihil fœdius sibi, nihil impurius videri in-*
« *fima mulieris suæ parte, qua mulier est (et mu-*
« *lierem duxit pulcherrimam) ; Stymphalidas in illa*
« *habitare sentina purulentas, in hac meram Vene-*
« *rem, meros Amores* » (*ori dabat osculum Chryso-*
gonus). « *Igitur specum fugit illam, et odit, quæ*
« *exhalat mephitem, purum os amat et illecebrosum*
« *caput. Uni fidit, uni arrigit. Uxor illi tam est in-*

faithful to her husbands such a one as is praised by Martial in *Epigr*. X., 63.

« My couch is lighted by the rarest glory, —
one member, one mentula alone has known
my chastity. »

To the preceding examples of *fellators* and *fel-
latrices* we will now add, from Aloysia Sigaea's
book, that of Crisogono, who cleverly persuades
Sempronia to lend him her mouth :

« The day before yesterday (it is Ottavia
speaking), Crisogono came to see my mother
in the afternoon. All was quiet and silent. He
had scarcely begun to wanton a little with her,
when be became very importunate. « Yesterday
morning », he said, « I learned a new kind of
pleasure. One of our grand personages, who had
certainly tasted it, says that there is nothing so
disgusting and repulsive as those parts of his
wife which stamp her as a woman, — and he
has a very pretty wife, mind ! In that sink every
thing is foul, while in this (kissing my mother
on the mouth), dwells the true Venus. He therefore abominates that illfavoured cavern, and
adores that pure mouth, that charming head.
He looks to nothing else, his member rises
for nothing else. His wife is as spirited as she
is beautiful, and even more obliging. She

« *geniosa quam formosa, sed magis obsequens. Hæc*
« *voluptatem agnoscit nullam, quæ non sit mariti :*
« *bene sibi est, cum illi. Omnibus assentitur mariti*
« *libidinibus et paret. Ore præstat obsequium. Quid*
« *vero tu facies, Sempronia, si rogaverim ? nam si*
« *negaveris, negabo et ipse promissi meminisse et fidei*
« *datæ. Demum non te fugit, pulchrum venustæ*
« *fœminæ corpus aliud esse nihil, quam vivum quen-*
« *dam, ut dicere solebat Socrates, libidinum thesaurum,*
« *ubi suas homines condant et quærant voluptates, in*
« *quem libidinis suæ calidos derivent fluctus. Utrum*
« *hoc puro* » (*osculabatur*), « *an illo scelesto* » (*imam*
« *digito designabat alvum* « *id canali fiat, quid ama-*
« *bo interest, si officii habebis rationem?* » *Persuasit*
cui jubendi jus erat, quod ipsa in se constituerat. —
« *Heus tu,* » *inquit subridens, ut surgentem exceptura*
erat mentulam, « *quos et quali tibia modos facere me*
« *jubes in his ludis ?* » *Post mucronem spiculi pri-*
moribus capit labiis, lingua involvit, novas subeunti
sedes delicias mentulæ facit novas. Præsensit illa ad-
fluentes gari Venerei impetu rivos. Exhorruit refugit-
que. « *Non vis, puto, intingi me tanto flagitio ?* »
« *dicebat mater.* « *Liquidum ego bibam hominem ?* »
Dixerat, et vestes deciduus imber multa corrupit copia.
Ille subirasci : — « *Ausa es,* » *inquit,* « *insana, tam*

knows no other pleasure than her husband's;
what he thinks right she thinks proper, and
abets all the caprices of her husband; so she
lends him the service of her mouth. What would
you do, Sempronia, if I asked you? If you were
to refuse I should say that you have forgotten
all your promises and your pledged faith. You
know that Socrates said, the beautiful body of
a pretty woman is nothing but a living treasure
chamber of voluptuousness, the storehouse
whereto men resort to find their pleasures,
whereto they direct the burning floods of their
lubricity. « What matter whether you fulfil your
duty through that pure canal (kissing her
mouth), or through that other (touching below),
which is infect? » He persuaded her to what she
was willing to do without persuasion. « Oh! »
she said, smiling, « what an air you want me to
play, and upon what a flute, in our concert! »
taking in her hand his member, which began to
rise. Se seized the point of his dart betwen her
lips and turning her tongue around it, caused
novel transports of delight to the member that
slid into its new receptacle. But feeling that the
fountains of the brine of Venus were on the point
of bursting forth, she recoiled with horror. « You
would not degrade me so far », said my mother,
« as to make me drink a man in a liquid form? »

« egregium opus perdere ? — Ignosce, » inquit illa,
« habebis obsequentiorem. » Stetit promissis, et liqui-
dos bibit homines. Salsam rem! nam salsa seminis
vis. »

Ore morigerabatur Mancia Marino, narrante
Eleonora apud Aloisiam, ibid. :

« Nupsit Mancia, cognata mea, Marino Neapoli-
tano. Sulphureis Stygiisque nequissimarum libidinum
incendiis torretur Marino pectus. Fœminam vecors
quærit in Mancia etiam supra papillas, qua incipit
desinitve fœmina. Buccam petit, quasi in eam puellæ
fugerit cunnus, aut ipsa sibi bucca in quadam sit cum
cunno societate ad participandos Veneris ludos. Objur-
gabam, quod hanc sibi sexuique fieri pateretur injuriam.
— « Quid vis! » respondit. « Occupat Marinus oris
« aream libidinibus suis, nec queri possum... Maritis
« hoc uno placemus nomine, quod fœminæ sumus; quæ
« quacunque petetur se probabit fœminam, hæc omnium
maxima placebit. »

Eeodem modo ipsam Eleonoram sumere tentavit
Alphonsus, ibidem :

She had scarcely spoken, when an abundant shower fell upon her robe. He showed some anger. « How could you be so foolish, » he cried, « as to spoil such good work ! » She replied : « Forgive me, the next time you will find me more obedient. » She kept her word, and actually drank men in a liquid state, — a spicy thing, for indeed the seed is spicy with salt ! » (Dial. VII.)

Mancia also proved complaisent in that way to Marino; Eleanor tells it in Aloysia Sigaea :

« My cousin, Mancia, has married a Neapolitan of the name of Marino. Marino is burning all over with debauchery. The libertine looks for the woman in Mancia even above the breasts ; he wants her mouth, as though tne vulva of the young wife had taken refuge there, or as if the mouth had made a bargain with the vulva to participate in the games of Venus. I blamed her for allowing so unnatural an act. » What would you have ? » she said. Marino's instrument occupies my mouth, so I cannot complain. We please our husbands only by reason of being women. Never mind where she is taken, if a woman only proves that she is a woman, she will please. » (Dial. VII.)

So too Alfonso tries to engage Eleanor herself in the same fashion :

*« En, Octavia mea, Alphonsi furores, » addebat
Eleonora. Ante hos dies, postquam bis terve telum
misit vere militans, ori et applicuit, — « Huic, » aio,
« ostio verberando, Alphonse, » ista non est apta
« catapulta : furis, et me vis furere. — Te furere ve-
« lim, me nolim, » reponit Alphonsus; « nam quod
« me amas, furori tuo debeo; nullum debeo merito
« meo. Si furere incipio, honorem, quem tibi debeo,
« forte obliviscar, qui mori malim, quam tibi non
« vivere. » His movit durum pectus : flexit ad ludi-
bria. Adsilientem appetii libens semiulco suavio flam-
mescentem nervum. Nihil ultra : nam eo mox sponte
reversa est erudita mentula, unde aberrarat. Cotyttium
fas nefasve in media perfecit regione, quod in hac su-
periori aggressa erat impudens. »*

*Fuit etiam Gonsalvus Cordubensis hujus sche-
matis amator. Aloisia, ibid. :*

*« Narrant Gonsalvum Cordubensem, imperatorem
magnum, cum insenuisset, hoc voluptatis delectatum
genere. »*

*Novum fellandi genus commentum est procax
ingenium Tiberii. Suetonius in Tiberio, cap. 44 :*

« Majore adhuc et turpiore infamia flagravit, vix

« Look you! Ottavia », added Eleanor, how passionately loving Alfonso is. Some days ago, after having several times plied his javelin in the legitimate way, he presented it to my mouth. « Your catapult, my Alfonso », said I, « is not made for breaching this door; you are mad, and you want to make me the same. » « No! I would fain have you mad, not myself; for that you love me, I owe to your madness, not to any merits of my own. If I get delirious, I may forget the respect which I owe you, and I would rather die than cease to live for you alone. « These words softened my heart, and decided me to assist him in that game. I seized his inflamed dart with a good heart between my lips. But that was all, his member returned voluntarily to the place it had left, and finished its exploits, which it had impudently begun above, properly in the region of the middle. » (Dial. VII.)

Gonzalvo of Cordova was another amateur of this mode. Aloysia Sigaea :

« Gonzalvo of Cordova, a celebrated general, is said to have taken very much to this kind of voluptuousness in his old age. » (Dial. VII.)

The prurient ingenuity of Tiberius invented a new species of *fellation*.

« His turpitude went still farther, to such in-

ut referri audirive, nedum credi fas sit, quasi pueros primæ teneritudinis, quos pisciculos vocabat, institueret, ut natanti sibi inter femina versarentur ac luderent, lingua morsuque sensim appetentes, atque etiam quasi infantes firmiores, necdum tamen lacte depulsos, inguini ceu papillæ admoveret : pronior sane ad id genus libidinis, et natura, et ætate. »

Imaginem ingeniosi hominis pisciculis appetiti cernere est tabula XVIII, in Monuments de la vie privée des douze Césars.

Proniores fere sunt ad irrumandi libidinem ætate provecti, quibus mentula desiit dicto audiens esse. Huc redeunt Martialea illa, IV, 50 : « *Nemo est senex ad irrumandum* » *; XI, 47 :*

Summa petas : illic mentula vivit anus.

III, 75 :

Stare, Luperce, tibi jam pridem mentula desit :
  Luctaris demens tu tamen arrigere.

famous excesses, that it is as difficult to relate them as to listen to them; they are scarcely credible. He caused little children, of the tenderest age to be taught to play between his legs, while he was swimming in his bath, calling them his little fishes, to touch him lightly with tongue and teeth, and like babies of some little strength and growth, though not yet weaned, to suck his privates as they would their mother's breast. His age and his inclination predisposed him for this sort of pleasure before all others » (Suetonius, *Tiberius*, ch. 44).

A representation of this ingenious libertine while tickled by what he called his little fishes, is to be seen on plate XVIII. of the *Monuments de la vie privée des douze Césars*.

Men advanced in age, whose member will no longer obey their will, are more inclined to irrumate than others. To this circumstance the passage in Martial, IV., 50, refers :

« No man is too old to irrumate. »

XI., 47 :

« Gain the heights ; there your old member will revive. »

And III., 75 :

« Your mentula, Lupercus, has long ceased

Cœpisti puras opibus corrumpere buccas ;
Sic quoque non vivit solicitata Venus.

Quam ob causam irrumatores minus timendi
sunt maritis. Ideo Martialis facilem se præbuit
Lupo, Pollæ suæ irrumatori deprehenso, X, 40,
quem locum paulo ante laudavimus : nam ut irru-
masse potius quam futuisse Lupum credamus, pa-
ronomasia adducimur, quæ latet in irrupi. *Nec*
Glyceræ maritus, si quidem illi maritus, metuen-
dum, erat, ne res suæ agerentur a Luperco ; Mar-
tialis, XI, 41 :

> *Formosam Glyceren amat Lupercus,*
> *Et solus tenet, imperatque solus.*
> *Quam toto sibi mense non fututam*
> *Cum tristis quereretur, et roganti*
> *Causam reddere vellet Æliano,*
> *Respondit, Glyceræ dolere dentes.*

Num vera sit Lepidini sententia in Hermaphro-
dito, *I,* 13, *qui semel irrumaverit, nunquam posse*
dediscere, judicium esto penes expertos. Aloisia qui-
dem consentit, III, 42 : « *Qui semel usi sunt perdite*
amant. »

to stiffen; nevertheless, in your folly you strive
to make it rise. You are fain now to corrupt pure
lips for gold; but even so your Venus is stimulated in vain. »

For this reason irrumators are less feared by
married men. Thus Martial dealt more lightly
with Lupus, whom he had surprised while irrumating his Polla, in the passage (X., 40) quoted
previously. The husband of Glycera, if so be
that she had one, also need not have feared that
Lupercus would do duty for him, Martial, XI.,
41 :

« Lupercus loves the beautiful Glycera ; he is
her lord and master, and he alone. He was com-
plaining bitterly he had not loved her for a
month; Aelianus asked the reason, — he replied
Glycera had the toothache. »

Lepidinius, in the *Hermaphroditus* (I., 13), is
of opinion, that anyone who has once irrumated
can never get rid of or renounce the habit. I
must leave it to experts to decide upon this. So
also thinks Aloysia Sigaea : « Such as have once
tasted it, are mad after this pleasure. » (Dial.
VII.)

No wonder that after fellation, the mouth

A fellando os aqua elui, qui est, qui miretur ?
Eo pertinet illud Martialis, II, 50 :

Quod fellas, et aquam potas, nil, Lesbia, peccas;
Qua tibi parte opus est, Lesbia, sumis aquam.

Inde et illustratur Priapeium, **XXX** *:*

Vade per has vites, quarum se carpseris uvas,
Quas aliter sumas, hospes habebis aquas.

Vult Priapus: Venisti ut aquam peteres ad bi-
bendum ; ubi autem uvas decerpseris, irrumabo te,
quo facto aqua tibi opus erit magis ad os eluendum,
quam ad sitim sedandam. Eodem spectat Martia-
leum de Chione, III, 87, quod, supra dedimus.

Quamvis improbius quiddam rogare sibi vide-
rentur, qui os rogarent, quam qui aut cunnum aut
culum ; Martialis, IX, 68 :

Lascivam tota possedi nocte puellam,
Cujus nequitias vincere nemo potest.
Fesus mille modis illud puerile poposci :
Ante preces totas primaque verba dedit.
Improbius quiddam ridensque rubensque rogavi :
Pollicita est nulla luxuriosa mora (81).

---

(81) *Pro prima igitur cœna dedit puella cunnum, pro se-*

has to be washed out with water. Martial alludes to this, II., 50 ;

« You lend your mouth, and then drink water, Lesbia; quite right, — where your work is, there you take water. »

Priapeia, XXX., says :

« Walk in the vineyards, and if you steal any of the grapes, you shall have water, stranger, to take in another way. »

Priapus means : « You came to get water to drink; but if you pluck any grapes, I shall irrumate you, and then you will want water to rince your mouth rather than to drink. » Martial says as much to Chioné in *Epigram* III., 87, quoted before.

To ask for the loan of the mouth is to demand a thing much more shameful than the other two orifices. Martial, IX., 68 :

« All the night long I possessed a lewd young girl ; I never knew anyone more naughty. Tired of a thousand postures, I asked for the puerile service; before I had done asking, she turned at once in compliance. Laughing and blushing, I asked something worse than that, — the wanton consented instantly » (81).

_____

(81) First the rogue lends her vulva, then her buttocks,

*atque diligenter, caverent, ne deprehenderentur :
idem, 46, XI :*

---

*cunda culum, pro tertia os. Sunt qui mammosam Spatalen
ita largam fuisse putent ; Martial, II, 52 :*

> Novit loturas Dasius numerare : poposcit
> Mammosam Spatalen pro tribus; illa dedit.

*Sed vereor, ne injuriam faciant bonæ Spatalæ. Nihil aliud
enim Dasius balneator voluisse videtur, quam ut Spatale, quæ
nimia corporis obesitate ac pinguedine trium fæminarum locum in solio impleret, pro tribus solveret. Omnibus modis
larga fuit Phyllis : Martialis, XIII, 65 :*

> Formosa Phyllis, nocte cum mihi tota
> Se praestitisset omnibus modis largam...

Jam intelliges, quid Martiali sit « nihil negare », XI, 50 :

> Nil tibi, Phylli, nego, nil mihi, Phylli, nega.

Item, IV, 12 :

> Nulli, Thai, negas; sed si te non pudet istud,
> Hoc saltem pudeat, Thai, negare nihil.

Item, XII. 72 :

> Nil non, Lygde, mihi negas roganti :
> At quondam mihi, Lygde, nil negabas.

Simpliciter, XII, 81 :

> Quisquis nil negat, Atticilla, fellat.

*Noluit autem nil negare Mallonia Tiberio : futui quidem
et pædicari forsitan tulerat, sed ut fellaret non potuit misera
fastidium vincere. Suetonianum locum nugis hisce nostris ante*

Those that found themselves thus situated

---

and lastly her mouth. Some suppose the full-bosomed Spatalé of Martial (II, 52) was just as prodigal :

« Dasius was astute at counting the bathers ; he asked full-bosomed Spatalé the fee of three women, and she paid. »

But I believe they wrong the good Spatalé. Dasius, the bathing man, wanted only that Spatalé, whose charms were ample and buxom, she taking up as much room as three other women, should pay for three.

The Phyllis of Martial (XII, 65), showed herself liberal in every way :

« The beautiful Phyllis, who throughout the whole night had proved herself right liberal in every way..... »

From this you will understand what Martial means by « refusing nothing » (XI, 50) :

« I will not deny you anything, Phyllis ; for you deny me nothing. »

And similarly, IV, 12 :

« You refuse no one, Thaïs. If you know no shame for this, blush at least that you refuse nothing, Thaïs ! »

And again, XII, 72 :

« There is nothing Lygdus, that you do not now deny me ; there was a time, when there was nothing you did deny ! »

And he says (XII, 81) right out :

« Whoso refuses nothing, Atticilla, sucks. »

It is in this sense that Mallonia refused to be entirely at the mercy of Tiberius ; she had already admitted him to her vulva and anus, but when it came to the mouth the poor girl could not overcome her disgust. We have before quoted the passage of Suetonius. Of a woman who refuses nothing, Arnobius (II, 42) says : « That she is

Intrasti quoties inscriptæ limina cellæ,
     Seu puer arrisit, sive puella tibi,
Contentus non es foribus veloque seraque,
     Secretumque jubes grandius esse tibi.
Oblinitur minimæ si qua est suspicio rimæ,
     Punctaque lasciva quæ terebrantur acu.
Nemo est tam teneri, tam solicitique pudoris,
     Qui vel pædicat, Canthare, vel futuit.

Non erat tamen, ut puderet veteres Romanos irru-
mare, quo vel ex contumelioso illo verbi usu Catul-
liano patet, sed pudebat fellare. Est enim aliquid
virtutis in audentia, nihil in patientia, præsertim
ejus, qui parti naturæ humanæ præstantissimæ tam
spurca ministeria imperat. Accedebat, quod fœtorem
oris a fellando contractum summo studio dissimulan-

---

inseruimus. Quæ nihil negat, Arnobio dicitur « nihil pati re-
nuens », II, 42. De ebria, quæ nihil potest negare, Ovidius,
de Arte amatoria, *III, 766* :

       Digna est concubitus quoslibet illa pati.

took good care not to be surprised; Martial, XI., 46:

« When you have crossed the threshold of a chamber with name ou signboard, whether it be boy or girl that smiled on you in welcome, doors and hangings and locks do not content you, and you want to be yet more certain you are not watched. Mystery is what you want; you look suspiciously on the smallest crack in the door and stop it; the same with the tiniest pinhole made by some inquisitive hand. Nobody can be more modest or circumspect in his doings, Cantharus, than the man who wants to pedicate or copulate. »

However, the old Romans did not blush to irrumate, as is evident by the use Catullus makes of that word, contemptuous though it be. What they *were* ashamed of was *fellation*. Indeed there is a certain bold audacity in playing the active part, but none in the passive one, particularly when the mouth, the noblest organ of the body, has to perform such vile offices. Add to this that a fetid breath was acquired by this

---

ready to undergo anything, » and of a woman that is drunk, « so much so as not to able to refuse anything. » Ovid says (*Art of Love*, III, v. 766):
« She is meet to undergo all kinds of assaults. »

dum putabant, fugam vel convivarum vel basiato-
rum metuentes. Adeo enim fellatores convivis erant
invisi, ut calices his propinare (82) *devitarent, et*
forte propinatos frangerent (83), *nec nisi inviti*(84)
occurrebant basiare minantibus. Hinc factum est,

---

(82) *Martialis, II, 15 :*

> *Quod nulli calicem tuum propinas,*
> *Humane facis, Herme, non superbe.*

Idem, VI, 44 :

> *Nemo propinabit, Calliodore, tibi.*

Seneca, de Beneficiis, *II, 21 :* « *Is* » (*Caius Cæsar*)
« *cum ab amicis conferentibus ad impensam ludorum pecunias*
acciperet, magnam pecuniam a Fabio Persico missam non
accepit. Et objurgantibus his, qui non æstimabant mittentes
sed missa, quod repudiasset : — « *Ego,* » *inquit,* « *ab eo*
beneficium accipiam, a quo propinationem accepturus non
sim ? « *Fellatorem fuisse Fabium Persicum, non cunnilin-*
gum, inde apparet, quod quæstionem instituerat Seneca de
eo, quid faciendum esset captivo, cui redemtionis pretium
homo prostituti corporis et infamis ore promisisset.

(83) *Martialis, XII, 75 :*

> *Hoc quoque non nihil est, quod propinabis in istis,*
> *Frangendus fuerit si tibi, Flacce, calix.*

Macedonius, in Analectis Brunckii, *III. 116 :*

habit, which *fellators* took every means to hide, afraid of putting to flight fellow-guests at table and acquaintances who should greet them with a kiss in the street.

Fellators were so repugnant to the guests at table, that no cups (82) were offered to them, or when they had been offered, they were afterwards broken (83), and that it was only with the

---

(82) Martial, II, 15 :
« You do not offer your cup to any man; it is discretion, Hermus, forbids, not pride. »

And VI, 44 :
« No one, Calliodorus, may drink from your cup. »
Seneca : When Caius Caesar accepted sums of money for the expense of the games from friends, who brought them to him, he refused to take a large amount from Fabius Persicus. His friends not looking at the character of the sender, but at the value of the sum sent, reproached him for having refused. « What! » said he, « am I to accept the service of a man fram whose cup I should decline to drink ? » (*De Beneficiis*, II, 21.) Fabius Persicus was a *fellator* not a *cunnilingue*; this is apparent from the controversy in which Seneca engaged about him, viz : what a prisoner should do whom a man promised to buy off, at the price of having his body prostituted, and his mouth sullied.

(83) Martial XII, 75 :
« It is no little matter, Flaccus if you drink with them; and then have to break the cup they touched. »

And Macedonius in the *Analecta* of Brunck, III, 116 :
« There drank a woman with me yesterday, whose

ut cinædi mallent videri quam fellatores (85), *uti*
Phœbus apud Martialem, III, 73 :

Ἐχθές μοι συνέπινε γυνὴ, περὶ ἧς λόγος ἔρρει
Οὐχ ὑγιής · παῖδες, θραύσατε τὰς κύλικας.

(84) *Martialis, XI, 96* :

Incideris quoties in basia fellatorum ;
In solio puto te mergere Flacce, caput.

Idem, I, 95 :

Cantasti male, dum fututa es, Ægle,
Jam cantas bene : basianda non es.

Idem, I, 84 :

Os et labra tibi lingit, Manneia, catellus :
Non miror, merdas si licet esse cani.

Seneca, de Beneficiis, *IV,* 30 : « *Quid nuper Fabium*
Persicum, cujus osculum etiam impuri vitabant, sacerdotem
fecit ? »

(85) *Ut improbos basiatores fuisse Romanos vel ex festivo*
illo epigrammate Martialis, I, 99, constat, ita non mirum
fecerunt fellatores, si ægerrime caruerunt basiationibus. Ho-
rum spurcum caput alias quoque perstringit Bilbilitanus ar-
tifex, ut II, 42 :

Zoile, quid solium subluto podice perdis ?
Spurcius ut fiat, Zoile, merge caput.

Item, VI. 81 :

greatest unwillingness any one would kiss their mouth (84), when presented for salute. Thus it was preferable to be taken for a *cinede* to being taken for a *fellator* (85), like Phœbus in Martial, III., 73 :

---

fame is anything but good; — go break the cups, my lads ! »

(83) Martial XI, 96 :

« Every time you happen to meet a *fellator's* kisses, I can fancy, O Flaccus, how you plunge your head in water. »

And I, 95 :

« You sung but badly, Aeglé, when you were loved *per vulvam*. Now no one kisses you, and you sing well. »

And I, 84 :

« Your lap-dog, Manneia, licks your mouth and lips I am not a bit surprised ; dogs like dirt. »

Seneca : « And mark ! he made that Fabius Persicus, whose kisses are shunned even by people who know no shame, a priest only the other day. » (*De Beneficiis*, IV 30.)

(84) It appears from Martial's *Epigram* (XI, 99), that the kiss on the mouth was the regular thing with the Romans ; *fellators*, therefore, could not be surprised at their kisses being avoided. The poet of Bilbilis makes yet another mock at their expense (II, 42) :

« Zoilus, why spoil the bath by bathing your bottom in it ? If your would make it still dirtier, plunge your head in. »

And VI, 81 :

« You bathe, Charidemus, as though you had a grudge against mankind, entirely submerging in the bath

Dormis cum pueris mutoniatis,
Et non stat tibi, Phœbe, quod stat illis.
Quid vis me, rogo, Phœbe, suspicari?
Mollem credere te virum volebam :
Sed rumor negat esse te cinædum.

Callistratus quoque apud eundem, XII, 35 :

Tamquam simpliciter mecum, Callistrate, vivas,
Dicere percisum te mihi sæpe soles.
Non es tam simplex, quam vis, Callistrate, credi :
Nam quisquis narrat talia, plura tacet (86).

hinc, ut Charidemum pathicum haberi nolentem,
et propter hanc causam et crura setosa et pectora
villosa præferentem, id juberet operam dare, ut vi-

Iratus tanquam populo, Charideme, lavaris,
Inguina sic toto subluis in solio.
Nec caput hic vellem sic te, Charideme, lavare,
Et caput ecce lavas : inguina malo laves.

(86) *Latent in versu ultimo aculei : unus in* « *tacet* » *quod supra vidimus ut adjunctum dici de fellando; alter in* « *narrat* », *probo linguæ opere posito pro improbo, quemad-modum III,* 84 :

Quid narrat tua moecha? non puellam
Dixi, Tongilion. Quid ergo? linguam.

« You sleep with youths whose members are full size, and what rises with them, will not rise with you. Pray, Phœbus, tell me, what must I suspect ? If I could think that you were but effeminate ! But rumour says, you are not a *cinede* ! »

The case of Callistratus, in XII., 35 of our author, is a similar one :

« You are very frank, Callistratus, with me, and you tell me that they often do it to you. You are not quite so simple, as you would appear ; the man that tells such things does not tell of others worse (86). »

For the same reason, as Charidemus will not be called a *patient*, and shows his legs and chest covered with hair. Martial tells him (VI., 56),

---

your privates. I should not like you to wash your head that way, Charidemus ; and now look ! you are washing your head. I had rather it were your privates ! »

(86) In the last verse there are two furtive stings ; the first is about not telling (*tacet*, — is silent), an expression, which was used as denoting a *fellator* ; the second is the word « tell, » (*narrat*), the honourable use of the mouth being put for the dishonourable, as in Epistle III, 84 :

« What tells (*narrat*) your harlot. — No ! I dont mean your girl, Tongilion ! — What then ? — Your tongue ! »

deretur potius pathicus, quam fellator, VI, 56:

> *Quod tibi crura rigent setis, et pectora villis,*
>   *Verba putas famæ te, Charideme, dare.*
> *Exstirpa, mihi crede, pilos de corpore toto.*
>   *Teque pilare tuas testificare nates,*
> *Quæ ratio est? inquis. — Scis multos dicere multa :*
>   *Fac pædicari te, Charideme, putent.*

Fellare, ut par erat, emebatur, nec parvo inter-
dum, Martialis, XI, 67:

> *Et delator es, et calumniator,*
> *Et fraudator es, et negotiator,*
> *Et fellator es, et lanista. Miror*
> *Quare non habeas nummos.*

Idem, III, 75 :

> *Stare, Luperce, tibi jam pridem mentula desit :*
>   *Luctaris demens tu tamen arrigere.*
> *Sed nihil erucæ faciunt bulbique salaces,*
>   *Improba nec prosunt jam satureia tibi.*
> *Cæpisti puras opibus corrumpere buccas :*
>   *Sic quoque non vivit solicitata Venus.*
> *Mirari satis hoc quisquam, vel credere possit,*
>   *Quæ non stat, magno stare, Luperce, tibi.*

Explicanti autem de fellando nefas videtur tac

to arrange himself in such a way as to appear a minion rather than a *fellator* :

« Because your legs are covered with bristles, your chest with hair, you think, Charidemus, to hand down your words to posterity; take my advice, and pluck the hair from all over your body, and get it certified you depilate your buttocks. Why so? you ask. — You know the world tells many tales; try to make them believe you are merely pedicated. »

Fellation, as was but fair, received payment, and high payment. Martial (XI., 67) shows this :

« Informer you are and blackmailer, swindler and trickster, *fellator* and bully. The wonder is you have no money. »

And again, III., 75 :

« Your member, Lupercus, has long ceased to stiffen; nevertheless in your folly, you strive to make it rise. Of no avail is cole-wort or salacious onions, of no use to you the provocative savory. You are fain now to corrupt pure lips for gold; but even so your Venus is stimulated is vain. But, — a thing to be marvelled at and scarce believed, — what will not rise, Lupercus, does rise if you pay a heavy fee. »

But when on the subject of fellation, we must

ere corvum, quem fellatorem dixit perpetuus noster,
XIV, 74:

> *Corve salutator (87), quare fellator haberis?*
>   *In caput intravit mentula nulla tuum,*

id quod vulgi opinione corvus putabatur ore coire.
Plinius, Hist. nat., X, 12:

> *Ore eos parere aut coire vulgus arbitratur. Aristo-*
> *toles negat, sed illam exosculationem, quæ sæpe cerni-*
> *tur, qualem in columbis esse.*

Negavit Erasmus, in Adagiis *sub* Lesbiari,
p. 409 *exemplaris Francofurti* 1670 *editi, sua*
ætate adhuc exstare irrumandi libidinem:

> « Λειχάζειν *ni fallor tale quiddam est Græcis,*
> *quale fellare Latinis. Nam vox etiamnum manet, ta-*
> *metsi rem jam olim e medio sublatam arbitror.* »

---

(87) *Causam appellationis petas a Macrobio,* Saturnal.,
II, 4: « *Sublimis Actiaca victoria revertebatur* » *(Augus-*
tus); « *occurrit ei inter gratulantes corvum tenens, quem*
instituerat hoc dicere: « *Ave, Cæsar victor, imperator!* »
Miratur Cæsar officiosam avem, viginti millibus nummum
emit. »

not pass over in silence the raven, whom our standing authority (Martial, XIV., 74), calls a *fellator* :

« Saluting raven (87), why do they call thee *fellator* ? Never a mentula entered your beak. »

The fact is ignorant people believed the raven fulfilled the coitus with his beak :

Pliny says : « The vulgar herd believes that it operates the coitus and procreates with its beak. Aristotle denied this, saying that ravens merely exchange kisses in the same way, familiar to everybody, that pigeons do. » (*Natural History*, X., 12.)

Erasmus denies in his *Adagia*, under the word *Lesbiari* (p. 409 of the Frankfort edition, 1670), that in his time the obscene practice of irrumation was still known :

« Λειχάζειν (to lick), if I am not mistaken, is with the Greeks the same thing as *fellare* with

---

(87) You will find in Macrobius (*Saturnalia*, II, 4), why he was called saluting. Augustus returned as victor from Actium ; amongst those who came to congratulate him was a man holding a raven, which he had taught to cry : « I salute thee, Caesar Victor and Emperor ! » Caesar, admiring this flattering bird, bought it for 20.000 sesterces.

Vereor ut vere : certe audio, ne ab nunc hominum quidem moribus plane abhorrere id schematis, quod viderunt ii, quibus magnas urbes adire licet. Imaginem fellantis præbet tabula XXI, in Monuments de la vie privée des douze Césars, *quanquam venusta illa tabula magis ad spintriacum genus, de quo infra, quam ad hoc nostrum pertinet.*

FINIS

TOMI PRIMI

the Latins. The word indeed romains ; but the thing itself has been, I think, long done away with. »

I fear this is not really the case. At any rate I am informed that this practice is not entirely opposed to the habits of libertines of the present day ; those must decide whose opportunities take them to great cities. Plate XXI., in the *Monuments de la vie privée des douze Césars* represents a *fellator*. However the graceful picture in question really belongs more properly to the category of « spintrian postures », of which more anon, than to the present chapter.

END

OF THE FIRST VOLUME

MANUAL

OF

Classical Erotology

(De figuris Veneris)

BY

Friedrich Karl Forberg

LATIN TEXT AND LITERAL ENGLISH VERSION.

SECOND VOLUME

CHAPTER IV

OF MASTURBATION

CAPUT IV

DE MASTURBANDO

MASTURBARE *dicitur qui manu perfricando mentulam semen elicit, voce ex* manu stuprare *corrupta. Ac fieri id potest aut propria manu, aut aliena. Cum fit propria manu, læva fere solet adhiberi. Hinc* pellex læva *apud Martialem, IX,* 42 :

> *Pontice, quod nunquam futuis, sed pellice læva*
> *Uteris, et Veneri servit amica manus,*
> *Hoc nihil esse putas? scelus est, mihi crede, sed ingens,*
> *Quantum vix animo concipis ipse tuo.*

CHAPTER IV

OF MASTURBATION

To excite the member by friction with the hand until the sperm comes spirting out of it is what the Ancients called masturbation, from *masturbare*, that is *manu stuprare*, — to pollute with the hand. This may be done by one's own hand, or by borrowing someone else's. If by one's own, it is generally the left hand that is employed, hence the expression, « left-hand whore » in Martial (IX., 42) :

« You never, Ponticus, enter a woman, but use your left-hand whore, making your hand the mistress for your pleasure; think you this is nothing? Believe me, it's a crime, yes! a crime, and worse than you can imagine. Old Horatius copulated once at any rate to beget his

Nempe semel futuit, generaret Horatius ut tres;
    Mars semel, ut geminos Ilia casta daret.
Omnia perdiderat, si masturbatus uterque
    Mandasset manibus gaudia fœda suis.
Ipsam crede tibi Naturam dicere rerum :
    Istud quod digitis, Pontice, perdis, homo est,

Eo spectat illud quoque ejusdem, XI, 74:

Venturum juras semper mihi, Lygde, roganti,
    Constituisque horam, contituisque locum.
Cum frustra jacui longa prurigine tentus,
    Succurrit pro te sæpe sinistra manus.

et Ramusianum sextum, pagina 62 *Parisiensi :*

Quid facias ? numquid læva est tibi sana valensque ?
    Utare hac, alia pellice non opus est.
Non eme, quod possit gratis tibi læva parare.

   Sed fuerunt etiam, qui dextra uterentur. Idem
Ramusius Ariminensis carmine quarto, pag. 61 :

Usque uaeo, Donate, premor tentigine, quod, ni
    Auxilium præbes, mentula no tra cadit.

three sons; Mars once to get chaste Ilia with twins. Neither of them could have done it, if by masturbation they had procured by the use of their own hand pleasures so shameful. Believe me, that nature's voice confirms it, — what escapes 'twixt your fingers, Ponticus, is a human being. »

To the same subject also *Epig.*, XI., 74 refers :

« Oftentimes, Lygdé, you swear you will grant my prayer, even appointing the place, even appointing the hour. Longtime I lay consumed with longing, till often my left hand comes to my help in your stead. »

And this passage of the VIth. book of Ramusius, p. 62 of the Paris edition :

« What are you to do? Is your left hand safe and sound? Well use it, then you will not want a whore. Why pay for what your left hand gives you gratis? »

There were of course also people who used their right hand; the same Ramusius of Rimini, book IV., p. 61, tells us :

« I suffer, dear Donatus, from so frightful an erection, I am fearful for my member, if you do not help me. My right hand, being wounded,

Nec possum dextra, læsa est, mihi ferre salutem,
    Nec mihi sunt nummi, nec mihi pulcer Hylas.
Cunnus abest nobis, futuendi copia nulla;
    Ut vivam, Venerem solve, quod asse potes.

Pacificus Maximus, Elegia *XII, pagina Parisiensi*
126:

Sed jam quid faciam ? sera tentigine rumpor,
    Impleremque utres terque quaterque graves;
Jamque diu nullum novit mea mentula cunnum,
    Effoditque maris viscera nulla diu.
Illa die tenta est, tenta est et nocte, nec unquam
    Decidit ; arrectum est nocte dieque caput.
Non puer hæc audit, non audit verba puella,
    Nemo venit : solitum dextrã frequentet opus!

Modo vidimus, quam severe castigaverit Martia-
lis Ponticum masturbatorem, eo quod digiti homi-
nem perderet ; neque tamen ispse castigator dubitavit,
manu officiosa uti, cum tentigine rumpebatur; II,
43:

At mihi succurrit pro Ganymede manus,

et *XI,* 74:

Succurrit pro te sæpe sinistra manus.

can do nothing; I have no money; Hylas is not here; no vulva opens for me — no chance of fornication, appease my desire, that I may live, and you can do it cheaply. »

Pacificus Maximus, *Elegy* XII., p. 126, Paris edition :

« What shall I do? I am so stiff — I'm bursting, and I could easily fill three or four large bottles. It is long since my member has known a vulva, long since it has stirred the entrails of a man. It is stiff day and night, and will never relax, — night and day it lifts its head. No youth, no girl will listen to my prayer, no help — my right hand must then do the service! »

We have seen just above, with what severity Martial reproached Ponticus, a masturbator, for losing between his fingers the substance of a man. Nevertheless this fine moralist did not hesitate to put his own hand to similar use under the pressure of erection, *Epigr.* 43, book II. :

« Another Ganymede, my hand assisted me. »

and XI., 74 :

« Often my left hand comes to my help in your stead. »

Nor was his severity given to whining when

Neque in mentem venit severitatis plorare iubenti
Telesphorum cinædum, XI, 59 :

Cum me velle vides, tentumque, Telesphore, sentis,
    Magna rogas : puta me velle negare nihil (1)?
Et nisi juratus dixi : « Dabo, » subtrahis illas,
    Permittunt in me quæ tibi multa, nates.
Quid si me tonsor, cum stricta novacula supra est,
    Tunc libertatem divitiasque roget?
Promittam; nec enim rogat illo tempore tonsor,
    Latro rogat : res est imperiosa timor.
Sed fuerit curva cum tuta novacula theca.
    Frangam tonsori crura manusque simul.
At tibi nil faciam; sed lota mentula læva
    Αἰάζειν *cupidæ dicet avaritiæ* (2);

---

(1) *Simili interrogatione per verbum infinitum et* puta
pro scilicet *usus est, III, 26 :*

    ..... *Hoc me puta velle negare*

Nihil opus videtur iis, quæ in utroque loco moliuntur viri
eruditi.

(2) *Vult : Succurret læva mentulæ laboranti, et ubi*
perfecto opere manus uda fuerit reddita seminis effluvio,
uti pecten, siquidem pecten, Ravolæ apud Juvenalem, IX, 4 :

    Ravola dum Rhodopes uda terit inguina barba,

he exhorted (XI., 59), the cinede Telesphorus:

« Soon as ever you see I want it, and know that I am in erection, Telesphorus, then you demand a heavy price, — can I say nay (1)? If I will not swear to pay you, you will withdraw those posteriors of yours, which are so precious to me. If with his razor set to my throat my barber, whilst shaving me, demands my liberty and fortune, I promise all; 'tis not the barber asks, but a cut-throat, and fear compels me to say « Yes ». But once I see the razor returned to its curved case and harmless, why! I will break every limb of the fellow. Not that I will harm you, but my left hand once washed, my member will say « Go hang! to your grasping avarice (2). »

---

(1) Martial had made use of the same interrogative phrase with the verb in the infinitive and *puta* put instead of *scilicet* also in Epigram III.,26. *Hoc me puta velle negare?* (Can I say nay to this?) Scholars have found occasion for a pile of annotations on the two passages: these need not detain us.

(2) Martial's meaning is : My left hand will console my suffering mentula; the business done, my hand covered with the ejaculation of the sperm, like the fleece on the pubis of Ravola in Juvenal (IX., 4), — if indeed it is the fleece of his pubis that is intended :

« Whilst Ravola with wet beard rubs the groin of Rhodopé »... the greedy cinede will be told to go to the

neque ab uxore in puero deprenso, XI, 44, quod epigramma non illepidum supra proposuimus ; neque Thelesinam volenti, II, 49 :

> *... Pueris dat Thelesina : volo;*

neque edicenti nescio cui, XI, 23, utatur culo Galesi ut parte sua :

> *Divisit Natura mares; pars una puellis,*
> *   Una viris genita est : utere parte tua.*

An istud quod culo perdit pædico minus homo est, quam quod digitis masturbator ?

> *Cum mentulæ sit vel adspectu surgere fœminæ*

---

valeat cinædus avarus, abeatque tristi vultu Horatiani illius, qui invenit

> *Nil sibi legatum praeter plorare suisque,*

Sat., II, v. 69. *Ceterum lota læva in memoriam revocamur mœchæ Juvenalis, XI, 186,* « *humida suspectis referentis multicia rugis.* »

The same when his wife surprised him engaged with a youth (XI., 44), — a witty epigram quoted above, as also when he intended to marry Thelesina (II., 49) :

« Thelesina makes presents to young lads; all the better. »

The same when he recommends somebody, I do not know who (XI., 23), to make use of the posteriors of Galesius only, as the part that would suit him;

« Youths are divided by nature; one part is reserved for girls, and the other for men — use your own portion. »

Is what the pedicon loses in the anus of the cinede anything else but the substance of a man, which the masturbator wastes between his fingers?

As it is in the nature of the virile member to

---

deuce, to slink off with drooping head, like the man in Horace (*Satires* II., 69), who finds :

« Nothing is left to him and his but to weep. »

This moist hand reminds us of the adulterous woman in Juvenal (XI.. 186), who :

« Shows humid traces in the doubtful pleats of her tunic. »

*pulchræ nudæ, imperiose tum sæpe jubet succurri
tentigo : nam* (3) οὐδὲν μέγα φρονεῖ ἐστυχὼς ἀνήρ.
Hoc est, quod, onerosis palliis amicæ jactatis.

*Abditus interea latet accersitus adulter,
Impatiensque moræ silet, et præputia ducit* (4),

---

(3) *Suidas sub* ἐστυχώς, *ex Ælio Dionysio, ut videtur.*

(4) *Non libidinis, sed decoris causa, præputia adduceban-
tur ab iis, qui, cum a Judæis ad ceteras gentes defecissent,
indigne ferentes et verpi videri et curti audire, operam dabant,
ut glandem nudam tegerent. I* Macc., *1, 15 :* Καὶ ἐποίησαν
ἑαυτοῖς ἀκροβυστίας. *I* Cor. VII, *18 :* Περιτετμημένος τις
ἐκλήθη; μὴ ἐπισπάσθω. *Celsus,* De Medicina, *VIII, 25 :*
« *Si glans nuda est, vultque aliquis eam decoris causa tegere,
fieri potest, sed expeditius in puero quam in viro; in eo, cui
id naturale est, quam in eo, qui quarundam gentium more
circumcisus est.* » *Exposita curatione eorum, quibus id naturale est, pergit :* « *At in eo, qui circumcisus est, sub circulo
glandis scalpello diducenda cutis ab interiore cole est. Non ita
dolet, quia summo soluto diduci deorsum usque ab pubem*

rise at the mere sight of a pretty woman's naked body, the amorous desire in that state often craves imperiously for relief, for « man in erection is not overwise » (3). This is why, when the fair one's heavy coverlets have been thrown back :

« Meantime the adulterer she has sent for lurks in furtive concealment, and impatient of the delay, yet says never a word, but pulls his foreskin (4). » — Juvenal, VI., 236, 7.

---

(3) Suidas under the word ἐστυχώς, after Aelius Dionysius apparently.

(4) It was not out of voluptuousness, but for decency's sake that Jews, who had renounced their nation, had their prepuce redressed over the gland, as they did not wish it to be seen thatd they had been circumcized, so they took means to get their bare gland recovered. « And they made for themselves new prepuces » (Maccabees, I., 1., 15), « Is there anyone that has been brought to believe, circumcised? Let him not recover his gland » (Corinthians, I., vii., 18). Celsus, De Medicina, VII., ch. 25: « If the gland is bare, and it is desired for convenience sake to recover it, this can be effected, but more easily with a child, than with a grown man, more easily with the man born so, than with the man who has been circumcised after the custom of certain people. After having explained the method of cure applicable to men, with whom it is a natural accident, Celsus continues : « With people that have been circumcised, the skin must be detached behind the crown of the gland. This

apud Juvenalem, VI, 236, 37 ; hoc quod.

> *Masturbabantur Phrygii post ostia servi,*
> *Hectoreo quoties sederat uxor equo,*

apud Martialem, XI, 105 ; hoc quod Gaditanarum puellarum saltatione, haud dubie non multum diversa ab ea, qua ad hodiernum usque diem Hispanos

---

manu potest, neque ideo sanguis profluit. Resoluta autem cutis rursus extenditur ultra glandem, tum multa frigida aqua fovetur, emplastroque circumdatur, quod valenter inflammationem reprimat. Ubi jam sine inflammatione est, deligari debet a pube usque circulum, super glandem autem adverso emplastro imposito induci. Sic enim fit, ut inferior pars glutinetur, superior ita sanescat, ne inhæreat. » Ex quo loco intelligitur, Celsi ætate nondum incessisse morem denudandi caput penis, qui post invaluit apud Judæos, ita quidem, ut, Buxtorfio auctore in Lexico Talmudico, post præputium abscissum remanens cutis per ungues pollicis acuminatos a circumcidente retrorsum traheretur. Nam si invaluisset, non opus erat præcepto de cute scalpello diducenda ab interiore cole. Fuit cum conjiciebam, dici Judæos recutitos a cute penis*

and why :

« The Phrygian slaves would be masturbating behind the doors, each time his bride mounted the Hectorean horse. » — Martial, XI., 105.

This is why during the dances of the young Gaditanian girls, which were without doubt very like the dances that are still so much appreciat-

---

operation is not very painful as the prepuce being loosened, you can draw it with the hand back to the pubis without any loss of blood.

Then the loosened integument is drawn once more over and beyond the gland. This done the verge is dipped frequently into cold water, and then covered with a plaster, which has a strong tendency to minimize inflammation. As soon as it is quite free from inflammation, the verge is to be bandaged from the pubis to the annular incision; the skin is then drawn over the gland, but kept separate from it by a plaster. In this way the lower part of the skin grows on again, while the upper part heals without adhering. » From this passage it would appear that at the time of Celsus the method of laying bare the gland which afterwards prevailed with the Jews was not discovered yet, by which, according to Buxtorf (Dictionnaire Talmudique), after the prepuce has been cut away, the circumcisor takes hold of the remaining skin between the thin edges of his thumb nails, and draws it forcibly back. If this practice had been customary it would have been superfluous to separate the prepuce with the scalpel. I conjecture from this, that

mirifice delectari constat (5), *vel pannuceas senum verpas sæpe legimus moveri. Martialis, VI,* 71 :

> *Edere lascivos ad Bætica crusmata gestus,*
> *   Et Gaditanis ludere docta modis,*
> *Tendere quæ tremulum Pelian, Hecubæque maritum*
> *   Posset ad Hectoreos solicitare rogos.*

Juvenalis, XI, 162-165 :

> *Forsitan exspectes, ut Gaditana canoro*
> *Incipiat prurire choro, plausuque probatæ*
> *Ad terram tremulo descendant clune puellæ* (6),
> *Irritamentum Veneris languentis...*

---

isto modo, sine quo circumcisio consummata non putatur, re-tracta; sed vetor Celso.

(5) *Jul.-Cæsar Scaliger,* Poetices *libro primo, p. 64 :* « *Ex fœdis* » (*saltationibus*) « *erat* ῥίκνωμα; ῥικνοῦσθαι *est lumbis et femoribus fluctuare. Crissare Latini dicunt. Apud Hispanos adhuc exercetur abominando spectaculo.* »

(6) *Hoc age, Lector, ne te prætereat forte saltationis Gadi-tanæ ratio. Tremulo clune ad terram descendere puellæ, ad extremum supinæ jacere, libidini paratæ. Ab hoc igitur sal-tandi genere diversa erat* βίβασις *Laconica, qua ita subsultare*

ed by the Spaniards (5), the limp appendages of even grey-headed spectators began to move visibly, as many authors tell us. Martial, VI., 71 :

« Cunning in the wanton gestures that go with the Baetican castanets, skilled in dancing to the Gaditanian measures, she might well stiffen trembling Pelias, and excite Hecuba's husband to emulate vigorous Hector. »

Juvenal, XI., 162-165 :

« Perhaps you may wait while the Gaditanian dancer begins to feel the wanton stimulus of the loud strains of her accompanying band, and the girls, fired by the applause sink to the ground with quivering buttocks, — a sight to sting languid senses to love... » (6).

---

the Jews were called *recutiti*, from having this skin of the gland drawn back, which, not being done, the circumcision was not considered complete ; but Celsus makes me doubt this.

(5) Julius Caesar Scaliger, *Poetica*, book I.,p. 64 : « One of these infamous dances was the ῥίκνωμα, ῥίκνοῦσθαι, meaning wriggling the haunches and thighs, the *crissare* of the Romans. In Spain this abominable practice is still performed in public.

(6) Do not miss, reader, the motive of this dance ; with their buttocks wriggling the girls finally sunk to the ground, reclining on their backs, ready for the amorous contest. Different from this was the Lacedæmonian dance βίβασις, when the girls in their leaps touched their but-

Neque vero adspectu tantum fœminæ pulchræ nudæ mentula solet excitari, verum solæ etiam mentis imagines, præsertim nocturnæ, quis nescit? eam vim habent, ut seminis fiat jucunda profusio. Ipse Priapus ita resolvi passus est; Priap. *XLVIII:*

> *Quod partem madidam mei videtis,*
> *Per quam significor Priapus esse,*

---

solebant, ut nates pedibus ferirent. Aristophanes in Lysistrata, *v. 82 :*

Γυμνάδδομαί γε καὶ ποτὶ πυγὰν ἅλλομαι.

Pollux, IV, cap. 14 : Καὶ βίβασις δέ τι ἦν εἶδος Λακωνικῆς ὀρχήσεως, ἧς καὶ τὰ ἆθλα προυτίθετο, οὐ τοῖς παισὶ μόνον, ἀλλὰ καὶ ταῖς κόραις· ἔδει δὲ ἅλλεσθαι καὶ ψαύειν τοῖς ποσὶ πρὸς τὰς πυγὰς, καὶ ἀνηριθμεῖτο τὰ πηδήματα· ὅθεν ἐπὶ μιᾶς ἦν καὶ ἐπίγραμμα· χίλια πόκα βίβαντι.

Artificiosius etiam saltationis genus ἐκλάκτισμα, *quo calce oportebat humerum contingere. Pollux ibidem :* Τὰ δὲ ἐκλακτίσματα γυναικῶν ἦν ὀρχήματα, ἔδει δὲ ὑπὲρ τὸν ὦμον ἐκλακτίσαι.

Nec recentioribus id genus inauditum : J.-C. Scaliger, Poetices *libro I, p. 651 : « Nunc quoque Hispani calce occiput aliasque contingunt partes. »*

But it is not only by the sight of a beautiful naked female the member is excited; who does not know that it is also roused merely by images called up by the imagination, particularly in the night. And the power of such fancies is such as to provoke a pleasurable ejaculation of sperm. Priapus himself has experienced this. *Priapeia* XLVIII :

« You see this organ after which I am called by my name Priapus, is wet; this moisture is not dew, nor yet hoar-frost. It is the outcome

---

tocks with their heels. Aristophanes in the *Lysistrata*, 82 :

« Naked I dance, and beat my buttocks with my heels». Pollux, IV., ch. 24 : « As to the βίβασις, this was a Laconian dance. There were prizes competed for, not only amongst the young men, but also amongst the young girls; the essence of these dances was to jump and touch the buttocks with the heels. The jumps were counted and credited to the dancers. They rose to a thousand in the βίβασις. »

Yet more difficult was that kind of dance which was called ἐκλάκτισμα, in which the feet had to touch the shoulders. Pollux, *ibid.* : « The ἐκλακτίσματα were dances for women : they had to throw their feet higher than their shoulders. »

This kind of dance is not unknown in more modern times. J. C. Scaliger, *Poetica*, book I., p. 651 : « To this day the Spaniards touch the occiput and other parts of the body with their feet. »

Non ros est, mihi crede, nec pruina,
Sed quod sponte sua solet remitti,
Cum mens est pathicæ memor puellæ.

Famam quandam masturbando consecutus est Diogenes Cynicus, quem publicitus tradunt pudenda perfricantem dixisse : « Utinam pariter ventrem perfricare possem latrantem » (7) !

At cum aliena manu masturbatur, id fieri potest non solum ut delectetur qui patitur, sed et qui facit.

Ac digitis quidem uti pertinet ad artem meretriciam, ut languens fascinum provocetur. Potest autem fascinum languere propter ingravescentem ætatem aut fœminæ ; Martialis, VI., 23 :

Stare jubes nostrum semper tibi, Lesbia, penem ;
Crede mihi, non est mentula quod digitus.

---

(7) Diogenes Laertius, VI, 2, 46 : Ἐπ' ἀγορᾶς ποτε χειρουργῶν, εἶθε, ἔφη, καὶ τὴν κοιλίαν ἦν παρατρίψαντα μὴ πεινᾶν. Plutarchus, *De Stoicorum repugnantiis*, p. 1044 tomi secundi Operum : (Χρύσιππος) ἐπαινεῖ τὸν Διογένην τὸ αἰδοῖον ἀποτριβόμενον ἐν φανερῷ καὶ λέγοντα πρὸς τοὺς παρόντας, εἶθε καὶ τὸν λιμὸν οὕτως ἀποτρίψασθαι τῆς γαστρὸς ἠδυνάμην.

given of its own sweet will, on recalling memories of a complaisant maid. »

It is said that Diogenes, the cynic, was a masturbator; once caught in the act of handling his mentula, he said : « I wish to heaven I could in the same way satisfy my stomach with friction when it barks for food (7). »

When the masturbation is done by the loan of another person's hand, it is possible that the pleasure is participated on the part of the agent.

It forms part of the business of a courtezan to be clever with her fingers; a languid member may by their use be invigorated. The inertness of the virile member may be caused by the inconveniences of age, and this either on the part of the woman, as in Martial, VI., 23 :

« You require my penis, Lesbia, to be ever in erection for you; believe me a man's mem-

---

(7) Diogenes Laertius, VI, 2, 46 : « One day, whilst masturbating himself in the middle of the market he said : « I wish to heaven that I could prevent my stomach from « being hungry by rubbing it. » Plutarch, *De Stoicorum repugnantiis*, 1044, vol. II, of his works : « Chrysippus praised Diogenes for masturbating himself in public, and for saying to the bystanders : « Would to heaven « by rubbing my stomach in the same fashion, I could « satisfy my hunger. »

Tu licet et manibus, blandis et vocibus instes,
Contra te facies imperiosa tua est;

idem, XI, 30 :

Languida cum vetula tractare virilia dextra
Cœpisti, jugulor pollice, Phylli, tuo.

aut viri; Martialis, XI, 47 :

Jam nisi per somnum (8) *non arrigis, et tibi, Mœvi,*
Incipit et medios meiere verpa pedes.
Truditur et digitis pannucea mentula lassis,
Nec levat exstinctum solicitata caput (9).

---

(8) *Vide quantum diligentiæ præstiterint egregia Prisco-*
rum ingenia Naturæ perscrutandæ! quam ingenue sensa men-
tis exprimenda duxerint! Quotusquisque est, qui hunc versum
ponere ausus non veritus hodie fuisset, ne communi usui tri-
bueret, quod suæ forsan mentulæ solœcismus esset?

(9) *Similiter in Bassi, rumpere latus in comatis soliti*
languidius ad torum reversa excitanda laborabant digiti uxo-
ris. Martialis, XII, 99 :

Rumpis, Basse, latus, sed in comatis,
Uxoris tibi dote quos parasti.
Et sic ad dominam reversa languet

ber is not like a finger. True, you strive to excite me with hands and tender words, but your face is a stubborn fact and counteracts all your efforts. »

and again in the same author, XI., 30 :

« When you set your old hand the task of rousing my member, your thumb, my Phyllis, will but strangle me. »

or of the man, Martial, XI., 47 :

« Only in dreams you get stiff (8), Maevius, and your verge begins to make water right onto your own feet; in vain your wearied fingers ply your wrinkled member, — rouse it as you may, it will not raise its drooping head (9). »

---

(8) Mark with what minuteness the Ancients scrutinized nature; with what ingenuity they gave expression to all their sentiments! Who dares nowadays write such a verse describing as a natural thing what might be but a solecism of his mentula.

(9) Bassus, who was in the habit of taking his pleasures with young minions, longhaired and slim, set the hands of his wife to work to excite his mentula, when he came back to the conjugal couch fatigued and languid. Martial, XII., 99 :

« You tire yourself, oh Bassus, but with minions, paying them from the dowry of your wife; thus when you return to her side, that member bought at the price of many million sesterces, lies languid. In vain her ten-

Aristophanes, in Vespis, *v.* 735-38 :

Καὶ μὴν θρέψω γ᾽ αὐτὸν, παρέχων
Ὅσα πρεσβυτῃ ξύμφορα ·
Πόρνην, ἥτις τὸ πέος τρίψει
Καὶ τὴν ὀσφύν...

Ibidem, v. 1334, 35 :

... Σαπρὸν τὸ σχοινίον,
Ὅμως γε μέντοι τριβόμενον οὐκ ἄχθεται.

Sed placet etiam iis, qui sunt integra ætate, puellisque adhuc vivunt idonei, habere amicas, quarum manus in lecto non jaceant inertes, et inveniant digiti, quod agant in partibus illis, in quibus occulte spicula figit Amor. Id officii sibi non præstari questus est Martialis ab invida uxoris gravitate, XI, 105 :

Nec motu dignarus opus, nec voce juvare,
Nec digitis, tanquam thura merumque pares (10);

Multis mentula millibus redemta,
Sed nec vocibus excitata blandis.
Molli pollice nec rogata surgit.

(10) *Eandem lumborum duritiem fœminæ istæ Aristophaneæ, versu* 227 *Lysistratæ, viris maligne minantur :*
Κακῶς παρέξω, κοὐχι προσκινήσομαι.

Aristophanes in the *Wasps*, 735-38 :

« Yes, I will nurse him and get him all that lis wanted for an old man : beef broth to lap, soft wool, and a rug to keep him warm, and a courtezan to rub his member and his loins... »

The same author, *ibid.*, v. 1334, 35 :

« ..... The cable is rotted away, yet is it still fond of being rubbed. »

Nor is it unwelcome to men in the vigour of life, and who are fit to caress young girls, to have mistresses whose hands are not lazy in bed, and whose fingers know how to act in the dark regions where the arrow of love is hidden. Martial (XI., 105), complains about the unseemly gravity of his wife, which forbade her to render him that service :

« You will not help me on by movement or by word, not yet with your fingers, as though you were preparing the incense and the wine for sacrifice (10). »

---

der thumb tries to excite it, vain are her tender words, it will not stand. »

(10) The women of Aristophanes (*Lysistrata*, v. 227) threatened their husbands with a similar rigidity of body :

« Though you may have your way, I shall be crabbed and never move. »

Præstitit autem Penelope Ulyssi; Martialis eodem epigrammate:

> *Et, quamvis, Ithaco stertente, pudica, solebat*
> *Illic Penelope semper habere manum.*

Præstitit etiam, etsi frustra, Nasoni amica infelici ista nocte, qua ea pars, quam pessimam dicit sui, velut præmortua inimico numine jacuit, et puella, ne suæ possent intactam scire ministræ, dedecus hoc sumta dissimulavit aqua, Amor., *III,* VII, 73, 74:

> *Hanc etiam non est mea dedignata puella*
> *Molliter admota solicitare manu.*

Et Juvenali vis digitorum in Venere ob oculos versabatur, VI, 195 96 :

> *..... Quod enim non excitat inguen*
> *Vox blanda et nequam? digitos habet!*

Nec ea res incognita erat auctori Priapeii *LXXX :*

> *At non longa satis, non stat bene mentula crassa,*
> *Et quam si tractes, crescere posse putes.*

Penelopé, on the other hand, contented Ulysses well that way, as Martial has it in the same epigram :

« Chaste though she was, when the king of Ithaca lay snoring, Penelope liked to have her hand always on it. »

Ovid's mistress did him the same service, but all in vain one miserable night, when a hostile divinity seemed to have smitten to death that most pitiful part of him, to use his own expression, and the girl, in order that the servants might not think that she had remained untouched, pretended to make her ablutions all the same (*Amores*, III., vii., 73, 74) :

« My darling did not disdain even to put her hand to it and gently try to rouse it. »

This virtue of the fingers in procuring erection is alluded to by Juvenal (VI., 195, 96) :

« ..... How well a soft and libertine voice will erect your member; it is as good as fingers ! »

The author of the *Priapeia* was also well aware of to fact; LXXX. :

« My member is not very long nor very thick, — handle it, and you'll see it grow apace. »

nec Jano Dusæ, de quo ad hoc ipsum Priapeium,
Scioppius, qui est nasus hominis :

« *Dusa ad Petronium* DOMI DOCTUS *docet nos rem
istam crescere et grandire, si tractatrix accedat.*

*Inde intelliges, quid sit, quod tantopere, ut etiam-
num Turcis, ita veteribus et tractatores commenda-
verit et tractatrices, quibus articulos non sine arte
malacissandos, digitos leniter et per vices premendos
et ducendos, omnia deinceps membra teneris manibus,
quippe manicarum usu a sole defensis, demulcenda
porrigerent, Seneca,* Epistola 66 :

« *An potius optem, ut malacissandos articulos
exoletis meis porrigam? ut muliercula, aut aliquis
in mulierculam ex viro versus, digitulos meos du-
cat? Quidni ego feliciorem putem Mucium, qui sic
tractavit ignem, quasi illam manum tractatori præs-
titisset ?* »

Martialis, III, 82 :

And so was Janus Dousa, quoted by Scioppius à propos of this same *Priapeia,* cleverly scenting out the man's character :

« Dousa, commenting upon Petronius, informs us that he knows *by home experience* how this object grows in thickness and length when shampooed by a woman. »

You can estimate the importance of this function by the value set by the Ancients, as in our days by the Turks, upon shampooers, men and women, who are employed for manipulating the joints with artistic expertness, their fingers softly pressing and turning them, and their hands kept soft by the constant use of gloves, kneading tenderly all the limbs. Seneca, *Letter* LXVI. :

« Would I rather offer my limbs for shampooing to my superannuated mignons? or to some little woman, or some weakling man, more woman than man, to draw and crack my fingers ? Should I not rather envy yonder Mucius, who put his hand in the fire with the same equanimity as though he tendered it to a shampooer. »

Martial, III., 82 :

Percurrit agili corpus arte tractatix,
Manumque doctam spargit OMNIBUS *membris* (11).

Joannes Sarisberiensis in Policratico, *libro III,*
cap. 13, ex vetere aliquo scriptore. Clearcho forsan,
Lipsio judice :

« *Cum lascivientis divitis luxus libidini vota sua*
præcingit, recumbentis pedes calamistratus comatulus
excipit, et in aliorum conspectu pedes, et ne plus dicam,
teneris manibus tibias tractat. Chirothecatus enim
incessit diutius, ut manus soli subtractas emolliret,
ad divitis usum. Deinde licentia paulum procedente
totum corpus impudico tactu oberrans pruriginem
scalpit, quam fecit, et ignes Veneris languentibus in-
flammat. »

Huc referre etiam juvat, nescio quo aptius, id
schema coeundi, si quis alius, sed artis doctæ,
fœminæ officiosa manu utitur ad testiculos molliter

---

(11) *Nec minus doctam sparsit manum callidus ille aliptes*
apud Juvenalem, VI, 422, 23, qui... cristæ digitos impres-
sit,

Ac summum dominae femur exclamare coegit.

« A woman shampoos your body all over with nimble skill; her trained hand manipulates *all* your members(11). »

John of Salisbury states in his *Policraticus*, book III., ch. 13, after some ancient author, perhaps Clearchus, as Lipsius thinks :

« When a rich libertine turns in his luxurious ways to effeminacy, a youth with frizzly hair takes before all the world his feet while he is lying on his couch, and shampoos them and his legs, not to go further, with his delicate hands. That youth is always wearing gloves, so as to preserve them white and soft for the benefit of rich people. Then, using his hands more licentiously, he runs them over all the body with impudent touchings and ticklings, raising the desires and stirring the amatory flames of his employer. »

I may very well describe here, for I could not find a better place, a performance for which the friendly hand of a woman is in request, but of

---

(11) He had a hand of no less experience (Juvenal, VI., 422-23), that cunning shampooer who put his fingers to the lady's clitoris.

« And made his mistress's thigh resound beneath his hand high up. »

comprimendos natesque blande mulcendas, quo sche-
mate nihil suavius, nihil dulcius esse perhibent.
Hujusmodi coitum Octaviæ cum Roberto juvante
Manilia peractum mira ubertate, varietate, copia
dicendi pinxit inexhaustum Aloisiæ ingenium,
Colloq. VII, Octaviam ipsam loquentem ponens :

« *Dein duxit Manilia ad pugilatum, veste exuit,*
nudam collocat in lecto. Insilit Robertus. « *En*
mihi, » *inquit amplexans,* « *summum bonum, omne*
« *bonum!... Hoc ego tuo vectus curru, Octavia, ibo*
« *tenebricosum istud per iter* » (*pubem vellicabat*),
« *ibo ad gloriam.* » *Uterum, femina, pectus pererrabat*
inspectans curiose. Demum intumuit puero nervus :
« *Fave,* » *inquit,* « *fave, Venus mea!* » *Suavium de-*
dit. — « *Favebo,* » *inquam;* « *qualem me cupies,*
« *talem habebis.* — *O nugacem!* » *clamat advolans*
Manilia; « *facto opus est, non dicto. Volo utrique*
« *præstare operam, et ope mea voluptati vestræ accres-*
« *cere delicias novas. Belle arrigis, Roberte. Agedum,*
« *candidum hoc in Octaviæ pectus libidines et te effunde.* »

a woman that is an expert, which will gently
press your testicles and stroke your thighs ; it is
said that nothing can be pleasanter or more voluptuous. Aloysia Sigaea describes, with her
inexhaustible ingenuity, such a scene, executed
by Ottavia and Roberto, with the assistance of
Manilia ; the fullness, variety and richness of the
description, placed in the mouth of Ottavia, are
admirable :

« Manilia then conducted us to the trysting
place ; she undressed me, and placed me naked
on the couch. Roberto jumped on to the couch.
« Now », he said, « I shall enjoy the most supreme unalloyed bliss. Carried on your chariot,
Olympia, I shall take my way through this dark
thoroughfare (he was pinching my pubis the
while), I shall take my way to glory ». His
hands were straying over my belly, my thighs,
examining everything. His member was swelling.
« Permit me, my Venus ! » he said, giving me a
kiss. « Willingly », I answered, « you shall have
me in any way you like. » Manilia interposed,
« Why so much talk ! Do not talk but act ! I will
assist both of you, and add new delights to your
voluptuous sensations. You are in excellent trim,
Roberto ! Come, down with you upon Ottavia's
snowy bosom, and have your fill ! » Roberto

*Dicente Manilia supervolat Robertus : ballista ferit
uterum; at exerrantem et resilientem intercipit caudam
Manilia, officiosam insinuans manum. « Veni, fugi-
« tiva, tuum id in ergastulum Dionæum; huc te vo-
« cant, » dicebat, « quas dominæ debes operæ. » Post
impacta in pueri lumbos manu impellit : momento
voro puerum, absorbeo surgentem. Velat commoveri
me Manilia. « Tolle id femur lævum, Octavia, » inquit, « contende alterum. » Fit. « Tu, Roberte, leni
« et spissa concute amores tuos subagitatione. At tu,
« Octavia, osculare, nec move. » Fit. « Cum sentietis
« alter et alter, » adjicit, « e libidinis vena exsilire
« vobis prurientes salaciæ spumas, tu, Octavia, mitte
« suspirium; tu, Roberte, morsiunculis Octaviam
« pete. » Subagitat ille vegeta, sed molli et lenta concussione. Amplector, osculor, nec moveo... Sentio me
remitti, suspirium mitto. « Nunc, nunc, Roberte, » in-
geminat nutrix lena, « fave, fave Octaviæ. Rapidi tibi
« ferveant lumbi. » Ille urgere, permolere. Mox collum appetit dente, cutem carpsit; gemitum dedi. « Nunc,
nunc, » repetit Manilia, « crissanti fave Roberto suc-
« cussu; tolle lumbos, succute pernix. Bene est, alumna;
« non ita, puto, lumborum placuit flexibilitate et mo-
« bilitate Lais. » Cæpit colliquescere dulcis puer, et*

precipitates himself upon me, and his engine
strikes against my belly. Manilia's soft hand in-
tercepts the erring tool. « Come », she says,
« you vagrant, enter the lovely prison, and do
the task set to you by your mistress`. » With
her other hand she pushes the young man's back,
and I take him in, entirely in. Manilia tells me
not to move. « Raise your left thigh, Ottavia »,
she says, « and stretch out the other one. » I
obey. « You, Roberto, you now push gently and
quickly! As to you, Ottavia, kiss him but without moving! » We do so. She added. « When
you both feel the boiling foam running over,
you, Ottavia, give a sigh, and you, Roberto,
gently bite Ottavia's lips! » He then begins to
poke vigorously, but without haste or violence,
in and out; I press him on to me, kissing him
but not moving. I feel it coming. I sigh. « Now!
now, Roberto! » cries Manilia, « help Ottavia!
Work away! » He shakes me and pounds me.
Soon I feel a slight bite on my neck. I heave a
sigh. « And now, Ottavia », cries Manilia, « you
assist Roberto; move your buttocks briskly,
raise up your loins, quick! quick! Well done,
my child! « Laïs, herself I think, could not have
shown more flexibility nor agility! » The sweet
youth begins to ejaculate, and I feel my inside
inundated by the fiery spring of love. I moved

ego intimos amoris sentio mihi sinus liquido exundare incendio. Nec lateribus peperci, nec animæ. Celeriori nunquam itum cursu ad Veneris metam. Altera manu Manilia mulcebat mihi nates, altera Roberto. Apprehensa identidem summis digitis cadurda stringebat, comprimebat, et incubantis testiculos molli emulgens compressione exprimebat. Defecit puer, et refugit nutrix, plaudens manibus, acta fabula.

Venustas imagines Cleopatræ et Julii Cæsaris et Marci Antonii virilia molli manu tractantis spectare poteris in Monuments de la vie privée des douze Césars, *tabulis IV et XII ; Liviæ eodem modo gratificantis Augusto in* Monuments du culte secret des dames romaines, *tabula XVI, et Bacchæ Fauno, ibidem, tabula V. masturbantem proprie sic dictum cernes ibidem, tabula IV, puellamque opus Tiberii Othonem pædicantis officiosa manu juvantem in* Monuments de la vie privée des douze Césars, *tabula XLIV.*

Sed sit quoque, ut delectet libidinosos manu solicitare aliena virilia, quo nihil indignius tulit Martialis, XI, 23 :

Mollia quod nivei duro teris ore Galesi
  Basia quod nudo cum Ganymede jaces,

with body and soul. I never arrived more quickly at the acmé of voluptuousness. Manilia caressed with one hand my buttocks, and with the other hand Roberto's; at the same time she pressed with the points of her fingers the lips of my vulva and his testicles, which were close up. The youth swooned, and our nurse withdrew, and clapped her hands applauding! » (Dialogue VII.)

Plates IV. and XII., in the *Monuments de la vie privée des douze Césars*, show you Cleopatra titillating with a delicate hand the virile parts of Julius Cæsar and Mark Anthony, while in the *Monuments du culte secret des dames romaines;* plate XVI., represents Livia bestowing the same caresses on Augustus; plate V., a Bacchante doing it to a Faun ; plate IV., a masturbator — expressly so called. In plate XLIV. of the *Monuments de la vie privée des douze Césars*, again, is a picture of a girl helping Tiberius with her benevolent hand in pedicating Otho.

Again it sometimes happened that lewd men found pleasure in handling the genital parts of other men. Martial knew nothing more infamous (XI., 23) :

« That your coarse lips should receive the

Quis negat hoo nimium ? sed sit satis ; inguina saltem
    Parce fututrici solicitare manu.
Lævibus in pueris plus hæc quam mentula peccat,
    Et faciunt digiti præcipitantque virum.
Inde tragus, celeresque pili, mirandaque matri
    Barba, nec in clara balnea luce placent.
Divisit Natura mares; pars una puellis,
    Una viris genita est : utere parta tua.

Vult, mentulam datam esse maribus, qua uteren-
tur puellæ, culo, quo viri. Utatur ergo culo potius,
quam mentula Galesi. Eodem spectat illud ejus-
dem, XI, 7 ɪ, in Tuccam, pueros vendere volentem .

Ah facinus ! tunica patet inguen utrinque levata,
    Inspiciturque tua mentula facta manu.

Nefas esse ait, pueros, quos mollis Tucca ad libidi-
dinem aluisset, jam venum exponi, eorumque men-
tulas exspectatas et manu tractatrice domini cres-

delicate kisses of fair-skinned Galesus, that you should sleep with your naked Ganymede — is not this enough yet? It ought to be! Cease at any rate to touch the privates with provocative hand. With boys of tender age this does more harm than the member does. The fingers hasten virility and make them prematurely men. Hence the goaty smell, the quick-coming hairs, and the beard that make the mother wonder, while they no more love to bathe in the open light of day. Nature has divided boys; one part is reserved for girls, the other for men. Keep to the part which is yours. »

Martial means to say that the member was given to boys for the purpose of using it with girls, while their buttocks were for the service of men, and that this pedicon should therefore make use of Galesus' buttocks rather than play with his mentula. Of similar import is also *Epigram* XI., 71, directed against Tucca, who wanted to sell young lads :

« Oh, for shame! there is the groin with the tunic all open, and a member appears fashioned and trained by your hand. »

He says it is a crime to put up for sale those lads whom the infamous Tucca has trained for

cere jussas emtoribus tradi inspiciendas. Similiter Eumolpus fricuit nervum Encolpio, capite 140 Petronii :

« *Hæc locutus* » (*Encolpius loquitur*) « *sustuli tunicam, Eumolpoque me totum adprobavi. At ille primo exhorruit, deinde, ut plurimum crederet, utraque manu Deorum beneficia* » (*nervum rigentem*) « *tractat.* »

Restat, ne quid promissi transiisse videamur, ut dicamus de cognata libidine, quæ per cetera cava corporis recipitur. Paucis defungemur. Ac de mammis quidem Aloisiani sermonis pulegio uti liceat :

« *Per Veneris concham utramque !* » (*Octaviæ verba sunt, Colloq. VII*) « *pudore suffundi me sentio. Pudet meminisse, id mammarum mearum interstitium viam factum esse ad Venerem... Pergula est in ædibus nostris, quæ amœnissimas, et, nosti, hortorum spectat areas omni florum consitas genere. In ea spatiabamur ego et Caviceus. Amblexabatur, suaviabatur, labella appete-*

debauchery, and to let the buyers see their fully
formed mentulas, accustomed to rise under the
provocative hand of the master. Eumolpus subjects in the same way the verge of Encolpus
to friction, Petronius, chap. 140 :

« After these words » (Encolpus speaking)
« I lifted up my tunic, and exhibited myself in
ull vigour to Eumolpus. He first recoiled as it
horror-struck; but, like a man who expected
worse, he got hold with his two hands of God's
gift, viz. : the verge in erection. »

I have still to treat, in order to complete my
task, of other pleasures belonging to this category, meaning those which can be taken in any
interstice of the body. A few words will suffice.
Taking in the first place the breasts, I have recourse to Aloysia Sigaea :

« By the twin conch-shells of Venus! » (Dialogue VII., Ottavia speaking) « I am ashamed.
I blush to think, that the valley between my
breasts has done duty as the avenue of Venus.
You know there is in our house a gallery giving
on the garden-parterres, which are full of all
sorts of flowers. There Caviceo and I were pro-
menading; he embraced me, kissed me, bit my
lips. . . . . He put his left hand in my bosom.

bat, morsiunculis... Demittit in sinum lævam : « Mo-
lior, « inquit, « improbum quid. Depone vestes, corcu-
« lum. » Quid facerem ? depono. Defigit in nudum
pectus oculos. « Video, » subjicit, « tuas inter papillas
« dormientem Venerem. Vis excitem ? » Projicit dicens
suspinam in torum, mentulam fervidam, flammescen-
tem (arrigebat præclarissime) interserit mammis. Qui
me huic eximerem impotentiæ ? Ferenda erant ultro ci-
troque omnia... Molli manuum nisu utramque conjun-
gens urgebat mammam, quo scilicet lata minus via
procurreret sibi nervus ad voluptatem hanc novam. Quid
plura ? Conspersit attonitam insolenti ridiculæ Veneris
imagine, calentique perfudit rore : perfecte. »

De aliis autem corporis cavis, alis, puto, femi-
nibus, poplitibus, natibus (natibus, inquam, non
ano), nominasse suffecerit Heliogabalum ; Lampri-
dius, cap. 5 :

« Quis enim ferre posset principem per cuncta cava
corporis libidinem recipientem, quum ne belluam qui-
dem talem quisquam ferat ? »

et Commodum ; idem Lampridius, cap. 5 :

« I am after trying a naughty trick, » he said. « Undress, my darling l' » What was I to do? I undressed. His eyes rested on my bare bosom. « I see, » he said, « Venus sleeping between your breasts. May I waken her! » While he was talking he had thrown me on my back in the bed, and being in a noble state of erection, slides his hot, burning member between my breasts. How could I escape his blind passion? I had no choice but to bear it. His hands softly pressed my breasts together, so as to narrow the space, in which his mentula had to travel towards a new experience. Why make a long story? Stupified as I was at this vain ridiculous imitation of Love, he inundated me with a burning libation : he had his will. »

As to other interstices of the body, e. g. the armpits, between the thighs, the calves, the buttocks (mind, I do not say the anus, but between the buttocks), be it enough to mention Heliogabalus; Lampridius, ch. 5 :

« How put up with a Prince who sought for pleasure in every cavity of the body, when you would not suffer a brute beast to do as much? »

Also Commodus, according to the same Lampridius, ch. 5 :

« *Nec irruentium in se juvenum carebat infamia,
omni parte corporis atque ore in sexum utrumque* »
(fellando et cunnum lingendo) « *pollutus.* »

*Licebitne huc referre etiam libidinem eorum, qui
aut mortuas fœminas, aut statuas polluunt? neque
enim verus coitus est, ubi non sunt duo coeuntes. In
Ægypto quidem Herodotus refert, II, 89, depren-
sum quendam esse, recenti cadavere muliebri libidi-
nose abutentem :*

Λαμφθῆναι γὰρ τινά φασί μισγόμενον νεκρῷ προ-
σφάτῳ γυναικὸς, κατειπεῖν δὲ τὸν ὁμότεχνον.

*Qua de causa lege sancitum esse, ne fœminæ nobiles
et formosæ prius traderentur conditoribus, quam
triduo aut quatriduo post obitum. Et quis nescit,
quid Veneri Praxitelis Gnidi acciderit ? Plinius,
Hist. nat., XXXVI, 5 :*

« *Ferunt amore captum quendam, cum delituisset*

« He gave himself up to the infamous assaults of young men, polluting every part of his body, even his mouth, and that with either sex, » — i. e. he was both a *fellator* and a *cunnilingue*.

Is it necessary to speak here of the debauchery of those who assault the corpses of females, or statues? This is not real coitus, there being no two parties to the act. Nevertheless, according to Herodotus (II., 89), in Egypt a man was taken in the act of abusing the corpse of a woman just dead :

« It is said that a man was surprised in the act of working in the fresh corpse of a woman, and denounced by a fellow-workman. »

In consequence of this a law was promulgated forbidding the corpses of noble and beautiful women to be given into the hands of the embalmer until three or four days after their decease. And who does not know the story of the Venus of Cnidos, the work of Praxiteles, as related by Pliny, *Historia Naturalis*, XXXVI., ch. 5 :

« It is related how a certain youth fell in love with her, and having hidden himself one night

noctu, simulacro cohæsisse, ejusque cupiditatis esse in-dicem maculam. »

*Consimilis error tauri, qui, narrante **Valerio Maximo VIII**, II, « ad amorem et concubitum æneæ vaccæ Syracusis nimiæ similitudinis irritamento compulsus est ».*

in the temple, cohabited with the statue, leaving a stain as the mark of the gratification of his passion upon the marble. »

There is a similarity in this with the mistake made by a bull which, according to Valerius Maximus, VIII., ch. II., fell in love witch a bronze cow, and copulated with the same at Syracuse, being deceived by the perfection of the resemblance.

CAPUT V

DE CUNNILINGIS

ATIS multa de opere Venereo, quod per mentulam editur ; sequitur ut quo modo Veneri sacra fieri etiam possint sine men-tula videamus. Fieri possunt aut lingua aut clito-ride. Erit igitur dicendum primum de cunnilingis, deinde tribadibus.

Quemadmodum fellatoris fellatricisve est lingere virilia, ita cunnilingi, muliebria. Cunnilingus peragit opus linguam arrigendo in cunnum. Rem portentosam dilucide satis et perspicue expedivit Martialis, XI, 62 :

> *Lingua maritus, mœchus, ore Mannejus,*
> *Summœnianis inquinatior buccis,*

CHAPTER V

CUNNILINGUES·

W E have now said enough about the work of Venus performed by the virile member; it remains for us to explain how a sacrifice may be offered to Venus without one. This may be done by means of the tongue or of the clitoris. We have accordingly first to treat of the cunnilingues, those who lick women's privates and then of the tribads.

As it is the office of the *fellator* or *fellatrix* to suck the virile parts, so is it the business of cunnilingues to lick the female. The cunnilingue operates by introducing his tongue into the vulva. Martial (XI., 62) has described this monstrous act very clearly :

« Manneius, husband with his tongue, adulterer

Quem cum fenestra vidit a Suburana
Obscena nudum lena, fornicem clausit,
Mediumque mavult basiare quam summum ;
Modo qui per omnes viscerum tubos ibat,
Et voce certa consciaque dicebat,
Puer an puella matris esset in ventre
(Gaudete, cunni, vestra namque res acta est),
Arrigere linguam non potest fututricem.
Nam dum tumenti mersus hæret in vulva,
Et vagientes intus audit infantes,
Partem gulosam solvit indecens morbus,
Nec purus esse nunc potest, nec impurus.

Quæ linguæ fututrici Manneji, eadem accidit paralysis linguæ Zoili; Martialis, XI, 86 :

Sidere percussa est subito tibi, Zoile, lingua,
Dum lingis. Certe Zoile, nunc futuis.

Cunnilingus erat Bæticus, Cybeles ille sacerdos eviratus, in quem Martialis, III, 81 :

Quid cum fœmineo tibi, Bætice Galle, barathro ?
Hæc debet medios lambere lingua viros.

with his mouth, — more foul than the mouths
of harlots of the Summoenium; whom seeing,
as he stood naked, from a window, the filthy
procuress closed her brothel; whose middle she
had rather kiss than his head. He who of old
knew all the channels of the inwards, and could
declare with a sure and certain voice, whether
'twas a boy or girl in the mother's belly (be
glad, all vulvas, for your part is done), can no
longer erect his fornicating tongue. For lo! as
he lurks with tongue plunged in a swelling
vulva and hears the babes wailing inside their
mother, a shocking malady paralyses his greedy
mouth, — and now he can no more be either
clean or unclean. »

By the same paralysis of the tongue Zoilus
was struck; Martial, XI., 86 :

« An evil star, Zoilus, has struck your tongue
of a sudden, even while licking a vulva. Of a surety, Zoilus, you must now use your member. »

Bæticus, the castrated priest of Cybelé, against
whom Martial has direct *Epigram* III., 81, was a
cunnilingue :

« What have you, Bæticus, a priest of Cybelé,
to do with the female pit ? That tongue of yours
by rights should lick men's middles. For what

Abscissa est quare Samia tibi mentula testa,
  Si tibi tam gratus, Bætice, cunnus erat ?
Castrandum caput est : nam sis licet inguine Gallus,
  Sacra tamen Cybeles decipis : ore vir es.

*Absque hoc loco minime dubio esset, hæreres in
ambiguitate epigrammatis 77 ejusdem libri :*

*Nescio quod stomachi vitium secretius esse
  Suspicor. Ut quid enim, Bætice, σαπροφαγεῖς ?*

*Nam putrida edere posset æque dici fellator et
cunnilingus, sicut in loco Galeni, quem supra
protulimus, uterque vocatur κοπροφάγος. Sed Bæ-
tico res est cum fœmineo baratro ; lingit igitur,
non fellat. Contra ea lingua mœcha Tongilio-
nis (III, 84) fellat, non lingit : nam lingua cun
nilingi mœchum imitatur, quia init ; fellatoris
autem mœcham, quia initur. Sæpe in his nugis
minus accurate versati sunt viri docti. Cunnilingus erat alter ex geminis fratribus, diversa
inguina lingentibus, apud Bilbilitanum nostrum,
III, 88. Priapi ille vicinus, « per quem misella*

was your member amputated with a Samian potsherd, if the woman's parts had so much charm for you? You must have your *head* castrated; true, you are a castrated Gallus in your secret parts, but none the less you violate the rites of Cybelé; you are a man so far as concerns your *mouth*. »

If this passage were in the least doubtful, *Epigram* 77 of the same book might offer difficulties, not othervise :

« Some latent sickness of your stomach I suspect. Why, I wonder, Bæticus, are you an *eater of filth*? »

In fact the *fellator* as well as the *cunnilingue* may be called eaters of filth, as in the passage of Galen quoted previously, where both of them are called *coprophagi* (dung-eaters). Bæticus however has only to do with the female pit; he is a *cunnilingue*, not a *fellator*. On the contrary, the lewd tongue of Tongilion (III., 84) is that of a *fellator*, not of a *cunnilingue*; for the tongue of a *cunnilingue* plays the part of a lover, being active; while that of a *fellator* acts the part of a prostitute, remaining passive. Sometimes for want of attention the most learned commentators are at fault in elucidating these playful pas-

Landace vix posse jurat ambulare præ fossis, » di-
serte dicitur cunnilingus Priapeio *LXXVIII, quem*
Scioppius quidem nihil vult fuisse nisi fututorem;
sed quid est quod discedamus a significatione verbi
et propria et perpetua? an fossæ? quasi cunnus ut
strenua fututione, ita non posset etiam lingua cun-
nilingi nimio plus lacessitus laxior reddi! Nec Ti-
berius Cæsar in secessu Capreensi cunnilingorum
voluptatem sprevisse videtur : cujus enim alius tur-
pitudinis notam omini isti omnium notarum inus-
tam putemus in Atellanico exodio, teste Suetonio in
Tiberio, *capite* 45, *assensu maximo excepto* :

    Hircum vetulum capreis naturam ligurrire...

nisi cunnilingi : Spectare vis Tiberium ligurrien-
tem? Suggerent tibi imaginem Monuments de la
vie privée des douze Césars, *tabula XXII.*

sages. One of the twin brothers, who in our friend of Bilbilis (the poet Martial) (III., 88), are licking different groins, was a *cunnilingue*. The neighbour of Priapus, « by whose fault it is unhappy Landacé swears she can hardly walk, she is so enlarged, » is covertly designated as a *cunnilingue* (*Priapeia* LXXVIII.); yet for all that Scioppius maintains he was only a fornicator; but why should we turn away from the proper sense of the word on account of the enlarged aperture? As if the vulva could not be enlarged, or relaxed by the tongue of the *cunnilingue* equally as much as by active cohabitation!

Tiberius Cæsar in his retreat at Capri does not seem to have disdained the voluptuousness of the *cunnilingue*. Blasted by every other kind of abomination, of what else is the Emperor accused in the Atellanian song, mentioned by Suetonius (*Tiberius*, ch. 45), which was so much applauded :

« An old buck licking the vulvas of goats. »

but this of being a *cunnilingue*? Do you want to see Tiberius employed at his licking? Plate XXII., in *Monuments de la vie privée des douze Césars*, represents it.

Sextus quoque Clodius iste, cui Cicero sæpius oris exprobrat impuritatem ac linguæ spurcitiem, Pro domo, *c.* 10 *et* 18, Pro Cœlio, *cap.* 32, *cunnos videtur linxisse. Hinc aculeus ille Ciceronis,* Pro domo, *c.* 18 :

« *Sexte noster, bona venia, quoniam jam dialecticus es, et hoc quoque liguris.* »

Certe, si linxit, Clodiam, Publii Clodii sororem (12), *Quinti Metelli uxorem, amicam omnium, linxit :* Cicero, Pro domo, *c.* 31 :

« *Quære hoc ex Sexto Clodio, jube adesse ; latitat omnino. Sed si requiri jusseris, invenient hominem apud sororem tuam* » (*Publium Clodium alloquitur*) « *occultantem se capite demisso.* »

Advertas quæso « *caput demissum* » : *mox recurret in Græcis.*

---

(12) *Sed non sororem tantum fuisse Clodiam Publio Clodio, apparet ex festivo joco Ciceronis,* Pro Cœlio, *cap.* 13 : « *Nisi intercederent mihi inimicitiæ cum istius mulieris viro !... fratrem volui dicere ; semper hic erro !* »

So also Sextus Clodius, whom Cicero frequently reproaches with the impurity of his mouth and the obscenity of his tongue (*Pro Domo*, chs. 10 and 18; *Pro Cœlio*, ch. 32), appears to us to have been a *cunnilingue*. Hence, that hit of Cicero, in his *Pro domo*, ch. 18 :

« My good Sextus, allow me to tell you, as you are already a good dialectician, you are also a good licker. »

Certainly if he was one, he was bound to lick Clodia, the sister of Publius Clodius (12), the wife of Metellus, the woman that was intimate with all the world. Cicero, *Pro domo*, ch. 31 :

« Ask Sextus Clodius as to this, cite him to appear; he is keeping quite in the background. But if you will have him looked for, he will be found near your sister (he is addressing Publius Clodius), lurking somewhere with his head low. »

Pay attention, pray, to this expression : « the

---

(12) But Clodia was something more tham a sister for Publius Clodius; this would appear from the spirited pleasantry of Cicero, *Pro Cœlio*, ch. 13 :

« If there had not arisen differences between me and that lady's husband,... brother, I would say; I always make that mistake. »

Neque enim Græci ab lingendi libidine abhorrue-
runt. Huc pertinent epigrammata LXXIV, LXXV
et LXXVI, in Analectis Brunckii, *tomo III,*
p. 165 :

LXXIV

Τὴν φωνὴν ἐνοπὴν σε λέγειν ἐδίδαξεν Ὅμηρος,
  Τὴν γλῶσσαν δ' ἐνοπὴν τίς σ' ἐδίδαξεν ἔχειν;

Ludit ignotus poeta in ambiguitate verbi ἐνοπή, *pro-*
bum linguæ usum subjicientis, si ab ἔπω *dico, im-*
probum, si ab ὀπή *foramen fluxisse statuas.*

LXXV

Αλφειοῦ στόμα φεῦγε · φιλεῖ κόλπους Ἀρεθούσης,
  Πρηνὴς ἐμπίπτων ἁλμυρὸν ἐς πέλαγος.

Et hoc epigrammate aucupatur poeta incognitus
ambiguitatem verborum στόμα, κόλπους, πρηνὴς *et*
ἁλμυρὸν πέλαγος, *quæ cum ad Alpheum, Arcadiæ*
fluvium, et Arethusam, Syracusanum fontem, re-
ferri possunt, tum ad os demissum cunnilingi, mersi

head low, » it will soon re-appear, when we speak of the Greeks.

The Greeks, in fact, felt no repugnance to the pleasure in question. *Epigrams* LXXIV., LXXV., and LXXVI., in the *Analecta* of Brunck, vol. III., p. 165, allude to this :

LXXIV.

« Homer taught you to call voice ἐνοπή; but who taught you to have the tongue ἐνοπή (in a slit)? »

The unknown poet plays upon the ambiguity of the word ἐνοπή, which is used with respect to the tongue in an honest sense, when derived from ἔπω, I speak, but as a vile usage when derived from ὀπή, a slit.

LXXV.

« Avoid Alpheus' mouth, he loves Arethusa's bosom, plunging head-first into the salty sea. »

In this epigram also the poet draws upon the ambiguity of the words mouth, bosom (bay), head-first, salt sea. which may refer to the river Alpheus in Arcadia and to Arethusa, a spring near Syracuse. but also to the mouth of a *cunnilingue*,

hærentis in vulva pathicæ, id quidem non sine cogitatione quadam adjuncta, de qua post paulo monemus.

LXXVI

Χείλων καὶ Λείχων ἴσα γράμματα · ἐς τί δὲ τοῦτο;
Λείχει καὶ Χείλων, κἂν ἴσα, κἂν ἄνισα.

Lusus in Chilonem cunnilingum. Hunc ait jure quodam suo lingere, qui vel nomine iisdem literis constante præ se ferat lingentem, et lingentem quidem tum labra oris, ut labris lingentis similia, tum cunni, ut dissimilia.

Ejusdem argumenti videtur esse Meleagri distichon in Phavorinum, ab Huschkio in Analectis criticis, *p.* 245, *editum :*

Εἰ βινεῖ Φαβορῖνος ἀπιστεῖς · μηκέτ' ἀπίστει.
Αὐτός μοι βινεῖν εἶπ' ἑτέῳ στόματι.

Uti Martialis, non minus quam Horatius felicissime sæpe audax, III, 84, narrat posuit de eo, qui lingua abutitur ad fellandum, six Meleager εἶπε *de eo, qui ad lingendum.*

that goes and plunges in the vulva of a woman;
not to mention yet another idea connected with
this, to which we shall return presently.

LXXVI.

« Cheilon and λείχων have the same letters,
and why? It is because Cheilon will lick things
that are like and unlike. »

This mockery is addressed to the cunnilingue
Cheilon. The epigram tells him that he has some-
how a right of licking, as his name, composed of the same letters as λείχων, announces at
once the licker, whether he may lick the lips of
a mouth, similar to his own, or those of a vulva,
which are very dissimilar.

The distich of Meleager upon Phavorinus,
published by Huschkius in his *Analecta critica*
(p. 245), seems to bear upon the same subject :

« You doubt whether Phavorinus does the
thing. Doubt no more ; he told me himself he
did, — *with his own mouth.* »

As Martial uses often very happily the word
narrat (III., 84), when he speaks of the abuse of
the tongue for *fellation*, and Horace the same,
so Meleager says εἶπε (he told) of the man, who
employs his for licking the vulva.

Aliquanto obscurius est illud Ammiani in Analectis *Brunkii, tomo H, p.* 386 :

Οὐχ ὅτι τὸν κάλαμον λείχεις, διὰ τοῦτό σε μισῶ,
     Ἀλλ᾽ ὅτι τοῦτο ποιεῖς καὶ δίχα τοῦ καλάμου,

*quo scholiastæ quidem auctor carpere videtur homi-
nem ignavum et calamum scriptorium lingendo, ut
alii ungues rodendo, tempus terentem, ita tamen,
ut subinde etiam lingat sine calamo, cunnum. Sed
possis etiam, atque haud scio an rectius, tactum
existimare hominem, qui linguam exserendo obscenum gestum cunnilingi præferre consuexerit, vel
sine cunno, in vita communi.*

*Eo insolentiæ processit monstrosa libido, ut, in-
credibile dictu, ne siccos quidem cunnos lingere contenti, madidos etiam aut menstruo aut alio humore
lingerent. Aristophanes in* Equitibus, *v.* 1280-
1283, *de Ariphrade :*

Οὐδὲ παμπόνηρος. ἀλλὰ καὶ προσεξεύρηκέ τι·
Τὴν γὰρ αὐτοῦ γλῶτταν αἰσχραῖς ἡδοναῖς λυμαίνεται,
Ἐν κασαυρίοισι λείχων τὴν ἀπόπτυστον δρόσον,
Καὶ μολύνων τὴν ὑπήνην, καὶ κυκῶν τὰς ἐσχάρας.

The following epigram of Ammanius from the *Analecta* of Brunck, vol. II., p. 386, is somewhat more obscure :

« It is not because you suck your pen that I dislike you ; ' tis because you do so, — without a pen. »

The scholiast imagined the author wanted to upbraid a lazy pupil who passed his time sucking his pen, as do others biting their nails, and to scold him at the same time for sucking without a pen, meaning for being a *cunnilingue.* But it may be taken to refer, and I think with more reason, to a man who is in the habit of putting out his tongue for the obscene act of the *cunnilingue*, and who is so accustomed to it that he puts it out in the ordinary intercourse of life.

This monstrous practice was pushed to such lengths that, it is almost incredible, there were people who, not content to lick vulvas which were dry, did it when tney were humid with the menses or any other secretion. Aristophanes says of Ariphrades in the *Knights*, v. 1280-83 :

« He is not only lewd ; his fancy goes astray ; he pollutes his tongue with shameful pleasures, licking up in his orgies the abominable dew, foulngi his beard and tormenting women's privates. »

Lacessere vulvas, lambere rorem, inquinare barbam, ecce tibi homo vel madidos lingere cunnos nequaquam dedignans! ecce ejusmodi barba, qualem deprensus habebat Ravola Juvenalis, XI, 4, « dum Rhodopes uda terit inguina barba!» quanquam, ne quid diffitear, uda barba Ravolæ possit etiam de udo pectine fututoris accipi. Ex hoc loco Aristophanis, satis et fere plus quam satis est perspicuo, intelligimus, illud quoque γλωττοποιεῖν, *de eodem Ariphrade in* Vespis, *v.* 1274, *ambigue positum, cunnilingum magis quam fellatorem notare :*

. . . .
Εἶτ᾽ Ἀριφράδην πολύ τι δυμοσσφικώτατον,
Ὄντινά ποτ᾽ ὤμοσε μαθόντα παρὰ μηδενὸς
Ἀλλ᾽ ἀπὸ σοφῆς φύσεως αὐτόματον ἐκμαθεῖν
Γλωττοποιεῖν, εἰς τὰ πορνεῖ᾽ εἰσιόνθ᾽ ἑκάστοτε.

Rursus id occurrit in Pace, *v.* 885, *quo, sublata omni ambiguitate, humorem muliebrem pro jusculo haurit :*

Τόν ζωμὸν αὐτῆς προσπεσών ἐκλάψεται.

Tormenting women's privates, licking the dews, staining the beard, there you have the man whom humid vulvas do not disgust! there you have a beard like that of the Ravola of Juvenal (IX., 4), « when he with beard all moist was rubbing against the groin of Rhodopé ». However, not to be dogmatic, it may be admitted that by Ravola's moist beard may have been intended merely the wet hair of a fornicator's pubis. From the above passage of Aristophanes we may deduce surely enough that the expression « working with the tongue, » which he also uses, rather ambiguously, with respect to the same Ariphrades, applies to a *cunnilingue* rather than to a *fellator*, *Wasps*, 1847-77 :

« Then Ariphrades, the best endowed of all, of whom his father said once, he never had a teacher, but prompted by nature, of his own free will, learned how to work his tongue, visiting every brothel! »

The same personage re-appears in the *Peace*, 885, where he is described without any circumlocution as imbibing the feminine secretion by way of a sauce :

« And throwing himself on her he will drink up all her juice. »

*Quid? nec in hoc genere Romanorum defuit imitato-
rum pecus.* Senecæ debet famam Mamercus Scaurus, De beneficiis, *IV*, 31 :

« *Quid tu, cum Mamercum Scaurum consulem fa-
ceres, ignorabas, ancillarum suarum menstruum ore
illum hiante exceptare? numquid enim ipse dissimula-
bat? numquid purus videri volebat?*

Item Natalis; Epistola 87 :

« *Nuper Natalis tam improbæ linguæ quam impu-
ræ, in cuius ore in cui fœminæ purgabantur...* »

Fuit ergo uterque καταμηνίου πίνων, *quo nomine Ga-
lenum appellare cunnilingos capite tertio vidimus.*

*Jam plane apparet, quid sibi velit Nicarchi in
Demonactem epigramma, tomo III, pag.* 334, Ana-
lectorum *Brunkii* :

Δημώναξ, μὴ πάντα κάτω βλέπε, μηδὲ χαρίζου
   Τῇ γλώσσῃ. δεινὴν χοῖρος ἄκανθαν ἔχει.
Καὶ συξῆς ἡμῖν, ἐν Φοινίκῃ δὲ καθεύδεις,
   Κοὺκ ὢν ἐκ Σεμέλης μηροτραφὴς γέγονας.

The Greeks however had in this kind of voluptuousness a host of imitators amongst the Romans. Mamercus Scaurus is known to us through Seneca (*De Beneficiis*, IV., ch. 31), in this light :

« Did you not know when you appointed Mamercus Scaurus as Consul, that he swallowed the menses of his servant girls by the mouthful? Did he make a secret of it? Did he pretend to be a blameless man? »

Similarly with Natalis, letter LXXXVII. :

« Lately Natalis, that man with a tongue as malicious as it is impure, in whose mouth women used to eject their monthly purgation. . . »

Both of them were consequently « imbibers of menses, » an appellation which, as we have seen in chapter III, Galen applies to *cunnilingues*.

Now too we can clearly understand the meaning of Nicarchus' epigram against Demonax, vol. III., p. 334 of Brunck's *Analecta* :

« Do not, Demonax, regard all things with downcast head, and do not spoil your tongue with over-gratification ; the sow has threatening bristles. You live amongst us, but you sleep in Phœnicia, and though no son of Semelé, you are thigh-reared. »

Adspicit nihil sursum, Materni pathici illius Mar-
tialei 1, 97, instar : gratificatur linguæ arrigendi
cupidæ; cunnus sit pilosus an depilatus flocci fa-
cit; interdiu videtur in Græcia vivere, sed dormire
tamen in Phœnicia, quippe qui cruore menstruo
Phœnicei sive rutili, quis nescit? coloris (13) *ore*

---

(13) *Non multo secus lusisse Gonsalvum Cordubensem
Aloisia narrat,* Dialog. VII : « *Erat et* liguritor, *provectæ,
nam aliud mihi nihil persuaserint, ætatis vitio. Inserviebat
vero libidini formosa viginti annorum puella. Cum vellet
mediam lambere, se velle dicebat in* Liguriam. » *Poterat
eandem rem, adjuncta tamen cogitatione cunni humentis, tecte
etiam significare ita, ut diceret, velle se ire in Phœniciam,
aut in mare Rubrum, aut in mare Salsum; nunc demum
penitus intelliges* ἁλμυρὸν πέλαγος *quo incidit Alpheus in
epigrammate* Anthologiæ. *Nec multum abludunt salgama
Ausoniana, de quibus paulo mox; nec* « *putri cepæ alece na-
tantes* », *quas vorat Bæticus Martialæus, III, 77. Num
mirum foret, si, ut fellatores ab imitando Phœniceorum morem, ita et cunnilingos a natando in mari quodam Phœnicei
coloris dixissent* φοινιχίζειν? *Ecce autem dixerunt! Hesychius :* Σκύλαξ σχῆμα ἀφροδισιακὸν, ὡς τὸ τῶν φοινικιζόν-
των. *Quid enim? schemate quodam Veneris utuntur* φοινιχι-

He never looks up, exactly like the Cinede
Maternus of Martial, I., 97 ; he gratifies his tongue, which likes erection ; whether the vulva be
covered with hair or depilated, he does not mind;
during the day he lives in Greece, but sleeps in
Phœnicia, because he stains his mouth with the
monthly flux, which is, as every one knows, of
the Phœnician dye, viz., purplish red (13); like

(13) Gonzalvo of Cordova, according to Aloysia Sigaea
(Dialogue VII.), made similar jokes : « He also, I am
sure, in spite of his age, was a great tongue-player (lin-
guist). A pretty girl of some twenty years had to amuse
him. When he wanted to put his tongue to her *juste
milieu*, he declared he wanted to go to Liguria. » He
could play with words upon the same matter, always
implying the idea of a humid vulva, saying that he was
going to Phœnicia, or to the Red Sea, or to the Salt
Lake; you now understand what is meant by the Salt
Lake or Salt Sea, into which Alpheus threw himself according to the epigram in the *Anthology*. Nearly related
to this are the salgamas of Ausonius, of which we shall
speak shortly, and the « onions swimming in putrid
brine, » which the Bæticus of Martial (III., 77) devours.
As it was said of the fellators that they « Phœnicized »,
because they followed the example set by the Phœnicians,
so probably the same word was applied tho the *cunnilingues* as loving to swim in a certain sea of Phœnician
red; and, in fact, this was the case. Hesychius : « Scylax, an erotic posture, like that assumed by Phœnici-
zers. » The Phœnicians assumed a certain posture, called
Scylax, or *the dog*. There could be nothing better for de-

exceptato inquinetur; ceu Bacchus alter femori-
bus (14) *alitur. Quid multa? nonne oculis tuis*
vides cunnilingum inguinebus hærentem, patran-
tem ?

Nec inferiore ætate omnino defecit mira cunnilin-
gorum libido. Castoris quidem et Euni nomina im-
mortalitati haud invidendæ ita tradidit Ausonii in-
genium epigrammatis 120,123,125,126,127,128.

Epigramma 120 :

Lambere cum vellet mediorum membra virorum
Castor (15), *nec posset vulgus habere domi,*

ζόντες, *quod dicitur* σκύλαξ, *canis. Quis est, qui ullo putet*
sensu commodo caninum dici posse aut irrumandi schema,
aut fellandi, et non oppido sentiat, nihil potuisse aptius ex-
cogitari ad cunnilingorum libidinem significandam canini
schematis nomine, cum canes inde a legatorum infamia cun-
nilingos esse satis superque constet ?

(14) *Ovidius,* Metamorph., *III, 308-312 :*

> ... *Corpus mortale tumultus*
> *Non tulit aethereos, donisque jugalibus arsit.*
> *Imperfectus adhuc infans genitricis ab alvo*
> *Eripitur, patrioque tener, si credere dignum,*
> *Insuitur femori, maternaque tempora complet.*

(15) *Fortassean hic Castor idem est, qui tradente Auso-*
nio in Professoribus Burdegalensibus, XXII, 7, *librum*
Cunctis de Regibus ambiguis *ediderat.*

another Bacchus, he draws his nourishment
from a thigh (14). This scarcely needs an expla-
nation. You can picture the *cunnilingue*, with his
mouth glued between the thighs, at work.

This strange depravity was still in favour in
succeeding centuries. Ausonius, in his *Epigrams*
CXX., CXXIII., CXXV., CXXVI., CXXVII.,
and CXXVIII., has bequeathed a very unenvia-
ble notoriety to the names of Castor and of Eunus :

Epigram CXX. :

« Castor (15) wanted to lick the middle part of

---

scribing the depraved action of a *cunnilingue* than this
canine epithet with regard to the posture taken for irrumating or fellation ; dogs are *cunnilingues* as anybody
knows, and have been so ever since that abominable
adventure which their ambassadors met with (allusion
to Phædrus' fable).

(14) Ovid, *Metamorphoses*, III., 308-12 :
« ... Mortal woman could not survive the celestial fire ;
she was consumed by her spouse's favours. The infant
but half formed is torn from the mother's womb, and, if
we may believe the tale, is sown still immature in the
father's thigh, and there cómpletes the period of gesta-
tion. »

(15) This Castor is perhaps the same who, according
to the statement of Ausonius (Epigram *in Professoribus
Burdegalensibus*, XXII., 7) had published a book with the
title *Cunctis de Regibus ambiguis*.

Repperit, id nullum fellator perderet inguen :
Uxoris cœpit lingere membra suæ.

Epigramma 123 *cum lemmate :* In Eunum liguritorem :

Eune, quid affectas vendentem Phyllida odores ?
Diceris hanc mediam lambere, non molere.
Perspice, ne mercis fallant te nomina, vel ne
Aere Seplasiæ decipiare, cave,
Dum costum cysthumque putas communis odoris,
Et nardum ac sardes esse sapore pari.
Diversa infelix et lambit et olfacit Eunus :
Dissimilem olfactum naris et oris habet.

Vide, jocatur, ne Phyllidis unguentariæ tuæ Ca-
puensis (Seplasia enim platea Capuæ, in qua un-
guenta vendebantur), diversa dona communis putes
odoris esse saporisve. Neque enim costum (16) *olet*
ut cysthus (17), *neque nardus* (18) *sapit ut sardæ,*

_____

(16) *Plinius,* Hist. nat., *XII,* 12 : « *Radix costi gustu*
fervens, odore eximio, frutice alias inutili. »
(17) *Cysthus est Græcum* κύσθος, *pudendum muliebre.*

men, but he could not persuade any one to go with him; however the *fellator* did not miss his treat; he went and licked his own wife's privates. »

Epigram CXXIII, entitled *In Eunum liguritorem*. — On Eunus the Licker :

« Eunus, why do you pay court to Phyllis, the perfume seller? Men say your tongue knows her parts, but not your member! Mind you make no mistakes in the names of her scents and perfumes, and that Seplasia's atmosphere play you no tricks; think not costus and cysthus have the same odour, — that sardines and nard exhale the same savour. Poor Eunus! the things that he tastes and smells are very different ; his mouth and his nose have tastes widely dissmilar! »

He says mockingly ; think not the sundry wares in the shop of Phyllis your little perfume seller of Capua (Seplasia is in fact a street of the town of Capua, where perfumes were sold), are all of the same odour and savour. The costus (16) does not smell like the cysthus (17), the

---

(16) Pliny, *Nat. Hist.*, XII, ch. 12 : « The Costus-root has a burning taste and an exquisite smell; its berries are otherwise useless. »

(17) The Cysthus, Greek κύσθος, is the private parts

*pisciculorum genus sale condiri solitum, quo salsa-
mento nihil aliud significare vult Ausonius, quam
quod mari salso auctor epigrammatis Græci, quam
quod ipse mox salgamis, humorem madidi cunni.
Euno tamen quid lambat, quid olfaciat, minus
pensi est ; diversa lambit et olfacit. Unguenta bene
olentia olfacit, muliebria male olentia lambit. Aliam
igitur sequitur legem nasus, aliam os hominis.*

   Epigramma 125, in eundem Eunum :

   *Salgama non hoc sunt quod balsama ; cedite odores :
   Nec male olere mihi, nec bene olere placet.*

*Ludit circa eundem fere sensum. Balsama dicit
odores quos Phyllis vendit, salgama, quos axhalat
concha. Salgama proprie sunt radices herbæque
sale conditæ in hibernum usum, quarum non est*

Aristophanes in Lysistrata, *v.* 1160 : 'Εγὼ δὲ κύσθον γ'
οὐδέπω καλλίονα (ὅπωπα).
   (18) *Plinius*, Hist. nat., *XII, 12 : « De folio nardi plura
dici par est, ut principali in unguentis. »*

nard (18) has a different flavour from the sardines, — a sort of little fish preserved in salt. By
this salty condiment Ausonius means to imply
precisely the same as the author of the Greek
epigram signifies, when he speaks of the Salt
Sea, and which he himself has called salgama,
meaning the secretion of the humid vulva. But
Eunus shows no discrimination between what
he licks and what he smells; the two have nothing in common. He inhales perfumes which
smell beautifully, and licks the vulva, which
smells abominably. His nose obeys one law, his
tongue another.

Epigram CXXV, directed against the same
Eunus :

« The salgamas are no balmy odours; give
place, all other perfumes. I would rather not
smell at all, either good or bad ».

Here again the poet plays with the words. The
perfumes which Phyllis sells he calls balms, and

---

of a woman. Aristophanes, *Lysistrata*, v. 1160 : « And
a more beautiful cysthus I never saw. »

(18) Pliny *Nat. Hist.*, XII, ch. 12 : « The leaves of
the nard must be considered more minutely, for they are
a principal ingredient in perfumery ».

*omnium narium odor. Quod addit, nec male nec
bene olere sibi placere, expressit illud Martialis,
VI, 55, in Coracinum, qui et ipse erat cunnilingus :*

Malo quam bene olere nil olere.

Epigramma 126 :

Λαὶς, Ἔρως *et* Ἴτυς, Χείρων *et* Ἔρως Ἴτυς *alter :*
  Nomina si scribis, prima elementa adime.
Ut faciam ve rbum, quod tu facis, Eune magister,
  Dicere me Latium non decet opprobrium.

Primæ literæ sex nominum Græcorum efficiunt
λείχει, *lingit. Similis lusus poetæ phallici carmine*
LXVII, *in verbo* pædicare :

PEnelopes *prima* DIdonis *prima sequatur,*
  Et primam CAni *syllaba prima* REmi :
Quodque fit ex illis, mihi tu deprensus in horto
  Fur dabis : hac pœnà culpa luenda tua est.

salgamas those which her vulva exhales. Properly speaking, salgamas are roots and greens, which are preserved in salt for winter use, and the odour of which is not pleasant to every one's nose. His saying that he would rather smell nothing at all than smell something bad is borrowed from Martial VI, epigr. 55, against Coracinus, who was a *cunnilingue* :

« Rather than smell bad scents I would not smell at all ».

Epigram CXXVI :

« Lais, Eros and Itys, Chiron and Eros, Itys once again, — if you write the names, and take the initial letters, they make a word, and that word is what you do, Eunus. What that word is and means, decency lets me not say in plain Latin. »

The initial letters of the six Greek names form the word λείχει, he licks. The phallic poet (*Priapeia* LXVII) plays in the same way upon the word *paedicare* (to pedicate) :

« Take the first syllable of *P*enelopé; add to it the first of *D*ido; then to the first of *C*anis append the first of *R*emus : what they make, I will do to you, thief, if I catch you in my garden. This is the penalty your crime will meet. »

Ludit vero etiam Ausonius in ambiguitate faciendi
verbum. *Non vult ipse facere, id est ponere, verbum
lingere, ut Latinis auribus turpius : Eunus tamen
illud verbum non dubitat facere, id est agendo
exprimere.*

Epigramma 127 :

> *Eune, quod uxoris gravidæ putria inguina lambis
> Festinas glossas non natis tradere natis.*

*Videris, inquit, jam natis tuis nondum natis glos-
sam (linguam intelligit) arrigendo, munus tuum
grammaticum ita præstare, ut glossas (obscuriorum
verborum nunc intelligit interpretationem)* (19) *iis*

---

(19) *Quintilianus*, Instit. orat., *I, 1 : « Potest interpretationem linguæ secretioris, quas Græci* γλώσσας *vocant,
ediscere.* » *Alcuinus in* Grammatica, *pag. 2086 operis Putschiani : « Glossa est unius verbi vel nominis interpretatio,
ut : catus, id est, doctus. » Qua occasione data liceat biblio-
thecæ aulicæ Coburgensis præfecto adnotare, esse in ea egregium operis Putschiani exemplar cum adscriptis iu margine
libri quarti et quinti Prisciani variis lectionibus manu Joannis Schefferi, qui anno 1679 Upsaliæ obiit, ita præfantis :
« Quæ in hoc libro ad Prisciani lib. IV et V ad marginem
notata reperiuntur, facta sunt ad exemplar manuscripti per-*

Ausonius plays on the words *doing* and *making*. The initials of the Greek words *make* a word he cannot say in Latin, — it is too indecent. Yet Eunus has no hesitation in *doing* it, — putting it in action.

Epigram CXXVII :

« Eunus, when you lick the groins of your wife, she being with child ; 'tis because you would be betimes in *teaching the tongues* to your babes yet unborn. »

You seem, he says, to send out your tongue to meet your unborn children, and fulfilling your duty as a Grammarian, to teach them lessons of tongue, and the interpretation of obscure terms (19). The Manneius of Martial,

---

(19) « Quintilian, *Instit. orat.*, I, ch. 1 : « He can learn the interpretation of the occult languages, what the Greeks call « γλώσσας ». Alcuin, *Grammatica*, p. 2086, in Putschius' *Collection* : « *Glossa* is the interpretation of a verb or a noun; e. g. *catus* is the same thing as *doctus* ». On this occasion it may be permitted to the Director of the Court-Library at Coburg to state, that this library contains a remarkable copy of the collection of Putschius, by the hand of John Scheffer, who died at Upsala in 1679, beginning thus : « The notes to be found in this volume, on the margin of books IV and V, of Priscian, have been made after a very ancient and most beautifully written manuscript, in which a number of traces of primitive Lat-

tradere festines. Sic gravidas etiam linxit Manne-
jus Martialeus, quem supra in partem vocavimus.

Epigramma 128 *cum lemmate :* Ad eundem
pædagogum liguritorem :

> *Eunus Syriscus inguinum liguritor,*
> *Opicus magister (sic eum docet Phillis),*
> *Muliebre membrum quadriangulum cernit :*
> *Triquetro coactu Delta literam ducit ;*
> *De valle femorum altrinsecus pares rugas*
> *Mediumque, fissi rima qua patet, callem*
> *Psi dicit esse ; nam trifissilis forma est.*
> *Cui ipse linguam cum dedit suam, Labda est,*
> *Veramque in illis esse Phi notam sentit,*
> *Quid imperite Rho putas ibi scriptum,*
> *Ubi locari Iota convenit longum ?*
> *Miselle doctor, Tau tibi sit obsceno,*
> *Tuumque nomem Theta sectilis signet.*

Opicum dicit liguritorem, quia frequentissimus
fuit, Festo teste, Oscis sive Opicis, spurcarum libi-

---

antiqui atque optimæ notæ, in quo multa pristinæ Romanæ
scripturæ vestigia reperiebantur, e.g. dirivare pro derivare,
peneultimus et antepeneultimus pro penultimus et antepenultimus, Oratius pro Horatius, et plura alia. »

whom we have spoken of above, was also in the habit of licking pregnant women's privates.

Epigram CXXVIII., entitled *On the same Eunus, the Learned Licker* :

« Eunus, the little Syrian pedagogue, licker of privates, Opican doctor ('tis Phyllis he owes his knowedge to), beholds the feminine engine in fourfold different fashions : Opening it triangularly, he makes it the letter Delta (Δ.); seeing the pair of folds side by side along the valley of the thighs with the line in the middle where the slit of the vagina opens, he says it is a Psi (Ψ.); in fact its shape is triple-cloven then. Then when he has put his tongue in, it is a Lambda (Λ.), and he makes out therein the true design of a Phi (Φ.) Why! ignoramus, do you think you see a Rho (P.) written, where merely a long Iota (I.) should be put? Contemptible doctor, foul pedant, you deserve the Tau (T.) yourself; the crossed Theta (Θ.) should by rights be put against your name. »

Ausonius calls Eunus an Opican, because these filthy practices were, according to Festus, most

---

in orthography are found, as for instance : *dirivare* for *derivare, peneultimus* and *antepeneultimus* for *penultimus* and *antepenultimus, Oratius* for *Horatius,* etc. ».

*dinum usus. Jocatur deinde, vel potius Eunum
proponit jocantem in forma pudendi muliebris* (20)
*quod illi ait videri aut quadriangulum, aut trian-
gulum, ut respondeat figuræ Græci* Δ, *quemadmodum et Aristophanes cunnum* δέλτα *dixit in* Lysistrata, *v.* 151 : Δέλτα παρατετιλμέναι ; *aut simile* Ψ

---

(20) *Quoniam forte sermo incidit de forma pudendi muliebris, non erit instituti nostri ratione alienum, semel sub-
jicere illius membri nomina Latina, maximam partem ex
Aloisiæ thesauris collecta :* ager, annulus, arvum, caverna,
clitorium, concha, cunnus, cymba, cysthus, fossa, hortus, in-
terfemineum, navis, ostium, porcus, porta, rima, saltus,
scrobs, sulcus, vagina, virginal, vulva. *Et quid impedit,
quo minus adjiciamus virilium quoque nomina ? En hæc illa
sunt :* arma ventris, catapulta, cauda, caulis, colei, columna,
contus, coleata cuspis, fascinum, hasta, inguen, machæra,
mentula, mutinus, muto, nervus, nota virilis, palus, peculia, penis, pessulus, phallus, pilum, pomum, pyramis, sca-
pus, sceptrum, seminale membrum, subula, taurus, telum,
tormentum, trabs, thyrsus, vasa, vasculum, vena, veretrum,
verpa, verpus, virga, vomer. *Sed plus satis!*

common among the Osci or Opici. He then in-
dulges in a series of jests, or rather represents
Eunus as doing so, on the shape of the female
organ (20). He says it seems to him either qua-
drangular, or triangular, in the latter case corresponding to the Greek Δ (similarly Aristophanes called it a Delta, — « their delta plucked clean of hair », *Lysistrata*, 151), and also
likens it to the letter Ψ, owing to the folds which

---

(20) As we are on the subject of the shape of the female organ, it will not be amiss to enumerate in this
place all tne various names by which it was known in
Latin; the greater part of them we have gathered from
the treasure-house of Aloysia Sigaea : « The field, the
ring, the furrow, the cavern, the clitoris, the couch-shell,
the cunnus, the little boat, the cysthus, the pit, the garden,
the between-thighs, the barque, the swine, the wicket,
the slit, the precipice, the hole, the trench, the sheath,
the virginal, the vulva. And what should hinder us from
giving at the same time the names of the virile member :
The armature of the belly, the catapult, the tail, the stem,
the parcel, the column, the pole, the lance with balls,
the amulet, the pike, the groin, the hanger, the mentula,
the mutinus, the muto, the nerve, the virile sign, the
stake, the peculia, the penis, the stopper, the phallus, the
javelin, the tree, the obelisk, the shaft, the spectre, the
seminal member, the awl, the bull, the dart, the balista,
the beam, the thyrsus, the vessel, the little vessel, the
vein, the private, the verpa and verpus, the verge, the
ploughshare. Here you have more than enough.

literæ, ita quidem, ut rugæ, vulvam ab utraque (21)
parte cingentes, labra sint cunni, medius callis,
qua patet rima fissi, sit os vulvæ, forma autem tri-
fissilis Ψ *literæ, quam in* Technopægnio, *versu*
140, *tricornigeram furcam vocat, repræsentet spe-*
ciem rimæ per lineam mediam, labrorum per
brachia utrinsecus annexa. Addit, Labdam esse
Eunum, cum lingat, a prima litera verbi λείχειν,
neque eum posse, quin in partibus istis hærens veram
linguæ fututricis notam Φ *esse sentiat. Quæ omnia*
luce ipsa clariora nescio cur obscura esse questus sit
eruditissimus Elias Vinetus. Nec ita multo plus
laboravi in eo quod subjungit Ausonius de Rho et
Iota literis. Si quidem lectio sana est, id mihi velle
videtur: Non est, Eune, quod hastam tuam pa-
trantem similem esse prædices P *literæ Græcorum,*
coleatæ cuspidis speciem præ se ferenti, qui non alia
hasta utaris ad Venerem, quam lingua, cujus for-

---

(21) *Nam* altrinsecus *Ausonio est idem quod* utrinsecus,
ab utraque parte. Sic Lactantius, De Opificio Dei, *cap. 8 :*
« *Quarum* » (aurium) « *duplicitas incredibile est quantam*
pulchritudinem præ se ferat, quod tum pars utraque simili-
tudine ornata est, tum ut venientes altrinsecus voces facilius
colligantur. »

surround the vulva on either side (21), and form
the outer lips, the lane in the middle being
the opening of the vulva, and so together form
the trifid letter Ψ; in the *Technopaegnium*, 140,
he calls it a three-pronged fork, the slit being the
middle and the lips the outer prongs. Then he
says that Eunus is a Lambda when he is licking,
on account of the first letter of the word λείχειν.
All this is clear enough. and I do not understand how the very learned Vinet can complain
of its obscurity. Neither has it given me much
trouble to make out what Ausonius means by
the letters Rho and Iota. The solution seems to
me to be as follows : « Do not tell us, Eunus,
that your pike in action resembles the letter P of
the Greeks, a letter which evidently looks like a
lance with balls; in your amorous diversions
you use no other lance than your tongue, which,
as you will not deny, looks more like a javelin

---

(21) *Altrinsecus*, in Ausonius, is equivalent to *utrinsecus*, meaning, from either side. Lactantius employs
that word in *De Opificio Dei*, ch. 8 : « It is incredible
how the fact of their being double (the ears) adds to their
beauty, as much on account of the symmetry thus produced, as because the sounds which arise on all sides,
can more easily be received on both sides (altrinsecus).»

*mam ipse non negabis magis convenire cuspidi non
coleatæ, qualis est figura Iota literæ : nempe me non
fallis, scientem, velle te videri non tam cunnilingum, quam fututorem, ut Gargilius ille, de quo
Martialis, III, 96 :*

> *Lingis, non futuis meam puellam,*
> *Et garris quasi mœchus et fututor !*

*Postremum imprecatur homini crucem per Tau,
mortem per Theta. Ac de hoc quidem res certa :
constat enim* Θ *literam in Græcorum judiciis notam
fuisse condemnationis, a prima litera vocabuli*
θάνατος *ductam* (22). *De illo autem utique est du-
bitationi locus. Nam te latere nolo, in libris et
scriptis et excusis pro Tau dari* ४, *quod licet præeunte magno Josepho Scaligero haud absurde accipi
possit de laquei collum obstringentis figura, hoc
tamen mihi aliquid scrupuli injicit, quod litera
composita, minor, per compendium dubiæ antiquitatis scripta, in serie literarum simplicium, majo-
rum, plene scriptarum, locum minus aptum occu-*

---

(22) *Persius, VI, 13 :*

> *Et potis es nigrum vitio praefigere Theta.*

Videsis etiam Martialem, VII, 36.

without balls, something like the letter Iota;
you cannot deceive me, who well know that
you would rather be taken for a fornicator than
for a *cunnilingue,* like that Gargilius, of whom
Martial, III, 96, says :

« You do not enter, only lick my mistress;
yet you boast yourself adulterer and copulator! »

Lastly and finally by the Tau he threatens his
man with the gallows, and by the Theta with
death. Of this there can be little doubt; it is a
proved fact that the letter Theta, the initial of the
word θάνατος, signified with the Greeks condem-
nation to death (22). With regard to Tau, there is
room for doubt; instead of Tau some of the copies of Ausonius give ȣ, and although this sign
may, according to Scaliger, very well signify the
rope for hanging, the difficulty I feel is this, that
a composite letter, a small letter, an abbreviation
of doubtful antiquity, thus placed amongst simple, capital, unabbreviated letters seems to come
in very inappropriately. It may be that Ausonius
originally wrote ταυ; then τ having been left out
by an inadvertence of the copyist, the αυ might

---

(22) Persius, VI, 13 : « And you may mark the crime
with a black Theta. » See also Martial, VII, 36.

*pare videtur. Quare haud scio an Ausonii manus
dederit* ταυ, *unde, litera prima alicujus librarii
mendo neglecta, facile nasci potuit* αυ, *deinde* ου.
Crucis certe signum Tau esse, neminem fugit. Tertullianus, Adversus Marcionem, III, 22 : « *Ipsa
est enim litera Græcorum Tau ; nostra autem T,
species crucis.* »

   *Ut irrumare, ita, et multo etiam magis, cunnum
lingere in seniores potissimum* (23) *cadere videtur,
quibus mentula stare negat. Aloisia (Colloq. VII) :*
« *Erat et* » (*Gonsalvus Cordubensis*) « *liguritor,
provectæ, nam aliud mihi nihil persuaserint, ætatis
vitio.* » *Martialis, XI, 48 :*

   Cur lingit cunnum Blatara ? ne futuat.

Idem, VI, 26 :

   Arrigere desit posse Sotades : lingit.

Idem XII, 88 :

   *Triginta tibi sunt pueri totidemque puellæ ;
   Una est, nec surgit mentula : quid facies ?*

---

   (23) *Potissimum inquam : nam placuisse interdum et junioribus lingere quos molere potuissent cunnos, per singularem quandam lasciviæ impotentiam, cognoscimus ex Martialeo XI, 86 :*

   *Sidere percussa est subito tibi, Zoile, lingua.
   Dum lingis : certe, Zoile, nunc futuis.*

easily have been turned into ου. The Tau, as the reader will see at once, represents a gallows. Tertullian, *Adversus Marcionem* : « This letter Tau of the Greeks is with us the T, a sort of cross ».

As was the case with irrumation, so with even more reason the licking of women's privates was particularly adopted by old men, whose tool will not raise its head (23). Aloysia Sigaea, Dialogue VII, says : « He (Gonzalvo of Cordova), was likewise a mighty *cunnilingue* by reason of his great age ».

Martial XI, 48 :

« Why does Blatara lick? because he cannot manage otherwise ».

The same author, VI, 26 :

« Lotades has lost the power of stiffening; so licks ».

And again, XII, 88 :

« Thirty young boys you have at command,

---

(23) I say it was adopted by them particularly; that there were also young men, who by a singular depravity licked the vulvas they might have entered legitimately, Martial tells us, XI, 86 :

« An evil star, Zoilus, has struck your tongue of a sudden, even while licking a vulva. Of a surety, Zoilus, you must now use your member. »

nempe linget, ut Linus apud eundem, XI, 25 :

> Illa salax nimium, nec paucis nota puellis,
>> Stare Lino desit mentula : lingua cave !

Fortasse et linxit Sextillus ; Martialis, II, 28 :

> Rideto multum, qui te, Sextille, cinædum
>> Dixerit, et digitum porrigito medium (24).
> Sed nec pædico es, nec tu, Sextille, fututor,
>> Calda Vetustillæ nec tibi bucca placet.

---

(24) *Cum digitus medius porrectus, reliquis incurvatis, tentam repræsentet mentulam cum coleis suis, factum est, ut medium digitum hoc modo ostenderent (Græci uno verbo dixerunt* σκιμαλίζειν) *cinædis, sive pelliciendis, sive irridendis. Martialis, I, 93 : « Sæpe mihi queritur Cestus tangi se digito, Mamuriane, tuo », atque etiam aliis, quos vellent despicatui habere : idem, VI, 70 :*

     Ostendit digitum sed impudicum.

(medicis, Martianus semper bene valens). Tulit et infamis nomen miser ille digitus ; Persius sine ulla obscena cogitatione adjuncta, II, 33 : « Avia puerum infami digito expiat. »

and as many girls ; yet you have only one member, and that will not rise. What then will you do » ?

Lick, no doubt, as we are told Linus did, in Epig. XI, 25 :

« This too frisky mentula, Linus, so well known to girls in plenty, will longer stand ; so mind your tongue ».

Sextillus (Martial II, 28), was in all probability also a *cunnilingue* :

« Have your laugh at those, Sextillus, that call you cinede, and show them your middle finger (24). You are not, Sextillus, a pedicon nor

---

(24) When the middle-finger is pointing, the other fingers are turned inside, representing thus a mentula with its accessories ; for which reason it was thus pointedly shown to Cinedes (the Greeks expressed this in a single word : σκιμαλίζειν), either by way of invitation or to tease them. Martial, I, 93 : « Cestus has often complained to me, Mamurianus, that you tease him with your finger. » It was also pointed at people held in contempt. The same author, VI, 70 :

« He points with the finger and that the impudent finger » (that is Martianus, who is never ill, does to the doctors). Thence this unlucky finger had the epithet « infamous. » Persius says without any obscene afterthought, II, 33 : « The grandmother cleanses the babe with the infamous (middle) finger. »

Ex istis nihil es, fateor, Sextille : quid ergo es ?
Nescio; sed tu scis, res superesse duas.

Duæ res supererant Sextillo, fellare et lingere, ut
qui nec fututor, nec cinædus, nec pædico, nec irru-
mator esset. Utram prætulerit, non liquet.

Eadem causa lingendi est eunuchis(25) *quæ*
senioribus non amplius pene potentibns. Gregorius
Nazianzenus in Epitaphio Basilii magni:

---

(25) *Eunuchos tamen, quibus testiculi tantum aut excisi*
sunt, aut collisi, non penis resectus, neutiquam deficit libido :
futuere etiam possunt, idque eo securius, quod nihil generant.
Res bene nota erat matronis Romanis. Martialis, VI, 67 :

> *Cur tantum eunuchos habeat tua Gellia, quaeris.*
> *Pannice. Vult futui Gellia, non parere.*

Juvenalis, VI, 365-67 :

> *Sunt quas eunuchi imbelles, ac mollia semper*
> *Oscula delectent, et desperatio barbae,*
> *Et quod abortivo non est opus...*

Hieronymus in Vita Hilarionis : « *Procurator calamistra-*
tus, et in longam et securam libidinem factus spado. . » Ut
certior esset libido, testiculos non prius exsecandos callidæ cu-
rabant, quam penis in justam magnitudinem crevisset, ve-

yet a fornicator, nor does Vetustilla's burning mouth tempt you. — You are none of these, I allow, Sextillus; then what are you ? I know not, but remember ! there are two sorts yet. »

Two sorts are still left for Sextillus, to suck the virile member and to lick the vulva, while he is neither a fornicator, nor a cinede, nor a pedicon, nor an irrumator. Which did he choose to be ? This we are not told. Eunuchs, just as impotent as aged men, adopt the practice for the same reason (25). Gregory Nazianzen says in his funeral sermon on Basil the Great :

---

(25) Nevertheless, Eunuchs who have been deprived of their testicles, but not of their mentula, are by no means wanting in lubricity; they can do the business without any danger for a woman, inasmuch as they cannot generate children. The Roman matrons were well aware of the fact; Martial, VI., 67 :

« You ask me, Pannicus, why Gallia keeps so many Eunuchs; she loves to be enjoyed, but wants no children. »

Juvenal, VI, 365-67 :

« There are women who like feeble eunuchs, and kisses that are ever harmless, and the absence, nay! the impossibility, of a beard, for they need use no abortive. »

St. Jerome, in the *Life of Hilarion* : « A steward with curled locks, castrated for the sake of longer pleasure and perfect safety... » To make more sure of their enjoyment, experienced dames did not allow the testicles of their Eunuchs to be cut off until the member had at-

Τοὺς ἐκ τῆς γυναικωνίτιδος, τοὺς ἐν γυναιξὶν ἄνδρας, ἐν ἀνδράσι γυναῖκας, τοὺς τοῦτο μόνον ἀνδρικοὺς τὴν ἀσέβειαν, οἵ τὸ φυσικῶς ἀσελγαίνειν οὐκ ἔχοντες, ᾧ δύνανται μόνον, τῇ γλώττῃ πορνεύουσιν.

Male cunnilingis olebat os, unde basiationes cunnilingorum æque vitabantur ac fellatorum. Martialis, XII, 87 :

> *Pædiconibus os olere dicis.*

---

rentes, id si ante diem fieret, ne pusillus exiguusque jaceret. Spadones poscunt bene mutoniatos, qui possint vel Priapum provocare, vel exoletorum podices discerpere. His futui cupiunt, partus securæ. Juvenalis, VI, 367-377 :

.. Illa voluptas
Summa tamen, quod jam calida matura juventa
Inguina traduntur medicis, jam pectine nigro.
Ergo exspectatos ac jussos crescere primum
Testiculos, postquam coeperunt esse bilibres,
Tonsoris damno tantum rapit Heliodorus.
Conspicuus longe cunctisque notabilis intrat
Balnea, nec dubie custodem vitis et horti
Provocat a domina factus spado. Dormiat ille
Cum domina, sed tu tam durum, Posthume, jamque
Tondendum eunucho Bromium committere noli.

« They of the gynaeceum, those men, who amongst women are men, and amongst men women : who have nothing virile about them but their impiety; those that cannot give them-selves up to voluptuousness in the natural way, have recourse to their tongue as their only alter-native. »

The *cunnilingues* exhaled an evil smell from the mouth, and their kisses were as much shunn-ed as those of *fellators*. Martial, XII., 87 :

« You say the mouths of pedicons smell badly; if

---

tained full proportions, apprehensive that it might remain puny and inactive if the operation were made earlier. They wanted their Eunuchs well furnished, capable of challenging Priapus himself. By such they liked to be worked, being sure of not becoming enceinte. Juvenal, VI , 367-77 :

« With those however is love's pleasure most exquisite, whose testicles, when they are lusty and fully matured, are delivered to the surgeons, the pubis being already black with hair. The organs are spared till they are full and ready; then at last, when they have reached two pounds in weight, Heliodorus cuts them, to the preju-dice of the barber. The observed of all observers, stared at by all, see him enter the baths and challenge the god of vineyard and garden, castrated thus by his lady's or-der. He may sleep now with his mistress; still beware, Posthumus, how you trust him with your Bromius, now fully developed and ready for the razor. »

Hoc si sic, ut ais, Fabulle, verum est,
Quid tu credis olere cunnilingis ?

Idem, XI, 59 :

Te vicinia tota, te pilosus
Hircoso premit osculo colonus,
Fellatorque recensque cunnilingus.

Hirci videntur et cunnilingi et fellatores propter
oris fœtorem dici Catullo, XXXVII, 3, 4, 5 :

Solis putatis esse mentulas vobis,
Solis licere quidquid est puellarum
Confutuere, et putare ceteros hircos ?

Cave putes, hircos vocari hoc loco capros castratos,
contra perpetuum loquendi usum, hircos jubentem
capros esse integros. Redit sententia eodem, via autem diversa. Putatis, inquit, solis esse penes vobis
legitimos ad futuendum ; ceteros oris hircino fœtore
prodere cunnilingorum fellatorumve olidam spurcitiem, atque illa ipsa spurca libidine inertiam in-
guinum effœtasque vires, per quas nihil possint, nisi
aut fellare aut lingere, more solito eorum, qui arrigere dedidicerint ? Nunc plenius intelliges aculeum
illum Atellanicum in Tiberium Cæsarem · « Hircum vetulum capreis naturam ligurrire. »

this is true, Fabullus, as you say, tell me! what think you of the breath of *cunnilingues*? »

And the same, XII., 59 :

«The neighbours kiss you every one, from the bearded cowherd, whose kisses have flavour of the he-goat, down to the *fellator* and the *cunnilingue* fresh from his business. »

Cunnilingues and *fellators* are compared to he-goats by Catullus (XXXVII.), on account of their fetid breath :

« Think you you alone have members, that you alone are entitled to satisfy women, and may consider all other men he-goats? »

Do not suppose for a moment that Catullus is speaking here of castrated he-goats, which would be against the sense of the word, one invariably used to designate entire he-goats. The sense is the same, but got at in another way. He says : « Do you believe that you alone have members fit to do the girls' business? that all the others betray by their goatish breath their vile trade as *cunnilingues* or *fellators*, and consequently the inertness of their mentulas, their feebleness, their inability for erection? You will better appreciate the sting of the Atellane

Malebant fututores haberi quam cunnilingi, pri-
mum ne deterrerent basiatores : Martialis, VII, 94 :

Centum occurrere malo cunnilingis;

Suetonius, De illustribus Grammaticis, *c.* 23 :

« *Sed maxime flagrabat* » *(Remmius Palæmon)*
« *libidinibus in mulieres, usque ad infamiam oris,*
dictoque non infaceto notatum ferunt cujusdam, qui,
cum in turba osculum sibi ingerentem, quanquam re-
fugiens, devitare non posset : « Vis tu, ·, inquit, « ma-
« *gister, quoties festinantem aliquem vides, abligurire?* »

vel convivas : Aristophanes in Equitibus, *v.* 1285,
86, *de Ariphrade:*

῎Οστις οὖν τοιοῦτον ἄνδρα μὴ σφόδρα βδελύττεται,
Οὔτε ποτ᾽ ἐκ ταυτοῦ μεθ᾽ ἡμῶν πίεται ποτηρίου.

deinde vero etiam ne lumbos exhaustos jacentemque
exigulum cum ramice nervum præ se ferre videren-
tur. Martialis, III, 96 :

verse respecting Tiberius Cæsar : « An old « buck licking the she-goats' parts. »

It was thought better to be taken for a fornicator than for a *cunnilingue*; in the first place, because your friends would not kiss you; Martial, VII., 94 :

« I had rather confront a hundred *cunnilingues*. »

Suetonius, *De Illustribus Grammaticis*, ch. 23 :

« He (Remmius Palaemon) was passionately fond of women, so much so as to prostitute his mouth to please them, and it is said that he was one day rebuked in the following way by a man, who in the throng could not contrive to avoid one of his kisses : « Master, » he said, « if you see a man in a hurry to get away, will you lick him off? »

In the second place for fear of scaring away your guests. Aristophanes says of Ariphrades, in the *Knights*, 1285, 86 :

« Whoever does not execrate that man, may he never drink from the same cup with us » — lastly, for fear of letting it be plainly known how shrunken one was, and how miserable one's member. Martial, III, 96 :

Lingis, non futuis, meam puellam,
Et garris quasi mœchus et fututor.

Proinde operam dabant cunnilingi, non minus quam
fellatores, ut unguentorum odore spurcetiem oris
dissimularent. Martialis, VI, 55 :

> *Quod semper casiaque cinnamoque*
> *Et nido niger alitis superbæ*
> *Fragras plumbea Nicerotiana,*
> *Rides nos, Coracine, nil olentes :*
> *Malo, quam bene olere, nil olere.*

Ne dubites, fellator fuerit Coracinus an cunnilin-
gus, palam et aperte cunnilingus dicitur, IV, 43 :

> *Non dixit, Coracine, te cinædum :*
> *Non sum tam temerarius, nec audax.*
> *Quod dixi tamen, hoc leve et pusillum est,*
> *Quod notum est, quod et ipse non negabis,*
> *Dixi te, Coracine, cunnilungum.*

Venerem putabant injurias et sibi et suis illutas
non tantum ita ulcisci, ut rei essent pathici, verum

« You lick my mistress, but you do not enter her; yet you boast yourself adulterer and copulator! »

Hence the *cunnilingues* took no less care than the *fellators* to hide the fetidness of their breath by means of essences and perfumes, Martial VI, 55 :

« Always scented with cassia and cinnamon, and your skin darkened with perfumes from the Phoenix' nest, you reek of the leaden jars of Nicerotus' shop. You mock at us, Coracinus, because we are unscented. Rather than smell sweet like you, I'd not smell at all ».

To remove every doubt as to Coracinus being a *fellator* or a *cunnilingue*, we will quote *Epigr*. IV, 43, where he is expressly called a *cunnilingue* :

« I did not say you were a cinede, Coracinus; I am not so rash and reckless. What I did say is a light, insignificant matter, one perfectly well known, that you will not deny yourself, — I said, Coracinus, you were a *cunnilingue*. »

It was believed that Venus revenged injuries done to herself or to hers, not only by condemning the guilty to submit to be the passive par-

etiam ut cunnilingi. Hinc pathica libido Philoctetis,

Herculis hæredis, quam Lemnia suasit egestas,

ut verbis utar Ausonii, epigrammate LXXI, qua libidine Venus vindicasse fertur vulnera Paridis; Martialis, II, 84 :

> *Mollis erat facilisque viris Pœantius heros;*
> *Vulnera sic Paridis dicitur ulta Venus.*

Hinc Martialis loco modo citato cunnilingum esse jocatur Sertorium, quasi si Erycem, filium Veneris, occidisset :

> *Cur lingat cunnum Siculus Sertorius, hoc est,*
> *Ex hoc occisus, Rufe, videtur Eryx.*

Videntur cunnilingi fere palluisse, cujus rei causam ut aperiant medici curent. Hinc demum intelliges, quid salis insit in epigrammate Martialeo de Charino, I, 78 :

> *Pulchre valet Charinus, tamen pallet.*
> *Parce bibit Charinus, et tamen pallet,*

ty, but by turning them into *cunnilingues*. Hence
the pathic tastes of Philoctetes :

« With which the destitution of Lemnos inspired the heir of Heracles. »

To use the very words of Ausonius, *Epigr*.
LXXI; and by inflicting these tastes Venus is
said to have avenged the wounds of Paris, Martial, II, 84 :

« The son of Poeas was effeminate and prone
to man-love; thus they say did Venus avenge
Paris' wounds. »

In the same epigram Martial rallies Sertorius
on being cunnilingue, giving as a possible reason his having killed Eryx, the son of Venus :

« Why does Sicilian Sertorius lick women's
privates; because, Rufus, it would seem it was
he killed Eryx. »

Cunnilingues appear to have been generally
pale-faced; it is for medical men to say why. This
may help you to discern the salt in Martial's epigram on Charinus, I, 78 :

« Charinus is well and strong, and still he is
pale ;
Charinus drinks with moderation, and still he
is pale ;

Bene concoquit Charinus, et tamen pallet.
Sole utitur Charinus, et tamen pallet.
Tingit cutem Charinus, et tamen pallet.
Cunnum Charinus lingit, et tamen pallet.

Scilicet in causis non pallendi numeratur denique et vera causa pallendi. Similiter videntur etiam fella-tores palluisse. Catullus, LXXX :

Quid dicam, Gelli, quare rosea ista labella
    Hiberna fiant candidiora nive,
Mane domo cum exis, et cum te octava quiete
    E molli longo suscitat hora die.
Nescio quid certe est. An verum fama susurrat,
    Grandia te medii tenta vorare viri?
Sic certe clamant Virronis rupta miselli
    Ilia, et emulso labra notata sero.

Rupta ilia sunt irrumatoris, labra emulso Virro-nis semine notata sunt Gellii fellatoris; re ipsa lo-cum paulo ambiguum sic accipi jubente. Ceterum Virronis pathici, nescio an ejusdem, supra mentio-nem fecimus ex Juvenale, IX, 35 :

Charinus digests well, and still he is pale;
Charinus loves the open air and sun, and still
he is pale;
Charinus dyes his skin, and still he is pale;
Charinus licks a woman's privates, and still
pale is he ».

That is to say, amongst the causes that should
prevent paleness the one last enumerated is the
veritable cause of his paleness. *Fellators* would
also seem to have had pale faces, Catullus, LXXX:

« How is it, Gellius, that those rosy lips of
yours grow whiter than the winter's snow, when
at morn you leave your house, and the eighth
hour calls you from your long-protracted soft
repose? I know not what to think. Can it be
true what rumour whispers, that you devour
the middle parts of men? This at any rate is
evidenced by wretched Virro's sunken flanks
and your own lips masked with the milky juice
sucked from him. »

The withered flanks are those of Virro, the
irrumator, the lips those of Gellius; the passage
is somewhat ambiguous, and only thus to be explained. One Virro, accustomed to take the passive part, has been already mentioned by us, in
quoting Juvenal, IX, 35. I do not know whether it is the same:

*Quamvis te nudum spumanti Virro labello
Viderit...*

*Nec minus videntur pathici quam fellatores pal-
luisse. Juvenalis, II, 50 :*

Hispo subit juvenes et morbo pallet utroque.

*Pathicus erat, ut qui subiret juvenes ; fellator, ut
quem opponeret poeta fœminis, sibi pudenda invicem
non lambentibus :*

Tædia non lambit Cluviam, nec Flora Catullam.

*Rarissimæ enim cunnilingæ, etsi non prorsus inau-
ditæ : unius certe memoriam servavit Martialis, de
qua capite proximo.*

« Though Virro has caught sight of you all naked, and the foam has come to his lips. »

Pathics too, no less tham *fellators*, appear to have had pallid faces. Juvenal, II, 50 :

« Hispo submits to young men ; he is pale with either kind of infamy. »

He served as *patient* to young men. and was moreover a *fellator*, as is shown by the difference which the poet institutes between him and women, who do not lick each other's secret parts :

« Taedia does not lick Cluvia, nor Flora Catulla. »

Women, in fact, are rarely *cunnilingues*, although there *are* examples. Martial only mentions one woman as belonging to that category ; we shall come across her again in the next chapter.

CAPUT VI

DE TRIBADIBUS

*T*RIBADES *dictæ a* τρίβω, frico, frictri-
ces (26), *sunt quibus ea pars naturæ
muliebris, quam clitoridem vocant, in
tantam magnitudinem excrescit, ut possint illa pro
mentula vel ad futuendum vel ad pædicandum uti.
Excrescere quidem solet clitoris* (27), *quæ est carun-*

---

(26) *Dictæ etiam sunt* ἑταιρίστριαι. *Hesychius :* Ἑταιρίστριαι τριβάδες. *Et* διεταιρίστριαι, *eodem auctore :* Διεταιρίστριαι γυναῖχες αἱ τετραμμέναι πρὸς τὰς ἑταίρας ἐπὶ συνουσίᾳ, ὡς οἱ ἄνδρες, οἷον τριβάδες.

(27) *Aloisia, Colloq. III :* « *Sed de clitoride* » (*Tulliæ
verba audis*) « *me fugit dicere. Speciem penis refert mem-
branosum corpus in extrema fere pube. Ac si penis esset, ob-*

CHAPTER VI

OF TRIBADS

HE tribads, also called frictionists (26), from the Greek τρίβω, I rub, are women, with whom that part of the genital apparatus which is called the clitoris, attains such proportions, that they can use it as a mentula, either for fornication or pedication. The clitoris (27), which is a very sensitive caruncle

(26) They were also called hetairistriae : — Hesychius : « Hetairistriae tribads » — and likewise dietairistriae, according to the same author : « Dietairistriae, women who go after prostitutes (hetairae) for carnal intercourse, just as men do; same as tribads. »

(27) Aloysia Sigaea, Dialogue III. : « But I forgot (Tullia speaking) to tell you of the clitoris. This is a membranous body, situated at the bottom of the pubis, and representing in a reduced form the virile verge. As is the case with the verge, the amorous desire excites it to erec-

cula perquam irritabilis, palpitans, peni haud absimilis, omnibus fœminis, non in coitu solum, cujus delicias titillatione adaucta creditur mirifice juvare, verum etiam prurientibus ; tribadibus vero aut lusu Naturæ, aut crebro usu præter modum crescit (28).

---

durescit tentigine : improba adeo titillatione fœminas inflammat vividioris paulo naturæ, ut adhibita manu, si irritentur ad Venerem, plerumque non exspectato conscensore ipsæ sponte colliquescant. »

(28) *Nisi tribas fuit, potuit certe illa esse, quam vidit Platerus, teste Venetto in libro de* Arcanis rei Venereæ *Francogallice scripto, I, 1, 3, cui clitoris, quæ aliis, cum maxime excrescit, solet esse plus minus dimidium digiti minimi longa, non brevior erat anseris collo. Quid mirum, si fœminæ pensilibus nimis peculiatæ de tanto incommodo tollendo valde sollicitæ sunt? Amputatio tamen periculosa. Platerus saltem jam institutam non ausus est persequi ; ne instituere quidem, etsi regina flagitante, Rodohamides, medicus Ægyptius sæculi XI, narrante Venetto, IV, 2. An audaciores fuerunt illi, quibus mulieres castrandas tradidit Adramytes Lydorum rex? Athenæus, XII,* II : Ὁ δ' οὖν Ξάνθος ἐν τῇ δευτέρᾳ τῶν Λυδιακῶν Ἀδραμύτην φησὶ τῶν Λυδῶν

(a small fleshy cone), capable of movement and resembling the verge, gets into erection with all women, not only during the coitus, the delights of which it is said to enhance immensely by increased titillation, but also in consequence of mere amorous longing; with tribads, either by a freak of nature or in consequence of frequent use, it attains immoderate dimensions (28).

---

tion, and in certain women of an ardent temperament it inflames them with pruriency to such a degree that by the mere caressing of it with the hand they very often discharge their fluid without the help of a rider at all. »

(28) If that woman whom Plater saw, according to Venette in his *Tableau de l'amour conjugal*, vol. I., ch. 1., 3, was not a tribad, she might well have been one; her clitoris, which with other women attains in its utmost erection the length of the half of the little finger or thereabouts, was as long as the neck of a goose. Is it surprising that women furnished with such an implement should wish to get rid of it ? Amputation is however dangerous. Plater did not venture to finish an amputation which he had commenced, and Rodohamidès, an Egyptian physician of the XIth century, had not courage to even undertake one, although commanded by a queen to perform the operation (Venette, IV., 2). Those whom Adramytes, the king of the Lydians, ordered to castrate women, were they more courageous? Athenæus, XII., 2 : « Xanthus states in the second book of his Lydiacs, that Adramytes, king of the Lydians, was the first to have women castrated and employ them as eunuchs. » However that may be, these female eunuchs

Arrigit tribas, fodit cunnum culumve, lætissima

βασιλέα πρῶτον γυναῖκας εὐνουχίσαντα χρῆσθαι αὐταῖς ἀντὶ ἀνδρῶν εὐνούχων. *Quicquid fuerunt, fuerunt male torquendis interpretibus hæ eunuchæ. Sunt qui de fibulis cogitent, quales hodieque ferunt Italos Hispanosve zelotypos uxorum pudendis, ut pudicitiæ cingula, imponere ; sunt, qui de suturis, quibus cunnos puellarum tueri solent Angolitani et Congitani ; sed haud scio an ita explicare sit desperare. Neque istæ id passæ videntur, quod etiamnum pati constat puellas apud Arabes, Coptos, Æthiopes, et in regionibus quibusdam Persiæ et Africæ nigræ, quibus præputium clitoridis præciditur, cujus rei testes bene multi satisque locupletes nominati sunt in* Encyclopædia *Erschii et Gruberi sub voce* Beschneidung; *nam qui fieri potuit, ut quod institutum esset, ut fœcundis parerent, id ipsum* εὐνουχίζειν *diceret Athenæus? Fuit cum illas tribadas fuisse putabam, resecta clitoride immani eunuchas factas ; nunc autem magis adducor ut credam, transtulisse regem ad mulieres, quod factum esse novimus in fœminis subus. Aristoteles in* Historia animalium, *IX, 50 :* Ἐκτέμνεται δὲ καὶ ἡ καπρία τῶν θηλειῶν ὑῶν, ὥστε μηκέτι δεῖσθαι ὀχείας, ἀλλὰ πιαίνεσθαι ταχέως. Ἐκτέμνεται δὲ νηστεύσασα δύο ἡμέρας, εἶτα κρεμάσαντες τῶν ὀπισθίων σκελῶν τέμνουσι τὸ ἦτρον, ᾗ τοῖς ἄρρεσιν οἱ ὄρχεις μάλιστα φύονται · ἐνταῦθα γὰρ ἐπὶ ταῖς ἡμέραις ἐπιπέφυκεν ἡ καπρία. *Plinius,* Hist. nat., *VIII, 51 : « Castrantur fœminæ » (sues) « quoque, sicuti cameli, post bidui inediam suspensæ pernis posterioribus »* (vulgatum prioribus *ex compendio scribendi male intellecto natum videtur),* « vulva recisa : celerius ita pinguescunt. » Columella, *VII, 9, 5 : « Fœminis quoque »*

The tribad can get it in erection, enter a vulva

---

have very much exercised the commentators. Some suppose that straps and buckles did in their case the same service as the chastity-belts, which, it is said, Spaniards and Italians to this day compel their wives to wear if they think they have reason to be jealous : others believe that it was a question of suture, as is the case with the natives of Angola and the Congo, who stitch the vulvas of young girls for the protection of their maidenheads ; but I believe that nobody knows anything certain in this respect. Nor does it appear that these women had to submit to an operation, which is certainly practised upon the young girls by the Arabs, Copts, Ethiopians, in some parts of Persia and Nigritia, and which consists in cutting off the prepuce of the clitoris ; this is proved by abundant evidence, and reported in the Encyclopaedia of Ersch and Gruber under the word : « Beschneidung » (Circumcision); how indeed could Athenæus describe as *Eunuchize* that which is calculated to increase the fecundity of women. I thought first that these women were tribads changed into eunuchs by the removal of their immoderately large clitoris; I am now inclined to believe that the king caused that to be done to these women, which according to Aristotle, *Nat. Hist*. IX ,50, was done to sows : « Sows are castrated, so that they shall no longer desire the coitus and get quickly fattened. They are castrated, suspended by their hind legs, after fasting two days, by an incision in that place where with a man the testicles are situated, in fact in the female matrix. » Pliny, *Nat. Hist.*, VIII., 51 « Sows are castrated in the same way as female camels, after a fast of two days, suspended by their hind legs, by an incision in the vulva; they thus fatten much quicker. » Columella, VII., ix. 5 :

permulcetur voluptate, præstat titillationem nisi justam, aliquam tamen, fœminæ quam subigit. Quid multa ? omnia facit, quæ fututor, quæ pædico, præter effluvium seminis, quanquam ne sic quidem tribadis coitus semper plane siccus erit, cum etiam fœminæ soleant saltante libidine colliquescere (29).

(subus) « *vulvæ ferro exulcerantur, et cicatricibus clauduntur, ne sint genitales.* » *Nec hodie rem exolevisse, adnotavit Schneiderus ad Columellæ locum modo prolatum : castrari enim fœminas sues, vaccas, equas, oves, ita quidem, ut ovaria aut tubæ Fallopianæ resecentur. Quidni statuamus, Adramytem simili ratione grassari cœpisse in alterum sexum, ut recisis locis, ubi ova muliebra delitescant, steriles redderet fœminas? Verum prisci Ægyptii, qui teste Strabone. libro XVII, p. 824,* περιτέμνειν, καὶ τὰ θήλεα ἐκτέμνειν *consueverunt, mihi quidem videntur non tam Lydorum more resecuisse locos ovorum intus reconditos, quam præputium* clitoridis *præcidisse, ut in illis oris adhuc fieri paulo ante monuimus : nam cum* τὸ ἐκτέμνειν *junctum sit* τῷ περιτέμνειν, *consentaneum est, rem similem potius intelligere, quam longe dissimilem.*

(29) *Ecce iterum Aloisia, Colloq. III : « Profecto dum me »* (Tullia loquitur) « *Callias nequitiis suis conscelerat, dum demulcet, dum attrectat, id ipsum »* (colliquescere) « *sæpe sæpius experta sum. Intra ipsius manus in his locis liberius ludentes copiosus decidit ex horto meo roscidus humor.*

or anus, enjoy a delicious voluptuousness, and procure if not a complete realisation of cohabitation, at least something very near to it, to the woman who plays the passive part. What more is there to say? She plays the man's part with the omission of the ejaculation of the semen, not that this sort of coitus is an altogether dry affair, as women are in the habit of emitting their liquid during the joys of love (29).

« Sows also are castrated by incision in the vulva; the wounds cicatrice, and they cannot conceive any more. » This practice has by no means disappeared; Schneider notes it in the passage of Columella. sows, cows, mares, sheep, are still castrated by excising their ovarium. Why should we not believe that Adramytes wanted the same process to be applied to the fair sex, in order to make women sterile? However the ancient Egyptians, who (see Strabo, book XVII., p. 824) undoubtedly circumcised themselves, and also their women, appear to me to have had in view not so much ovariotomy as the circumcision of the prepuce of the clitoris, a practice still in use with them, as stated above; cutting the female parts being thus something like circumcision, it is to be assumed that a similar operation was intended rather than any other one.

(29) Let us consult again Aloysia Sigæa, Dialogue III. : « It has happened sometimes to myself (Tullia), when Callias tries on me his lubricities, when be tickles me and excites me. Then I sometimes water his too libertine hands with an abundant dew from my pleasue

Hujus voluptatis insolentiam Lesbiis mulieribus

Hinc illi in me jocorum larga seges, et facetiarum campus. Sed quid facerem? In cachinnos erumpit, rideo ego. Petulantiam ejus increpo, increpat libidinem meam : ludus sumus alter alteri, et dum ludimus verbis, re prosilit in me, sternit volentem nolentemque, init jacentem, et quod humoris hortum meum amisisse jocatur, vi magna refundit e suo, nihil ut querar per ejus culpam mihi periisse. » Item, Colloq. *IV* : « Compressit me » *(Tulliam) « arctius Callias, promovit in uterum meum ea vi caudam ardentem, ut etiam videretur velle se totum in corpus meum immergere. Defluxit tunc in me deliciosus imber, et simul sentio etiam me liquescere, sed tanta et tam incredibili cum voluptate, ut nulla amplius in hoc Veneris furore habita honestatis ratione urgerem ipsa Calliam, subsultibus crebris fatigarem, rogarem ut properaret. Ita defecimus, resolutis quasi artubus ambo eodem temporis puncto. »* Jam facile perspicies, quo intendat epigramma Sosipatri in* Analectis Brunkii, *I, 504 :*

Μέχρις ἀπεσπείσθη λευκὸν μένος ἀμφοτέροισι,
Καὶ Δωρὶς παρέτοις ἐξεχύθη μέλεσι.

Reiskius quidem λευκὸν μένος *censebat sudoris esse guttas ; vah! virus est, quo in ultimo voluptatis æstu diffluit uterque sexus. Aloisia, Colloq. IV : « Cum dicerem »* (iterum audis Tulliam), « ipse superincumbens*

Intorquet summis innixus viribus hastam,

implet fœcundo rore uterum, distillat etiam mihi album virus. Voluptatum magnitudini impares ambo alter in alterius*

This depravity of voluptuousness, whether

---

grounds. And that gives him an opportunity for letting
off a whole sheaf of sarcasms and jokes But what can I
do? I begin to laugh, and so does he; I tell him he is
too impudent, he tells me I am too lewd; we call each
other names right and left, and in the midst of our mutual recrimination he will throw himself upon me, turn
me on my back, and force me to submit to his assault,
saying he will give me his dewdrops for those he has
drawn from me, so that I may not be a loser. » Farther
on, Dial., IV.: « Callias, pressing me more closely to him,
buried his weapon deeper into my belly, almost as though
he were trying to get himself in altogether. Soon a delicious stream spirted into me, and at the same time I
felt my liquid boiling over, causing me such delight that
I forgot all reticence, and myself excited Callias more
and more, pressing him against me and begging him to
quicken his pace. Thus we expired both together with
our muscles relaxing at one and the same instant. » You
will understand by this the meaning of the epigram to
Sosipator in the *Analecta* of Brunck, I , p. 504 :
« Until the white liquor ran over with both of them,
and Doras unwound her wearied limbs. »
    Reiske thought the « white liquor » in this passage meant
drops of perspiration. Nonsense! it means the virus secreted by both sexes, and liberated in the last spasms of
lust. Aloysia Sigæa, Dialogue IV.: « As I finished speaking » (it is still Tullia that speaks), « he got upon me,
and collecting all his strength he pushed the arrow into
me, he filled my womb with his fecundating dew, and I
also shed the rivulet of white liquid. Incapable of enduring any longer so intense a voluptuous feeling, we sank
back exhausted in each others's arms. » We have quoted

(*utrum cœli temperie, an soli fontiumve singulari virtute, an aliis de causis, parum liquet*), *admodum familiarem fuisse, antiquitus fama exiit. Lucianus Dialogo meretricio quinto, p. 349 tomi VII Operum;* Τοιαύτας (ἑταιριστρίας) ἐν Λέσβῳ λέγουσι γυναῖκας, ὑπὸ ἀνδρῶν μὲν οὐκ ἐθελούσας αὐτὸ πάσχειν, γυναιξὶ δὲ αὐτὰς πλησιαζούσας, ὥσπερ ἄνδρας. *Id si Lesbidinis in usu quotidiano positum erat, sane videntur Natura ipsa duce* (30) *rem excogitavisse, ut prurigine intoleranda levarentur. Tribadum omnium celebratissima et regina cui non dicta Sappho, et ipsa Lesbis? quam quidem post Maximum Tyrium plures tali scilicet infamia optimo consilio liberatum iverunt; sed audias ipsam Ovidianis verbis (an dubitas, reddi his firmam ratam-*

---

amplexu sumus resoluti. » *Plura exempla huc facientia passim protulimus ex Aloisiæ divitiis.*

(30) *Quæ enim nimia clitoride laborant, iniri nequeunt, unde libidinantes vix aliter sibi consulere possunt, nisi ut tribadas agant. Conferas, si tanti, Venettum, IV, 2, 4.*

caused by the warmth of the climate, or by a
peculiarity of the soil or waters, or other reasons unknown to us, was especially common
with the women of Lesbos; this is attested by
all the old writers. Lucian, in his « Dialogues
of Courtezans », No. V. (Works, vol. VII,
p. 349.): « This is one of those tribads, as they
are to be found in Lesbos, who will have nothing to do with men, and do the men's business
with women ». If such things were an every
day occurrence with the Lesbian women, we
must believe that they were pushed to them by
natural instigation (30), and to allay an intolerable pruriency. Who has not heard of that most
celebrated queen of all tribads, Sappho, herself
a Lesbian? Some authors, Maximus of Tyre
the first amongst them, have with the best intention tried to exonerate her from this infamous
vice; but hear her in Ovid (and he represents
the Ancients in sentiment and feeling), repudiat-

---

besides on different occasions extracts from the rich treasures of Aloysia Sigæa, on this subject.

(30) Women, whose clitoris is too prominent, are thus
prevented from having intercourse with men, so that
when they are seized with amorous designs they cannot
well find any other way of satisfying their desires than
by playing tribadism. (Venette IV, ii, 4.)

que Antiquitatis sententiam?) importunos liberato-
res deprecantem, Heroid. xv, 15-20:

Nec me Pyrrhiades Methymniadesve (31) *puellæ,*
   Nec me Lesbiadum cetera turba juvant.
Vilis Anactorie, vilis mihi candida Cydno,
   Non oculis grata est Atthis, ut ante, meis,
Atque aliæ centum, quas non (32) *sine crimine amavi.*
   Improbe, multarum quod fuit, unus habes...

et versu 201 :

   Lesbides, infamem quæ me fecistis amatæ!

En hæ sunt primum generatim, quas subagitavit
Sappho, Pyrrhiades Methymniadesque puellæ, deinde

---

(31) *Pyrrha et Methymna civitates Lesbi sunt.* Mela, *II,*
7 : « *In Troade Lesbos, et in ea quinque olim oppida : An-*
tissa, Pyrrha, Eresos, Methymna, Mytilene. »

(32) *Parum refert, legatur* « *quas non sine crimine amavi.* »
an *cum libris quibusdam* « *quas hic sine crimine amavi.* »
Nam et si « *hic* » *præferas, erit in ipsa excusatione confessio*
accusationis ; neque aliud poscimus, nisi ut concedatur, opi-
nionem de tribadica Sapphus libidine non recens esse commen-
tum, sed jam antiquis temporibus, quo jure nescio, percre-
buisse. An potuit mutuus puellarum amor ullo unquam
nomine aliter infamia adspergi, quam tribadico?

ing her would be apologists, *Heroides*, XV, 15-20 :

« Neither the maidens of Pyrrha, nor those of Methymna (31), nor all the host of Lesbian beauties please me. Vile to me seems Anactoria, vile the fair Cydno, Atthis is no more so dear to my eyes as once she was, nor yet a hundred others I loved not innocently (32). Villain! yours is now what belonged to many women...»

and verse 201 :

« Lesbian women, beloved, who made me infamous! »

Sappho speaks first in general of those that have submitted to her caresses, the maidens of

---

(31) Pyrrha and Methymna are towns in Lesbos. Pomponius Mela, II, 7 : « In the Troad is Lesbos, and in Lesbos there were formerly five cities, viz. : Antissa, Pyrrha, Eresos, Methymna, Mytilené.

(32) Not innocently, or rather, « not without crime »; some read « which I loved not without crime » others, « which I loved here without crime », but the difference is not great. If you prefer « which I loved here », the excuse itself is a confession. All we want is the admission that the tribad-tastes of Sappho are no modern invention, but originated, how we know not, and prevailed in very early times. The love of woman for woman was never known under any other name than the notorious one of tribadism.

nominatim Anactorie, Cydno, Atthis : quibus addit Suidas Telesippam et Megaram :

Έταῖραι δὲ αὐτῆς καὶ φίλαι γεγόνασι τρεῖς, Ἀτθις, Τελεσίππα. Μεγάρα, πρὸς ἃς καὶ διαβολὴν ἔσχεν αἰσχρᾶς φιλίας.

Quæ veterum loca cum satis sint aperta, et nihil habeant justæ dubitationis, licebit inde explicare ea, quæ alias utique obscuriora et ambigua videri possent : ut « masculam Sappho » Horatii Epist., *I*, 19, 28, *« querentem puellis de popularibus », ejusdem* Od., *II*, 13, 25 ; *Ovidiana de Arte, III*, 331 :

Nota sit et Sappho : quid enim lascivius illa?

et Tristium, *II*, 363 :

Lesbia quid docuit Sappho, nisi amare puellas ?

Martialeum, VII, 68 (33) :

Carmina fingentem Sappho laudavit amatrix :
Castior hæc, et non doctior illa fuit.

---

(33) *Vide, num sine causa factum sit, ut proximum epigramma 69 Philænim, tribadem tribadum, sugillet.*

Pyrrha and Methymna; then she mentions by name Anactoria, Cydno and Atthis, — to whom Suidas adds Telesippa and Megara :

« Her favourites, whom she loved well, were three in number, Atthis, Telesippa, Megara, and for those she burnt in impure passion. »

These passages from the Ancients are clear enough, and do not admit of any doubt; they even assist us in explaining other sentences, which otherwise seem obscure or ambiguous; for instance the « masculine Sappho » of Horace (*Epistles* I, XIX, 28); « making plaint against the maids of her country » (*Odes* II, XIII, 25); also Ovid, *Art of Love*, III, 331.

« Sappho should be well known too; what more wanton than she? » *Tristia*, II, 363 :

« What was the lore Lesbian Sappho taught, but to love maids? »

and Martial, VII, 68 (33).

« Sappho, the amorous, praised our poetess; the latter was more pure, the former not more perfect in art. »

---

(33) See whether it is with good reason or no that the succeeding epigram, no. 69, calls Philaenis the tribad of tribads.

Aliam tribadem Lesbiam, Megillam, liberrim-um notabilitavit Luciani ingenium Dialogo laudato, lepidissimo illo, nec ultra modum obsceno, nam abrumpitur, cum maxime dicendum erat, quod res esset; quamvis hunc Germanice ut verteret virgineus Vilandi nostri pudor neutiquam tulit. Leænam introducit philosophus Samosatensis expo-nentem, quibus artibus a Megilla sit ad obsequium allecta. Leænæ quidem interroganti: Οὐκοῦν σὺ καὶ τὸ ἀνδρεῖον ἐκεῖνο ἔχεις, καὶ ποιεῖς τὴν Δημώνασσαν *(nam et Demonassam tribadico more permolebat Megilla)* ὅπερ οἱ ἄνδρες; *hæc fere respondet:* Ἐκεῖνο μὲν, ὦ Λέαινα, οὐκ ἔχω· δέομαι δὲ οὐδὲ πάνυ αὐτοῦ. ἴδιον δέ τινα τρόπον ἡδίω παραπολὺ ὁμιλοῦντα ὄψει με. Ἐγεννήθην μέν ὁμοία ταῖς ἄλλαις ὑμῖν, ἡ γνώμη δὲ καὶ ἡ ἐπιθυμία καὶ τἄλλα πάντα ἀνδρός ἐστι μοι. Πά-ρεχε γοῦν, εἰ ἀπιστεῖς, καὶ γνώσῃ οὐδὲν ἐνδέουσάν με τῶν ἀνδρῶν. Ἔχω γάρ τι ἀντὶ τοῦ ἀνδρείου, ἀλλὰ πάρεχε, ὄψει γάρ. *Tandem precibus, donis, procul*

Lucian's witty and licentious pen has made famous another tribad, Megilla, in the above quoted Dialogue. This Dialogue is not outrageously obscene, for it breaks off just at the moment when things would have had to be said very plainly; nevertheless, the virginal modesty of our Wieland has not dared to translate it into German. The philosopher of Samosata brings Leaena upon the scene, and makes her disclose by what artifices Megilla gained her consent. Leaena asks Megilla :

« Are you then made like a man, and do with Demonassa (whom Megilla used after the manner of tribads), as men do? I have not got exactly all that, my Leaena », answers Megilla, « but I am not entirely without it. However, you will see me at work, and in a very pleasant manner. I have been born like all of you, but I have the tastes, the desires and something else of a man. Let me do it to you, if you do not believe me, and you will see that I have everything that men have. Give me leave to work you, and you will see ». Leaena confesses that she at last consented, moved by her solicitations and promises, and no doubt also by the novelty of the thing. « I let her have her way », she says, « yielding to her entreaties, seconded by a mag-

*dubio etiam rei novitate mota se dedisse fatetur
Leæna :* Παρέσχον, *inquit*, ἱκετευούσης πολλὰ, καὶ
ὅρμον τινά μοι δούσης τῶν πολυτελῶν, καὶ ὀθόνας τῶν
λεπτῶν. Εἶτα ἐγώ μὲν ὥσπερ ἄνδρα περιελάμβανον,
ἡ δὲ ἐποίει τε καὶ ἐφίλει καὶ ἤσθμαινε καὶ ἐδόκει μοι
ἐς ὑπερβολὴν ἤδεσθαι. *Verum enimvero Clonarium
curiose sciscitantem :* Τί ἐποίει, ὦ Λέαινα, ἢ τίνα
τρόπον; τοῦτο γάρ μάλιστα εἰπὲ, *fallit :* Μὴ ἀνά-
κρινε ἀκριβῶς, αἰσχρὰ γάρ · ὥστε μὰ τὴν Οὐρανίαν,
οὐκ ἂν εἴποιμι, *dolente lectore, rei prodigiosæ peni-
tius cognoscendæ cupido.*

In tribadum numero poni quoque debent Philænis, eadem haud dubie, quæ de schematibus scripsisse
fertur, Luciano teste in Amoribus, *p.* 88, *tomi V
Operum :* Πᾶσα δὲ ἡμῶν ἡ γυναικωνῖτις ἔστω Φιλαινὶς,
ἀνδρογύνους ἔρωτας ἀσχημονοῦσα (34); *Sophoclidisca*

---

(34) *Ne dubites quid sit* ἀνδρογύνους ἔρωτας ἀσχημονοῦσα, *expende contextum sermonis :* Ἄγε νῦν, ὦ νεώτερε
χρόνε, καὶ τῶν ξένων ἡδονῶν νομοθέτα, καινὰς ὁδοὺς ἄρρενος
τρυφῆς ἐπινοήσας, χαρίσαι τὴν ἴσην ἐξουσίαν καὶ γυναιξίν ·
ἀλλήλαις ὁμιλησάτωσαν, ὡς ἄνδρες, ἀσελγῶν δὲ ὀργάνων ὑπο-
ζυγωσάμεναι τέχνασμα, ἀσπόρων τεράστιον αἴνιγμα, κοι-
μασθωσαν γυνὴ μετὰ γυναικὸς, ὡς ἀνήρ · τὸ δὲ εἰς ἀκοὴν
σπανίως ἧκον ὄνομα, αἰσχύνομαι καὶ λέγειν, τῆς τριβαδικῆς

nificent necklet and a robe of fine linen. I took
her in my arms like a man; she went to work
caressing me, panting with excitement and evidently experiencing the extreme of pleasure. »
Clonarion asks her inquisitively : « But what
did she do to you Leaena, and how did she manage ? » But Leaena eludes the question. « Do
not ask me anything more; these are nasty
doings; by Urania, I shall not breathe a word
more ! » she answers, to the great regret of
the reader, who would like to penetrate further
this mystery.

Amongst the tribads is still to be named Philaenis, the same, no doubt, who according to
Lucian (*Amores*, ch. 28, — Works vol. V, p.
88), wrote about erotic postures : « Let our
women's apartments be filled by women like
Philaenis, dishonoured by androgynic (34) loves

------

(34) To make yourselves quite sure about what the
author means by androgynic loves, look at the passage
as a whole : « Come, you man of the new age, you
law-giver of unknown amours, if you open out new
ways to the lubricity of men, you may grant to the
women equal licence. Let them cohabit together as the
men do; let woman lie with woman, and simulate with
their lascivious organs conjunctions, sterile though they
be, as man lies with man ! Let the word one hears so
very rarely, and which I am ashamed to pronounce, let

Plauti in Persa, *II, 2, 45, cui Pægnium :* « *Ne me attrecta, subagitatrix !* » *et Folia Ariminensis, quam* « *masculæ libidinis* » *dixit Horatius,* Epodo *V, 41 ; sed has leviter tangunt scriptores verecundiores quam pro impatientia lectoris curiosi. Quo nomine erit etiam, quod queraris de parsimonia* Senecæ Controversia *secunda extrema :*

« *Hybreas cum diceret controversiam de illo, qui tribada deprehenderat et occiderat, describere cœpit mariti affectum, in quo non deberet exigi inhonesta inquisitio.* »

At multo plenior, locupletior, explanatior est optimus Bilbilitanus noster. Age, hunc audias tribadicam Bassæ artem ita perspicue enarrantem, ut nihil possit supra, I, 91 :

ἀσελγείας, ἀναίδην πομπευέτω. *Animadverte primum, tribades rarius exstitisse ac secretius ; deinde clitoridem tribadis naturalem modum excedentem* τέχνασμα *dici* ἀσελγῶν ὀργάνων ὑποζυγούμενον, *eodem fere sensu, quo Seneca in* Controversia secunda *tale prodigium* ἄνδρα *dixit* προσερραφθέντα *virum adsutum ; postremo* « *portentosi ænigmatis sterilium* » *nomen, illi ipsi clitoridi inditum, ad coitus tribadici siccitatem referri.*

ves! — Sophoclidisca in Plautus, to whom Paegnion says : « Do not caress me, subagitatrix! » (*Persa*, act II, 41); — and Folia of Ariminum, who according to Horace (*Epodes*, V, 41) was « of masculine lubricity ». However writers as a rule touch upon these points more lightly than is agreeable to the curiosity of the reader. For the same reason the too great reserve of Seneca (*Controversia*, II) is to be regretted, where he says at the end :

« Hybreas having to plead in favour of a man who had surprised and killed a tribad, described the grief of the husband; on such a subject one must not ask for a too particular investigation. »

Much more complete, full and explicit is our good friend of Bilbilis (Martial). Hear him! he is disclosing the tribadic doings of Balba, so clearly that it could not be done better; I, 91 :

---

the lubricity of our tribads triumph without blushing ». Observe in the first place how tribads were seldom spoken of, and that they kept themselves in the dark ; in the second place how the immoderate clitoris of the tribad is said to simulate lascivious organs in conjunction. Seneca, *Controversia Secunda*, in a similar sense, calls such a monstrosity ἄνδρα προσερῥαφθέντα, an *artificial man* ; lastly the epithet « sterile » is applied to the clitoris, and points to the dry unproductiveness of the tribadic coitus.

Quod nunquam maribus junctum te, Bassa, videbam
    Quoque tibi mœchum fabula nulla dabat,
Omne sed officium circa te semper obibat
    Turba tui sexus, non adeunte viro,
Esse videbaris, fateor, Lucretia nobis ;
    At tu, pro facinus ! Bassa, fututor eras !
Inter se geminos audes committere cunnos,
    Mentiturque virum prodigiosa Venus.
Commenta es dignum Thebano ænigmate monstrum,
    Hic, ubi vir non est, ut sit adulterium !

Putasne solis luce clarius esse, quid feccrit Bassa, inter se geminos ausa committere cunnos? Nihil minus. Fuerunt interpretes haud sane contemnendi, qui rem planissimam pessime ita intelligerent, ut aliarum fœminarum pudenda pene scorteo sive ὀλίσβῳ *perfricuisse Bassam putarent : de quo voluptatis genere, a Bassa virum mentiente alienissimo, in extremo hoc capite erit quædam dicendi locus.*

Nihil portentosius Philænidis libidine, quæ non modo istarum tribadum cunnos clitoridis tentigine perforabat; Martialis, VII, 69 :

« As no one, Bassa, ever saw you go with
men; as rumour never assigned you a lover, as
every office about you was fulfilled by a troop
of women, no man ever coming nigh you, you
seemed to us, I admit, a very Lucretia. But, oh!
shame on you, Bassa, you were a fornicator all
the time! You dare to conjoin the private parts
of two women together, and your monstrous
organ of love feigns the absent male. You have
contrived a miracle to match the Theban riddle :
that where no man is, there adultery should be » !

Surely it is clear enough what Bassa did, in
conjoining the privates of two women together.
By no means! There are expounders, and very
good ones too, who have quite misunderstood
this very easy passage, and have imagined that
Bassa misused women by introducing into their
vagina a leathern contrivance, an olisbos, a *godemiche*; we shall speak at the end of this chapter of this kind of pleasure, but it was quite unknown to Bassa, who simulated the man in her
own person.

Nothing could be more monstrous than the
libertine passion of Philaenis; she did not content herself with introducing her stiff clitoris in
the vulva of tribads, Martial, VII, 69 :

Ipsarum tribadum tribos, Philæni,
Recte, quam futuis, vocas amicam;

aliasque puellas, et undenas quidem in die, tribadico more subagitabat, verum etiam pueros pædi-
cabat; idem, VII, 67 :

Pædicat (35) pueros tribas Philænis,
Et tentigine sævior mariti
Undenas vorat in die puellas.

atque adeo cunnilingorum lasciviam tentabat, ne
quid virilis voluptatis inexpertum relinqueret; in
fine ejusdem epigrammatis :

Post hæc omnia, cum libidinatur,
Non fellat : putat hoc parum virile :
Sed plane medias vorat puellas.
Di mentem tibi dent tuam, Philæni,
Cunnum lingere quæ putas virile !

---

(35) Pro « pædicat pueros » poterat etiam, si per metri
legem licuisset, dicere « init pueros ». Nihil aliud sibi vult
Senecæ illud, Epist. 95 : « Viros ineunt, » in quo misere
setorsit magnum Lipsii ingenium : « Libidine vero nec maribus quidem cedunt pati natæ. Dii illas Deæque male per-
dant! adeo perversum commentæ genus impudicitiæ : viros
ineunt! » Ecce tibi retecta Stygiis tenebris digna fœditas
Lipsii : tribades sunt pædicantes.

« Tribad of tribads, you, Philaenis, you are well justified in calling her your mistress whom you work »; or in those of other young girls, and to get a dozen of them under her in a day; but she even pedicated boys; Martial, VII, 67 :

« Philaenis the tribad pedicates boys (35), and stiffer than a man in one day works eleven girls ».

In order to leave nothing untasted in the way of virile lusts she was also a *cunnilingue*; same epigram, at the end :

« After all that, when she is in good feather, — she does not suck, that it too feminine; she devours right out girls' middle parts. May all the gods confound you, Philaenis, who think it manly work to lick the vulva. »

---

(35) Instead of « pedicating boys », Martial might have said, if the metre had allowed it, « entering boys ». Seneca's expression (Letter XCV), *viros ineunt*, » which was a source of great trouble to the great Justus Lipsius, signifies nothing else : « The women will contest for the crown of lubricity with the men. May the gods confound them! one of their refined lubricities reverses the laws of Nature : they have connection with men! » There you have in plain words the turpitude which Justus Lipsius considered worthy of the infernal regions; tribads pedicating.

Ipsam quoque se lingi passam esse Philænim, nimio plus subantem, non obscure prodit, XI, 41 :

> Tarpejas Diodorus ad coronas
> Romam cum peteret Pharo relicta,
> Vovit pro reditu viri Philænis,
> Illam lingeret ut puella simplex,
> Quam castæ quoque diligunt Sabinæ.

Vovet pro reditu mariti, ut cunnum sibi lingat puella simplicitatis pudicitiæque spectatæ. Ab impudicis enim lingi jam in consuetudinem verterat Philænidi; nunc desiderabat experiri etiam pudicæ officium, ut summa hominibus solet voluptatis inesse in novitate rei et insolentia. Rarissime enim accidisse, ut mulieres a mulieribus lingerentur, intelligitur ex Juvenale, II, 47-49 :

> ...Non erit ullum
> Exemplum in nostro tam detestabile sexu :
> Tædia non lambit Cluviam, nec Flora Catullam.

Quid autem fortius, quid nervosius, quid lec orem in medias res, non secus ac notas, ad rapiendum aptius unquam reperias iris illis, quibus Juvenalea severitas excanduit in tribadum orgiâ, ea tempestate Romæ noctu celebrari solita, VI, 308-333?

Philaenis, when overmuch in rut, caused herself also to be served by *cunnilingues*; this is clear enough from Martial, IX, 41 :

« When Diodorus, wanting the Tarpeian crowns, left Pharos behind and sailed for Rome, Philaenis vowed that to celebrate her mate's return an innocent maid should lick her, such a one as the chaste Sabine women still cherish ».

She vowed if her husband returned to have her vulva licked by a young girl, well-known for her innocence and chastity; to have it done by prostitutes was for Philaenis nothing new; she wanted on that occasion to experiment with a virgin, exactly like men, who always want something new and strange to spur their lust. How rare it was for women to use other women for that purpose appears from Juvenal II, 47-49 :

« ..... There will no other instance be found so abominable in our sex ; Taedia does not lick Cluvia, nor Flora Catulla ».

But what could you find stronger, more energetic and plainer to enlighten the reader completely on this subject than the following verses in *Satire* VI, 308-333, where Juvenal's ire against the tribadic orgies in Rome breaks out in words of fire ?

Noctibus hic ponunt lecticas, micturiunt hic,
Effigiemque Deæ longis siphonibus implent,
Inque vices equitant, ac luna teste moventur,
Inde domos abeunt. Tu calcas luce reversa
Conjugis urinam, magnos visurus amicos.
Nota Bonæ secreta Deæ, cum tibia lumbos
Incitat, et cornu pariter vinoque feruntur
Attonitæ, crinemque rotant, ululantque Priapi
Mænades ! O quantus tunc illis mentibus ardor
Concubitus! quæ vox saltante libidine! quantus
Ille meri veteris per crura madentia torrens
Lenonum ancillas posita Laufeja corona
Provocat, et tollit pendentis præmia coxæ
Ipsa Medullinæ frictum crissantis adorat.
Palmam inter dominas virtus natalibus æquat.
Nil ibi per ludum simulabitur, omnia fient
Ad verum, quibus incendi jam frigidus ævo
Laomedontiades et Nestoris hernia possit.
Tunc prurigo moræ impatiens, tunc fœmina simplex
Et pariter toto repetitus clamor ab antro :

« At night they stop their litters here, make water here, and flood with long syphons the Goddess' statue, and ride turn and turn about and go through the motions under the eye of the conscious moon; then they make for home. When the morning light returns, you walk through your wife's piss, to visit your great friends. Known are the secret rites of the *Bona Dea*, when the flute excites their wanton loins, when drunk with music and with wine they rush along, whirling their locks and howling, these Maenads of Priapus! How they yearn for instant copulation! how their voice trembles with passionate longing! what floods of old wine gush down their dripping thighs! A prize is offered, and Laufeia challenges the brothel-master's girls, and wins the first place for nimble hips; while herself is mad for the pleasure Medullina's artful movements give her. Amongst these dames merit carries off the palm from noble blood. There nothing must be feigned, all must be done in very truth and deed, — enough to set on fire, however chilled with age, Laomedon's son and old Nestor with his rupture! Then is seen mere lust that will brook not a moment's more delay, woman in her bare brutality, while from every corner of the subterranean hall rises the reiterated cry : « The hour « is come, admit the men ». Is the lover

Jam fas est, admitte viros. Jam dormit adulter?
Illa jubet sumto juvenem properare cucullo :
Si nihil est, servis incurritur ; abstuleris spem
Servorum, veniet conductus aquarius; hic si
Quæritur, et desunt homines, mora nulla per ipsam,
Quo minus imposito clunem submittat asello!

Quid ergo? duplex erat orgiorum tribadicorum ge-
nus, quorum altero mulieres Urbis nil sibi non
permittentes aræ Pudicitiæ illuderent, altero sacra
Bonæ Deæ obirent. Vides primum ad Pudicitiæ
aram, ut ipsa rei indignitas irritamentum sit Ve-
neri saturæ, tribadas de nocte lecticis portari, mictu-
rire (36), *effigiem Deæ mingendo inquinare, urina*

---

(36) *Prurientes fœminas Natura jubet micturire. Juvena-*
lis, VI, 63-65 : « *Chironomon Ledam molli saltante* » (*Le-*
dam, lascivis gestibus Jovem excipientem, saltando repræsen-
tante) « *Bathyllo* »

Tuccia vesicae non imperat, Appula gannit,
Sicut in amplexu...

Idem, XI, 166-168 :

... Major tamen ista voluptas
Alterius sexus; magis ille incenditur, et mox
Auribus atque oculi concepta urina movetur.

(*Quod dicit Juvenalis, majorem esse voluptatem alterius sexu,*
eo pertinet, quod fœminarum in Venere voluptatem majorem
esse censebat, quam virorum ; hinc etiam illud, VI, 254 :
« *Nam quantula nostra voluptas !* » *Tiresia quidem judice*

asleep? she bids the first young man to hand
snatch up his hood and come at once. Is none
to be found? resort is had to slaves. No hope of
slaves? a water-carrier will be hired to come. If
he comes not, and men there are none, she will
not wait an instant more but get an ass to mount
her from behind ».

The tribadic orgies were divided into two
kinds; in one of them the Roman dames, giving free course to their lust, defiled the altar
of chastity; in the other they celebrated the mysteries of the *Bona Dea*. You see in the first place
the tribads go at night in litters to the altar of
chastity, there pass their water (36) against the

---

(36) When women are in rut they pass their water,
nature wills it so, Juvenal VI, 63-65 : « Let lewd Bathyllus dance the pantomime of Leda » (representing
Leda receiving Jupiter in a dance with wanton gestures » :

« Tuscia cannot command her bladder, Appula is sigh-
ing as if in amorous trance... «
The same XI, 166-168 :
« The other sex however feels more pleasure, is
much sooner fired, and lets the water off, excited through
eyes and ears ».
(What Juvenal says here as to this greater enjoyment
on the part of the opposite sex is connected with his general opinion that women experience more pleasure in
Love than men do. So his words in VI, 254 : For how
insignificant is our pleasure! » Tiresias, called upon to

longo tractu circum reddita, an in os Deæ pro-
jecta (37) *? mane illa calcanda maritis patronos salu-*
tatum euntibus, alternis vicibus subagitare et suba-
gitari : en plus una Philænis, tribas tribadum l Aliæ
deinde properare ad Bonæ Deæ mysteria scilicet, post
Clodii (38) *audaciam in vulgus nota; et tibiarum*
cornuumque cantu et vino illic ad cunnorum certamen

---

apud Lucianum in Amoribus, *p. 85, voluptas fœminarum*
altero tanto major est virili : « Εἴ γε μὴ δικαστῇ Τειρεσίᾳ
προσεκτέον, ὅτι ἡ θήλεια τέρψις ὅλη μοίρᾳ πλεονεκτεῖ τὴν ἄρ-
ρενα.) *Martialis, XI, 17 :*

> O quoties rigida pulsabit pallia vena,
>   Sis gravior Curio Fabricioque licet!
> Tu quoque nequitias nostri lususque libelli,
>   Uda puella leges, sis Patavina licet.

(37) *Ambiguitas quædam in* « *longis siphonibus.* » *Sunt*
enim aut stagna urinæ adj aram] missæ, aut intelligit, ut
Grangæi verbis utar, « *ipsam urinam longo tractu in effigiem*
Deæ projectam, quod faciebant mulieres impudicæ, manu suos
locos premendo, diutuleque eam retinendo : sic enim urina
prius coacta majori prosilit impetu. »

(38) *Mox versiculis 335-39 :*

> ... Sed omnes
> Noverunt Mauri atque Indi, quae psaltria penem
> Majorem, quam sint duo Caesaris Anticatones,
> Illuc, testiculi sibi conscius unde fugit mus,
> Intulerit..

statue of the Goddess, and having perhaps spirted their urine up to her face (37) they at all events wet the area all about, (their husbands walking right through it in the morning, when they go to see their patrons), and then they ride or allow themselves to be ridden alternately ; here we have more than one Philaenis, tribad of tribads ! Other ladies go to celebrate the mysteries of the *Bona Dea*, well known to the public since the adventures of Clodius (38). You observe them rousing themselves with the sounds of flutes and

---

arbitrate on this point in Lucian (*Amores*, p. 85), declared women's enjoyment to be double that of men : « Unless indeed we are to agree with Tiresias' arbitrement, that the woman's pleasure is twice that of the man »).

Martial XI, 17 :

« How often will your rigid nerve lift up your tunic, though you be as stern as Curius or Fabricius ! You too have to read our pages, be they ever so lascivious, young maiden, though you come from Padua ».

(37) There is some ambiguity about the « long syphons ». They are rivulets of urine passed near the statue, or perhaps Juvenal means, to use the expression of Grangé, « Urine spirted right up into the Goddess' face, which may be done by impudent women compressing with the hands their parts, and thus retaining for some time the water; thus collected it will spurt out with greater force ».

(38) Verse 335-339.

strenue ineundum excitari : furere, crines passos hinc indejactare, gannire, micturire. Tum præmium poni, ut fere in convivio Alexandri sexti, acerrimæ subagitatrici : Laufeja provocare ancillas subagitandas; victrix ipsa tollere coronam (39); nulla melius dare quam Medullina, crissandi artis peritissima vibratasque movere nates doctissima ; palma virtutis obscenæ hic fastu posito dominas æquare ancillis, infimo loco natis : nihil simulari per ludum, omnia fieri ad verum (40), tribadico quidem more; tandem

---

(39) *Coxa pendens est femur tribadis superincubantis pro figura Fotidis Apulejanæ*, Metam. *II, 122, quæ pendulæ Veneris fructu Lucium suum satiavit.*

(40) *Prorsus omnino omnia facta sunt ad naturæ veritatem Parisiis, anno 1791, in theatro publico, quo, referente Gynæologiæ auctore, III, 423, ferorum hominum personis effictis nudus nudam ingenti spectatorum utriusque sexus plausu rite compressit. At nil novi sub sole. Erat enim vetus Romanorum mos, ut prostibula in scenam producta post Ludos exactos, ne deesset spectatoribus, quæ modo natantibus*

trumpets, as also with the fumes of wine, to undergo valiantly the jousts of mutual love; you see their amorous frenzy, their hair flying in the wind; you note their sighs of longing, and how they piss with excitement. A prize is set, as in the feast of Pope Alexander VI, to be given to the most intrepid tribad : Laufeia calls upon the brothel-girls to let her ride them, and carries off the crown (39); there is none there of better heart than Medullina, expert in plying her loins and buttocks; there all etiquette ceases, mistresses and servants alike contest for the palm of obscenity; there is no sham, all is tribadic reality (40);

« But all the Moors and Indians well know the flute-girl who showed a bigger penis than great Caesar's two anti-Catos, in that place from which a rat will fly, conscious of possessing testicles... ».

(39) The « nimble hips » are those of the tribad, who is riding another in the posture of Apuleius' Fotis, *Metamorph*. II, p. 122, when she gratified Lucius with the joys of a superincumbent Venus.

(40) All this was actually represented in Paris, 1791, on the stage of a theatre, where, according to the author of the *Gynaeology* III, 423, a man completely naked had connection with a woman as naked as himself, both representing savages, accompanied by the plaudits of both sexes. There is however nothing new under the sun. With the Romans it had long been customary, after the public games were finished, to bring prostitutes into the

natura vincere, tribas finire, fœmina simplex
redire, missa tribadica umbra prurigini levandæ
haudquaquam pari ; undique clamor : Jam fas est
admitti viros, actutum cieri juvenes ingenui ; qui
si desunt, servi ; ne servi quidem sunt iu promtu,
vilissimi quique de trivio arripi ; ademta facultate
et horum conditionibus fruendi, nulla esse mora per
ipsas impudicas, quo minus clunes etiam submittant
asello (41) !

---

oculis vidissent, nunc re vera agendi opportunitas, ibi pros-
ternerentur, non sine prædicatione publica præconis. Tertullianus, De Spectaculis, *c. 17 :* « *Ipsa etiam prostibula,*
publicæ libidinis hostiæ, in scena proferuntur, plus miseræ
in presentia fœminarum, quibus solis latebant, perque omnis
ætatis, omnis dignitatis ora transducuntur, locus, stipes,
elogium, etiam quibus opus est, prædicatur. » *Isidorus,*
Orig., *XVIII, 42 :* « *Idem vero theatrum, idem et prosti-*
bulum, eo quod post Ludos exactos meretrices ibi prosterne-
rentur. » *Non ita multo secus lusisse videntur raptores illi*
scortorum apud Livium, II, 18 : « *Eo anno Romæ cum per*
Ludos ab Sabinorum juventute per lasciviam scorta rapieren-
tur, concursu hominum rixa ac prope prælium fuit. »

(41) *Ne te fugiat dicendi subtilitas poetæ :* « *imposito*

but, after all, finally nature got the upper hand
again, the tribad disappeared, and the woman
became again a woman, leaving alone tribadism,
as a phantom only of pleasure, and not satisfying
them ; from all parts a cry is raised : « Now is
the time for the men to come in : go and find
young men; if you cannot find any, then slaves
will do ; if they are lacking, bring the first
men you can find in the streets. » And if all
fails, in their shameless wantonness, they will
offer their buttocks to an ass (41). On the origin

---

arena, and set them to work, so that the spectators might
have an opportunity to perform what they had been
looking at with greedy eyes; a herald proclaimed what
was to come. Tertullian, *De Spectaculis*, ch. 17 : « Prostitutes, the victims of public incontinence are brought
upon the stage, shamefaced with respect to the women
only; to the men they were known; they are exposed to
the laughter of all, high and low; their dwellings, their
prices, even their recommendations were proclaimed by
the crier ». Isidorus, *Origines*, XVIII, 42 : « The theatre
is like a brothel; when the games are over, public women are prostituted there ». The rape of the Sabines
described in Livy (II, 18) would seen to have been a not
dissimilar form of amusement : « In this year young Sabines in Rome having, in the midst of the games, ab-
ducted some prostitutes, the tumult ensuing thereupon
degenerated into a riot, in fact nearly into a battle ».

(41) Observe the subtlely of the expression adopted by
the poet : « offers her buttocks to an ass to get on them ».

De origine (42) *tribadum exstat fabula Phæ dri, IV, 14 :*

> Rogavit alter tribadas et molles mares
> Quæ ratio procreasset. Exposuit senex.
> Idem Prometheus auctor vulgi fictilis,
> Qui simul offendit ad Fortunam, frangitur,
> Naturæ partes, veste quas celat pudor,
> Cum separatim toto finxisset die,
> Aptare mox ut posset corporibus suis :
> Ad cœnam est invitatus subito a Libero,
> Ubi irrigatus multo venas nectare,
> Sero domum est reversus titubanti pede.
> Tum semisomno corde et errore ebrio
> Adplicuit virginale generi masculo,
> Et masculina membra adplicuit fœminis :
> Ita nunc libido pravo fruitur gaudio.

Masculinum quidem membrum fœminis adplicitum

---

clunem submittat asello. » *Scit mulierem vix aliter posse commode iniri ab asello, nisi aversam.*

(42) *Aliam originem finxit Plato in* Convivio, *p.* 205 *tomi X Operum Biponti editorum, ubi in eo est, ut exponat notum illud commentum de hominibus in duas partes a Jove divisis :* "Οσαι δὲ τῶν γυναικῶν γυναικὸς τμῆμά εἰσιν, οὐ πάνυ αὗται τοῖς ἀνδράσι τὸν νοῦν προσέχουσιν, ἀλλὰ μᾶλλον πρὸς τὰς γυναῖκας τετραμμέναι εἰσί·καὶ αἱ ἑταιρίστριαι ἐκ τούτου τοῦ γένους γίγνονται.

of tribads (42) Phedrus has a fable, IV, 14 ;

« Another asked the reason why tribads and cinedes were created. The old man thus explained : The same Prometheus, modeller of the human clay, that if it knock against Fortune is shivered in pieces, once when he had been fashioning all day long separately those parts that modesty keeps hidden beneath a garment, to fit them presently to the bodies he had made, was unexpectedly invited to supper by Bacchus. There he imbibed the nectar in large drafts, and returned late home with unsteady foot ; then what with fumes of wine and sleepiness, he joined the female parts to male bodies, and fixed male members on to the women. Thus it is we find lust indulging in depraved pleasures. »

The masculine member applied to women is evidently that clitoris of such proportions in

---

Juvenal knows that a woman has no chance to have an ass's mentula in her except by turning her back to the beast.

(42) Plato, *Symposium* (Works, Zweibrücken edition, vol. X, p. 205) imagines another origin ; in the passage where he relates the celebrated fable, according to which Jupiter had cut the men in halves, he says : « As to those women who are halves of women, they are not much harassed by desires after men ; but are much more given to amuse themselves with women ; the hetairist-riae descend from that category ».

clitoris est immanis tentiginis, qua tribades possint pro pene uti; virginale autem maribus aptatum quid erit aliud, nisi postica caverna, pathicis ita pruriens, ut fœminis solet antica?

Neque Tertulliani ætate defuerunt tribades, quas frictrices vocat; De Pallio, *c. 4 :*

« *Aspice lupas, popularium libidinum nundinas, ipsas quoque frictrices.* »

Item, De Resurrectione carnis, *c. 16 :*

« *Et tamen calicem non dico venenarium, in quem mors aliqua ructarit, sed frictricis, vel archigalli, vel gladiatoris aut carnificis spiritu infectum, quæro an minus damnes quam oscula ipsorum?* »

Nec Aloisiæ ævo tribadum artes exoleverant :

« *Noli,* » *inquit Tullia (Colloq. II)* « *me putare proterviorem. Nam hic mos ubique fere terrarum inolevit: Italæ, Hispanæ, Gallæ fœminæ invicem amant altera alteram, et si pudor absit, omnes confestim, altera in alteram, ruant prurientes.* »

erection, that the tribads can use it like a penis; the female apparatus fitted on to man is nothing else but the posterior orifice, which itches in the case of cinedes, just as the vulva titillates women. Tribads were not wanting in the times of Tertullian; he calls them frictrices. *De Pallio*, ch. 4 :

« Look at those she-wolves who make their bread by the general incontinence; amongst themselves they are also frictrices. »

The same author says in the *De Resurrectione Carnis*, ch. 16 : « I do not call a cup poisoned which has received the last sigh of a dying man; I give that name to one that has been infected by the breath of a *frictrix*, of a high-priest of Cybelé, of a gladiator, of an executioner, and I ask if you will not refuse it as you would such persons' actual kisses. »

Nor was the trade of tribad out of date in the time of Aloysia Sigaea :

« Nay! do not think me », says Tullia, Dialogue II, « worse than others. This taste is spread almost over the universe. Italians, Spaniards, French, are all alike as to the tribadism of their women; if they were not ashamed, they would always be rutting in each other's arms. »

Quid? quod exempla etiam profert tribadici furoris et sudoris; Colloq. VII :

« *Erat Enemonda forma excellens, Fernando Portio soror, et Enemondæ erat amica, Francisca Bellina, etiam forma præstans. Nesciebant inter se, quæ magis amaret, quæ magis amaretur. Cubabant frequenter una in domo Fernandi. Secretis petebat, quales amat Venus, insidiis Franciscam Fernandus; se peti sciebat puella, gratulabatur suæ formæ. Surrexerat impatiens libidinis surgente Aurora e lecto adolescens; frigido aeris halitu mitigabat ignes in pergula. Tremula strepebat argutatione proximo in cubiculo sororis lectus. Patebat vero ostium: hanc amanti commodarat puellarum negligentiam Venus favens. Intrat, nec vident libidine cœcæ, libidine ebriæ. Superequitabat Francisca, Enemondam impellebat ad cursum, nuda nudam.* « *Ambiunt,* » *dicebat Francisca,* « *meam quoti-* « *die pudicitiam nobiliores et salaciores mentulæ: pulchrio-* « *rem ex iis, amica, legam ego, sed tibi. Sic volo indulgere genio tuo et meo.* » *Dicens subagitabat accerrime. Conjicit Fernandus se in lectum nudus. Territæ puellæ nec fugere*

More, she quotes herself some examples of the hot transports of tribads, Dialogue VII :

« Enemunda, the sister of Fernando Porcio, was very beautiful, and not less so was a friend of hers, Francisca Bellina. They frequently slept together in Fernando's house. Fernando laid secret snares for Francisca; the latter knew that he desired to have her, and was proud of it. One morning the young man, stung by his desires, rose with the sun, and stepped out upon the balcony to cool his hot blood. He heard the bed of his sister in the next room cracking and shaking. The door stood open; Venus had been kind to him and had made the girls careless. He enters; they do not see him blinded and deafened by pleasure. Francisca was riding Enemunda, both naked, full gallop. ' The noblest and most powerful mentulas are every day after my maidenhead', said Francisca, ' I should select the finest, dear, but for you ; so fain am I to gratify your tastes and mine'. Whilst speaking she was jogging her vigorously. Fernando threw himself naked into the bed ; the two girls, almost frightened to death, dared not stir. He draws Francisca, exhausted by her ride, into his arms and kisses her : ' How dare you, abandoned girl' he says, ' violate my sister, who is so pure and chaste ? You shall pay me for this ; I will

ausæ sunt: amplexu Franciscam ligat cursu fessam; oscu-
latur. « *Audes tu, improba, vitiare sororem meam,* » *ait,*
« *tam sanctam, tam castam? Pœnas dabis; domus ulciscar*
« *meæ injurias. Patiere furores meos, ut illa tuos.* — *Frater*
« *mi, frater mi,* » *respondit Enemonda, ignosce amanti-*
« *bus; noli nos traduci ludibrio.* — *Nemo sciet,* » *inquit;*
« *faveat hæc mihi cunno, favebo ego utrique lingua.* »

At multo etiam fortius ac vividius est colloquium
Octaviæ cum Tullia tribade in ipso opere sertum
(Colloq. II) :

Tullia. *Nec refuge, amabo; aperi femora.*

Octavia. *En, totam me jam occupas; os ore premis,*
pectus pectore, uterum utero; amplectar etiam te, cum me
amplecteris.

Tullia. *Tolle altius crura, superinjice femoribus meis*
femora. Artifex tibi sum ego Veneris novæ, quæ nova es.
Quam excellenter pares! non ita egregie possim imperare,
ut tu obsequeris.

Octavia. *Ah! ah! Tullia mea, hera mea, domina mea,*
ut me pulsas! ut te agitas! Velim exstinctos cereos illos;
pudet lucem testem habere patientiæ meæ.

Tullia. *Age intente quod agis. Ut ego adsilio, tu sub-*

revenge the injury done to our house; answer now to my flames as she has answered to yours. ' My brother! my brother!' cries Enemunda, ' pardon two lovers, and do not betray us to slander!' ' No one shall know anything', he answered, ' let Francisca make me a present of her treasure, and I will make you both a present of my silence ».

The conversation of Ottavia with Tullia, acting as tribad, in the same work (Dialogue II) is still bolder and more to the point :

TULLIA : Pray do not draw back; open your thighs.

OTTAVIA : Very well! Now you cover me entirely, your mouth against mine, your breast against mine, your belly against mine ; I will clasp you as you are clasping me.

TULLIA : Raise your legs, cross your thighs over mine, I will show you a new Venus; to you quite new. How nicely you obey! I wish I could command as well as you execute!

OTTAVIA : Ah! ah! my dear Tullia, my queen! how you push! how you wriggle! I wish those candles were out; I am ashamed there should be light to see how submissive I am.

TULLIA : Now mind what you are doing!

*sili ; exagita crissantes nates, ut agito, et in aera mitte,
ut poteris altius. Times te anima deficiat?*

Octavia. *Sane me rapidis his fatigas concussionibus!
opprimis me; vim tam efferatam ab alio paterer?*

Tullia. *Tene, amplectere, Octavia, excipe... En, en
fluit, furit pectus, ah! ah!*

Octavia. *Hortus mihi tuus hortum meum incendit;
abscede.*

Tullia. *Agedum, Dea mea, tibi ego vir fui, mea
sponsa! mea conjux!*

Octavia. *O utinam mihi vir esses! quam amantem
haberes uxorem! quam amatum haberem virum! Enimvero etiam tu hortum meum imbre proluisti, quo me
sentio perfusam! Quam ignominiam depluisti in me,
Tullia?*

Tullia. *Nempe perfeci opus, et Venereum virus ex
cœca navis meæ sentina projecit in cymbam virgineam
tuam amor cœco impetu.*

*Fessanarum tribadum mentionem facit Leo Afri-
canus in* Descriptione Africæ, *p. 336 exemplaris
Elzeviriani anno 1632 excusi :*

« *Verum qui sanioris sunt judicii, mulieres has* »
(*fatidicas*) « *Sahacat, quod Latinis fricatrices sonat,*

when I push, do you rise to meet me; move your buttocks vigorously, as I move mine, and lift up as high as ever you can ! Is your breath coming short ?

OTTAVIA : You dislocate me with your violent pushing; you stifle me ; I would not do it for any one but you.

TULLIA : Press me tightly, Ottavia, take... there! I am all melting and burning, ah! ah! ah!

OTTAVIA : Your affair is setting fire to mine — draw back !

TULLIA : At last, my darling, I have served you as a husband ; you are my wife now !

OTTAVIA : I wish to heaven you were my husband ! What a loving wife I should make ! What a husband I should have ! But you have inundated my garden ; I am all bedewed ! What have you been doing, Tullia ?

TULLIA : I have done everything up to the end, and from the dark recesses of my vessel love in blind transports has shot the liquor of Venus into your maiden barque.

Leo Africanus, in his *Description of Africa*, p. 336 (edition Elzevir, of 1632), mentions the tribads of Fez :

« But those who have more common sense, call these women (he is speaking of witches)

appellant, quod illis damnanda sit consuetudo, Venerem inter se ipsas exercere, quod honestiori vocabulo exprimere non possum. Si quando contingat, ut formosæ quædam mulieres illas adeant, veneficæ harum amore non secus atque adolescentes puellarum accenduntur, et in Dæmonis specie rogant, ut concubitum pro mercede patiantur. Hoc modo sæpenumero fit, ut, dum se dæmoniorum dictis paruisse putànt, rem cum veneficis habuerunt. Neque desunt, quæ ejus rei voluptate allectæ veneficarum consortium ambiant, et morbum fingentes unam earum ad se vocent, vel miserum eo mittant maritum : quæ ubi rem intellexerint, mulierem a dæmone quodam vexatam affirmant, eamque ob causam nullo modo liberari posse, nisi se illarum adjunxerit numero. »

Num ad hodiernum usque diem tribades supersint, quæris. Nisi supersunt, certe superfuerunt Parisiis proxime ante conversionem rerum, si credere par est auctori Gynæologiæ, III, 428. Collegium ibi justum tribadum, Vestalium nomine adscito ; certi conventus certis locis ; sodales haud

« Sahacat », a word which corresponds with the
Latin *fricatrices*, because they take their pleasure
with each other. I cannot speak more plainly
without offending decency. When good-looking
women visit them, these witches fall at once in
hot love with them, not less hot than the love
of young men for girls, and they ask them in
the guise of the devil to pay them by suffering
their embraces. So it happens that very often
when they think they have been obeying the
behests of demons, they have really only had
to do with witches. Many too, pleased with the
game they have played, seek of their own im-
pulse to enjoy intercourse again with the witches , and under pretence of being ill, summon
one of them or send their unfortunate husbands
to fetch her. Then the witches, seeing how
matters stand, asseverate that the wife is possessed by a demon, and can only be liberated by
joining their association ».

You ask whether tribads are still to be
found in our days? If there are none now, there
certainly were some in existence in Paris only
a short time before the Great Revolution, if we
are to trust the author of the *Gynaeology*, III,
p. 428. There was a veritable college of tribads
in Paris, who went by the names of Vestals,

paucæ et summi ordinis; certæ leges, quibus in fidem reciperentur novæ; tres gradus desiderantium, postulantium, initiatarum; difficilis per triduum perseverantiæ tentatio, priusquam fieret interioris admissionis postulans, cubiculo clausa, ab lascivissimis imaginibus Priapisque mentulatissimis illecebrosissime instructo, ignem alere jussa, nescio qua arte ita comparatum, ut materie aut parum aut nimis injecta pariter exstingueretur: in quatuor aris Templi, Sapphus, Lesbidum amatarum, Eonis equitis, cui sexum tam diu dissimulare contigerat, statuis lautaque supellectili splendide adornati, ignis perpetuo ardens. Nec Anglicanas fœminas plane abhorrere a re tribadica, idem auctor est, III, 394. Londini enim refert exstitisse non procul a fine sæculi superioris collegia quædam, etsi parva, tribadum, Alexandrina dicta.

holding regular meetings in particular localities. There were a great many members, and of the highest classes; they had their statutes with respect to admission; the affiliated were divided into three degrees : aspirants, postulants, the initiated. Before the postulant could be admitted to the secret of the order, she had to undergo for three days a difficult probation : shut up in a cell tapestried with lewd pictures, and ornamented with carved Priapi of magnificent proportions, she had to keep up a fire with I do not know how many ingredients, and arranged in such a manner that it would go out if there was taken too much or too little of any of the materials; on the four altars of the temple, which was adorned with Statues of Sappho, of the Lesbians she had loved, and of the Chevalier d'Éon, who for so many years successfully dissimulated his sex, and with splendid hangings, perpetual fires were burning. Kept English women too did not recoil at Tribadism, as the same author states, III, p. 394. He affirms that not long before the close of the last century, confederacies of tribads, called Alexandrine confederacies, were still in existence in London, though in a small number only.

*Hæc quidem de tribadibus proprie sic dictis suf-
ficiant. Sed nomen tribadum latius patet. Nam
tribades etiam eæ dicuntur fœminæ, quæ vera mentula defectæ aut digito aut pene scorteo vulvæ
immisso libidinem titillationis aliqua specie fallunt.
Ac de digitorum quidem abusu isto magnis memini
Germaniam nuper querelis personare, quæ ut solet
conticuerunt tandem. Penem autem ex corio (43)
confectum, quem* ὄλισβον *dixerunt, olim ante alias
ferunt in deliciis fuisse Milesiis mulieribus. Aristophanes.* in Lysistrata, *v.* 108-110 :

> Ἐξ οὗ γὰρ ἡμᾶς προὔδοσαν Μιλήσιοι,
> Οὐκ εἶδον οὐδ᾽ ὄλισβον ὀκτωδάκτυλον,
> Ὃς ἦν ἂν ἡμῖν σκυτίνη ᾽πικουρία !...

Suidas sub Ὄλισβος :

Αἰδοῖον δερμάτινον, ᾧ ἐχρῶντο αἱ Μιλήσιαι γυναῖκες, ὡς τριβάδες καὶ αἰσχρουργοί. Ἐχρῶντο δὲ αὐτοῖς
καὶ αἱ χῆραι γυναῖκες.

---

(43) *Alium usum penis scortei supra capite secundo adno-
tavimus.*

Enough now of those who are, strictly speaking, included under the name of Tribads ; but the word has a more extended signification. The term is also applied to those women who in default of a real mentula, make use of their finger or of a leathern contrivance, which they introduce in their vulva, and so attain a fictitious enjoyment. Germany, I have lately heard, has been ringing with complaints about this abuse. As regards the leathern engine (43), called by the Greeks olisbos, the women of Miletus, above all others, made it their instrument of pleasure. Aristophanes, in the *Lysistrata*, 108-110 :

« For since the day the Milesians left us in the lurch, not an olisbos have I set eyes on, eight inches long, — that might give us its leathern aid... »

Suidas under the word Ὄλισβος :

« A virile member made of leather which was used by Milesian women, as being tribads and immodest. It was also made use of by widows. »

---

(43) Another use of these leathern engines has been noted in chap. II.

Idem sub Μισητή.

Καὶ ὁ Κρατῖνός που τοῦτο ἔφη · Μισηταὶ δὲ γυναῖκες ὀλίσβοισι χρήσονται.

Quem locum etiam profert Hesychius. Num hodieque sit, rogas, ut confugiant spretæ formæ injuriam passæ ad scorteum auxilium. Responsum feras ab Aloisiæ simplicitate, Colloq. II :

Milesiacæ compingebant sibi e corio veretra octo digitos » (transversos) *« longa et pro modo crassa. Aristophanes auctor est, his uti solitas fœminas sui ævi. Ac hodie quoque Italis Hispanisque maxime, sicut et Asiaticis mulieribus, id instrumentum mundi muliebris et pretiosioris supellectilis præcipua pars est : magno in pretio habetur. »*

Cum matronas Romanas (44) *constet in deliciis*

─────────────────────

(44) *Sed erat id genus draconum etiam in oblectamentis virorum : Suetonius, in* Tiberio, *c.* 72 : « *Erat ei in oblectamentis serpens draco, quem ex consuetudine manu sua ciberatus cum consumtum a formicis invenisset, monitus est, ut vim multitudinis caveret. » Rem tangit Plinius,* Hist. nat., *XXIX,* 4. « *Anguis Æsculapius Romam advectus est, vulgoque pascitur et in*

The same author under the word Μισητή :

« Cratinus also says on this head : *Lewd*
women will be using the olisbos. »

Hesychius quotes the same passage.

If you ask whether modern women, who
have suffered the wrong of seeing their beauty
slighted, actually have recourse to this leathern
substitute, Aloysia Sigaea (Dialogue II) shall
answer you :

« The Milesian women made for themselves
imitations in leather, eight inches long and thick
in proportion. Aristophanes tells us that the women of his day habitually made use of such. And
to this very day Italian, Spanish and Asiatic women honour this instrument with a place in their
toilet apparatus ; it is their most precious possession, and one very highly appreciated. »

It is an undoubted fact that the Roman matrons cherished a species of inoffensive snake (44),

---

(44) This sort of snake served also to amuse men.
Suetonius, *Tiberius*, ch. 72 : « He kept for amusement a
snake; one day, when he went as usual to feed it, he
found it devoured entirely by ants, which he took as a
warning to guard against being attacked by a mob ».
Pliny, *Nat. Hist.* XXIX, ch. 4 : « The Aesculapian serpent was brought to Rome from Epidaurus; it was kept
in the public edifices, and also in private houses ». Seneca,

habuisse genus quoddam draconum innoxium, quibus, ut gelidissimæ naturæ, æstivis mensibus se refrigerarent; Martialis, VII, 86 :

> *Si gelidum collo nectit Gracilla draconem...*

Lucianus in Alexandro, *p.* 259 *tomi IV Operum :*

Ἐνταῦθα ἰδόντες δράκοντας παμμεγέθεις, ἡμέρους πάνυ καὶ τιθασσούς, ὡς καὶ ὑπὸ γυναικῶν τρέφεσθαι, καὶ παιδίοις συγκαθεύδειν, καὶ πατουμένους ἀνέχεσθαι, καὶ θλιβομένους μὴ ἀγανακτεῖν, καὶ γάλα πίνειν ἀπὸ θηλῆς κατὰ ταῦτα τοῖς βρέφεσι·

haud sane improbabilis videtur conjectura elegantissimi Bœttigeri nostri in Sabina, *multæ et reconditioris doctrinæ libello Germanice scripto,*

---

domibus. » *Seneca quoque,* De Ira, *II, 31, commemorat* « *repentes inter pocula sinusque innoxio lapsu dracones.* » *Non parvos fuisse, apparet ex Philostrato, in* Heroicis, *VIII, 1 :* Εἶναι δὲ αὐτῷ καὶ χειρόηθη δράκοντα πεντάπηχυν τὸ μῆκος, ὃν ξυμπίνειν τε καὶ ξυνεῖναι τῷ Αἴαντι, καὶ ὁδῶν ἡγεῖσθαι, καὶ ξυνομαρτεῖν, οἷον κύνα.. *Tales dracones multos nasci apud Pellam in Macedonia, auctor est Lucianus loco citato :* Πολλοὶ δὲ γίνονται τοιοῦτοι παρ' αὐτοῖς. *Nec hodie desunt in Italia, Lipsio ad Senecam teste.*

the cold skin of which served as a refrigerator in summer, Martial VII, 86 :

« If Glacilla winds an icy serpent round her neck... »

Lucian *Alexander* (Works, vol. IV, p. 259) :

« In that country one sees serpents of an enormous size, but so quiet and mild that they are fondled by women, sleep with the children, do not get angry on being trodden on or handled, and suck the nipples of the breast like a nursling. »

This being so, our eminent Böttiger was probably right, when he wrote page 454 of his *Sabina* (45) a profoundly scientific work in

---

in the *De Ira*, II, ch. 31, speaks of : « Those snakes that glide harmlessly amid the cups and into the bosoms of the guests ». They were not of a small size ; this appears from what Philostratus says in his *Heroics*, VIII, 1 : « Ajax had a tame snake of five cubits length, which kept close to him, guided him on his way, and followed him about like a dog ». This kind of snake was very common at Pella, in Macedonia, as Lucian says in a passage quoted in the text : « There are many such in their country ». They are still to be found in Italy, according to Justus Lipsius in his Notes to Seneca.

(45) « Sabina, or the Morning Toilette of a Roman Lady at the end of the First Century », translated into French by Clapier, 1813, 8vo.

p. 454 proposita, fuisse hos dracones libidinan-
tibus fœminis anguineo etiam auxilio. Tum penitus
intelliges, quid acciderit, certe accidere potuerit,
Atiæ, Augusti matri, de qua Suetonius in Augusto,
cap. 94 :

« *In Asclepiadis Mendetis* Θεολογουμένων *libris*
lego, Atiam cum ad solenne Apollinis sacrum media
nocte venisset, dum ceteræ matronæ dormirent, obdor-
misse, draconemque repente irrepsisse ad eam, paulloque
post egressum, illamque expergefactam quasi a concubitu
mariti purificasse se.

Nam quid mirum, hujusmodi draconem, licet
injussu Atiæ, locos ex aliarum consuetudine sibi
notos investigasse, atque expergefactæ eundem fere
sensum reliquisse, ac si justum coitum passa
fuisset?

German, that very likely snakes were used as instruments to satisfy the lubricity of amorous women. You may understand now what happened, or what might have happened to Atia, the mother of Augustus, of whom Suetonius (*Augustus*, ch. 94) wrote :

« I read in the treatise of Asclepiades of Mendé called the *Theologumena*, how Atia the mother of Augustus, having gone at midnight to the temple of Apollo, to assist at a solemn sacrifice, fell asleep, and so did the other women present; how a serpent suddenly glided close to her, and after some little time withdrew again, and how on waking she purified herself as though she had left the arms of her husband. »

There would be nothing surprising in the fact that a serpent of that sort should have investigated even without incitation on Atia's part, a certain locality which was well known to it by the lubricity of other women, and that Atia felt on awakening the very same sensation, as though she had undergone a real coitus.

CAPUT VII

DE COITU CUM BRUTIS

AT quoniam ad hoc ventum est, non ab re fuerit subtexere quædam de intemperantia eorum, qui cum brutis coiverunt. In Ægypto constat Mendesios, hircum (46) divino cultu prosequi solitos, sacra illi ita peregisse, ut, fœminas palam etsi invito, substernerent. Herodotus, II, 46 :

Ἐγένετο δ' ἐν τῷ νομῷ τούτῳ (Μενδησίῳ) ἐπ' ἐμεῦ τοῦτο τὸ τέρας · γυναικὶ τράγος ἐμίσγετο ἀναφανδόν.

---

(46) *Plutarchus*, De brutis ratione utentibus, *p. 989 tomi II. Operum* : Ὁ Μενδήσιος ἐν Αἰγύπτῳ τράγος λέγεται πολλαῖς καὶ καλαῖς συνειργνυμένος γυναιξὶν οὐκ εἶναι μίγνυσθαι πρόθυμος, ἀλλὰ πρὸς τὰς αἶγας ἐπτόηται μᾶλλον.

CHAPTER VII

OF INTERCOURSE WITH ANIMALS

I T will not be out of place to say something here of the incontinence of those who have carried out carnal intercourse with animals. It appears that in Egypt the Mendesians, who paid divine honours to a he-goat (46), prostituted to him publicly women, even against his inclination, in celebrating his rites. Herodotus II, 46 :

« A monstrous affair was connected with this district (viz. the Mendesian) in my time; a he-goat covered a woman in public. »

---

(46) Plutarch, *Of Animals that have Reason*, p. 989, vol. II, of his works : « It is reported in Egypt the he-goat Mendes, shut up with a great number of women, all of them beautiful, refused to have anything to do with them, and prefers goats by far ».

Strabo, XVII, 802 :

Μένδης, ὅπου τὸν Πᾶνα τιμῶσι, καὶ ζωὸν τράγον. οἱ τράγοι ἐνταῦθα γυναιξὶ μίγνυνται (47).

Rem non incognitam fuisse Hebræis, discimus ex lege Mosis. Levit. xx, 15-16 :

« *Qui cum jumento et pecore coierit, morte morietur ; pecus quoque occidite. Mulier quæ succubuerit cuilibet jumento, simul interficietur cum eo.* »

An Juvenali putes unquam in mentem venisse, ut caneret, VI, 332-33 :

> ... *Mora nulla per ipsam,*
> *Quo minus imposito clunemsubmittat asello,*

nisi interdum evenisset, ut asinos paterentur fœminæ ? an Apulejo, ut Lucii, Fotidis errore in asinum transformati, coitum cum matrona tam

---

(47) *Si Venetto fides, II,* iv, *3, nihil frequentius fit in Ægypto ad hodiernum usque diem, quam ut puellæ coeant cum hircis.*

Strabo, XVII, p. 802 :

« Mendes, where they worship Pan, and a live he-goat ; the latter in that place have intercourse with women (47). »

The Jews also knew something of the practice ; as we know from the law of Moses, Leviticus xx, 15-16 :

« And if a man lie with a beast, he shall surely be put to death : and ye shall slay the beast. And if a woman approach unto any beast, and lie down thereto, thou shalt kill the woman, and the beast : they shall surely be put to death »......

How should Juvenal have come to tell us, Satire VI, 332-33 :

« ... no more delay is there ; she hastens to make a donkey ride her from behind, »

if it had not been known that women sometimes submitted themselves to asses ? Would Apuleius have thought of describing to us with no less minuteness than wit the scene in which Lucius, changed into an ass by a mistake of Fotis,

---

(47) If we may believe Venette (II, iv. 3), there is nothing more common in Egypt at the present day than for young women to have intercourse with he-goats.

copiose quam festive describeret? Metamorph. *libro X, p.* 249 :

« *Sed angebar plane non exili metu reputans, quemadmodum tantis tamque magnis cruribus possem delicatam matronam inscendere, vel tam lucida tamque tenera et lacte ac melle confecta membra duris ungulis complecti, labiasque modicas ambrosio rore purpurantes tam amplo ore tamque enormi et saxeis dentibus deformis saviari; novissime quo pacto quanquam ex unguiculis perpruriscens mulier tam vastum genitale susciperet... Molles interdum voculas, et assidua suavia, et dulces gannitus commorsicantibus oculis iterabat illa.* — « *Et in summa, teneo te,* » *inquit,* « *teneo meum palumbulum, meum passerem.* » *Et tum dicto vacuas fuisse cogitationes meas ineptumque monstrat metum : arctissime namque complexatum me totum prorsus, sed totum recepit. Illa vero, quotiens ei parcens nates recellebam, accedens totiens nisu rabido et spinam prehendens meam appliciore nexu inhærebat, ut, Hercules ! etiam deesse mihi aliquid ad supplendam ejus libidinem crederem.* »

Tusca puella canem experta est tempore Pii V, pontificis Romani, narrante Venetto, II, IV, 3 ; et

effects intercourse with a matron? *Metamor-phoses*, book X, p. 249 :

« But I was a prey to grave apprehensions ; I asked myself how I, with my long and coarse legs, could mount a delicate woman, clasp with my hard hoofs her soft and tender limbs that looked like milk and honey ; how I could with my enormous mouth, furnished with teeth as big as tomb-stones, kiss those small, rosy, scented lips; how lastly this lady, although in rut to her very finger nails, could take in such a big genital verge..... She, however, doubled her tender allurements, her endless kisses, her sweet murmurings, interspersed with sweet glances like stings : ' I hold you at last,' she cried, ' I hold my dove, my sparrow ! ' and having said this, she showed me how vain my fears had been for embracing me as closely as she could, she received me inside entirely, out and out. Even more than that, whenever I drew back in order to spare her, she pushed closer to me, and clasping my backbone like mad, she clung to me so closely that, by Hercules, I began to think that I was not well enough furnished to assuage her passion completely. »

A young girl of Tuscany got herself covered by a dog in the time of Pius V, the Roman

Parisiis anno 1601 mense Octobri, adnotante Elmenhorstio ad Apuleji locum modo laudatum, p. 297, « inventa mulier, quæ cum cane rem habuerat : ideoque leges citavere, ut vindicarentur, exque communi sententia Senatus mulier adultera canisque maritus vivi comburio periere. » Quid ? quod crocodilum etiam subire ausa est fœmina, si credere fas est Plutarcho, De solertia Animalium, *p. 976, tomi secundi Operum :*

Ἔναγχος δὲ Φιλῖνος ὁ βέλτιστος ἥκων πεπλανημένος ἐν Αἰγύπτῳ παρ' ἡμῖν διηγεῖτο γραῦν ἰδεῖν ἐν Ἀνταίου πόλει κροκοδείλῳ συγκαθεύδουσαν ἐπὶ σκίμποδος εὖ μάλα κοσμίως παρεκτεταμένῳ.

Nec viri spreverunt brutos cunnos. Imaginem viri capram ineuntis præbet tabula III, in Monuments du culte secret des Dames Romaines, *quanquam ab interprete locus alienus ex Virgilio* Bucol. *III, 8, non debebat afferri :*

Pope, as reported by Venette II, iv., ch. 3 ; and according to a note of Elmenhorst on the above quoted passage of Apuleius, a woman was discovered in Paris, in October, 1601, to have had connection with a dog. The law was appealed to, and in conformity with the unanimous verdict pronounced by the parliament, the adulterous woman and the dog were both burnt alive. Nay! more, a woman has been known to submit to a crocodile, if we may believe Plutarch, who reports in his treatise *On the Sagacity of Animals* (p. 976, vol. II, of the complete Works :

« Quite lately our excellent Philinus, on returning from a long voyage to Egypt, told me that he had seen at Antaeopolis an old womansleeping with a crocodile stretched comfortably beside her on her pallet. »

Nor have men despised the vulva of animals. Plate III of the *Monuments du Culte Secret des Dames Romaines*, shows the picture of a man working away in a goat, though the annotator ought not to have quoted in illustration of it a passage of Virgil (*Bucolics* III., 8.), which has nothing whatever to do with this matter :

Novimus et qui te (pædicaverit) *tranversa tuentibus hircis.*

Et nostris regionibus, præter capras, oves etiam, vaccas, equasque nonnunquam et pastoribus placuisse et aliis infimæ fortunæ hominibus, acta forensia loquuntur.

« We know who (pedicated) you, while the he-goats looked at you askance. »

In our countries legal cases show that not only goats, but also sheep, cows, and mares, have sometimes charmed shepherds and other people of low breeding.

CAPUT VIII

DE SPINTRIIS

*I*N *his libidinum generibus, quæ adhuc explicavimus, plerumque duo secum rem habebant. Fit autem, ut rem etiam secum habeant plus duo, aut tres, aut plures quod Tiberio auctore spintriarum genus dicimus. Sueto-nius, in* Tiberio, *c.* 43 :

« *Secessu vero Capreensi etiam sellariam excogitavit, sedem arcanarum libidinum, in quam undique conquisti puellarum et exoletorum greges, monstrosique concubitus repertores, quos spintrias appellabat, triplici*

CHAPTER VIII

OF SPINTRIAN POSTURES

I N the sundry kinds of voluptuous enjoyment which we have studied so far, there are almost always only two persons in action. It happens, nevertheless, that more than two, three or even more, may enjoy themselves together; this is what we call after Tiberius, the spintrian kind. Suetonius, *Tiberius*, ch. 43 :

« In his retreat at Capri he had a *sellaria*, the scene of his secret debaucheries, in which chosen groups of young girls and worn-out voluptuaries, the inventors of monstrous conjunctions, called by him *spintries*, forming a triple chain, surrendered themselves to mutual defilements in his presence, so as to re-animate by this spectacle his languishing desires. »

*serie connexi, invicem incestarent se coram ipso, ut ad-
spectu deficientes libidines excitaret.*

*Sellaria quidem vi originis haud dubie fuit locus
sellis instructus. Qui sese mutuo in his sellis constu-
prabant, sellarii dicti a loco, spintriæ a nexu; nam
Festo teste, pag.* 443, *spinter est* « *armillæ genus,
quo mulieres utebantur brachio summo sinistro* »;
voce, ut videtur, corrupta ex sphincter, *Græce*
σφιγκτήρ, *a* σφίγγω, *constringo, quasi dicas brachii
vinculum. Tacitus,* Annalibus, *VI,* 1 :

« *Tuncque primum ignota ante vocabula reperta
sunt, sellariorum et spintriarum, ex fœditate loci ac
multiplici patientia.* »

*Spintriæ igitur sunt, qui velut annuli spinteris
inter se cohærentes Veneri vacant. Possunt ita cohæ-
rere duplici serie tres, ut medius sit fututor vel pædico, ante puella vel pathicus, pone pædico. Tali
catena tenebantur illi apud Ausonium. Epigrammate CXXIX* (48):

_____ _____

(48) *In Latinum convertit Ausonius epigramma Græcum
Stratonis, quod legitur in* Analectis Brunkii, *II, 380.*

This *sellaria*, by the etymology of the word, was evidently a room furnished with seats; those who prostituted each other on these seats were called « *sellarii* », from the place, and « *spintriae* », from the chain they formed. Spinter, according to Festus, p. 443, signified, « a kind of bracelet worn by women on the upper part of the left arm. » The word is probably a corruption of *sphincter*, the Greek σφιγχτήρ from σφίγγω, « I clasp, » as for instance, a band surrounding the arm. Tacitus, *Annals*, VI, ch. 1 :

« Then there were invented names never known before, as for instance, *sellarii* and *spintriae*, names taken from the turpitude of the place or from the complicated infamies undergone. »

Spintries then are those who, linked like the rings of a bracelet, thus accomplish the pleasures of Venus. Three can link themselves thus, two and two, in such a way that while the middle one is a fornicator or a pedicon, in front is a woman or a cinede, behind a pedicon. Such was the chain formed by those Ausonius (*Epigram* CXXIX.) describes (48) :

---

(48) Translation by Ausonius of a Greek Epigram of Strato, to be found in Brunck's *Analecta*, II, 380.

Tres uno in lecto : stuprum duo perpetiuntur,
Et duo committunt. — Quattuor esse reor.
— Falleris. Extremis da singula crimina, et illum
Bis numeres medium, qui facit et patitur.

Vis tu spectare medium futuentem ? præbet tabula XL
in Monuments de la vie privée des douze Césars ;
medium pædicantem ? ostendit tabula XXVII.

Neque vero opus est, ut medius aut futuat, aut
pædicet. Is enim potest etiam ita inter admissarios
distribui, ut a postica parte draucum patiatur, ab
antica aut irrumet, aut fellet, aut lingat. Hæc
omnia tentavit et nove variavit Hostius ille, miri
in lasciviendo ingenii, ut exemplar apud posteros
habeatur, in quem Seneca pæne vehementius quam
pro philosophi moderatione et æquitate invehitur,
Nat. Quæst. *I,* 16; *ita tamen, ut nescio quid tacitæ*
voluptatis ipsum pectus virtutis rigidi satellitis per-
mulcere videatur :

« Hoc loco, » inquit, *« volo tibi nabrare fabellam,*

« Three in one bed ; two submit to the infamous act, two perform it. — Four there are, I
suppose. — Wrong! to the outermost ones give
a villainy apiece; count the man in the middle
twice, for he both acts and submits. »

Do you want to see the one in the middle
working a woman. Plate XL. of the *Monuments de la Vie Privée des douze Césars* shows you
an example. Do you wish to see the middle one
pedicating? look at plate XXVII.

There is, however, no need that the middle
actor should fornicate or pedicate. He may be
placed between his two companions in such a
way that while he is enduring the assault of a
pederast behind, he may in front irrumate, suck
a member or lick a vulva. Hostius whose mind
was so fertile in inventing obscenities that he
was held up as an example to future ages, has
tried all these postures and even added fresh variations. Seneca (*Nat. Quaest.*, I., 16) has inveigh-
ed against him more vehemently than is perhaps fit for a philosopher. It seems to me as
though some secret voluptuousness had been
acting here on the sense of this rigid guardian
of virtue ; he says :

« I will tell you here a story which will show

ut intelligas, quam nullum instrumentum irritandæ voluptatis libido contemnat, et ingeniosa sit ad incitandum furorem suum. Hostius quidam fuit obscenitatis usque in scenam productæ. Hunc divitem avarum, sestertii millies servum, divus Augustus indignum vindicta judicavit, cum a servis occisus esset, et tamen non pronuntiavit jure cæsum videri. Non erat ille tantummodo ab uno sexu impurus, sed tam virorum, quam fœminarum avidus fuit. Fecitque specula ejus notæ, cujus modo retuli, imagines longe majores reddentia, in quibus digitus brachii mensuram et longitudine et crassitudine excederet. Hæc autem ita disponebat, ut cum virum ipse pateretur, aversus omnes admissarii sui motus in speculo videret, ac deinde falsa magnitudine ipsius membri tanquam vera gauderet. In omnibus quidem agebat ille dilectum et aperta mensura legebat viros, sed nihilominus mendaciis quoque insatiabile malum delectabat. I nunc, et dic, speculum munditiarum causa repertum ! Fœda dictu sunt, quæ portentum illud lacerandum ore suo dixerit feceritque, cum illi specula ad omni parte opponerentur, ut ipse flagitiorum suorum spectator esset, et quæ secreta quoque conscientia premuntur et quæ accusatus quisque fecisse se negat, non

you that lust will not disdain any artifice which
is calculated to rouse desires, and to stimulate
its own fury. The lasciviousness of Hostius was
of the extremest kind. It was this rich miser, this
slave of a hundred million sesterces, whose
death, when he had been assassinated by his
slaves, Augustus would not avenge, although
he would not say that they were right to kill
him. His lewdness was not contented with one
sex; he was as passionate for men as for women. He had mirrors made which magnified the
reflections so much that a finger appeared as
big as an arm. These mirrors were placed in
such a manner that when he had a man under
him he could watch every movement of his accomplice, and enjoy as it were the fictitious
size of his member. He chose his men carefully,
the measuring tape in hand, and still had to
deceive his insatiable passion. It would be too
outrageous to report everything which this
monster, that ought to have been torn into
pieces, dared to say and do with his mouth;
when surrounded on all sides by his mirrors he
was the spectator of his own turpitudes, and
those secret infamies which every man would
deny, if accused of them, of such he took his fill
not with his mouth only, but also with eyes.
And, by Hercules, generally speaking crimes

*in os tantum, sed in oculos suos ingereret. At Hercules!
scelera conspectum suum reformidant; in perditis quoque, et ad omne dedecus expositis, tenerrima est oculorum verecundia. Ille autem, quasi parum esset, inau-
dita et incognita pati, oculos suos ad illa advocavit, nec
quantum peccabat videre contentus, specula sibi, per
quæ flagitia sua divideret disponeretque, circumdedit.
Et quia non tam diligenter intueri poterat, cum compressus erat, et caput merserat, inguinibusque alienis
obhæserat, opus sibi suum per imagines offerebat. Spe-
culabatur illam libidinem oris sui, spectabat sibi ad-
missos pariter in omnia viros. Nonnunquam inter ma-
rem et fœminam distributus, et toto corpore patientiæ
expositus, spectabat nefanda. Quidnam homo impurus
reliquit, quod in tenebris faceret? Non pertimuit diem,
sed ipsos concubitus portentosos sibi ipse ostendit, sibi
ipse approbavit. Quid? non putas, eo ipso habitu voluisse pingi? Est aliqua etiam prostitutis modestia, et
illa corpora, publico objecta ludibrio, aliquid, quo infelix patientia lateat, obtendunt : adeo quodammodo lupa-
nar quoque verecundum est. At illud monstrum obscenitatem suam spectaculum fecerat, et ea sibi ostentabat,
quibus abscondendis nulla satis alta nox est. « Simul, »*

shun their own reflection; men who are bare
of every feeling of honour and exposed to every
insult, still have some sense of shame, and do
not like to appear as they are. But he feasted
his eyes on unheard of and unknown infamies,
and, not content to see simply how he dishonoured himself, he surrounded himself with mirrors, for the sake of multiplying and grouping
his lubricities. As he could not see unaided everything distinctly when, pedicated by one man,
he had his head between the thighs of another,
he saw by his mirrors what he was doing and
how. He saw the lewd work of his mouth, and
watched himself absorbing men by every orifice. Sometimes placed between a man and a
woman, playing both ways the passive part, he
was able to see the greatest abominations. Darkness was not for him! So far from being afraid
of the light of day, he wanted it for his monstrous copulations, and was proud to have them
illuminated by it. Nay, more, he even wanted
to be painted in these attitudes. Even prostitutes
have a certain reserve, and those that abandon
themselves to the outrages of all, veil to some
extent their poor complaisances, and the very
brothel keeps some relics of decency; but this
monster turned his obscenities into a spectacle
for himself.

inquit, « et virum et fœminam pctior : nihilominus illa
« quoque supervacua mihi parte alioqui contumeliam
« majorem exerceo. Omnia membra stupris occupata
« sunt : oculi quoque in partem libidinis veniant, et
« testes ejus exactoresque sint. Etiam ea, quæ ab ad-
« spectu corporis nostri positio submovit, arte visantur, ne
« quis me putet nescire, quid faciam. Nihil egit Natura,
« quod humanæ libidini ministeria tam maligna dedit,
« quod aliorum animalium concubitus melius instruxit.
« Inveniam, quemadmodum morbo meo imponam et sa-
« tisfaciam. Quo nequitiam meam, si ad Naturæ mo-
« dum pecco ? Id genus speculorum circumponam mihi,
« quod incredibilem imaginum magnitudinem reddat.
« Si liceret mihi, ad verum ista perducerem ; quia non
« licet, mendacior pascar. Obscenitas mea plus quam ca-
« pit videat, et patientiam suam ipsa miretur ! » Faci-
« nus indignum ! Hic fortasse cito et antequam videret
occisus est : ad speculum suum immolandus fuit ! »

Tiberii imaginem singulari prorsus nec illepida
ratione spintriam agentis exhibet tabula xxi *in*
Monuments de la vie privée des douze Césars,
in qua semisupinus ita jacet imperator, ut unius
puellæ superimpendentis cunnum lingat, alteri pe-
nem fellandum præbeat.

« Yes, » he said, « I submit myself to a man
and a woman at the same time ; but nevertheless with the organs which are left free to me I
am still able to commit a worse ignominy. All
my limbs are polluted; then shall my eyes also
take part in my enjoyments, they shall be wit-
nesses and judges. What I cannot see in a natural way let me see by the help of art, so that I
may not be ignorant of what I am doing. No
matter to me that Nature has provided man with
such insignificant organs of voluptuousness,
the same nature which has furnished animals so
well; I find means to deceive my passion, and
to satisfy myself. Where is the harm, if I try to
imitate nature ? I will have mirrors which shall
reflect images of incredible dimensions. If I
could, I would make these images real; as I cannot, I must be satisfied with phantoms. Let me
see these objects of obscenity larger than they
are in reality, and surprise myself by the sight
of them ! »

Plate XXI. of the *Monuments de la Vie Privée
des douze Césars* shows the picture of Tiberius
in a very strange spintrian posture, which however is not without charm; the emperor, half
reclining on his back, licks one girl's privates who
is kneeling over him, while he offers his penis
to be sucked by another.

*Sed possunt etiam plus connecti tres, ut longior
spectetur catena. Si quis futuit puellam, cum interea et ipse et puella pædicatur, habes quatuor triplici serie connexos Tiberii apud Suetonium loco
dudum adducto. Junge alterutri extremo rursus
pædiconem, habebis symplegma, quo quinque qua-
druplici serie copulentur; Martialis, XII, 43 :*

> *Sunt illic Veneris novæ figuræ,*
> *Quales perditus audeat fututor,*
> *Præstent et taceant quid exoleti,*
> *Quo symplegmate quinque copulentur,*
> *Qua plures teneantur a catena.*

*Ecce autem symplegma quinque copulatorum artifi-
ciosius variatum tabula* XXXVI *in* Monuments de
la vie privée des douze Césars. *Nero pronus
puellam supinam futuere, alteramque stantem lingere, ipse pædicari, stans illa pati quoque pædiconem.
In infinitum extendi posse talem catenam. per se
intelligitur.*

There are also arrangements where more than three can join, making thus a longer chain. Let a man put his member into a woman while both of them are being pedicated at the same time, and you have four people forming a triple chain, like those of Tiberius in the passage of Suetonius quoted above. Suppose then another pedicon on each end, and then you have a group of five, forming a quadruple interweaving. Martial, XII, 43 :

« There are to be found novel figures of Love, such as the impassioned fornicator may try, such as experienced libertines perform and keep the secret of; how five can copulate in a group, how more still may be connected in a chain. »

Look ar Plate XXXVI. of the *Monuments de la Vie privée des douze Césars*, with a group of five copulators artistically diversified. Nero, lying face downwards, enters one girl who is on her back, at the same time licking the privates of another who is standing; he himself is being pedicated, while the girl standing also submits her behind to a pedicon. That such a chain may be extended infinitely, is self evident.

FIGURARUM VENERIS

ENUMERATIO

—◆◆—

1. *Pronus supinam pedibus protensis jacentem intra femina recipiens.*

2. *Pronus a supina pedibus divaricatis jacente intra femina receptus.*

3. *Supina alterum crus equitis intra femina recipiens.*

4. *Supina pedibus in lumbos equitis decussatim sublatis.*

ENUMERATION

OF THE

EROTIC POSTURES

1. The man face downwards taking between his thighs the woman, who lies on her back with her legs stretched out straight.

2. The man face downwards taken between her thighs by the woman, who lies on her back with the legs apart.

3. The woman lying on her back taking only one leg of her cavalier between her thighs.

4. The woman lying on her back with her feet crossed over the loins of the man.

5. *Supina altero pede protenso, altero in lumbos viri sublato.*

6. *Supina cum equite averso.*

7. *Supina cum equite transverso.*

8. *Jacens cum semisupina in latus jacente, pedibus protensis.*

9. *Jacens cum semisupina in latus jacente, altero pede protenso, altero in lumbos viri sublato.*

10. *Semisupina cum equite averso.*

11. *Ingeniculans cum supina pedibus divaricatis jacente.*

12. *Supina pedes in lumbos ingeniculantis tollens.*

5. The woman lying on her back with one of her legs stretched out, and the other over the man's loins.

6. The woman lying on her back with the cavalier mounted on her with his back towards her face.

7. The woman lying on her back, with the cavalier mounted athwart her.

8. The man lying with the woman half couched on her side with the legs stretched out.

9. The man lying with the woman half couched on her side, one leg stretched out, the other one over the man's loins.

10. The woman half couched, the man mounted with his back to her.

11. The man on his knees, the woman on her back with her legs open.

12. The woman on her back with her legs resting on the man's loins, who is kneeling.

13. *Pes alter supinæ protensus, alter in lumbos ingeniculantis sublatus.*

14. *Supina pedes in humeros ingeniculantis tollens.*

15. *Pes alter supinæ protensus, alter in humeros ingeniculantis sublatus.*

16. *Pes alter supinæ in lumbos, alter in humerum ingeniculantis sublatus.*

17. *Ingeniculans sedentem pedibus divaricatis futuens.*

18. *Alter pes sedentis protensus, alter in lumbos ingeniculantis fututoris sublatus.*

19. *Uterque pes sedentis in lumbos ingeniculantis fututoris sublatus.*

20. *Alter pes sedentis protensus, alter in humerum ingeniculantis fututoris sublatus.*

13. The woman on her back, one leg stretched out, the other one resting on the loins of the man, who is kneeling.

14. The woman on her back with her legs on the shoulders of the man, who is kneeling.

15. The woman on her back with one leg stretched out, and the other one on the shoulder of the man, who is kneeling.

16. The woman on her back with one leg resting on the loins of the man, who is on his knees, and the other one on his shoulder.

17. The man kneeling gets into the woman, who is in a sitting position with her thighs open.

18. The woman sitting with one leg stretched out, and the other resting on the loins of the man, who is kneeling.

19. The woman sitting, with her two legs resting on the loins of the kneeling man.

20. The woman sitting with one leg stretched

21. *Uterque pes sedentis in humeros ingeniculantis fututoris sublatus.*

22. *Alter pes sedentis in humerum, alter in lumbos ingeniculantis fututoris sublatus.*

23. *Ingeniculans cum aversa.*

24. *Supinus cum adversa.*

25. *Supinus cum aversa.*

26. *Supinus cum transversa.*

27. *Supinus cum sublata.*

28. *Sedens cum adversa.*

29. *Sedens cum adversa pedibus sublatis.*

out, and the other on the shoulder of her cavalier on his knees.

21. The woman sitting with her two legs on the shoulders of her cavalier on his knees.

22. The woman sitting, one of her legs on the shoulder of the man on his knees, the other one stretched out.

23. The man on his knees, the woman with her back to him.

24. The man on his back, the woman facing him.

25. The man on his back with the woman turning her back to him.

26. The man on his back, the woman athwart him.

27. The man on his back, with the woman lifted up.

28. The man sitting with the woman facing him.

29. The man sitting, the woman facing him, with her legs in the air.

30. *Sedens cum aversa.*

31. *Stans cum stante.*

32. *Stans cum stante, altero pede sive viri sive fœminæ sublato.*

33. *Stans cum supina pedibus divaricatis jacente.*

34. *Supina pedibus in lumbos stantis sublatis.*

35. *Supina altero pede protenso, altero in lumbos stantis sublato.*

36. *Supina pedibus in humeros stantis sublatos.*

37. *Supina altero pede protenso, altero in humerum stantis sublato.*

38. *Supina altero pede in humerum, altero in lumbos stantis sublato.*

30. The man sitting with the woman turning her back upon him.

31. Man and woman standing.

32. Man and woman standing, with one leg of the man or the woman lifted up.

33. The man standing, with the woman on her back, her legs open.

34. The woman lying on her back, with her legs lifted on the loins of the man, who is standing.

35. The woman lying on her back, one leg stretched out and the other lifted on the loins of the man, who is standing.

36. The woman on her back, with her two legs on the shoulders of the man, who is standing.

37. The woman on her back, one leg stretched out and the other one on the shoulder of the man, who is standing.

38. The woman on her back, with one of her legs on the shoulder of the man, who is standing, the other over his loins.

39. *Stans cum semisupina in latus jacente.*

40. *Stans sedentem pedibus divaricatis futuens.*

41. *Stans sedentem pedibus sublatis futuens.*

42. *Stans sedentem altero pede protenso, altero
     sublato, futuens.*

43. *Stans cum sublata.*

44. *Pedes sublatæ humeris stantis impositi.*

45. *Stans cum aversa ingeniculante.*

46. *Stans cum aversa conquiniscente.*

47. *Stans cum aversa ita sublata, ut inferior pars
     corporis tollatur, superior jaceat.*

39. The man standing, the woman half lying on her side.

40. The man standing, getting into the woman, who is sitting with her legs open.

41. The man standing, getting into the woman sitting with her legs in the air.

42. The man standing, the woman sitting with one leg stretched out and the other one lifted up.

43. The man standing and the woman lifted up.

44. The woman lifted up, with her legs on the shoulders of the man, who is standing.

45. The man standing, the woman on her knees, with her back towards him.

46. The man standing, the woman crouching down, with her back towards him.

47. The man standing, the woman with her back towards him, the lower part of the body elevated, and the upper part resting on the bed.

48. *Stans cum aversa, inferiore parte corporis arti
ficiose sublata.*

49. *Pædicatur jacens.*

50. *Pædicatur stans.*

51. *Pædicatur ingeniculans.*

52. *Pædicatur conquiniscens.*

53. *Irrumator jacens.*

54. *Irrumator sedens.*

55. *Irrumator stans.*

56. *Irrumator ingeniculans.*

57. *Irrumator conquiniscens.*

58. *Cunnilingus jacens.*

59. *Cunnilingus sedens.*

60. *Cunnilingus stans.*

61. *Cunnilingus ingeniculans.*

62. *Cunnilingus conquiniscens.*

63. *Fellatrix cum cunnilingo.*

48. The man standing, thee woman turning her back to him with the lower part of the body artificially raised.

49. A man lying down and being pedicated.

50. A man pedicated standing.

51. A man on his knees being pedicated.

52. A man pedicated crouching down.

53. Irrumator lying, down.

54. Irrumator sitting.

55. Irrumator standing.

56. Irrumator kneeling.

57. Irrumator crouching.

58. Cunnilingue lying down.

59. Cunnilingue sitting.

60. Cunnilingue standing.

61. Cunnilingue kneeling.

62. Cunnilingue crouching.

63. Fellatrix and cunnilingue.

64. *Masturbator.*

65. *Manus officiosa.*

66. *Manus officiosa tertiæ.*

67. *Auxilium digiti.*

68. *Auxilium scorteum.*

69. *Coitus cum quadrupede mare.*

70. *Coitus cum quadrupede fœmina.*

71. *Tribas futuens.*

72. *Tribas pædicans.*

73. *Spintriæ tres : fututor pædicatur*

74. *Spintriæ tres : pædico pædicatur.*

75. *Spintriæ tres : fellator pædicatur.*

76. *Spintriæ tres : fellator futuit.*

77. *Spintriæ tres : fellator pædicat.*

78. *Spintriæ tres : fellator irrumat.*

79. *Spintriæ tres : fellatrix futuitur.*

64. Masturbator.

65. The helping hand.

66. A third hand helping.

67. The finger helping.

68. The assistance of a leathern *godemiche.*

69. Coitus with a male animal.

70. Coitus with a female animal.

71. Tribad at work on a woman.

72. Tribad pedicating.

73. Three spintries : a fornicator pedicated.

74. Three spintries : a pederast pedicated.

75. Three spintries : a fellator being pedicated.

76. Three spintries : a fellator entering a woman.

77. Three spintries: a fellator pedicating.

78. Three spintries : a fellator irrumating.

79. Three spintries : a fellatrix entered by a man.

80. *Spintriæ tres : fellatrix pædicatur.*

81. *Spintriæ tres : fellatrix lingitur.*

82. *Spintriæ tres : cunnilingus futuit.*

83. *Spintriæ tres : cunnilingus pædicat.*

84. *Spintriæ tres : cunnilingus irrumat.*

85. *Spintriæ tres : cunnilingus pædicatur*

86. *Spintriæ tres : cunnilingus futuitur.*

87. *Spintriæ tres : cunnilinga pædicatur.*

88. *Spintriæ quatuor duplici serie nexi.*

89. *Spintriæ quatuor triplici serie nexi.*

90. *Symplegma quinque copulatorum.*

FINIS

80. Three spintries : a fellatrix pedicated.

81. Three spintries : a fellatrix offers her vulva for licking.

82. Three spintries : a cunnilingue fornicating.

83. Three spintries : a cunnilingue pedicating.

84. Three spintries : a cunnilingue irrumates.

85. Three spintries : a cunnilingue being pedicated.

86. Three spintries; a female cunnilingue is entered by a man.

87. Three spintries : a female cunnilingue is pedicated.

88. Four spintries forming a double chain.

89. Four spintries forming a triple chain.

90. Group of five copulators.

THE END

INDEX

OF EROTIC WORDS AND PHRASES

A

Abligurire. II. 98.

Abusus digitorum. II. 160.

Abuti lingua. II. 60.

Adlaborare ore. I. 220.

Admissarius, II. 182, 184.

Adsilire. II. 152.

Agilitas clunium. I. 130.

Agitare. I. 76.

Agitare clunem. I. 128, 130.

Agitare equum supinum. I. 44.

Αἰδοῖον δερμάτινον· II. 160.

Basiare medium. II. 50.

Βίβασις. II. 16.

Bibere liquidos homines. I. 234.

Βινεῖν. II. 60.

Βινεῖν στόματι. II.

Brutis, Coitus cum. II. 168-177.

Buccæ Summœnianæ. II. 48.

C

Cacare mentulam. I. 164.

Cadurda. II. 36.

Calamistratus. II. 30.

Capiti non parcere. I. 46.

Caput demissum. II. 56.

Catamitus. I. 80.

Catapulta. I. 238; II. 82.

Catena. I. 16; II. 190.

Cauda. I. 172; II. 34, 82.

Caulis. II. 82.

Cava corporis. I. 154; II. 40, 42.

Caverna. I. 134, 204; II. 148.

Caverna postica, II. 148.

Cella inscripta. I. 170, 248.

Cevere. I. 98, 128. 162, 222.

Chia. I. 168.

Cinædulus. I. 94.

Cortegianæ. I. 212.
Cotyttium. I. 238.
Coxa pendens. II. 136, 142.
Crissare. I. 128; II. 16, 34, 136, 154.
Crista. II. 30.
Cruor menstruus. II. 68.
Culus. I. 22, 80, 92, 96, 100, 142, 162, 168, 182,
    184, 186, 244, 246; II. 10, 38.
Cunnilingæ. II. 106.
Cunnilingus. I. 198, 202, 222, 224; II. 48-107,
    50, 58, 62, 64, 70.
Cunnus. I. 22, 24, 52, 114, 118, 120, 168, 198,
    200, 218, 236, 244; II. 6, 44, 48, 50, 52, 54,
    56, 60, 62, 66, 68, 70, 76, 98, 100, 102, 104,
    112, 130, 132, 140, 152, 185.
Cunnus brutus. II. 174.
Cunnus humens. II. 68.
Cunnus madidus. II. 62, 64, 74.
Cunnus vulsus. I. 118.
Cuspis coleata. II. 82, 84, 86.
Cymba. II. 82, 154.
Cysthus. II. 72, 82.

D

Dedolare. I. 68, 78.
Deglubire. I. 204.
Delicatus. I. 80, 136.
Δέλτα. I. 118; II. 60.

Ἐταιρίστριαι. II. 108, 118, 146.
Εὐνουχίζειν. II. 112.
Eunuchæ. II. 112.
Eunuchi. II. 112.
Eviratus. II. 50.
Exagitare nates. II. 154.
Excipere Venerem. I. 156.
Exercere supinos. I. 48.
Exoletus. I. 14, 82, 102, 226; II. 190.
Exsugere. I. 190.

F

Facere. II. 182.
Facere modos tibia. I. 234.
Facilitas femoris. I. 130.
Fallere libidinem. II. 160.
Fascinum. I. 220; II. 20.
Fascinum scorteum. I. 82.
Favere cunno. II. 152.
Feles pullaria. I. 176.
Fellare. I. 190, 192, 194, 196, 198, 204, 206, 220,
   226, 238, 244, 246, 248, 254, 256, 260; II. 44,
   182, 188.
Fellator. I. 104, 198, 202, 222, 232, 250, 252, 256,
   258; II. 48, 52, 64, 70, 72, 100, 104, 106, 132.
Fellatrix. I. 194, 202, 232; II. 48.
Fides Socratica. l. 158.

Figuræ Veneris. I. 2, 14; II. 192, 209.

Fluctuare lumbis. II. 16.

Fodere. I. 22 ; II. 112.

Fœtor oris. I. 248.

Foramen. II. 58.

Fores. I. 38.

Fornix. I. 170; II. 50.

Fossa. I. 104; II. 82.

Fossor. I. 174.

Fricare nervum. II. 40.

Fricatrix. II. 154.

Frictrices. II. 108, 148.

Frictus. II. 136.

Frumen. I. 214.

Futuere. I. 24, 34, 42, 54, 56, 74, 164, 190, 204
  218, 220, 224, 226, 242, 246, 248; II. 2, 4, 6
  50, 100, 108, 132, 182, 190.

Fututio. I. 24, 80, 128; II. 54.

Fututor. I. 14, 42, 78; II. 64, 98, 100, 114, 130
  180, 190.

Fututrix. II. 38.

G

Gaditanæ. II. 14, 16.

Gannire. I. 132; II. 138, 142.

Garum Venereum. I. 234.

Gausape. I. 104, 112.

Genitale. II. 172.
Glans. I. 222, 224; II. 12.
Glossas tradere. II. 78.
Γλωττοποιεῖν. II. 64.
Gratificare linguæ. II. 68.
Gurgulio. I. 104, 112.

H

Habere rem. I. 36, 42.
Hasta. I. 38, 40, 50, 92; II. 82, 116.
Hernia. II. 136.
Hircus. II. 168.
Hortus. I. 36; II. 116, 154.
Humor. I. 94.
Humor menstruus. II. 62.
Humor muliebris. II. 64.

I

Illudere capitibus. I. 214.
Illudere ori. I. 114.
Illud puerile. I. 132, 244.
Imber. I. 40.
Impellere ad cursum. II. 150.
Improbius quiddam. I. 244.
Impudicus. I. 230.
Incestare. II. 180.
Incurvare. I. 162, 168, 170.

J

Juventus resinata. I. 112.

K

Κακουργία. I. 220.
Καθιππάζεσθαι. I. 138.
Καλλίπυγοι. I. 134.
Κατάγειν μετέωρα. I. 34.
Κάτω βλέπειν. II. 66.
Κέλης. I. 46.
Κελητίζειν. I. 46.
Κίναιδος. I. 198.
Κινεῖν τὰ αἰδοῖα· I. 130.
Κοπροφάγος. I. 200, 202; II. 52.
Κύσθος. II. 72, 74.

L

Λάβδα· I. 194; II. 80.
Labra cunni. I. 38; II. 60.
Lacessere vulvas. II, 64.
Læva pellex. II, 2, 4.
Lævigare. I. 102, 116.
Lambere. I. 222; II. 64, 74, 106, 134.

N

O

P

Pædagogium Trajani. I. 152.

Pæderastia. I. 156.

Pædicare, pædicari. I. 80, 82, 104, 114, 128, 130, 132, 138, 144, 162, 164, 186, 188, 204, 218, 220, 224, 226, 230, 246, 248, 256; II. 6, 26, 36, 108, 132, 182, 190.

Pædicatio. I. 80-189.

Pædicator. I. 80.

Pædico. I. 42, 80, 142, 144, 162, 178, 180, 182, 186; II. 10, 114, 180, 190.

Παιδεραστεῖν, I. 172, 174.

Palæstra Veneris. I. 48.

Palæstrita. I. 112.

Παλαίειν ἐπὶ γῆς. I. 76.

Palus. II. 82.

Papillæ. I. 236; II. 42.

Pars. I. 36.

Πάσχειν ἀπόρρητα. I. 198.

Pathica puella. II. 14, 18, 60.

Pathicus. I. 80, 82, 90, 94, 98, 100, 104, 114, 122, 124, 130, 142, 148, 164, 254, 256; II. 68, 100, 104, 106, 180.

Peccare superne. I. xvii, 44.

Pecten. I. 122; II. 8, 64.

Peculia. II. 82.

Peculiatus. I. 222; II. 110.

Πέλαγος ἁλμυρὸν. II. 58, 68.

Penis. I. 94, 178, 184, 190; II. 14, 20, 148, 188.

Penis circumcisus. I. 222.

— *ex corio.* II. 160.

— *scorteus.* I. 82, 130, 160.

Pensilia. I. 222; II. 110.

Πέος. II. 24.

Percidere, percidi. I. 190, 216, 213, 220, 254.

Percidere os. I. 216.

Perdere hominem digitis. II. 6.

Perforare. II. 130.

Perfricare. I. 190; II. 20.

Permolere. II. 34.

Perpeti stuprum. II. 182.

Pessulus. II. 82.

Petere buccam. I. 236.

Petere summa. I. 216, 218, 240.

Phallus. II, 82.

Phi. II. 280.

Pilare. I. 104, 118, 120, 122.

Pilum, I. 92.

Πίνων καταμηνίου. I. 202, 66.

Pisculi Tiberii. l. 240.

Plantaria. I. 112.

Plus quam futui. I. 226.

Podex. I. 82, 84, 90, 92, 94, 98, 102, 104, 114
120, 142, 176.

Q

Quadrantaria. I. 206.
Quærere fœminam supra papillas. I. 236, 238.

R

Raphanus. I. 120, 226.
Recipere libidinem. I. 154; II. 42.
Recutitus. I. 222, 224; II. 14.
Res salsa. I. 236.
— *tribadica.* II. 158.
— *Venerea.* I. 20.
Rho. II. 280.
'Ρίχνωμα. II. 16.
Rigere. I. 220.
Rima. I. 26. 38; II. 80, 82.
Rododaphne. I. 8.
Rogare culum. I. 244.
— *cunnum.* I. 244.
— *os.* I. 244.
Ros. II. 64, 116.
Rumor. I. 218.
Rumpere latus. II. 22.

S

Sacra Veneris. I. 56.

Φ

INDEX

OF AUTHORS QUOTED

—

ERRATA

VOLUME I

Page VIII, line last : *for* hwile *read* while
Page XII, line last : *for* th *read* the
Page XVII, line 14 : *for* ones *read* one's
Page XVII, line last : *for* 41 and 195 *read* 45 and 215
Page 17, line 24 : *for* countains *read* contains
Page 45, line 18 : *for* Sigea *read* Sigaea
Page 51, line 6 : *for* nnder *read* under
Page 52, line 16 : *for* bonitat *read* bonitati
Page 59, line 8 : *for* back *read* face
Page 64, line 6 : *for* amemtem *read* amentem
Page 68, line 9 : *for* alli *read* alii
Page 83, line 11 : *for* a *read* at
Page 92, line 9 : *for* cu *read* cum
Page 94, line last : *for* ade *read* adeo
Page 115, line 14 : *for* buttock *read* buttocks
Page 119, line 7 : *for* pratice *read* practice

Page 119, line 13 : *for* the reis *read* there is

Page 121, line 13 : *for* Tesmophoriazusae *read* Thesmophoriazusae

Page 127, line last : *for* believ edyo suaw *read* believed you
saw

Page 133, line 2ι : *for* Derdanian *read* Dardanian

Page 145, line 10 : *for* Roman *read* Romans

Page 148, line 4 : *for* improbit *read* improbis

Page 157, lines 14 and 16 : *for* Magira *read* Magirus

Page 161, line 22 : *for* noting *read* nothing

Page 166, line 12 : *for* ur *read* fur

Page 166, line 12 : *for* hnnc *read* hunc

Page 177, line 1 : *for* pratice *read* practice

Page 177, line 23 : *for* brids *read* birds

Page 182, line last but one : *for* judicie *read* judice

Page 187, line 24 : *for* grow *read* grew

Page 192, line 16 : *for* ἐλεσβίαζεν *read* ἐλεσβίαζεν

Page 200, line 7 : *for* ὁνιδός *read* ὄνειδός

Page 214, line 5 : *for* et eleta *read* elata

Page 221, line 16 : *for* 'Αῤῥητουργία *read* 'Αῤῥητουργία

Page 227, line 28 : *for* sels *read* sells

Page 228, line 2 : *for* ledtus *read* lentus

Page 232, line 4 : *for* pudiciti *read* pudicitiae

Page 235, line 21 : *for* Se *read* She

Page 235, line 21 : *for* betwen *read* between

Page 244, line 18 : *for* fesus *read* fessus

Page 249, line 4 : *for* ou *read* on

Page 257, line 23 : *for* is *read* in

Page 259, line 18 : *for* Λειχάζειν *read* Λειχάρειν

VOLUME II

Page 18, line 12 : *for* ἄθλα *read* ἄθλα
Page 18, line 15 : *for* ἦν *read* ἥν
Page 18, line 18 : *for* ὀρχήματα *read* ὀρχήματα
Page 24, line 16 : *for* dignarus *read* dignaris
Page 24, line 16 : *for* vocc *read* voce
Page 25, line 3 : *for* lis *read* is
Page 27, line 23 : *for* to *read* the
Page 40, lines 4 and 6 : *for* Encolpus *read* Encolpius
Page 41, line 8 : *for* ull *read* full
Page 47, line 6 : *for* witch *read* with
Page 51, line 22 : *for* direct *read* directed
Page 53, line 10 : *for* othervise *read* otherwise
Page 60, line 10 : *for* six *read* sic
Page 62, line 4 : *for* ποιεῖς *read* ποιεῖς
Page 63, line 1 : *for* Ammanius *read* Ammianus
Page 63, line last : *for* foulngi *read* fouling
Page 65, line 15 : *for* 1847,77 *read* 1274
Page 66, line 15 : *for* συξῆς *read* συζῆς
Page 69, line 26 : *for* tho *read* to
Page 71, line 23 : *for* sown *read* sewn
Page 73, line 16 : *for* dissmilar *read* dissimilar
Page 80, line 17 : *for* nomem *read* nomen
Page 100, line 4 : *for* spurcetiem *read* spurcitiem
Page 115, line last : *for* pleasue *read* pleasure
Page 132, line 1 : *for* tribos *read* tribas

Page 132, line 20 : *for* setorsit *read* se torsit
Page 147, line 11 : *for* drafts *read* draughts
Page 182, line last : *for* nabrare *read* narrare
Page 191, line 16 : *for* ar *read* at
Page 205, line 1 : *for* thee *read* the
Page 205, line 8 : *for* lying, down *read* lying down

Printed in the United Kingdom
by Lightning Source UK Ltd.
122317UK00001B/10/A

9 781410 206206